MW01230489

New Warleans

By: Kennaire Mathieu

&

Devon Wilson

ISBN-13: 9781799023715

Published by: Street Nation Publications
Email us at NewWarleans@gmail.com
Facebook account: streetnationpublication
Instagram: street_nation_publication

ACKNOWLEDGMENTS

First of all, we would like to thank YOU, the person who is holding this book. We realize that you could have selected any novel, and without you, this book would still be on the shelf. To show our appreciation, we gave you one of the best urban novels of all times; one that's gon make you feel like you're actually on the scene. When we wrote this book, we penned it with the intent of giving the readers a realistic vision of life on the bloody streets of New Orleans.

We hope you enjoy reading our first novel, just as much as we enjoyed writing it.

Thanks…

DEDICATION

This book is dedicated to my mother, Edna Hall Mathieu. She departed this life on October 2, 2007, and I miss her dearly. She was the one person who always reminded me of how special I actually am. I wish she were here today to see her son finally do something positive for a change. I know she would've been so proud of me, but then again before she passed away, she explained to me that she'd always be with me spiritually. Holding on to that one memory, I know she's smiling from heaven due to my accomplishment. I LOVE YOU MA! I promise I'ma continue to make you smile. 'Rest In Peace Ma." WE MISS YOU.

Your son Kennaire "Bul" Mathieu

In loving memories of my aunt Ophilia… We all must answer when God calls. Now that you are dwelling in the house of our heavenly Father, I ask that you continue to look down on us all... LOVE FOREVER

Your Nephew Devon 'Oreo' Wilson

CHAPTER 1

Summer 2005

The nappy headed youngsta woke up in a deep sweat from a nightmare of someone killing him. He rolled out of bed and peeped out of his bedroom window. Immediately, he spotted a group of dudes huddled around a dice game, talking shit. After he threw on his clothes, he grabbed his .380 handgun. Trying not to wake his crack craving mother Wanda, who was knocked out asleep on the living room sofa, he eased out of the apartment.

"Bet twenty, bet forty nigga, I got whatever on this easy eight! Who wanna bet?" Shitty inquired as he looked at the dudes standing around.

"Bet a hundred, fuck forty," Ben called out to Shitty.

"Bet nigga! You got me fucked up, what 'cha think you the only nigga getting money or something. We getting money back here too," Shitty stated as he picked up the dice to roll.

He shot the dice, and they landed on six, "Tre Tre running mates," Shitty said in his deep voice, snapping his fingers.

Shitty is a tall, black, ugly dude that weighs about 280 lbs. He looks like he should've been an offensive lineman in the

NFL, and due to his size and temperament, he's feared by a lot of people. His treacherous ways, which also cause pain among several families within the hood is a major factor as well. There are only a few people who like him, but almost everybody respects him.

"I got fifty, he hit that eight," Rell said, puffing on his blunt filled with purp.

"It's a bet!" Ben quickly hollered.

The moment Shitty picked up the dice to roll again, he started talking shit, "These bitches 'bout to cum in his face – 5:30 in the morning."

"Nigga if you feel like that, bet another hundred!" Ben shouted.

Shitty, with only three hundred dollars in his hand, let his pride get the best of him, "Bet nigga, it's more where this came from," he replied.

"Oh, yeah! You gon need it, cause you bout to miss this eight," Ben said as he quickly stopped the dice with his hand.

***

"Make a right when you get to Martin Luther King and S. Robertson," Cadillac told the white boy driving the truck. "...and stop by the store."

Cadillac is an around the way fiend who will hang around any drug spot that has the best drugs at the time. Back in the day, he used to be the ultimate hustler. Nonetheless, his mother died, and that lead to his intense abuse of drugs. He was well-known uptown, and some even wished he could kick his habit because when he was getting money, he made sure the entire neighborhood was taken care of.

The driver nervously pulled up; because he was in the heart of the ghetto, he was trying to be cautious. After placing his truck in park, he turned to Cadillac to make a point.

"I'm not trying to spend my money on some bullshit."

"Man, this shit's good. This is where I score from all the time, trust me, you won't regret it," Cadillac said.

"I hope not, cause lately these young guys around town been beating me, and I hate getting screwed out of my hard-earned money."

"You want the shit or not? Ain't nobody 'gon screw you out your damn money!" An aggravated Cadillac replied.

"Alright buddie calm down, here's two hundred dollars. If it's straight, I don't mine spending more money."

When Cadillac got out of the truck, he noticed a group of dudes standing on the side of the store located directly across the street from the Melphomene project.

"Where Ben at Lil' Mike?" Cadillac asked the youngsta that was standing on the corner.

"He not out chere. He left like thirty minutes ago, but whatever you want, somebody out chere got it," Lil' Mike replied.

"No, I'm straight, I'm 'bout to go in the Calliope and holla at Shitty." Cadillac expressed, getting back in the truck before speeding away.

***

Ben was constantly placing bets around the game. It seemed like it took forever for Shitty to crap out. Ben got on one knee, picked the dice up and before tossing them back to Shitty he talked noise.

"Nigga you got buzzard luck. Hurry up and crap out." Before Shitty replied, everybody turned their heads to see who slammed the car door to their left.

"Come here Shitty," Cadillac said as he quickly walked towards the dice game. But the closer he got, he noticed Ben and quickly changed his mind.

"What's up Ben? What you doing in my neck of the woods? I just came from round your way looking for you, let me holla at you right quick."

"Hold on a minute. I need to holla at him," Ben told Shitty as he turned to approach Cadillac.

"What's up, you got something?" Cadillac asked him as soon as they were a few steps away from the others.

"Yeah, I got something, but it ain't bagged up, how much you trying to spend?"

"I got two hundred right now, and I got this white boy in the truck waiting on me, and that bitch got money too. If the shit's good, he gonna spend all day."

"Don't my shit always be good!" An arrogant Ben questioned.

"Not always," Cadillac jokingly replied.

"Go run to the store for me right quick. Get me a box of aluminum foil, some keep moving cigars, and a 20oz Coca Cola. Once you come back, I'ma go handle that for you," he told Cadillac.

"Hurry up nigga, you holding up my fucking shot!" Shitty aggressively shouted cause Ben caught a sell on his set that was intended for him.

"Damn nigga, you ain't see me handling my fucking business?" Ben responded in an evenly aggressive tone.

"Nigga fuck your business, I'm trying to handle my business by throwing this eight in your face."

Shitty shot the dice using his spin shot, which caused the dice to rapidly spin as he continued to talk shit. Within seconds, one of the dice stopped and landed on six as the other one continued to spin. As soon as the dice was about to stop, Ben formed his hand like a gun. Using his two fingers and his thumb, he aimed at the dice.

"Pow, one to the head, Shitty's dead," he said, watching as seconds later the other dice landed on one.

"Seven out nigga, don't nobody move but me, give me my fucking money," Ben stated, picking up the money.

"I'm 'bout to take all this dum ass nigga money," Ben added.

"Damn my nigga, you talking real reckless right na. You better slow your fucking roll," Shitty angrily replied. "And shoot the dice, it's your shot."

"It ain't my shot, it's Rell's turn to get on the dice. I shoot after him," Ben quickly responded.

Rell, got on the dice and it looked like he couldn't miss a point. He hit a 10, 5, 4, and rolled two naturals before he caught a six to be his next point. Six is one of the easiest points to hit on the dice, but when he tried to hit it, he missed, crapping out four-tre.

"Now it's your shot, Ben. Shoot the dice so I can get my fucking money back," Shitty said.

"I see you anxious for me to take your money huh?" Ben responded. "But you know what, I ain't 'gon touch the dice," he added looking to his left at the lil' youngsta who was just standing there watching the game.

"Aye lil' homie, what's your name?"

"Fred! Why what's up?"

"So we can take this ugly motherfucker's money, I want you to shoot the dice for me. You wit' that?"

"I'm always with taking a nigga money," the youngsta shot back.

"I'm shooting 50," Ben stated.

"I got him faded," Shitty hollered, counting his money.

As soon as Fred was about to pick the dice up, Cadillac rode up in a charcoal gray Ford F-150. He rolled down the passenger window and yelled, "You ready Ben?"

"Hold on, give me one second Cadillac."

Fred picked up the dice and started shaking them, "Shitty, I'm 'bout to take all your money."

"Man, hurry up, shoot the fucking dice," Shitty insisted, mad cause Fred was trying to win his money. Fred rolled the dice and they landed on tre-one, making four his point. Shitty felt good cause he knew that a four was the hardest point to hit, so he felt like he had a chance to get his money back.

"Bet this buck fifty, take it all from me," Shitty said, referring to the hundred and fifty dollars he had left in his hand.

"No, fuck that! Bet your fifty," Ben responded.

"What! Nigga I just bet you two hundred on my eight," Shitty angrily shot back.

"So! That's on you. I bet my money how I wanna bet it," Ben sternly suggested.

"Man, this bitch ass nigga gamblin' bad as a motherfucker."

"Man, shut the fuck up, and watch Lil' Fred throw that four backdoor on your stupid ass." Ben aggressively replied.

Fred released the dice outta his hand, and they landed on two deuces.

"Two stupid deuces!" Ben yelled, laughing as he picked up the money.

After all the money was picked up, he looked at Fred, dapped him, and gave him fifty dollars.

"That's you lil' homie." He looked up at Shitty who was now standing on the porch. "I'ma do you a favor and leave you with that hundred dollars you got left, cause I got to go handle my business. Get yourself something to smoke with that."

"Nigga you think you bout to just leave with my money like that without giving me a chance to win it back?" Shitty stated.

"Nigga, this was your money. It's my money now, and I say I quit. As a matter of fact, I'm 'bout to go treat my hoe with yo money," Ben informed Shitty, turning to walk away from the porch.

As soon as Ben took about 7 steps, Shitty reached in his back pocket and retrieved a .38 special. He aimed it at Ben's back and gave specific instructions.

"Give me all that fucking money before I kill your bitch ass out chere!"

"Damn homie, that's how you 'gon play it?" A nervous Ben managed to get out his mouth.

"Homie! Nigga I ain't your fucking homie. Give me the fucking money, and this is my last time telling you!"

Ben took all of the money out of his pockets and as Shitty started walking closer to him to take the money out of his hand, 'POW POW' was all Ben heard, besides the tires burning rubber from the F150 as the driver accelerated on the gas.

Ben started panicking at the thought of being shot. Suddenly, he noticed Shitty fall to the ground and Lil' Fred standing there in shock with a handgun shaking in his hand.

Ben stared at Fred for a second. "Damn! I owe you lil' homie!" But Fred was still in shock behind what had just taken place.

Returning a favor, Ben grabbed Fred's arm and they both took off running to Ben's Monte Carlo. By this time, people started coming out their houses to see if somebody had been shot. Out of nowhere, Ms. Wanda ran from her house barefoot and screaming.

"Where is my baby? Oh, my baby!' She screamed after hearing gunshots and noticing her son wasn't in the apartment.

Once she made it to the crowd, she noticed Shitty was shot, so she calmed down a bit. She still didn't see her son as people crowded the murder scene, making all kinds of comments pertaining to the shooting.

"I can't believe somebody finally got his ass," Ms. Wanda said.

CHAPTER 2

"Dawg, stop fucking tripping!" Ben aggressively fussed as they pulled up at Paul's house.

"I'm good, Homie," Fred replied. "I just hope none of them niggas start talking. Ya, dig?"

"Man, look, it's whatever. Besides, these niggas know what it is when it comes to that rat shit," Ben said as they jumped out the whip. While approaching Paul's front door, Fred noticed Five-0 pulled up on the corner of Thalia and S. Roberson.

"Man, there go them, people," Fred nervously said.

"Homie, chill out," Ben stated, knocking on the door. At the same time, he was feeling the same nervous itch himself.

"Dawg let's get the fuck out of here, this nigga ain't home."

Fred turned to go back to the car, and Ben followed him. After a few steps, Ben looked back and noticed the blind open in the living room.

"There that nigga go!" He yelled to Fred as they both turned to head back to Paul's porch. Once they were back in front of the house, Paul stood on the top step dressed in a pair of camouflage cargo shorts, with no shirt, and a pair of Nike slippers on. He had this dumb ass smirk on his face that upset Ben.

"What's so fucking funny?" Ben spat out in frustration.

"Pump yo brakes, Homie," Paul shouted back as he focused on the dude that was unfamiliar to him. "Who lil' one is?" Paul asked, noticing that Ben always kept a youngsta around him.

"This Lil' Fred, Wanda's son," Ben replied.

"What Wanda?"

"Wanda out the Calliope, Big Fred's ole lady."

"Damn, now that you mentioned it, he looks just like his paw."

Big Fred was a grimy ass nigga that would do any and everything to make that money. He was the definition of an all-around hustler. He and Wanda were like Bonnie and Clyde back then, but Karma is a motherfucker.

"I heard you knocking, but I was knee deep in some ass; besides, when I heard the knock at the door, I was at my peak, and you know I wasn't gon stop until I got me."

"Them hoes gonna be the cause of your death," Ben replied in a serious tone.

"The way I see it, a nigga have to go someday, so why not be in some pussy when it happened," Paul said as he waved Ben and Fred in the apartment.

"Say, who that hoe is anyway?" Ben asked, curious to know who the bitch was, but Paul immediately changed the subject.

"What you niggas up to? Y'all looking like you just robbed a bank or something."

"Homie, get rid of that hoe, we need to lace you up on some shit." Ben insisted.

"Give me a minute," Paul said as he put on a Saints t-shirt that was on the coffee table with half a bottle of Hennessy and what looked to be at least a half-ounce of Orange Kush.

"Roll something up right quick," he told them before he headed to the bedroom.

Paul had always been that playboy type of dude in the hood that was fucking all kind of bitches, regardless of if they were black, white, Asian, you name it, he had 'em. It's like they couldn't resist his 6'2" frame, long shoulder length dreads and cocoa complexion. Not to mention the fact that he wore the best clothes, along with his crazy sense of humor. His only downfall was that he was easily distracted by a woman, which we all knew could cost him his life.

Moments later Paul and some brown skin hotty who stood like 5'5" weighing 135lbs, with long silky black hair flowing way past her shoulders, walked out the room. The highly attractive female spoke.

"What's up," she said with a look on her face that read y'all just stopped a bitch from getting hers.

"What's up," they said in unison in an evenly dry tone. "China this is my nigga Ben I was telling you about," he pointed in Ben's direction. "And this is Fred, a friend of Bens."

"Nice to meet y'all," China said dryly approaching the door, then she turned to Paul and made a hand gesture, implying that he should call her.

"So what is it, my nigga?" Paul anxiously asked, not completely closing the door.

Ben started to enlighten him on the details of the event that transpired in the Calliope. After he was brought up to speed, Paul turned to Fred, who by this time is high as a motherfucker.

"Since you, a friend of Bens, I'ma give it to you like I'd give it to him. You need to lay low for a few days to see if they have some type of buzz in the streets. You know the streets be talking, so just chill for a sec."

"On some real nigga shit, fuck what the streets have to say. If a nigga want to see me, I'm out here errday, I'm ready to cut loose on any nigga that want it." Fred said, not realizing he could be knee deep in some shit if he fell on a Murder Charge.

Paul looked at Ben, then back towards Fred, and said, "I like yo heart Lil' One, but heart without brains ain't worth shit, keep in mind Lil' Homie that it's not a physical game, it's a thinking game, and only the smart survive, always remember that."

Fred didn't want to hear that shit, combined with the smoke having his thoughts off balance, he shouted, "It's 'gon take more than smarts to survive in this game, the only thing these niggas respect is drama, and I got plenty of that!" "How old are you?" Paul asked.

"I'm 15, but what difference do that make?"

Who the fuck is this? Ben thought to himself as he looked down at his phone not trying to shift his focus from the situation at hand.

After the third ring, Ben answered, "Hello?"

"Say homie, put it on the news," Rell spit through the phone. Ben grabbed the remote and started searching for the news channel.

"What's up?" Paul asked as he and Fred ran to the TV.

"What's going on?" Fred asked as he eyed the screen upon seeing the Calliope.

"What she said?" Ben asked as the voice of Molly Robertson blast through the TV speakers.

"Anybody with information concerning the shooting in the Calliope Housing Development where a 21-year-old male was injured in what appeared to be two gunshot wounds to the mid-section of his back. It has been confirmed by EMS that the victim is in critical condition with life-threatening injuries. Anyone with information that can lead to an arrest can contact the Crime Stopper Hotline at 1-800-822-0000. Back to you Bob."

"Roll something else up, this shit got my nerves fucked up all over again," Fred said. "I hope none of them clown ass niggas don't say shit," he continued.

"Just lay low like I said and see how things play out," Paul suggested as he broke down the bud to twist it up.

"Look here my nigga, go meet Rell in the Calliope and see what the business is," Ben told Paul.

"I got you, my nigga, consider it done," Paul said as he headed for the door.

When he pulled in the project, he put his .40 cal on his waist, grabbed half of a blunt out the ashtray, got out of the truck and walked over to Rell.

"What it is my nigga?" Paul asked as he eyed the crowd that was standing around gossiping.

"It's the same ole shit," Rell replied extending his hand to reach for the blunt. "That nigga Shitty had it coming, if not Lil' Fred, somebody was going to get at that nigga. You know how reckless that fool can talk at times."

"Where the fuck Fredrick at?" Wanda yelled as she approached Rell and Paul, puffing on a Newport, looking like she hadn't slept in weeks.

"Ms. Wanda, I haven't seen him, but when I do, I'll tell him you looking for him," Rell said, giving Paul a look like she needed to get it together.

"Yeah, you do that," she replied as she stormed off mumbling to herself.

Rumors circulated fast that Fred smoked Shitty because he tried to rob the dice game. They were also saying that Fred smoked him cause Shitty handled his mother real bad from being short on her score money.

Paul's phone started to ring, initially he thought it was Ben calling to see what the word was, but when he looked at the phone, he realized it was China, so he simply sent her call to voicemail by hitting the end button. After clearing his line, he decided to call Ben to update him on the situation.

"What's up B?" Paul said the moment Ben answered the phone.

"Dawg, I was just about to hit you up," Ben said.

"Talk to me, I'll talk back," Paul said, curious to know what he had on his mind.

"I need you to go pass by Charity Hospital to see if homie made it or not."

"Bet," Paul said as he ended the call, dapped Rell, "I have to make a run."

Paul jumped in his truck, took out the Soulja Slim disc, replaced it with Lil' Wayne, and began pressing the skip button until he reached his favorite track #3, *Money on my Mind.*

As he approached the intersection of MLK and S. Claiborne, the traffic light turned red. A nice-looking bitch pulled up alongside him in a red Honda Accord and for some reason, they noticed one another. Paul gave her a head nod, and she obliged. With Paul being the player, he is, he signaled for her to pull over. She did as asked and the moment she got out her car and closed the door, he pulled in behind her, and parked. He got out and greeted her like a player would.

"What's good luv?" he asked, with a flirtatious smile that revealed his perfectly even white teeth. "I'm Joe," he lied for no reason at all, extending his hand to shake hers.

"I'm Roxanne, but everybody calls me Roc."

"So what were your eyes saying that your mouth couldn't at the light?" Paul asked.

"What you mean, you were looking down in my face, so what were your eyes saying?" Roxanne replied with a shy smirk on her face as if she was in 6th grade and had her first crush on a boy.

"Since you put it that way, my eyes was saying that ole girl is attractive as a motherfucker."

"You probably tell that to every girl you meet, huh?" Roxanne asked with one hand on her right hip.

"Damn, we been acquainted for 90 seconds, and you passing judgment already."

"I'm not passing judgment, I'm simply asking do you flirt with every attractive woman you see?"

"It's obvious we started out on the wrong foot, do you care to start over?" Paul asked.

"No, we good," she said, knowing she was enjoying the moment.

"So where you headed?" he asked the second he noticed he had full control of the conversation.

"I'm on my way home, I live a few blocks away."

"Where at?" Paul asked, feeling as if she lived a few blocks away, then he should've known her, considering that the Melph was only a few blocks away.

"I'm from off Josephine and LaSalle."

"Yeah," Paul responded, "well if you find yourself bored, hit me up, and we can go out to eat or whatever you want to do for entertainment."

"I can do that," Roxanne said as she accepted the offer. "How you gon call me if you don't have my number?"

"Because you gon give it to me," she said in a sassy tone.

"Now you giving me demands," he said then they exchanged numbers and went their separate ways. As Paul jumped in his truck, his phone fell under the driver seat as he pulled away.

"Fuck," he yelled as he tried to retrieve the phone and maintain the wheel.

***

"Man, if somebody mentions my name to the police, they would be a dead man before they catch me," Fred said.

"I know Paul made it to the hospital by now," Ben said as he paced the floor back and forth.

"Why the fuck this nigga ain't hit me back yet. It's been like an hour since I last talked to him," Ben continued.

"Hit that nigga up again," Fred told him.

He did as asked, but still didn't get a response. "This some crazy shit."

"What?" Fred asked.

"He ain't answering his phone."

"Take me home so I can get a change of clothes for a few days," Fred said.

"Nigga, don't get scared now," Ben said joking.

"You got me fucked up homie, the only thing I'm scared of is what I can't challenge," Fred said as he clutched his pistol through his front pocket.

When they pulled up in the Calliope, so Fred could get his clothes, they noticed a police car patrolling the area. Not knowing if someone had given a description of Ben's car or not, he didn't want to take a chance on going through the project. Especially, with Fred still having his gun on him. Instead, they went to a Hip Hop store on N. Broad St. and grabbed a few outfits.

"This should hold you down a few days," Ben said as he handed Fred the bags.

"Big Homie, I appreciate this," Fred said as he put the bags in the trunk of Ben's silver Monte Carlo. As they got into the car, Ben's phone rung twice.

"This is Paul right here," Ben said as he answered the call.

"So what's the status on the situation?" Ben asked, not knowing what to expect. "Homie, shit was crazy when I arrived at the hospital. Motherfuckers was screaming and crying, you know the usual reaction when a loved one gets touched. Dawg, it was hectic. I'm in route to the crib right now, meet me over there." Paul said as he sat in traffic at the corner of Tulane Ave. and N. Claiborne.

"What the deal is?" Fred asked as they sped away from the parking lot.

"From the sound of things, Shitty dead," Ben said as he headed in the direction of Paul house.

"Fuck that nigga, that's his family's problem, not mine," Fred said as they rode down N. Broad, heading back uptown.

Ben pulled in the parking lot of a Chevron and told Fred to hand over the .380 that was used in the shooting.

"Dawg, I ain't giving my shit up. What kinda time you on, Big Homie?" Fred rejected.

"I'm only trying to keep 'yo ass out of the LTI with juvenile life till 'yo ass 31," Ben said.

Fred thought about it for a few seconds then handed the gun to Ben after wiping his prints off. Ben wrapped it in a Burger Orleans bag that laid on the backseat from the day before and tossed it in a dumpster that was located on the side of the Chevron.

"Getting some heat is the easy part, I can get you twenty throwaways in one phone call," Ben said as he put his car in reverse, knowing they had an apartment in the Melph where they stashed so many guns, you would mistake it for an armory.

"Put 'yo seatbelt on, you know them people be smoking uptown, and we don't need that extra heat on us.

"I feel ya, Big Homie," Fred said as they approached the Broad St. overpass.

***

Paul made a right on N. Claiborne Ave., glanced at his watch, 1:45 read on his Movado. *It's odd to have all this fucking traffic at this time of day*, He thought to himself. The weather was beautiful, in the early 70's and while stuck in traffic, Paul just took in the scenery of the hot girls walking around in their come fuck me shorts. To his left, he saw what appeared to be some dude trying to mack on a female at a local gas station and thought of Roxanne, but instead of calling her, he decided to hit China back to see what it was hitting for. He picked up his phone, which was lying on the passenger seat and scrolled through the call log until China Doll showed up on the screen. He then pressed -*Send.* China answered the phone on the second ring.

"I know you saw that I called earlier, why it took you so long to call me back?" she said in a sassy tone.

"I had to wait until the opportunity presented itself," Paul said nonchalantly, "But if I called at a bad time, I'll hit you back later," he continued.

"No, it's not a bad time," she responded quickly. "I'm just saying, I know you saw I called over an hour ago."

"So what's up?" Paul asked, trying to change the subject. "Nothing, I'm at home chilling with my best friend, what's up with you?"

"I'm still in the midst of handling some business, you know how my line of work is, but I should be free tonight. If you want to get together, maybe we can go to the casino, and while we are there, we can get something to eat. Tonight, is seafood night and the buffet is going to be open all night. Afterward, we can get a room at the W and do us, if that's what you want to do," he said, forcing a smile to her face.

All China could do on the other end of the phone was think about them picking up where they had left off the last time they were together. The way he sexed her up was unexplainable, and she craved those exact types of pleasures every time she thought of him. However, more than likely, he was good for standing her up or simply just would not answer the phone.

"You know you play all kind of games. If you ain't sure 'bout this, tell me now, don't have me anticipating you picking me up, because I ain't gon be sitting around waiting on you, or wondering if you gon show up or not."

"Just be ready when I call," Paul said before hanging up.

By the time Paul made it home, Ben and Fred were already smoking a blunt waiting for him.

"Damn homie, 'bout time you got here, we been waiting on your ass for like 10 minutes. If you wouldn't have made it by the time we finished this blunt, we was gon push out. Cause you know Safe Home be swinging through, especially on Tuesday and Thursday."

Safe Home is a police unit that raids all the hot spots in the city. When they come, they're coming in at least 10 unmarked cars, normally, Expeditions. They're riding four deep, and any and every nigga that's out when they hit is going to be harassed. With niggas knowing that you'll see them throwing their packs, tossing bangers, or anything that could send them upstate.

Even with the thought of Safe Home hitting the block, the only thing Ben had on his mind was putting Fred somewhere to chill for a few days.

"Dawg, I was stuck in traffic, it's jammed packed, bumper to bumper on Claiborne. I thought it was a wreck or some shit like that, but it was just some fucked up traffic, especially at this time of the day. But fuck all that, what the business is?" Paul asked as he adjusted his tool on his waist.

"I'm about to take Fred to the Comfort Inn in the East on Read Blvd.," Ben said. The East is a section of the city where the upper-middle-class lives. It's like its own city within the city.

"Aight I'ma fuck with you later on," Paul said.

As they pulled in the parking lot of the hotel, Fred started to feel very uncomfortable with the fact that he was in Eastern, New Orleans with no transportation, and only $50, which he'd gotten from Ben at the dice game in the Calliope. Also, to him, being in this part of the city felt as if he were a thousand miles away from home; yet in reality, he was really 20 minutes away from uptown.

As they parked, the trunk opened, and Fred took his bags out before heading for the hotel lobby. Ben approached the receptionist, who was a rather short, but sexy light-skinned female. After securing a room and getting the key he paid in cash. Making sure Fred was good, he handed him three hundred dollars, and after giving him the key, he told him to hit him up if he needed anything.

***

It was 10:30 at night and China needed someone to vent to, so she called her best friend. Immediately after she answered the phone, China released all of the frustration that she had built up.

"Hello."

"Girl I don't know why I keep putting up with this shit. All he fucking do is lie," China complained.

"Slow down girl. Tell me what the hell you're talking about."

"He called me earlier today..." but before she could finish, her best friend cut her off.

"Who is he?"

"Paul! He told me we were going to the casino and afterward to get something to eat, but he ain't even bother to call to tell me he wasn't gon make it."

"You never know what came up, just hear him out before you start tripping."

"Girl, it's always some shit with him."

"China, I can't wait to see who this Paul dude is."

"Don't hold your breath."

"Just relax and stop tripping, you know you a drama queen."

"Girl, bye! I'ma talk to you tomorrow."

After hanging up the phone, China undressed and went to bed.

CHAPTER 3

The next morning Fred called Ben and told him to bring him something to smoke. The few nickel bags he had the night before had not lasted long. A few hours later, Ben brought him seven grams of purp and a couple of boxes of Swisher Sweet cigars. Despite the fact that the hotel offered complimentary breakfast, Ben also brought a dozen Krispy Kreme doughnuts.

"Dawg, how long I have to stay in this fucking hotel?" Fred asked, not liking the fact that he had to be in a hotel like he was hiding or something, because to him image and reputation was the only thing that mattered, even if it meant going to prison or dying, cause at the end of the day, when niggas spoke of him, he wanted to be spoken about as a standup guy.

"Out of sight, out of mind is the best solution right now," Ben replied, trying to get him to understand the severity of the situation. "I think you should lay low for at least another day or two. This should hold you down till then, if not, hit me up and let me know what you need," Ben said as he looked at his watch like he was going to be late for a meeting or something.

Before he left, he called Fred over to the window and pointed across the street to the Plaza Mall.

"Go over there and buy you some food, or to simply hang out if you got tired of sitting in the hotel," Ben said, knowing the chances were slim that anyone would recognize Fred in this part of the city. "Whatever you do, just try to stay under the radar," Ben said. After they pounded fists, he turned and headed for the door, but before leaving, he looked back at Fred. "I'll be back to get you in a few hours."

***

Before Ben could close the door on his Monte Carlo, Trap rushed him with urgency to get the dope from him, because there was a long line of impatient dope fiends waiting to score.

Business was doing extremely well for the Slum Godds. Actually, their clientele doubled after word traveled throughout the city that the Melph was giving twice as much product for their money. Plus, the dope was the best out right now, and Ben was loving every minute of it because the money was rolling through in lump sums, and everybody that was part of the SG's were eating.

When running a heroin shop, the two most important times of the day to be available for addicts is early in the morning so they can kill their morning sickness, and right before shop closes, because a true dope fiend refuses to go in for the night without scoring a couple of bags.

"Dawg you know shop opens at 7:00am. It's damn near 9 o' clock where the fuck you been?" Trap asked as all eyes focused in on Ben and the bag that he clutched in his hand. Everyone present knew he was the one responsible for the product they so desperately needed.

"Fred called first thing this morning, so I stopped by the hotel to bring him something to smoke," Ben shot back.

"How long is he gonna be in that fucking hotel?"

"A few more days. I'ma go look for a house to rent, and I was thinking 'bout letting him live in it, cause the way his momma living, I think it would be better if he got away from that shit."

Ben handed Trap a brown paper bag with 30 bundles of heroin inside of it. Each bundle contained twenty-five 20-dollar bags, which was equal to $15,000. With the line being as long as it is, there was a good chance that the 30 bundles were not going to be enough, so Ben figured he'd need at least 10 more bundles by noon.

Ryder and K-Dog both strapped with Mac-11 held their post, making sure no foul moves were made. Ryder stood at the bottom of the stairwell, while K-Dog stood on the second floor, watching Trap serve the work. This was necessary due to the heroin game being the most dangerous hustles of all. One reason being a fiend would do whatever it took to kill their sickness when they're sick.

Posted up by the corner store that sat on MLK and S. Robertson, Lil' Mike watched out for the law or anything out the ordinary. If he had to inform the crew of anything, he'd call it in by using his Cobra 2-way walkie talkie, which is what the entire crew used when their shop was open.

After every 5 bundles sold, Tre would collect the money from Trap and bring it to Paul who would count it and place it in the thousand-dollar stacks using rubber bands. At least this was their position for this week, cause next week it would be totally different. They made sure they rotated their operating process every week. That way, Ben would know the entire crew could be trusted on all levels of the operation. And after the heat settled, even Fred would be placed in rotation.

"This ain't no fucking Ben's shit. I don't hustle for no nigga," the old cat standing in the hallway said.

"Well if it ain't Ben's dope, I don't want it," the fiend shot back.

The old nigga instantly got in his feelings and started making all kinds of statements, not realizing that these addicts that use dope can be more dangerous than the ones that sell it in some cases.

"You better get from out of this project," the old timer said, not liking the fact that the fiend didn't want to score from him. These young cats were making it hard for him to sell his dope.

"You hear that?" K-Dog asked Trap after he heard the conversation between the old timer and the dope fiend.

"Yeah, Dawg, I heard that shit," Trap said kind of confused because he' know ain't nobody supposed to be hustling in that hallway.

"Let me go see who the fuck that is," K-Dog said as he went down a flight of stairs, ready to defend their territory.

When he got there, he saw one of their customers walking off and some old penitentiary looking ass nigga with two long plaits that hung to the middle of his chest. They were standing there looking up at him as he stood on the fifth step that led to the platform the old timer was standing on.

"Yo Ken," K-Dog called out to his customer.

He turned to see K-Dog standing there, so he walked back towards the hallway.

"Who that nigga is?" Ken asked, referring to the old timer who was looking crazy.

"I don't know, why what's up?" K-Dog asked.

"That nigga trying to get me to score from him like I'm new to this shit or something."

"That's what's wrong with you niggas, y'all got the game fucked up. That's what you do when you hustling, you try to make the sell. It's up to you to buy it," the old-timer shot back.

"I don't give a fuck how you hustle, just don't do it in this hallway," K-Dog said, not liking old timer's vibe.

"How the fuck you gon tell me where to hustle?" he said, disrespecting K-Dog and the gun in his hand. "I been in this project before you was born, go ask yo people about Jack Rabbit, they know me," he continued.

When K-Dog heard the name Jack Rabbit, that name rung a bell. He remembered hearing stories about how dangerous he was, but it didn't matter, cause he still had to protect his territory despite the fact that he was dealing with an old gangster.

"Say bruh, check this out, this is my second and last time telling you, don't hustle right chere," K-Dog said, knowing the old ass nigga was gonna be a problem.

"You right youngster, I'm gone chill, but you lil' niggas better start showing some respect," he said as he eyed K-Dog real hard before turning to walk towards the middle court.

"Dawg you got to watch that nigga," Ken told K-Dog who was thinking the same thing.

"So what you trying to get homie," K-Dog asked Ken.

"Let me get 3 for 50, I'ma be back at cha."

"Come upstairs, Trap got it," K-Dog said, walking up the stairs.

When they made it to the second floor, Trap asked what the deal was. K-Dog told him about the old nigga name Jack Rabbit trying to shortstop sells, and that he'd ran him off. "Jack Rabbit," Trap said more to himself.

"You heard of that nigga before?" K-Dog asked.

"Man, dude like a legend back here, that's the nigga they said killed a police who had his potna handcuffed on the police car. He's supposedly walked over to the officer to ask why he had his brother handcuffed, and in a blink of an eye he pulled a .38 special. Shooting the police once in the head and once in the chest. Back then if you ratted, you were getting whacked, so nobody said shit."

"Yeah!" K-Dog said as the thoughts of killing this old nigga crossed his mind, more now than ever.

"So what's up Ken?" Trap asked.

"I got 50 dollars, let me get three bags."

"You got that," Trap said, handing him the dope.

Ken was a killer also, he just couldn't shake the dope. The way that Jack Rabbit handle him, all he was thinking 'bout was how many times he was gon shoot him, cause he knew that the old timer had underestimated him simply because he was a heroin addict. An hour later, Ken came back in the project. This time it wasn't to score, but to set this old timer straight. When Ryder saw him come through the cut, he signaled for him to come over to him.

"How much you got?" Ryder asked him.

"I'm good right now, I came to holla at old timer right there," Ken said, pointing to Jack Rabbit who was now standing under a tree in the court way without a worry in the world. Ken walked up to Jack Rabbit carrying a .45 cal in his back pocket.

"What's up old school, you still straight?"

"Yeah, I'm still straight. Them young niggas must have sold you some weak shit, now you want to fuck with me, but I ain't tripping. What you trying to get?" Jack Rabbit asked.

"Let me get a bag," Ken shot back.

When Jack Rabbit looked down into the plastic bag to serve Ken, Ken reached into his pocket, pulled his gun, and pointed it into his chest.

When Rabbit looked up and saw Ken's gun pointed at his chest, he had to utilize his street experience. The number one rule is not to panic when you're boxed in, because if it's a way to get into a situation, then more than likely, it's a way to get out of one.

"Put it up young blood, there go the police," Rabbit said, looking over Ken's shoulder as if the police had just arrived.

Ken took his eyes off one of the most dangerous niggas the Melph had ever seen for what seemed like a tenth of a second, and Rabbit immediately pulled his .45cal off his waist. Immediately, he fired 3 quick shots, striking Ken twice in the head. Ken was dead before his lifeless body hit the ground.

Jack Rabbit then stood over him and fired five more shots, hitting him in the chest area. Afterwards, he took off running from the scene. Ryder had the urge to start shooting at Rabbit but decided to fall back, realizing that didn't have shit to do with them, so instead, he watched the entire scene from a distance.

"Churp...Churp, what's going on?" Lil' Mike asked on his walkie talkie.

"We good," Ryder said, looking at Ken's motionless body on the pavement.

By that time, all the SGs, along with some other cats from different crews in the Melph was on point after hearing the gunshots.

"Oh my god, somebody call the ambulance, an elderly woman screamed from her balcony. As the crowd grew larger and larger, spectators tried to get a look at Ken's corpse.

Rabbit returned back on the scene five minutes later, after putting away the gun he used, he found himself in a stare down with K-Dog, who was now on the murder scene.

CHAPTER 4

After picking Fred up from the hotel, they headed to the Lake Front which was jam-packed with the best of whips, the baddest bitches in the city, and low-level hustlers all the way up to the major niggas getting real paper. Everybody who was somebody was here to make their appearance. Usually, during the summer, every Sunday, Lake Shore Dr. was the place to be.

"Damn dawg, this is how it goes down out here?" Fred asked as his head was moving side-to-side like he was watching a tennis match. He was trying to look at every piece of ass moving.

"Yeah, nigga, this is how it goes down," Paul replied as Ben sat in the front passenger seat laughing at the fact that Fred was unfamiliar with this territory which was only 15 minutes away from his house.

"If you get out of the project sometimes, you'll be amazed at the things you see," Paul said.

"For real homie, cause this shit looks like Miami or something. I didn't know New Orleans had all these palm trees and shit, all I know is the project and the things that surround it. This shit looks like another city to me," Fred said staring out the window.

As they slowly rode down the strip checking out the scene, Ben shouted with urgency. "There's a parking spot right there," he pointed in the direction of an empty parking spot.

Paul put on his right turn signal and honked the horn three times to alert the nigga standing in front of the parking spot to move. As he talked on his phone, the nigga motioned for them to keep going as if the spot was occupied. Paul began to roll down the window to hear what the tall black dude was saying. Paul stuck his left hand out the window, clutched his .40 cal in the right, and confronted. "Look here my nigga, I'm trying to get here."

From the backseat, Fred noticed it was Black Larry from his hood that ran with the Cheddar Boys. The Cheddar Boys are one of the most dangerous crews in the Uptown area, and they also have a reputation for getting money by any means necessary.

"Let me holla at him right fast," Fred said, hopping out the Avalanche.

"What's good big homie?" Fred said, before his feet even touched the ground.

"Ain't nothing," Larry replied, and continued "What you doing with them, you running with them Melph niggas now?"

"We trying to get here," Fred replied, putting an end to the small talk.

"Naw homie, I'm holding this spot down for my homies," Larry said, standing his ground. "There they go right there," He continued, looking in the direction of Je'sus' truck.

As Fred turned to see what Larry was talking about, he noticed an all-white Range Rover with the left blinker on. It was occupied with three dudes, Je'sus, Curtis Mitchell, and 9 Finger Lou. Fred wasn't trying to make a big scene, so he simply said, "I respect that."

As he turned and walked back to the truck that was about nine feet away, his body language revealed that he was in his feelings. The moment he got in the truck, he told Paul to go find another spot with a mug on his face.

"What was that about?" Curtis asked the moment they got out of the Rover and greeted Larry cause he caught the fucked up vibes.

"It wasn't nothing, I was letting him know I was holding the spot down."

"It looked like a little more than that," Je'sus said. "Don't underestimate that lil' nigga."

"I should have run over that duck ass nigga," Paul said as Fred got in the truck.

"That's the only thing 'bout coming out here; you have to get out here early to get a decent parking spot," Ben said. "That's why most niggas just ride the strip and not worry about parking," he continued.

It took only twenty minutes to find a parking spot open at the corner of Franklin Ave. and Lakeshore Dr. They got out of the truck, checked to make sure no weapons on them was revealed. They were in fear of crossing paths with the undercovers that walk the strip like civilians.

"I'm good?" Ben asked, looking down at his waist hoping the extended clip wasn't showing.

"You good my nigga," Paul told him. "Let's just hope we don't have to use the motherfuckers."

"If we have to, we gonna do just that," Fred said still in his feelings with Black Larry.

Paul's phone started to ring, playing *'I'll pay for it'* ringtone by Soulja Slim. He removed the phone from its phone clip, looked down at it and in nearly a whisper said, "What this hoe want! Hello?" he said, answering China's call.

"Where you at?" she asked, staring him down from a spot by the red and black Bullz Eye BBQ food truck.

"What you mean, where I'm at?" Paul shot back.

"You heard me, where you at? Let me guess! By one of your hoes?"

"Listen!" Paul said. "Don't call me with that bullshit, besides, I'm in the midst of something right now so I'ma get back witcha."

"You still ain't answer my question," China said, giggling to herself.

"I'm on the Lakefront taking care of some business, so I'ma get with you later."

"You promise?"

"Yeah. I'ma hit you up later tonight."

"Why can't we get together right now?"

"Didn't I tell you I was taking care of some business?"

"I only need five minutes of your time," she said, instructing him to look to his left towards the Bullz Eye food truck on the opposite side of the street.

"What the fuck you mean?" he asked, not understanding her request.

"Boy just do what I asked you."

He complied, and after scanning the area, not knowing exactly what he's looking for, he locked eyes with her who was looking good and smiling from ear-to-ear, along with a bad bitch who was just looking. As Paul and his niggas approached the two highly attractive women, China met him. They embraced with a hug and kiss that lasted longer than expected, and then she introduced Paul to her friend.

"Paul this is my friend Diamond, Diamond this is my Boo I was telling you about."

"So this is Paul huh," which was more of a statement than a question. "I've heard a lot about you," Diamond said, extending her right hand to greet Paul.

"I hope the things you..." yet before he finished his statement, China interrupted, "Paul introduce us to your friends."

"I apologize for my rudeness," Paul replied, introducing them to the ladies.

Diamond looked at Fred and said, "Girl, how old is he? He can't be no more than 13 out here trying to be grown."

"I'm old enough," Fred said in his defense.

"So now that everyone has become acquainted, what y'all up to?" Paul asked, trying to end the conversation so he can push out and track down some new pussy.

"We just out and about enjoying the weather," which was perfect for the occasion. The sun was shining bright and it was mixed with a slight breeze coming off the lake.

"Damn those ribs smell good," Ben said, digging into his right front pocket to pull out a fist full of money. At the same time, he scanned the menu that hung on the back wall of the food truck. "Do you ladies want anything."

At first, they were acting bashful, "I'm good," but Ben insisted.

"Beautiful women have to eat too," which made both of them smile. Afterward he placed five orders of ribs, four cokes and one Pineapple Big Shot, which was for him.

"Is it separate," the cashier asked.

"Put it on one bill, she'll pay for it," Ben replied, pointing at Diamond, who had a surprised look on her face.

"Naw, I'm just bullshitting, I got it. How much?"

"That'll be $54.38," the cashier said, bagging up the food.

As they walked over to a picnic table in the area, Ben handed everyone their tray of ribs. They chit-chatted for a while before going their separate ways.

"Make sure you call me tonight," China yelled,

The moment they separated, Ben told Paul that Diamond was a bad bitch and that they all should get together someday. "Do you want me to set it up?" Paul asked.

"Yeah, Homie set it up," Ben replied. "I know niggas be fucking the dog shit out that hoe," he continued.

"You know I got China dick whipped, she'll basically do whatever I tell her, and with that being her best friend, it'll be easy to convince her to go through with it. All I have to tell her is that the 4 of us should double date and trust me, she gon see to it that it happens. But forget them, man look at all these boss bitches out here, we need to pull a few of these hoes before we leave," Paul said.

As they walked the strip, they crossed paths with the Cheddar Boys who were posted by the roadside talking to some bitches. Both crews noticed how Fred and Black Larry locked eyes as they passed, but no one said a word.

"What was really said between you and Larry?" Ben asked Fred the moment they walked past the Cheddar Boys. It was obvious tension was building up, based on the stares between the two.

"Fuck that nigga, if we wasn't out here, I would let him have it," Fred responded.

"You know what your problem is?" Paul asked.

"What my problem is?"

"You need some pussy," he said as him and Ben burst into laughter.

"Y'all laughing like I ain't fucking nothing," Fred said.

"Nigga you ain't got no game for these hoes," Ben added.

"I don't need no game, all these hoes want is a real nigga, they don't give a fuck bout no game."

"Okay! Let me see you pull her," Ben said, pointing at a pretty youngsta who was around Fred's age, or maybe a year older.

The moment Fred approached her and asked her name, shots went off about a block away. The crowd went crazy.

"Let's get the fuck out of here!" Ben yelled as the three of them maneuvered through the crowd trying to make it to their truck.

While running, they passed several undercovers who had their guns drawn. Once they made it to the truck, they sped off in the direction of the hotel to drop Fred off. As they were riding down Gentilly Ave., Paul noticed a police car riding behind them with their sirens blazing and lights flashing. His initial thought was to run them, but Fred told him to just give him all the guns and he'll get out and run. He let them know to pick him up when he calls.

After they made the first right, so Fred could run, he opened the door to make his move, but noticed Five-0 kept going down Gentilly Ave. After a sigh of relief, they made the block, and got back on track before continuing to head toward the hotel to drop Fred off.

Once they made it to the hotel, Paul pulled in the parking lot right in front of the lobby. The moment they left, Ben told Paul to stop by the barbershop once they made it uptown. He needed to get something to smoke from Duck, considering it had been a long day even though the day was still young.

"Damn nigga, you smoked that whole ounce already, you just got that shit two days ago. Joy got yo ass stressing, huh?" Paul asked, joking around.

Normally, an ounce lasted Ben at least a week, cause he didn't really smoke blunts. But when he with the fellas, he'd smoke.

"I ain't got shit to stress about when it comes to my baby, I make sure my household's in order. That's something you need to try instead of running around like you still in high school, chasing these nothing ass hoes. If you need to know, I took care of Fred's weed head ass, and the way he smokes weed, I hope he don't fuck around with no other drugs," Ben continued with a chuckle.

"Oh, yeah! Speaking of Fred, what you get out of that look him and Larry gave each other," Paul asked, trying to see if he and Ben were on the same page.

"I know that look too well homie, that's a look of animosity, and animosity lead to beef," Ben answered as he replayed the scene of Fred and Larry in his head.

"Homie check that hoe out right there," Paul told Ben as he pointed in the Plaza Mall parking lot where they saw a beautiful redbone, placing her bags in the back seat of her white Lexus coupe. She had the perfect shape of an hourglass and could have easily been mistaken for a model or actress.

"On some real shit homie, that bitch bad as a motherfucker, but you know I don't fuck with them type of hoes. Most of the time it's 'bout what a nigga have, and it's very rare that the attraction is genuine. That's one of the reasons why I don't trust them gold diggin' bitches. Hoes like her are the biggest threat to niggas that's winning out chere in these streets," Ben said.

"What you mean by that my nigga?" Paul asked, confused with Ben comment.

"What I mean by that is that hoes like her use' what they have to get what they want, and before you realize it, you'll be exposing shit to that bitch you ain't supposed to."

"That's how some niggas rock, I just fuck 'em and duck 'em. You know how I rock, besides, you act like you wasn't that same nigga that targeted boss bitches," Paul said, reminding Ben of his old ways.

"Yeah, I was that nigga, but I was that nigga with a purpose. My situation was bigger than just getting my dick wet, I was getting that bread fucking with them hoes, but playing them hoes the way you be doing it can be dangerous. For the simple fact that women love hard, and it's so easy for a woman to allow their feelings to get involved. When you play games with their heart, they'll do anything to get even, especially when you don't know shit about them besides they suck a good dick or have some good pussy. Keep in mind that some of them think like men, that's why I rock the way I do with them hoes, it a reason for everything."

Before Ben came up in the game, he was a grimy ass nigga that specialized in hitting licks. He would pull a bad bitch and after schooling her on how they could get that money from them sucker ass niggas, he would send her to the doughboys who would be blinded by all their success. As a result of this, they don't recognize when a bitch is using them for a target, and that's how he came up in the game. He was a true Slum Godd, and he made a promise to himself that he'd never be that naive when it came to them no good ass bitches. When it came to fuckin' around with hoes in the streets, Ben knew it was a dog-eat-dog world, and he understood his position. He never put himself in a situation where a bitch could undermind or cutthroat him. Ben would rather go to the strip club, pull one of those clueless hoe's, slaughter they pussy, and walk away with no strings attached.

Then he'd go be with Joy who was his first love and also the mother of his son BJ, which was short for Benjamin Jr. Lately, he'd been thinking about making her his wife, but he wasn't sure that he was ready to take their long-term relationship to the next level. Though he knew if marriage was in his future, Joy would be the one, cause she'd been down with him when he ain't have shit. Once they got on the interstate, the traffic was mild, so it only took 15 minutes to make it uptown.

"Fuck! I should have called and told that nigga I was going to stop by," Ben stated, pulling up to the barbershop. He didn't see Duck's car parked in front.

"We should've known that nigga wasn't going to be in the shop on his day off," Paul said. "So, what we gon do?"

"I don't know," Ben replied.

But as they were parked in front of the shop debating on where they were gon' score from, Duck came out to dump his trash and noticed Paul's truck.

Ben hopped out the truck and went in the shop. Moments later, Duck came in.

"What's up B?" Duck asked as they dapped each other.

"I was about to leave cause I didn't see your car. Let me get an ounce of that OG Kush," Ben said as he peeled off five hundred from his knot of bills.

"Tiffany's in my shit, she went to get a box of trash bags, she should've been back by now"

"You got to be fucking her, you keep her hanging around, even on your off days," Ben said.

"You know how Tiff is, let me get that for you though," Duck said as he went in a door that was in the back of the shop.

Ben called Paul and told him to come in the shop cause he got caught up in a *Hood-to-Hood* DVD that Duck was playing.

Paul and Duck entered the room at the same time. Duck handed Ben the ounce and then dapped Paul.

"You got something to roll up in?" Ben asked.

Duck went in his drawer on his workstation and grabbed a keep moving cigar. He tossed it to Ben.

"It's cool to smoke in here?" Ben asked, cutting the cigar with his thumbnail.

"Do you, Matter of fact, I'ma match yo blunt," Duck said as he grabbed another cigar out the drawer to roll up.

The moment Ben fired up the blunt, Tiffany walked in, carrying a Wal-Mart bag.

"What up y'all?" Tiffany spoke, referring to Ben and Paul.

"What's up Tiff?" Ben responded, but Paul was on some other shit.

"When you gon stop playing games with a nigga?" Paul asked, looking her up and down.

"I ain't playing no games, either it is or it ain't, and it ain't. I'm not fucking with you like that," Tiffany said. "But y'all can let a bitch hit the weed."

"And a bitch could let a real nigga hit that ass," Paul said while Ben and Duck laughed at his persistence to fuck Tiff.

"All you niggas talk that shit, and when a bitch let you hit, y'all don't even put it down like y'all claim," Tiffany said, making Ben and Duck laugh harder.

"You gon' slip up one day and give me that pussy, so just remember what you saying right now."

"Here, and don't be holding the weed, two hits and pass it," Ben said, handing her the blunt.

"I'm glad y'all here though, because I want to know what y'all beefing with the Cheddar Boys for," Tiffany asked, being nosey.

"That's some bullshit, we just saw them, niggas," Paul said.

"Well, that's the word on the street, so be careful."

"I'ma have to check into that," Ben said trying to make sense of the rumor.

After watching the DVD, they headed to the project. Within twenty minutes, Ben's phone rang.

"What's up Bae?" Ben said.

"This B.J."

"What's up, Lil' Man?"

"You still gon play the game with me?" BJ asked.

"Of course, Jr."

"Well, what time you coming, because my bedtime is in an hour"

"Okay, I'm on my way."

"Aight, bye daddy."

"Bye," Ben said, hanging up.

"I'ma holla at cha, my nigga, the lil' one wants me to play the game with him," Ben said as he dapped Paul.

"A'ight homie, be safe."

CHAPTER 5

Once Ben made it to the project, he called Rell and told him to meet him in the Melph.

"I'll be waiting by the first ramp on the S. Roberson end of the project. Park in the driveway," Ben said.

"I'll be there. Give me an hour. I'm handling some business," Rell told him.

By the time Rell arrived, it was raining, so all of the hustlers who typically hung out no matter what the weather was like, gathered under the breezeway which protected them from the rain.

"Yo Ben, ain't that your boy out the Calliope that just rolled up in that Maxima?" K-Dog asked as all eyes locked in on Rell running across the courtyard toward the crowd of niggas standing around.

"Yeah, that's my nigga Rell," Ben responded as he made himself visible.

"What's popping my nigga?" Rell asked as they embraced with a hug and a dap.

Ben pulled him away from the crowd of niggas before he got into the details of the requested visit.

"Before I say anything, what's yo' relationship with the Cheddar Boys?" Ben asked.

"I mean, I know them niggas, but I don't fuck with them like that ya dig. Why?" Rell asked, curious to know where this conversation was headed.

"It's like this, I was in the *Hot Spot* barber shop and Tiffany pulled me to the side. She told me I needed to be careful because the Cheddar Boys are planning on making a move on us or something of that nature. And if that's so, shit 'bout to turn out bad. I fuck with you and Fred, so if by any chance you hear of anything, let me know what the deal is," Ben told him, hoping he didn't make a mistake by exposing his hand.

"I didn't hear shit, but I'll see what I can find out and get back with you," Rell said. They dapped, and he ran back to his car trying not to get too wet.

Rell and Ben started fucking with each other back in 2001 at Booker T. Washington High School. They became cool after Ben was approached by two niggas out the Magnolia Project who Rell didn't like. At the time, the Melph and the Magnolia had a little beef, so they were about to crowd Ben, but Rell stepped in and helped Ben fight those niggas. They been potners ever since.

The moment Rell pulled out of the project, Paul asked Ben to fill him in on the private conversation he and Rell had. So Ben gave him detail after detail, but the more Ben talked, the more Paul came to the conclusion that he didn't think it was a good idea to expose their hand, especially if the rumor was true, or if they have to take action.

"I know we fuck with Rell, but do you trust him enough to possibly put our lives at risk?" Paul asked.

"I think homie good," Ben responded with a tone of uncertainty.

"Do you think, or do you know? Cause out here in these streets, ain't much room for error, one slip up, and it's over. So what we need to do is prepare for war just in case some flaky shit happens," Paul said, not liking the feeling in his gut that this shit was gonna end in bloodshed.

"Just to be on the safe side, I'll put the wrecking crew on standby," Ben said, which consisted of Tre, Ryder, K-Dog, and Trap.

"So we can all be on the same page, we have to get everybody together to discuss this potential problem, because that's gonna play a major part in our success," Ben continued.

"Do you think it's a good idea to let Fred know what's going on right now?" Paul asked, feeling that Fred was no different from Rell.

"Fred is a hundred, I don't have a doubt in my mind that if it comes down to war, he'd side with us," Ben said, hoping that his judgment was correct.

Later that night they all met up at the hotel where Fred was ducked off. As soon as Fred noticed that Ryder and his crew was on deck, he automatically knew something was about to go down. The only issue was finding out what it was, cause he'd always heard whenever those niggas hooked up, drama was sure to come.

After Ben explained the situation, and how they should handle it if it came down to it, K-Dog replied, "Let's just crush that nigga Rell. The process of elimination should start with him, because right now he's the only threat. Once he's out of the way, we can deal with Je'sus and them."

Tre spoke up, "Let Fred holla at Rell. I think he can put him in a comfort zone because I think we can always use somebody on the inside. With him being around those niggas daily, he can at least let us know how and when they move, or if we had to make a move."

"Or we could just say fuck it, and to send them niggas a message, I can go in the project and smoke that bitch ass nigga Black Larry," Fred said.

"That's what I'm talking bout, so how we gon' do this?" K-Dog asked.

"You know what, Tre made a lot of sense bout using Rell to keep us updated till we see if the rumor was true. In the meantime, go by Betty and get everything together," Ben told Ryder and Trap who were just listening to the plan without any input; yet, they were down to do whatever.

CHAPTER 6

Paul was on his way to the *Hot Spot* barber shop that sat on the corner of MLK and Simon Blvd., when he noticed an all-black F-150 at the red light. Just as the light turned green, the driver window rolled down, and the driver started letting off several shots in the direction of Paul as he ran behind a tree that was on the sidewalk to return fire. He put multiple holes in the driver door and bed of the truck.

Most of the people in the shop were startled by the fact that they just heard a gang of shots, and then saw Paul running inside in a frenzy, with his banger still in hand. One of the barbers took charge of the situation.

"Yo Homie you have to get out of here with all that," he zoned in on the .40 cal that was still clutched in Paul right hand. "This is a place of business, and as you can see, you have my customers very…" But before he could finish his statement, Paul cut him off.

"Be cool Duck dawg, not right now homie," he said still shook up at the fact that he was that close to getting killed. He really didn't know exactly who was shooting at him.

"Just give me a minute," Paul added.

"At least put that gun away," Duck said as he tried to relax but in reality, he was hoping that Paul just left.

"You got that dog," Paul said as he tucked the gun in his pants, and moved his dread locks out of his face with his free hand.

He asked Tiffany to go outside and see if it was cool for him to leave, but when she came in the shop, her expression said it all.

"Boy police are everywhere. I think somebody got shot, cause they have a big ass crowd on Simon Blvd. and Thalia."

Come to find out, an innocent bystander got shot in the thigh. So Paul used that incident as an escape route, knowing that everybody's attention was going to be on the person who got shot. He took that opportunity to dip out and headed toward the project, which was a block away where he saw Lil' Mike and K-Dog standing in the breezeway.

"Somebody just got at me," Paul began to tell K-Dog.

"I told Lil' Mike it sounded like somebody was getting it in, cause we heard the shots. Did you see who it was?" K-Dog asked.

"No, the shit happened so fast, all I had time to do was run for cover. I managed to get off a few shots, but niggas caught me slippin' like a motherfucker."

"That probably was Je'sus or somebody affiliated with them, cause who else would it be?" K-Dog said.

***

Ben stopped at a newspaper stand that's on the outside of the store on Martin Luther King Ave. and Magnolia St. to buy a paper before picking Fred up. He was hoping the classified section had houses in it for rent.

I got to get' one a phone, Ben thought to himself realizing he couldn't call Fred to let him know he was on his way.

When Ben closed the door on the newspaper stand, he turned to head for his car, but he noticed a police car slow rolling down Martin Luther King in his direction. They were two blocks away, so he decided to go into the store to avoid a run-in with the police.

Ben browsed around the store for at least 3 minutes before purchasing a couple of Keep Moving cigars just for the sake of buying something. As soon as he walked out of the store, he saw the same police car conducting a traffic stop a half block away from the store. Not wanting any problems, he moved quickly to his car, got in, and casually pulled away. Once he reached MLK and Claiborne, he picked up his speed and made a right to get on I-10.

When Ben made it to the hotel, he asked the front desk receptionist to call room 312 to tell Fred to come to the lobby. Fred didn't have a clue as to why he was told to come to the lobby. He didn't know what to think, but he did as told. Once he got off the elevator, he saw Ben.

"What's up big homie," Fred asked, relieved to see Ben.

"Let's take a ride," Ben suggested, exiting the hotel lobby.

"Dawg I ain't feeling this hotel shit," Fred said, running out of patience with the whole situation.

"I know homie, that's why we bout to go look for a house to put you in."

"Real talk!" Fred said with excitement in his voice.

"Yeah, real talk nigga," Ben shot back.

Fred opened the passenger door, and then quickly closed it. As soon as Ben started the engine, Fred realized he was forgetting something.

"Hold on homie, let me go get my tool out that fucking room," Fred said, opening the door.

"Hurry up nigga."

While Fred went to get his gun out of the hotel, Ben looked through the paper to see what was on the market. There were several houses listed for rent, but a house in the 7th Ward on N. Rocheblave, and a house in Mid-City caught his attention. So they went to check those out.

"You straight?" Ben asked after Fred got back in the car.

"I ain't gone be straight till I get out this hotel."

"Don't trip you'll be out there soon, maybe today," Ben told him. "We gon check out this spot in Mid-City, and if it's straight, I'ma get it, cause we need another stash house. With that, you can live in it if you want to," he continued.

"Fuckin right I want to live in it," Fred said with a big smile on his face.

As they pulled up in Mid-City, they parked in front of a white house.

"This it right here," Ben said, surveying the property from the driver window, as Fred looked at him.

Ben called the number on the rental sign to inform the owner that he was interested in renting the house.

"I can be there in 20 minutes, can you wait?" the owner asked.

"Yeah, I can wait. I'll see you when you get here," Ben replied.

When the homeowner arrived, which was 30 minutes later, he allowed Ben and Fred to walk through the house to see if they were satisfied.

"This will work, Fred do you like the house," Ben asked.

"I like it. Man, anything's better than that hotel room," Fred said as they both smiled.

"Well let's go over the lease, then it's all yours."

Ben filled out all the necessary paperwork, got the keys to the property, then gave Fred one of the keys. As they were about to leave the house Ben phone started ringing.

***

Paul called Ben to explain what happened.

"I'm on my way," Ben said, then quickly hung up.

Ryder and Tre came through the cut and asked K-Dog and Paul did they see Trap, but a fiend that overheard them said that Trap was at Betty's baggin up.

"Go up there and tell that nigga I said get down here ASAP. It's urgent," Paul told the Junkie.

Fifteen minutes later, Ben and Fred pulled up the same time Rell did. He was on a 250-dirt bike. "What's popping?" Rell asked.

"I'm 'bout to find out right now," Ben said, shifting his attention to Paul. "Some nigga just got at Paul, he told me the nigga was in a black F-150."

"A black F-150!?" Rell said. "I just saw a black F-150 parked on Erato St. with bullet holes all over that bitch.

"Where on Erato?" Ben asked, trying to envision the location. He knew if it was those niggas out the Calliope, that would confirm the rumors, and something had to be done ASAP.

"It's parked on Erato and S. Galvez," Rell said. While gathered in the courtyard, Ben told his crew what Rell expressed to him 'bout the truck in the Calliope.

"I told you niggas to let me go in the project and smoke that nigga Black Larry," Fred said, forming a gun shooting with his right hand. "I was gonna go platinum on that bitch ass nigga," he mumbled. "This ain't no game. Somebody gone end up dead, and if that's the case, let it be one of them niggas," Fred continued.

"Tre go rent a U-Haul, and everybody meet me back here at 8:00 p.m. sharp," Ben stated. In the meantime, he had to go hook up with his plug to purchased eighteen ounces of, Boy, well actually he was going to meet the mule. So he and Trap went to handle that while Ryder and K-Dog went to get the guns together. Fred and Lil' Mike stayed there hustling.

CHAPTER 7

BAM BAM BAM, was the sound of Cadillac as he knocked on the front door of the Cheddar Boys trap house.

"Who the fuck that is beating on the door like they the fucking police?" Donte' said as he approached the door.

"This Cadillac! Y'all good?" he asked as he fumbled in his right front pocket to get the 14 dollars he had crumbled up in it.

Donte' opened the door with seven 20-dollar bags of heroin in his hand, revealing a nickel plated .357 magnum tucked in his waist. Before Donte' could ask what, he wanted, Cadillac immediately shouted.

"Look dawg, I'm a lil' short right now, but you know I'ma make it up to you. I'll run sells your way all day dawg, but I need this wake up hit first. I need to knock off this sickness."

"Say brah, you know we don't take shorts," Donte' shot back at him.

"I know dawg, just do this for me this time. Please my nigga, I'm sick," Cadillac plead. "Oh, yeah! I wanted to tell y'all, y'all need to step y'all game up."

"What the fuck you mean, our shit is grade A," Donte said.

"Yeah, I know, but those SG niggas from the Melph got some serious heat back there for lower prices than y'all," Cadillac said.

"Why in the fuck you ain't go score from them? Better yet, fuck those bitch ass niggas from the Melph, we have a track record for having the best dog food in the city," Donte' replied.

"Everybody knows the Calliope is the home of the dope, so what the fuck you talking 'bout!" an aggravated Donte' said as he dropped one bag of foil in Cadillac's hand.

"I got to let Je'sus know he got to tighten up on his product," Cadillac said, walking away quickly from the door.

Business started to slow up for the Cheddar Boys because the Slum Godds had the best dope at the time, plus their bags were twice as big as any other heroin set in the city, and Je'sus didn't like it one bit, so he felt something had to be done, because it was fucking up his money. The only way he could have competed with the shit Ben was putting on the streets, was to put less cut on his product, which wasn't going to happen. Ben wasn't scoring within the city, he was getting some high-quality dope, for an unbelievable price out of Houston. At the time, bricks were going for anywhere from eighty to a hundred thousand, but he was getting half a brick for thirty-five thousand, plus it was taking a four easy, (meaning, he could put four half bricks of cutting mixture on it), but he was only putting two and a half on it, and then putting it back on the streets. The way it was, someone could overdose off that shit, and that's exactly what the user wanted, and that's exactly what he had.

When Rell told Curtis Mitchell bout the rumor that they were responsible for shooting at Paul, Curtis had no idea what he was talking about. He knew if anybody in his crew would have made a move like that, he would have been aware of it. So he called Je'sus to see what the fuck was going on, or even if the rumor was true. He felt like if it was, he should have been in on the decision to make a move or not. But when Je'sus told him he had no idea what he was talking about, he ordered that everybody meet him at the trap house to get some answers.

***

By the time Ben, Trap and a smoker named James made it to the Greyhound bus station, the bus was just pulling in the parking lot.

"Damn homie, we got here just in time," Trap said.

"Let's get this shit over with," Ben said as they got out of the car to head for the waiting area.

"Go ahead James and wait in the restroom, I'll be there in a minute," Ben said.

Two or three minutes after James went into the station, Ben headed for the entrance.

Ben met a mule twice a month, and every time they got together, he was nervous as a motherfucker, despite the fact that he changed locations all the time. That was his way of only having to do a pick up at the bus station once a month. The only thing that put his mind at ease was the fact that Ernest almost always sent a different mule to drop off the packages, and very seldom would he send the same one on two consecutive trips. The way they identified him was that he would always sit in the third seat on the third row to the right of the entrance, and the mule which was normally an older woman would sit directly behind him. They would address each other by simply saying "B" and he would give a head nod.

Ben was seated about ten minutes before a heavy set older woman took a seat behind him. The woman said their code word, "B" in a husky voice, and Ben simply gave her a head nod. The woman then placed a small shopping bag under Ben's seat and headed for the exit. Once there, Trap waited on her to give her a paper bag with money in it. Afterwards, he got back in the car and patiently waited on Ben. Ben waited about ten minutes before grabbing the shopping bag and headed for the restroom where James waited to strap the work onto him. Ben handed him the eighteen ounces and left the restroom carrying an empty shopping bag.

A couple of minutes later, James came out of the restroom and headed for the exit. He immediately started walking toward the project, which was only two blocks away.

***

By the time they all met up, twenty minutes passed. They were all anxious to see what the fuck Je'sus was talking 'bout. As he went on about the shooting by the Melph, no one in the room had any idea what he was talking bout.

"So what y'all telling me is that no one in this room made a move?" Je'sus asked.

"If I would have made a move on that nigga, they'd be getting funeral arrangements together," Nine Finger Lou stated. "Cause real talk, it ain't many niggas that I went at in these streets still alive to talk about it. But since the rumor is out there, we should strap up and make a move, cause if they believe we shot at that nigga, they'll handle the situation as if we actually did the shit."

"So that means we going to war," Black Larry added.

***

Rell saw the Cheddar Boys go into the apartment, so he had to think fast. He jumped on his dirt bike and rode to the Melph to explain what he witnessed to Fred. The Cheddar Boys all in one house surely meant they were probably plotting to make another move on them. He knew if they could hurry up and get back over there, they could catch them slipping, cause they wouldn't be expecting to get ambushed in their own hood.

Ten minutes later, Fred and Lil' Mike met Rell by Rosenward Gym in the Calliope to discuss how they were going to handle shit.

"Soon as they come out the apartment we gon charge them niggas," Fred said.

Him and Mike had their ski masks tucked in their back pockets, while the three of them waited patiently for the Cheddar Boys to exit the apartment. They knew they couldn't be seen by anyone, so they stayed ducked off in a hallway that was directly across from the apartment they had to come out of. They positioned themselves to ensure that whenever they decide to come out the apartment, it was no way they could miss them.

"When we move on them niggas, we ain't just shooting to send a message, we shooting to kill," Rell said. "Cause those niggas gon be strapped, so we have to move fast. That means we strike, and get the fuck… Ya dig?"

"Those niggas don't know me, I probably can walk up to them and let'em have it before they can react," Mike suggested.

"Naw homie, we gon move at the same time," Fred said, anxious to put it down.

***

Lou looked at Curtis Mitchell and asked him why he was so quiet. He hadn't had much to say since they'd met up.

"Dawg, I'm just thinking that something ain't right bout all this shit. I mean, a rumor started out the blue that we was beefing with the SGs, then some niggas get at one of them in broad daylight that came back to us, which we ain't know shit about, and on top of all that, the truck that was used in the shooting was parked in our hood, which connects us to the shit. I'm just thinking and trying to figure this shit out. I'm thinking about calling them niggas to let them..."

"Fuck them bitch ass niggas," Lou interrupted. "If they think we done it, then it is what it is!"

"We'll figure this shit out later," Je'sus said. "In the meantime, we have to prepare to go to war."

"I'm with that," Black Larry said, grabbing a 10mm off the table.

"Since we all together, we can go pass in the Melph now to see if we can catch them niggas slipping. We can split up. Some of us can come from Thalia driveway, those niggas be right there in Thalia Courtyard, we can't miss them," Larry continued.

They all agreed and started to exit the apartment.

***

"Heads up! There they go," Rell said as Mike and Fred removed their ski masks from their back pockets and put them on. Rell took a white T-shirt and pulled the arm part over his head until it came down right under his eyes. Afterwards, he covered his head with a black NY Fitty hat.

As soon as the Cheddar Boys approached the bottom stairwell that led to the first floor, Boca. Boca. Boca. Boca. Wop. Wop. Wop. Wop. Pop. Pop. was the sound of the shots that went off as Mike, Fred and Rell ambushed the hallway.

The attack happened so fast and unexpectedly, they didn't have a chance to return fire, all they were able to do was turn and run back towards the apartment.

"I'm hit, I'm hit!" Nine Finger Lou kept shouting in pain as he laid on the ground clutching his stomach in a pool of blood.

Fred noticed that Lou was hit as he laid on the ground, so he ran in the hallway. Lou looked up in disbelief that he'd been caught slipping, and it was about to cost him his life. When Fred put the Hi-Point 9mm to his head and squeezed, the gun jammed.

Let's get the fuck out of here homie!" Mike yelled, nervously looking around.

As they all took off running towards Earhart Blvd., Black Larry managed to let off seven shots in their direction. Curtis saw the three as they ran from the scene, but decided not to shoot due to the distance between them. Larry rushed over to pick up Lou and carried him into the apartment.

Covered in Lou's blood, Curtis was yelling for someone to call the ambulance, he had so much blood on him that it appeared as if he was shot also.

"Lay him on the sofa," Je'sus said, trying to help Lou relax. "Don't panic homie, just relax, the paramedic is on the way," Je'sus kept saying over and over.

Donte got the guns and the work and moved it to the other house, which was about seven apartments down from the one they were in.

Curtis' mind was racing cause as the three niggas ran from the scene, it was something about how one of them ran that was familiar, but he couldn't put his finger on it.

By the time the paramedics arrived on the scene, Lou had passed out from all the blood he'd lost. So to everybody present, it appeared as if he had died, but the EMS Medical Tech was yelling that he still had a faint pulse. They quickly strapped an oxygen mask to his face and headed to Charity Hospital.

Je'sus had a look in his eyes that nobody had ever seen before. It was pure evil, and a sincere look of destruction. While Larry and Donte' stood in the project contemplating their next move, him and Curtis got into his Rover and headed to the hospital.

CHAPTER 8

Lil' Mike and Fred were by the cut when Ben and Trap pulled up.

"Damn homie, that was quick," Fred said as they got out the car.

"When you have business in order, it'll always be quick," Ben shot back. "But when James comes through, I need you to get that package from him. He should be here in five minutes or so."

"Don't trip, I gotcha my nigga," Fred said. "But check this out homie..." he continued. "Me and Mike went in the Calliope and sprayed that bitch up, but I think the nigga Lou was the only one got hit, ya dig?"

"Where the fuck Paul at?" Ben asked with hostility in his voice.

"I don't know where he's at, I haven't seen him since earlier today. But what I do know is that this shit's 'bout to go down for real."

"Let me call this nigga Paul," Ben said as he pulled out his phone.

After calling Paul back-to-back without getting an answer, Ben became pissed off even more.

As they turned to enter the court way, Trap yelled, "There goes Tre," he pointed as Tre pulled into the driveway in a U-Haul.

Tre got out of the truck holding a Nextel phone in his left hand and looked at Ben.

"Whenever you ready to go punish that shit, we ready my nigga," he said.

CHAPTER 9

After two long hours of hard rough sex, Paul is still fully energized for more. He would normally last about an hour or so, but the Cialis he took on the way over to Ciera house had his dick hard as a rock. Ciera, still horny herself, laid back on the pillow with her legs spread wide open. Realizing she had his attention, she started fingering her pussy as Paul crawled towards her on the bed. She was so hot that she started screaming just at the thought of what he was about to do to her again.

As he penetrated his dick deeper and deeper inside of her, she screamed out in pleasure, "Ohhh, baby it feels so good, don't stop Paul, fuck me harder, ohhhh, yes," she moaned, matching the motions of his body.

"You like it like this?" he asked as he pounded her from the back while he fingered her ass.

"Yes, baby I like it," she said in-between moans. "Don't cum baby, please don't cum," she begged as she got closer to her climax. But seconds before she came, he pulled out of her and told her to get on top of him. Breathing heavily, she climbed on top, and let out a loud moan.

"Ohhhh, fuck," she loudly moaned, finding her rhythm as she dug her nails into his chest. He grabbed her around her waist as he guided her up and down on his dick.

"Who this pussy for?" he asked as she allowed him to go deeper inside of her.

"This your pussy baby so fuck me," she said as she bounced on his dick harder and harder until she screamed out in ecstasy. "OOOOHHHH baby, I'm cumming," she managed to say as she released her love juices that covered her inner thighs, which made its way down to his pubic hairs.

Paul laid her on her back and climbed on top of her and put one leg on his shoulder as he entered her hot, wet pussy. After repeatedly cumming, her pussy was very sensitive to the slightest touch.

"Ooohh baby, I can't take it no more, you have my pussy sore," she cried out as he tried to give her every inch of him.

His phone started to ring and he was about to reach for it , but he'd gotten her to the point where she's about to tap out, so he ignored the call and continued to fuck her, not giving it a thought that the call could be urgent.

After four sessions, Paul got dressed and they said their goodbyes. Just as he approached the door, she said, "I love you and be careful."

As Paul road down Banks Street on his way to the project, he noticed a beautiful young woman walking down the street talking on the phone.

"Damn Shorty nice," he mumbled under his breath before he lowered the music and rolled the window down. "What's up Shorty, where you headed walking in this hot ass sun?" Paul asked anticipating a response.

She briefly glanced in his direction as if she were trying to see if she knew him, then turned her head as if he didn't exist. But Paul refused to give up, so he quickly put his truck in park on the single lane street and jumped out completely blocking traffic in that direction.

"Damn luv, you deaf or something?" he asked as he approached the sidewalk in a slight trot trying to keep pace with the woman who was clearly not interested in what he had to say.

"No, I'm not deaf," she said. "Besides, don't you see me on the phone?" she continued with an attitude, as she kept walking. "Instead of trying to talk to me, you need to move your truck so them people can pass."

But with Paul determined to get her, he shot back, "I ain't moving shit until you give me a second of your time."

"Boy, you crazy! Girl let me see what this boy want, I'ma call you back. What you want?" she asked as she ended her phone call while wiping sweat from her forehead.

"Well, the first thing I want to know is your name so I'll know what to address you by. But what I'm more curious to know is why a pretty girl like yourself is walking in this heat. That alone gives me the impression you're not involved in a relationship, because if you were my girl, you most definitely wouldn't be walking."

"Well if you must know, my name is Garineka, and your speculation was correct. I'm not involved in a relationship, but even if I had a man, what's that got to do with me taking a walk?" With cars constantly piling up, she said, "You better move your truck out the street. I know you see cars lined up waiting on you to move."

"Fuck them, I want you and like I said, I'm not moving until I get your number. You are very attractive and single, it don't get no better than that. Plus, I'm a good judge of character and it seems that you deserve a nigga like me in yo' life," Paul said looking her directly in the eyes.

"And what type of nigga is that?" she asked allowing the conversation to progress.

"It's only one way to find out the answer to that question," he shot back.

"Well take my number so you can get out those people's way before you get us killed," she said in a joking way.

"You don't have to worry 'bout that, you in safe hands when you with me. What would be the best time for me to call?" Paul asked as he glanced at her number. "Would ten o'clock tonight be cool?"

"Yeah, that's cool," she replied. "But whom should I be expecting the call from?" realizing she didn't know his name.

"I'm Paul, I thought you'd never ask"

"Nice to meet you Paul."

"Nice to meet you too, Garineka."

***

After several hours in surgery, Lou pulled through with the help of a blood transfusion that was desperately needed. After waiting for so long on the paramedics to arrive, he lost over three pints of blood. The surgery was successful, and he was transferred from the surgical ward to ICU for observation. Attached to his side was a colostomy bag because of the damage the .40 cal bullet caused to his stomach when it ripped through his flesh and arteries. If treated properly, it could be removed within a six-month period.

Je'sus and Curtis waited patiently in the waiting room to hear the good news that their homie was going to be okay. It was the doctor's order that he be placed on bed rest for two to four weeks until he regained his strength.

After hearing that Lou was going to be alright, Je'sus headed home to get his money together, knowing he had to meet with Giovanni to score some more work. Giovanni told him that it was a new package, and that the shit was Grade A. It was so good that it took on the name (Light's Out) because the few people that sampled it went straight out, regardless if they shot it or snorted it, so Je'sus was most definitely trying to get his hands on that especially with the torcher they had in the Melph, but by the time he made it home he was exhausted from the events that happened earlier that day, so he decided to call Giovanni to let him know that they'll meet up 7:30 in the morning at the I-Hop on the I-10 service road off Bullard.

CHAPTER 10

As Paul pulled up in the driveway, he immediately felt something wasn't right when he noticed Ben walking towards his truck with a fucked up look on his face. Instead of boasting 'bout fucking Ciera, the expression on Ben face let him know that it wasn't the time for that, so instead he asked was everything straight, but Ben didn't reply to the question.

"Where the fuck was you, and why didn't you answer your phone? You must think it's a game out chere."

"Man, what the fuck you talking 'bout," Paul interrupted.

"I mean a nigga just shot at you last week and we don't have a clue who it was. So you should be playing the hood close, at least until we find out some answers about that situation," Ben said before he continued. "But the reason why I was calling is because Mike and Fred went in the Calliope and hit Lou up, so with that move you know it's all-out war now. You running around like you can't be touched..." but before Ben could finish what he was saying, Ryder yelled out.

"Fuck all that bullshit. All we need to be discussing is how we gon' put an end to this shit."

The thing about Ryder, Tre, K-Dog and Trap was whenever these niggas put it down, very seldom did a nigga live to do anything about it. They were all dangerous, but Ryder was the most treacherous of the crew. Tre was more of the thinker, the one who calculated all his moves before he made them. K-Dog was simply down with whatever, you name it, he was 'bout it, and Trap's name pretty much spoke for itself. That nigga could sell anything he put his hands on. But when those niggas were on a mission, it was sure to be a lot of slow singing and flower bringing.

"At this point those niggas gon' be at the top of their game, so we have to put ourselves in their position," Tre said, looking around at the crew before he continued. "What will we do if one of us got hit up and how would we react to that?" he said trying to weigh their options.

"If one of us get shot, we would do everything in our power to bring pain to whoever is responsible for it," Ben said.

"Well that's exactly what we have to prepare for, cause those niggas ain't no bitches. We can expect for them to seek revenge," Tre added.

"So, what's out next move?" K-Dog asked. "Cause whatever it is it need to be done soon. Like Tre said, them niggas coming!"

Paul turned to Mike and Fred and asked them how they managed to get so close to them niggas. So Fred explained how Rell came back there and told them that they could catch those niggas slipping if they went A.S.A.P.

"The only person with me at the time was Mike so we rode back there on Mike's go-cart, and when them niggas came out the apartment we ambushed them. That fool Lou was the only one got hit, cause he was the first one exiting the hallway. When he fell, I went and stood over that clown to close his casket, but the fucking gun jammed when I put it to that nigga head. So we got the fuck on."

"And where was Rell when all that went down?" Paul asked.

"He was shooting with us."

"Yeah!" Paul responded as he gave Ben that look like, you said Rell can be trusted.

"But them niggas really didn't know who we was cause we had masks on," Mike said.

"You still be fucking with that girl from the Calliope?" Tre asked Paul. "If so you need to hook up with that hoe and manipulate her to let us use her apartment to stake out, so we can make a move on them niggas. Cause it's proven they can get caught slipping. If she put up a fuss, make her an offer she can't refuse."

"Do you think it's a good idea to put that hoe in our mix like that, especially on this level?" Ben asked, not liking the sound of the idea.

"It really don't matter, cause if it go down like we plan, it ain't nothing to off that bitch," K-Dog said.

"And that's real shit," Trap said in agreement.

It seemed like out of nowhere a four-wheeler came speeding up the driveway with two niggas on it, both wearing biker masks. As Donte' hit the throttle to the Max, Black Larry, pulled his banger when he noticed the SG's and with biker masks on, they had no idea who was on the four-wheeler. But the closer they got, Donte' realized he could pull up on them. When they didn't get a reaction, Larry, who was already clutching his heat, started shooting rapidly, striking Tre twice in the chest and once in the head. Tre was dead before his lifeless body hit the ground.

Bap... Bap... Bap... Bap... Bap... Boom… Bap... Boom, was the sound of the automatics discharging several rounds, shattering the windows on the U-Haul as Ben and his crew ran behind it for cover.

Black Larry was getting off the four-wheeler when he noticed Fred creeping from the back of the truck. He quickly let off three shots striking Fred in the leg. When Lil' Mike saw Fred fall he came from behind the U-Haul letting off several shots. Boca... Boca… Boca... Boca… Boca, just enough to back them up.

Donte' was still letting off shots when Larry yelled "Pull off." Boom... Boom… Boom... Boom... Boom, "Let's go Dee" Boom… Boom "Come on let's get the fuck…," Larry said with a sense of urgency.

When they pulled off, Lil' Mike ran behind them shooting like a mad man Boca...Boca...Boca...Boca, grazing Larry in the shoulder. As the nosey neighbors came out of their apartments to see what had happened, someone yelled, "Call a ambulance!" When they saw Ben standing over Tre's body. The crowd grew bigger and the screams got louder for the fact that Tre was dead. But Ben didn't show any emotion, he just stood there looking down on his homie.

Fred sat up against a car holding his leg where he was shot as he called for Trap to get his gun before the police arrived.

"I got it homie," Trap said as he grabbed Fred's gun and tucked it in his pants.

"You gon be straight my nigga, it ain't nothing but a leg shot, you'll be back on yo feet in no time."

"Don't worry 'bout me, make sho Tre aight," Fred said as he looked at Tre's body lying motionless on the hot concrete, knowing in his heart Tre was dead.

Paul was already mesmerized at the fact that Tre was lying in a puddle of his own blood and Fred getting hit also. But when he saw blood running down Ben's neck he started to panic.

"Don't move Ben, you hit dawg," Paul told Ben in a crackling voice.

With his adrenaline pumping so hard, he didn't notice he was bleeding. But when he realized he was, he instantly panicked. Especially, with the injured area being on his neck, close to his jugular vein. As Paul examined the area where the blood was coming from, he realized Ben had only been cut by the glass from the window of the U-Haul when it shattered.

"Damn homie you good, it ain't nothing but a cut from the broken glass."

Within a couple of minutes, they heard sirens blaring in the distance. Ryder and K-Dog came through the cut with choppers in their hands because they heard shots, but when they got on the scene, they realized that Tre had been killed in a gun battle and that Fred was also hit.

"Who was it!? Who was it!?" Ryder kept repeating over and over as he stared at Tre's body with tears in his eyes.

While Tre's body laid on the ground, his phone kept ringing. When Ryder looked down at it he saw Curtis M. on the caller I.D. which confused him but too much was going on at the time to think about it.

"There go the police, let's get the fuck off the scene," K-Dog said, so they all took off running to Betty's apartment.

"I'm killing anything from that project," Ryder said as he stared out the window at the crime scene, where his mother was being restrained by two officers as she tried to cross the caution tape.

"We need to find a way to let Fred's mom know that he been shot," Ben said knowing that Fred was going to be okay. "Yeah, you right, but how?" Paul asked.

Bam, bam, bam, was the sound of knocking on the door. "See who that is," a nervous Paul said.

Lil' Mike looked through the peephole and saw it was James and said, "That's James," as he started unlocking the door to open it.

"Man, what happened out there? The police are everywhere, so I had to go the long way around the project and when I..."

"Do you have the package?" Ben cut him off.

"Yeah, I got it. It's right here," James said as he removed it from around his waist and handed it to Ben.

Ben took the package from him and gave him two hundred dollars.

"Here's another fifty dollars. I need you to go in the Calliope and let Wanda know her son had been shot, and for her to go to Charity Hospital."

"You talking 'bout Wanda who be smoking?" James asked.

"Yeah, her, let her know her son been shot."

"Alright, I'm on it."

"If you can't find her, look for Cadillac, he'll most likely know where she at."

Tre didn't really have any family other than his grandmother. His parents died in a car crash on their way from church when he was twelve years old. That's when his grandmother took him in but Ryder's mother. Ms. Grace practically raised him. She felt he was disobedient towards his grandmother, who was 67 at the time.

"...Reporting live with breaking news from the Melphomene Housing Development concerning a deadly shooting that left one dead and another with non-life-threatening injuries to the leg. The identity has been confirmed by the guardian that the death victim is twenty-three-year-old Trevon Miller."

The shooting was reported around 6:45 p.m., said Officer John Oliver, a NOPD spokesman. One of the victims was pronounced dead at the scene while the second victim was in stable condition and was taken to a nearby hospital. Evidence technicians bagged up a cellphone that laid in a puddle of blood near the death victim. The officers have placed twenty-five small yellow markers, typically used to mark the location of spent shell casings as you can see behind me. The shooting was the third in fewer than twenty-four hours in a five-block radius, coming two hours after a twenty-four-year-old was shot in the courtyard of Thalia and Tonti in the Calliope Housing Development. Authorities say they are working to determine a motive for the shooting and ask anyone with information to call homicide detective Brian Morrison at 504-586-3005 or Crime Stoppers at 1-800-822-0000. You're broadcasting live from the scene with Kelly Porter from Channel Six News, Back to you Sarah..."

"I want all them niggas dead," Ryder said as his eyes filled with tears. "And I ain't stopping until I see to it that they all die, or them bitch-ass niggas kill me. If you niggas ain't ready to go all out, don't fuck with it at all," he continued. "Because if we have to murder fifty motherfuckers to get them niggas, that's exactly what I'm willing to do. Mommas, sisters, kids, whoever. I don't give a fuck."

"We with you a hundred percent my nigga," Ben replied. "Yeah, Homie, we with you," they all agreed.

"We can't move on some crashed out shit, we have to think and plan out our next move, cause after seeing the news combined with the streets talking, those niggas gon be sitting and waiting for us to show up," Paul said trying to get them to focus, knowing they wasn't thinking straight at this point, but speaking out of anger.

"So what the fuck you suggest?" Ryder spoke up.

"At this moment I really don't know, but I do know they gonna be waiting on us to make a move," Paul shot back.

"What the fuck that's stopping cause they gon be waiting, eventually we gon have to bring the heat to them, so why not be now?" Ryder shot back.

"That's true, but we need a plan. Unless we're all ready to die," Paul responded looking around at everybody.

"Behind my lil' brother, I'm willing to die," Ryder said in a truthful tone.

"But being willing to die, and ready to die is two different things," Paul responded.

"Don't trip my nigga, Tre was like a brother to all of us," Ben said. "And if I have to spend every dollar I have on resources and ammunition, I'ma do that until those niggas pay with their lives."

Ben's phone started to ring.

"What's up son?" he said as he answered the phone.

"Where you at?" Rell replied. "I'm in the project by Betty."

"I'm on my way, we'll talk when I get there."

"One."

"Rell on his way," Ben said out loud for everybody to hear. "Maybe he'll have a drop on them niggas," Paul said in a hopeful voice.

"I hope so," K-Dog said, after being quiet since Tre was killed. "We have a 50/50 chance of making it out their project alive if we all show up with choppers with at least two thirty round clips taped together, because that's gon be the best odds we gon get no matter when we make our move, I'm just ready to move on them niggas," K-Dog added.

"Let's see what Rell talking 'bout," Ben said hoping he had some information that would lead them to catching those niggas slipping like Fred and Mike did.

"I'm the only one they don't know," Mike said.

"And what that supposed to mean?" Ben asked.

"That means my chances is good to get up on them niggas."

"No homie it's too dangerous to let you move alone. You won't have enough firepower to make it out alive," Ben said.

"Besides it's a Melphomene/Calliope beef and if we seen trying to creep down on those niggas by anybody in they project, they most likely gon' strike. This shit bigger than us against them, niggas that's not involved in this shit gon' be involved, feel me. When we decide to make a move, we going in with everything we got, on some Vietnam type shit, even if we have to link up with Tiger and his squad. Even if it cost us a few dollars, we all eating homie, so if it takes us a few dollars we all gon see to it that the bill gets paid if necessary," Ben added.

Tiger is a ruthless cat, him and his crew is responsible for a lot of the murders that happen in Melph. Everybody uptown knows about the Thalia Court Boys. They named their crew the Thalia Court Boys, because they hang out in the Thalia Courtyard of the project.

"I be serving Tiger, so I'll holla at him and see how he feels about linking up, cause you know those niggas is Melph to the bone," Paul said. "They might just ride on the strength."

"What's up with that lil' hoe Tre was asking you about?" Ben asked.

"Who, Brittany! I'm 'bout to see right now," Paul replied as he pulled out his phone.

***

Brittany was sitting on her front porch when her phone rang. She looked at it to see who the caller was and couldn't believe it when she saw Paul's name, because she hadn't spoken with him since he left her on hold to take another call, so she never tried to contact him again. She was about to refuse his call, but she decided to answer.

"Hello?"

"Yes! Who is this?" she asked as if she didn't know who it was.

"Now you acting like you can't recognize my voice," Paul replied.

"If I knew who it was, I wouldn't be asking," she responded.

"This Paul. How can you forget a nigga like me?"

"The same way you forgot a bitch like me. But anyway, why are you calling me?"

"Damn luv, it sounds like you in your feeling 'bout something."

"Boy please. You ain't that important to me for me to be in my feelings."

"That's good to know, but a nigga just got out of jail a few weeks ago, and I want to know if you wanted to go out to eat, my treat."

"Boy, stop fucking lying. I heard you got niggas shooting at you and everything, you ain't been in jail."

"Real talk! The day I got shot at was the same day I came home. I was heading to the barber shop when some nigga pulled up and started shooting. I still don't know if he was shooting at me or the other niggas sitting by the shop. "

"Boy, whatever."

"What you mean whatever?"

"Just like I said, whatever. All you do is lie."

"Do you want me to pick you up or not?"

"We can go out, but I don't think it's in your best interest to come back here," Brittany replied.

"Why not?"

"Because y'all name been ringing back here. They saying y'all beefing with the Cheddar Boys. Didn't one of your friends get killed?"

"What else they saying?" Paul asked not answering her question 'bout Tre getting killed.

"All I heard is that y'all was beefing."

"So what, you gonna meet me in the Melph?" Paul asked.

"I can do that, cause I ain't trying to get implicated in whatever y'all got going on."

"A'ight then, pass through 'bout 8:30, I'll be waiting for you."

"Where are we going to eat?" Brittany asked.

"Whatever you feel like eating."

"It's up to you, remember it's your treat."

"How 'bout some steak from Ruth Chris steakhouse," Paul asked.

"That's fine with me, to be honest with you, it's good hearing from you, I really thought you deleted my number. I can remember a time, when I would have done anything for you, you was one of the few niggas, I could say I loved. But you let that hoe, Ta'Quita come between us."

"If you really loved me, you would have fought to keep our relationship alive, but you gave up so easy, and I looked at that as a sign of weakness," Paul explained using reverse psychology.

"I'm far from weak, sometimes a bitch just knows when to let go."

"If love ain't worth fighting for what is?" Paul asked.

"When the love is true, neither party shouldn't be put in the position to fight for it," she answered.

"So tell me how do you feel right now?" Paul asked.

"I feel like it's worth trying again, I mean what can I lose?"

"I guess that was a part of your game when you said you would have done anything for me."

"Game, boy please! When you play games, somebody has to lose, and I know I ain't no loser, and if I thought you were one, I wouldn't have allowed my feeling to get involved."

"So you meant that?" Paul asked knowing he had her where he wanted her.

"Yeah, I meant it."

"Okay, hold that thought. I'll see you tonight. "

"I love you Paul."

"I love you too Brittany."

"Bye"

"I got that hoe right where I want her," Paul said to his crew that was sitting there looking at him.

CHAPTER 11

James was, familiar with damn near all the crackheads in the third ward area, mainly in the Melphomene, Magnolia, and the Calliope project. Because at one time or another he'd have ran through them all.

When he made it to the Calliope, he saw a smoker who he'd gotten high with in the past. He asked him had he seen Wanda lately, but the smoker thought he was trying to score and lead him in the direction of a dealer selling double-ups. That way he could have gotten a piece of the rock for leading him to the dealer, but once James recognized what the deal was, he stated, "No, I'm good."

But a true hustler wouldn't let a smoker walk away with money, so he flashed the huge rocks in James' face and said, "I need a straight ten for these."

James' eyes got big as saucers and he asked, "Those dimes?"

"Yeah, these dimes, they boulders bigger than yo' shoulders."

"Let me test it to make sure this ain't no dummies."

The guy that brought him to the dealer said, "It's good James, you know I'm not gonna lie."

"Okay give me one, and if I like it, I'll spend a few dollars with you," James told the dealer.

Him and the runner went in a nearby hallway and James broke him off a reasonable size piece and he put it on the glass dick and took a blast. The moment James seen the immediate impact the crack took on the runner, he knew it was some good coke. As soon as he put a piece on the pipe and took a hit, he heard a female screaming out loud.

"I been spending with you all day and you can't serve me for the seven, that's fucked up."

"I need straight ten for these here, come back when you get three 'mo dollars," the dealer said. But all the chaos made James spooked so he walked out of the hallway and when he did, he realized that it was Wanda who was making all that damn noise.

"Wanda."

"What the hell you want?" she shot back with aggression.

"If you calm down, I might just have something for you."

"What's up?" Wanda asked calmly.

James didn't respond, he simply handed her the remaining piece of the rock he had.

"But before you hit that, I need to tell you that your son Fred just got shot, but don't panic, he gonna be okay, he been shot in the leg."

"Where is my child?" a nervous Wanda asked.

"Check Charity Hospital. He was caught in a crossfire in the Melphomene."

"Oh my God, that boy gonna kill me!" Wanda said as she began walking off.

Before James left, he bought four more rocks knowing he could have made his money back and still had three flippers to smoke. On his way back to the Melph, he ran into a couple of sales in the neighborhood called *The Rat Hole*. There'd be crack smokers hanging around with three or four dollars trying to get a hit. He served them off one of the rocks making almost half of his money. But he knew once he made it to the Crackhouse in the Melph, that's where the real party was gonna be.

***

Ben was thinking about calling Rell when they heard a knock at the door.

"Who is it?" Paul asked.

"This Rell," Rell answered.

Once he entered the apartment he greeted everybody, and sat down at the table.

"So what's up?" Ben asked.

"I don't know if y'all know who that was or not, but that was the nigga Donte' and Black Larry," Rell said.

The room got uncomfortably quiet before Ryder yelled out in a loud outburst as he slammed his hand hard on the dresser.

"I'ma punish them bitch-ass niggas!" Ryder said as his anger grew.

"Those niggas was campaigning for their credit as the shooters especially Black Larry. He was bragging how his first shot hit Tre in the head and how the rest of y'all ran."

The more Rell talked, the hotter Ryder got, as his eyes filled with water. Ryder quickly grabbed his AK off the table and headed for the door. Defiant to the point where it took K-Dog, Ben and Paul to hold him back until he stopped resisting and just wept on the shoulder of K-Dog as the gun hit the floor.

"We gonna handle this my nigga, don't trip," K-Dog told Ryder as he rubbed his head.

"Them niggas killed my brother," Ryder sobbed as he tried to gather himself.

"Tre was all our brothers," K-Dog said as his emotion grew.

"For some reason, Curtis Mitchell reacted in a remorseful way as he was grilling Donte' and Larry 'bout making that move without letting him or Je'sus know," Rell started explaining what he witnessed. "The nigga Larry was like, we at war, if I can catch them niggas slipping again, I'll do the same thing. Besides, what difference it make if we would have to let y'all know?"

"At least we would have been on our shit," the nigga Curtis shot back at him.

"Nigga at this point all of us supposed to be on our shit, it's war." Larry told him.

"Them niggas was going back and forth, but I can tell Curtis Mitchell didn't agree with what went down, at least it seemed that way to me," Rell continued. "But you know I can be wrong."

By this time, Ryder had pulled himself together.

"Curtis Mitchell...Curtis Mitchell…" Ryder kept repeating in a whisper with a distant look on his face, then it came to him. "That nigga was calling Tre phone when I was standing over Tre body, but at the time I couldn't process everything, but that nigga was calling his phone."

"Calling his phone?" Ben said in a confused tone.

***

"Would you come this way ma'am?" a nurse asked as she escorted Wanda to the ICU.

Once she got to the room where Fred was, a detective was
already there questioning him.

"I told you, I don't know who shot me," Fred said with an attitude.

"Are you sure, cause if you know anything let us know so we can catch the son-of-a-bitch who done this to you."

"I don't know nothing, how many times I have to say it?" an agitated Fred responded.

"Excuse me officer, may I have a word with my child...Alone?"

"Sure, and you are?"

"I'm his mother, Wanda."

"Wanda what?" the detective asked.

"Wanda Coleman."

"You have five minutes, cause I need to finish my investigation, because I'm not sure if you're aware of it or not, but your son was a victim of a deadly shooting, that left a young man dead. I encourage you to talk to your son and let him know the severity of holding information in a murder investigation."

"First of all, he is only fifteen years old, you shouldn't have question him without an adult present, secondly, if my son don't know who shot him, then how can you expect him to tell you who it was?"

"I'ma step out and leave you two in here, hopefully you can get him to talk," the detective said.

As Wanda was standing there with tears in her eyes looking at Fred's leg, she thought about the time when three masked gunmen kicked in her door, put her, Big Fred, and Lil' Fred, who was only five at the time, on the floor with guns to their heads, demanding money and drugs. The intruders thought Big Fred was lying when he said he didn't have nothing, so they started burning Lil' Fred's legs with a hot iron, and when that didn't changed nothing, they shot Big Fred three times in the head right before exiting the apartment with nothing, leaving Wanda and Lil' Fred in the house crying hysterically.

"Are you alright baby?"

"Yeah, I'm good."

"Who done this to you?"

"Them fools out the project."

"What fools out the project and what project?"

"Our project! The Cheddar Boys shot me!"

"Oh my god! Are you sure about this?"

"Yeah, I'm sho Wanda, I'ma deal with them niggas."

Wanda paused for a second then stated, "Don't worry son, I'ma deal with their asses too!"

As the detective walked back in the room they both got quiet and just looked at him.

"You think you ready to talk now?" the detective asked Fred.

"Man, I told you, I don't know who shot me."

"Detective can I talk to you on the outside of the room?" Wanda asked.

"Yes, you can," he answered as they both headed for the door.

CHAPTER 12

"Before I get in the tub, let me call this boy and let him know that I'll be there soon," Brittany said to herself while taking her phone off the charger.

The first time she called, she didn't get an answer, so she automatically got discouraged, and she refused to leave a message. *I don't know why I even waste my time with him*, Brittany thought to herself. "If he don't answer this time, fuck him," she mumbled to herself. Deep in her heart she was disappointed, but on the second attempt, he answered right before the call went to voice mail, which was a sense of relief to Brittany.

"Hello" Paul answered.

"What's up, what you doing?" Brittany asked hoping that the plan was still on.

"Cooling, can't wait to see you," Paul responded.

"I'm 'bout to get in the tub, I'll be there in thirty minutes or so."

"That's what's up."

"Okay, I'll see you then," Brittany said.

Once they hung up Paul looked at his niggas and said, "Once my bitch, always my bitch."

Later that day the courtyard was packed with niggas and hoes, and with all the beef shit that had been happening lately. Damn near everybody was strapped and on point with all the people and cars that came and went in the Melph.

"Say Round, that's the second time that Malibu passed," Tiger told his right-hand man Poppa as they pulled their guns.

A few other niggas noticed them draw their weapons, and they pulled theirs as well, as they all keyed in on the car.

"Who the fuck that is?" Poppa asked Tiger as the car slowed up.

"Dawg I don't know," Tiger replied.

When the Malibu pulled to the side and parked, they all pointed their guns in its direction.

***

"I just spoke with my son and he told me who shot him and killed his friend."

The detective started jotting down her statement in a small notepad.

"So, who does your son think shot him?"

"He doesn't think, he knows who shot him. It was the gang out of the Calliope project. They call themselves the Cheddar Boys."

"Did he see their faces to know for sure who the shooters were?"

"He said they had masks on but he knew who they were."

"So he don't know for sure it was these Cheddar Boys you telling me about?"

"He knows for sure. All they do is sell drugs and kill people."

"Calm down Ms. Wanda, I'm just trying to get all the facts."

"The fact is, they shot my son and you keep asking all these stupid ass questions instead of arresting them motherfuckers."

"I need to investigate the case more thoroughly before I can get an arrest warrant. I might not ever get enough facts about the case that would lead to an arrest warrant."

"My child is lying in a hospital bed with a bullet in his leg, and his friend is dead, and you telling me you may not have enough facts about the case to arrest them?"

"I'm sorry ma'am, but without your son's cooperation, ain't much I can do at this point."

"What about them selling all those drugs?"

"Again, I'm sorry, but I'm with Homicide Division, but I can forward this information 'bout the drug sells to Lt. Moore. He runs a task force that targets drug distributors and firearms."

"Yeah you do that," Wanda said with an attitude.

"Thank you for your time Ms. Wanda. Oh, before you go, let your son know that I'll be back to talk to him soon. Just in case he has relevant information concerning the murder. By not letting us know, he could be charged with obstruction of justice. Until next time, I'll get somebody to check into this Cheddar Boy gang and hopefully we can get them off the streets."

"Yeah, we'll see," Wanda shot back.

***

Brittany's car had light tint on it, but the later in the day it got, the harder it was to see the inside of it. Brittany got out the car talking on the phone with Paul, letting him know she was there and she felt very uncomfortable, and for him to hurry up.

Nobody was taking many chances these days so Hood, who ran with the Thalia Court Boys, walked up to Brittany's car and looked through the front windshield to make sure nobody else was in the car, then looked up at Brittany and asked, "Who you looking for," still holding the .45 cal in his right hand.

"I'm waiting on Paul," she said nervously as she hung up the phone.

"Yo Poppa, run by Bettys and get Paul," Hood said.

By the time Poppa made it by Bettys, Paul was already coming down the stairway.

"Say homie, some lil' hoe talking bout she waiting on you." "Yeah, I know, where she at?" Paul asked.

"That's her parked right there," Poppa said pointing at the blue Malibu.

"Dawg who that hoe is, she fine as a motherfucker," Poppa shot at Paul.

"That's a lil' bitch out the Calliope I be fucking with."

"Dawg you got something," Poppa said giving Paul his props.

"That bitch ain't shit lil' homie," Paul replied as he began walking towards her car.

As soon as she saw Paul approaching her car, she felt relieved as she greeted him with a long hug and a kiss.

"What's up my baby?"

"Nothing much, ready to eat," Brittany answered while smiling.

"To be on the safe side, we gonna take your car," Paul said as he got in on the passenger side of Brittany's Malibu.

"Cause I don't want to chance nobody shooting at my truck while you in it."

"If you feel like your truck is marked for death, you need to get rid of it you got the money to buy a new one."

"I'ma take that into consideration," he responded.

"I hope so."

"But look at you, you looking good, I see you been keeping yo'self up," Paul said while placing a hand on her thigh.

"You ain't looking bad yo self," Brittany shot back as she was pulling off. In all reality, she wanted to strip him down right there and fuck him in the back seat.

"Here, put this in your purse," Paul said as he handed her his .40 cal.

"Why you got to bring this?" she asked while placing the gun in her purse.

"Because I'd rather get caught with it, than get caught without it."

"Boy, you really need to be careful out here."

When they pulled into the parking lot of the restaurant, Paul noticed that it wasn't a lot of cars parked. Hopefully, they wouldn't have to wait for a table to be available. As they entered the restaurant, they were greeted by a waitress. "Good evening sir... ma'am. I'll be your waitress for the evening, would you guys like a table for two?"

"That would be fine," Paul answered politely.

"Follow me this way," the waitress said as she seated them at a table that was too much in the open for Paul, so he asked, "Is there a corner table available?"

"Yes, this way please," the waitress said leading them to another table.

They were seated at a table in the far-right corner which was perfect because it faced the entrance which allowed him to see everyone that entered the restaurant. The waitress handed them two menus and told them to let her know when they were ready to order, and asked if they wanted an appetizer. They both declined the appetizer, but Paul stated that he was ready to order. The waitress wrote down his order, an eight-ounce steak, and two baked potatoes with sour cream and bacon bits on them.

"I'll have the same," Brittany said.

While waiting on their order, Paul started a conversation, by asking her, "How do you really feel about me?"

"To be honest, I don't know how I feel, you ain't the easiest person in the world to open my heart up to," she answered.

"But do you care?" Paul asked.

"Yeah I care, and that's the part that scares me."

"You scared because you care?"

"I care about you, but I'm scared you will hurt me if I allow you to."

"So, that's how you feel towards me?" Paul asked.

"You leave me no choice but to feel that way, and that's the only way I can protect my feelings," Brittany continued. "Enough 'bout my feelings, how do you feel about me? And don't lie," she said looking him directly in the eyes.

"I mean, I dig you like a motherfucker, but are you ole lady material? That's another question, but don't get me wrong, you have the potential, ya dig. My thing is this, my ole lady must be someone I can trust with my life. When a person put that title on someone, that's the closest you can get in a relationship without being married."

"Excuse me!" the waitress said as she placed their food on the table.

"Thank you," Paul said politely.

"But what was you saying?" Brittany asked, ready to finish their conversation.

"I was just saying what it would take for a person to be my ole lady. Most women ain't willing to sacrifice to be my woman."

"And what exactly would a person have to sacrifice?" Brittany asked curiously.

"First of all, my woman ain't allowed to do certain things, wear certain things, and go certain places. I expect my woman to represent me at all times, and to have the utmost respect for me and herself, whether I'm around or not. Most importantly, she needs to be loyal and truthful with me at all times, no matter what the topic or situation may be. Because if you've done something to the point where you need to lie, that will damage my trust in you and if I don't trust you, I don' t need you in my corner," Paul stated in between a mouth full of steak and potatoes.

"All y'all niggas say y'all want a woman to be a certain way, but I think the shit should be mutual. You niggas want to do whatever y'all want whenever y'all want, and we supposed to just sit back and accept it."

"Me personally, a woman that accepts just anything from a man could never be my woman. My woman has to be strong and independent, that's why I like you so much. You never put up with my shit like most of them hoes, and you've always had my back whenever I needed you."

"That's what true love is about," Brittany said while cutting up her steak.

"Brittany, remember when you told me you would do anything for me?"

"Yeah, I remember."

"Well, I need you to do something really important for me."

"Like what?" she asked very curiously.

"I need to hang out in your apartment for a few days."

"What exactly do you mean hang out, like sleep over for a few days?"

"I know you can see those niggas apartment from your living room..."

"And?" Brittany said in an unconcerned tone.

"I need you to let me and a few of my homies hang out for a few days."

"Listen Paul, I don't know what's going on and I ain't trying to find out, just leave me out of it. I don't want to see anything happen to any of y'all, even though I don't like Black Larry ugly ass. I don't want to get involved in y'all beef though Paul."

"You won't be involved, the last thing I want them niggas to know is that I'm in 'yo house," he explained to her.

"I don't know 'bout this Paul."

"How much would it take for you to consider it?"

"My life is worth more than any amount of money you can give me."

"I promise I won't allow anything to happen to you. It's just one of those kill or be killed situations," Paul explained, trying to get her to understand.

"So, that's why all those boys had those guns when I pulled up?"

"Brittany, you must think this shit a game huh?"

"No I just thought it was more of a rumor than anything."

"It is a rumor. The only thing is, it's true, so give me a price, I'll make it worth your time."

"I can use a few extra dollars," Brittany said while smiling.

"So how much?" Paul asked.

"I don't know, I never done anything like this before, would three hundred be too much?"

"Three hundred?!" Paul said while giggling.

"What?" she asked confused.

"Since I really like you Brittany, and I respect the fact that you still have my back, I'ma give you a thousand dollars."

"For real! You must really want them huh?"

"Not as much as I want you," he said as he grabbed her hand making her drop her fork.

They finished up their food, left a nice tip for the waitress and left the restaurant. As they walked out the door they noticed a black Expedition with dark limousine tint, coming in the parking lot of the restaurant. As soon as Paul noticed it, he immediately grabbed Brittany's purse to get his gun, because he wasn't familiar with the Expedition. Once he saw Rell get out of it with his two homies, J-rock and Creature, he was relieved and said, "What's good homie?"

Brittany was still scared to death because she knew that Rell and them was out the Calliope. With all the shit going on she didn't know what to expect.

"What's up Brittany?" Rell spoke. "I see you fucking with my people. That's a real nigga, you better treat him right too," he said as he dapped Paul and went in the restaurant.

"Do you know them boys out the Calliope?" Brittany asked not understanding the situation.

"Yeah, I know them, I fuck with Rell though."

"Boy, you better be careful."

On the way to drop Paul back off in the Melph, Paul saw a hotel and told Brittany to make a U-turn and pull in the Days Inn they just passed. As soon as Brittany parked in the parking lot, she looked at Paul and stated, "I appreciate you taking me out, I had a good time tonight."

"I enjoyed myself also, but tonight is far from over," he said as he slid his hand between her legs.

Brittany was enjoying the moment, so she leaned over and started kissing him on his lips.

"Let me go get us a room," Paul said in between kisses.

"What we need a room for?" Brittany said while unbuckling his pants.

The whole time she was sucking his dick, Paul was laid back in the passenger seat in a zone while a Mariah Carey CD was playing through the speaker. After he nutted in her mouth she made sure she swallowed it all before they moved to the backseat where they fucked for almost two hours before she dropped him back off in the Melph and called it a night.

CHAPTER 13

By the time Je'sus made it to the IHOP, Giovanni was already there waiting on him, but hadn't placed an order. Je'sus got off his motorcycle, peeped out his surroundings, and removed a Crown Royal bag from his backpack. He walked over to Giovanni Cadillac truck and placed the bag under the driver seat, then made his way towards the entrance of the restaurant, after placing the backpack on the seat of the bike.

Giovanni was a local drug lord that supplied at least one third of the city heroin spots, ranging from uptown to the lower ninth ward. He wasn't only involved in drug distribution, he was also a productive business man. He was established in the real estate business and owned several houses throughout the city. He also owned a small nightclub, and a hip-hop clothing store on the Westbank Expressway. When it came to business, he was fully aware of all competition, legal or illegal.

As Je'sus approached the table, Giovanni stood up to greet him with a firm handshake.

"So how's business on your end?" Giovanni asked Je'sus the moment he sat down.

"Business good, but it can always get better," Je'sus answered.

"So tell me what I can do to make it better for you, because as long as you making money, I'm making money," Giovanni said.

"It's like this, they have some cats in the Melph with some serious heat, not to mention the size of their bags are twice as big as any other set. At the moment those niggas got the shit on lock, but with better prices, I can at least put myself in a position to compete."

Giovanni put a hand under his chin as he pondered the thought. "What I can do is this, after this score, I can start giving you a kilo just the way I get it, but I need a hundred grand for it, fifty up front."

"What can it take?" Je'sus asked.

"It can take a four, five if you push it, but if you really trying to compete, I would suggest you put a three on it, and you still can't lose. The only reason I'm considering doing this is because we've been doing business for some time now and not once have you fucked me, not to mention you've made me a lot of money over the years. So this is my appreciation to you," Giovanni said.

"You won't regret it," Je'sus said with a smile on his face.

"Why didn't you bring Curtis with you this time? I like that guy," Giovanni asked.

"He was taking care of some business."

Moments later a waiter approached their table and asked if they were ready to order. They both ordered blueberry pancakes and orange juice.

Upon finishing their breakfast, Giovanni stood up and shook Je'sus' hand and told him it was a pleasure doing business with him. But before he left, he told Je'sus that the package was in a trash bag in the restroom. Before Je'sus went to recover the package, he asked the waiter for a to-go bag.

After getting a to-go bag, he went to the restroom and got the work and then left the restaurant. Je'sus placed the work in his backpack, immediately jumped on his motorcycle, and headed uptown.

CHAPTER 14

J-Rock was steady talking shit as he selected his play on Madden.

"Nigga you know the Saints can't fuck with them Cowboys," he told Rell cause he was on the goal line threaten to score.

"Those Cowboys can saddle up and ride the fuck out," Rell shot back at him. "After today, we ain't gonna be the New Orleans Saints no more, we gon' be the New Orleans Devils the way I'm 'bout to punish that shit," Rell continued. "Nigga you ain't 'bout to do shit but get your ass whip."

"How much you wanna bet?" Rell asked.

"Nigga, bet your ass," J-Rock said before laughing out loud. "But on some real shit homie, what's up with them niggas out the Melph, you trust them niggas, cause the shit been on my mind ever since we ran into ole boy at Ruth Chris," J-Rock continued.

"Trust is a powerful word my nigga," Rell replied. "But do I fuck with them niggas from time to time, yeah, but only the SGs, I don't fuck with the rest of them niggas from their project at all."

"How you start fucking with them niggas?" J-Rock asked.

"On some throwback shit at Booker T.," Rell shot back.

Out of nowhere, Creature burst through the door holding Cadillac by the back of his shirt. Holding a .38 special in his right hand he yelled at Cadillac 'bout stealing his stash.

"Give me my shit before I hurt you."

"You got me fucked up, I don't got yo shit, you must've misplaced yo shit or something," Cadillac said pleading his case.

"Nigga I know where I put my shit at," Creature shouted.

"Out all the motherfuckers out there, why you gon say I took yo shit?"

"Cause you the only one seen where I put my shit, now it's gone, and I don't appreciate how you talking like you a fucking gangsta either," Creature said while poking Cadillac face with his finger.

"Dawg don't get it twisted cause I get high," Cadillac said standing face to face with Creature.

"What the fuck that supposed to mean?" Creature shouted back.

"You talking to me like I'm a bitch or something, I ain't the average smoker dawg, and Rell you know I don't rock like that," Cadillac said pointing at Rell.

"I don't know a fucking thing, that's on y'all, matter a fact, both of y'all can go outside with that bullshit," Rell said not wanting to hear that shit no more.

A couple of seconds after they left out the house, "POP...POP" was all they heard from the inside. It was the sound of Creature putting two bullets in the back of Cadillac's head.

"What the fuck!" Rell said as they rushed to the door.

Once he made it out the apartment, he saw Cadillac laying face down with two holes in the back of his head, and Creature trying to explain how Cadillac tried to reach for the gun, and when he didn't get it, he tried to run so I shot him.

"How much work you have on you?" Rell asked J-Rock trying to clean up Creature's mess.

"I got about thirty stones, why?"

"Give em here," Rell said as he extended his hand.

Rell took the rocks and put them under Cadillac hand as he yelled for someone to call the ambulance. They all went back inside the apartment and the moment the door closed Rell went off on Creature.

"What the fuck was you thinking 'bout killing that nigga in front the spot dog, that's gonna bring unnecessary heat."

"That bitch reached for my gun," Creature shot back but Rell gave him that look like he knew Creature was lying.

"Let's just hope that they rule it as a drug related murder and close the case," Rell said while peeping out the window.

"Man, who gonna pay for my rocks, cause I need mines?" J-Rock asked.

"I'ma give it to you," Rell said knowing that them three hundred dollars could save Creature from spending the rest of his life in jail.

"Let me get that then," J-Rock demanded as he had his hand out.

Rell wasn't trippin' bout the money. He knew if everything went as planned, the Cheddar Boys and Slum Godds would be out the way and he'd soon be the man he's been striving to be.

***

Back at the police station, the homicide detective explained to Lt. Moore who ran the task force unit for 6th district what Wanda told him at the hospital about the Cheddar Boys. He assured him that it was worth looking into especially now that they had a lead. Lt. Moore gathered all the information and told the detective that he'd put some men on it. But before the detective left, Lt. Moore asked if Wanda gave any names, or said who the head of the group was. The detective made it clear that he wasn't interested in drug dealers, his main concern was to get a lead in Tre's murder.

***

The stress was building up by the day for Ms. Grace. Not only because of Tre's death but she had no idea how she was going pay for his funeral. He didn't have insurance, and she felt that it was her duty to bury him with dignity. Her thoughts were interrupted by a knock at the door.

"Who is it?" she called out.

"It's Ben and Paul," Ben yelled through the door.

When she opened the door they both extended their arms to give her a hug.

"How you holding up?" Paul asked because it was obvious that she was taking Tre's death hard.

"I'm managing, I'm just thinking 'bout the funeral."

"What about it?" Ben asked.

"Trevon didn't have insurance," she said between sobs.

"Don't worry 'bout that, you just make sure you send him home with the best of everything. That's why we came, so we could give you the money to pay for his funeral arrangements," Ben said while digging in his pocket.

Ben gave her twenty thousand dollars, and told her, "This should cover everything, and if not, give me a call."

"I'm truly thankful for this," Ms. Grace said while looking through the bills.

"No problem, Tre was family. Ms. Grace if you ever find yourself in a financial bind of any kind, feel free to let us know," Ben told her.

"Okay, thank y'all," she said sincerely.

She hugged them both telling them good night and to be safe.

CHAPTER 15

One week later, 5:02 a.m...

"I hate baggin' this shit up," Curtis Mitchell said as he folded the aluminum foil that contained twenty-dollar worth of heroin. "So how things went with Giovanni?" He continued.

"Homie we 'bout to be on for real."

"What the fuck you talking 'bout, nigga we already on," Curtis said with swag.

"We straight, but I'm talking 'bout making a power move." "Like what?" Curtis asked curiously.

"He gon start giving me a brick just the way he get it."

"How much do he want for it?"

"He gon charge me a hundred racks, but it's impossible to lose cause the brick can take a five."

"Damn! So that would be six bricks," Curtis said which was more of a statement than a question."

"That's what the fuck I'm talking 'bout," Je'sus said with a smile on his face. "But I need you to network, you know, put the word out," he continued.

"I gotcha my nigga, I know niggas all over the city. Just let me handle that part, you just focus on keeping the plug satisfied."

"I was thinking about shutting the bag shop down and focus on a bigger clientele," Je'sus said.

"Why not lockdown the city from the project," Curtis asked. "Cause if we have the best dope, and the bigger bags for the cheapest price, we can make ten times as much money that way, versus us selling weight," Curtis continued.

"That's true, but it's too risky. Can you imagine how much traffic we gon have in the project if we operate that way. We don't need that heat, that's why it's better if we spread that shit throughout the city. I was thinking if we step on it four times we can sell four and a half for eight racks and nine ounces for sixteen," Je'sus said.

"If we do that we gon pretty much be givin' the shit away," Curtis said in a confused tone.

"That's how you see it, but the way I see it, we gon' make over three hundred racks, now you do the math, and tell me if we giving the shit away. It's a difference between a drug dealer and a hustler," Je'sus said while scooping the dope off the plate with a razor blade, to put on the foil to make a bag.

"I feel that, just give me a few days to handle my end, and on some real shit homie, I appreciate you putting me in this position," Curtis said looking Je'sus directly in the eyes.

"Dawg I love you like a brother," Je'sus confessed. "And if I shine, you gon shine. It's nothing I wouldn't do for you Curt, I'd even take a bullet for you my nigga."

"I love you too homie, and believe me when I tell you, I'd do the same for you," Curtis shot back.

"Don't think I don't acknowledge that you play a big part in our success, without you I wouldn't have nearly as much as I have now. But it's all about to pay off, cause from now on we are fifty-fifty partners. If we score once a month, we gon average at least three hundred and twenty racks a month. Before you know it, I would be able to retire. When I get out,

I want you to get out, cause I ain't gon leave you dealing with the dogs alone."

"Nigga I'm a dog," Curtis said as he mocked the sound of a dog, then looked at Je'sus and asked, "How 'bout stepping on it two times instead of four?"

"Why would we do that?" Je'sus asked confused.

"Because we can charge three racks an ounce, but it will be able to take a three and that way we would eliminate all competition once word get out we got it like that, and we will still can make three hundred and twenty something racks off a brick."

"That ain't a bad idea," Je'sus said with a smile then added, "That's why we're partners."

"Then we can score our own two bricks, and when he sees we spending our own money, who knows what can come out of that," Curtis said.

"Ever since this stupid ass beef started, we can't even focus on making money," Je'sus said once the reality sat in about the beef situation.

"Say brah the shit crazy though, because we don't even know what the beef is about," Curtis said in response to Je'sus' statement.

"But fuck it, it is what it is now, and with that nigga Tre getting smoked, squashing it ain't an option," Je'sus said.

Just the sound of hearing Tre's name caused Curtis to reminisce about some of the good times they shared together, especially the time when the two were teammates on the varsity basketball squad.

Once after practice when Tre was in the shower a couple of guys took his clothes, and towel. He had to come out the shower naked, covering his dick with his hand as he yelled,

"Where my shit at? Y'all play too fucking much!"

Thinking 'bout those times made Curtis smile.

When Je'sus saw him smile after he mentioned Tre's death, he automatically assumed that was the reason.

"Nigga what you smiling at?" Je'sus asked expecting him to say something in reference to Tre death, but Curtis lied and told him, "I was thinking about all the money we bout to get."

"Nigga you better think about what you gon do with all this' money we 'bout to get," a cocky Je'sus said.

Once Curtis and Je'sus finished bagging up some of the dope, Curtis brought the work to the trap house so Donte' and Black Larry can begin distributing the bags, then he went to visit an old friend.

CHAPTER 16

"Damn! Homie shit packed like Soulja Slim shit was," K-Dog said as he observed the huge crowd when they pulled up to Rhodes funeral home.

"I'ma miss that nigga," Ryder said in a depressed tone.

"We all gon miss that nigga," Ben said.

Trap ain't respond to either statement made by K-Dog, Ryder, or Ben, it's like he was trapped in a thought.

"You straight homie?" Ben asked Trap.

"I ain't gon be straight until we end this beef shit, cause as long as this shit going on, it could easily be one of us next in that fucking casket," Trap said while opening the car door.

Mike and Fred rode with Paul, because Fred needed the back seat to himself, so he could have stretched his leg across the seat because of the cast he had on. Once the crew exited their cars, everybody grew quiet. Focusing on them as they entered the funeral home, where Ms. Grace stood with bloodshot eyes from crying and a lack of sleep.

"It's gonna be alright momma," Ryder told her as he hugged her tight.

"I know baby," she said while rubbing his back.

As they were signing the attendance book, Paul yelled out to Ryder who was still huggin' his momma.

"Come see this shit!"

"After seeing Curtis Mitchell name signed on the attendance book, all of them instantly got heated.

"What kind of games that bitch ass nigga playing," Ryder yelled out loud.

"What is it baby?" Ms. Grace asked.

"Nothing momma," he answered trying not to upset her more than she already is.

"Come on Ms. Grace," Ben said as he walked her to the first row to have a seat.

Ben returned to the entrance hallway where Ryder and the rest was still discussing how disrespectful it was for the nigga to show up there.

"He must've came during visitation hours," Paul said.

"I wish I could have caught his ass, I would have killed his bitch ass right in here," K-Dog said in a loud outburst.

"What's good my niggas?" Tiger said as him and his crew made their appearance to show they respect.

"Everything straight," Paul responded for everyone.

"Just give me the word when y'all ready to make a move," Tiger said as he flashed the gun that was on his waistline.

"Dig homie! And we appreciate the support," Paul shot back.

After the funeral service, the majority of the attendees went to the burial site, where Tre's death really took its affect, especially on Ryder and his mother.

Once they made it to the Melph, Rebirth Brass band immediately cranked up the second line. What constituted a second line is a group of musicians and often Mardi Gras

Indians. In situations, such as funerals, the Mardi Gras Indians aren't involved as the band plays unique music. While hundreds of people parade through the local neighborhoods dancing in a traditional way which is called Second Lining. The people from the hood wore black T-shirts with a picture of Tre holding a gun in one hand, and a big knot of money in the other. Everyone was caught up in the going home second line celebration for Tre. Except Ben he was constantly thinking 'bout this Curtis Mitchell shit. He kept replaying in his mind how Rell kept putting emphasis on how Curtis Mitchell didn't react in approval of Tre's murder, along with Curtis trying to call Tre, and now his name was on the attendance log for the funeral.

"What's on your mind my nigga?" Paul asked when he noticed how distant Ben was.

"It's something about Curtis Mitchell that's worth checking out," Ben answered.

"Like what?" Paul asked confused.

"I'm not sure," Ben said with a blank look on his face.

Normally second lines would travel from location to location. That wasn't what Ben wanted, he wanted his to be stationed in the Melph.

After the second line ended, D.J. Cheeks immediately got the hood jumping. The crowd got twice as big once the DJ got crunked up. Hoes from all over New Orleans came out. Some for support, and others were just there because that's where it was popping at that day. New Orleans have a very unique way of laying a love one to rest. A mother can go from grieving a child's death, to laughing and dancing in a matter of minutes.

Everyone was out enjoying themselves. The DJ was a success but it was a known fact that things could change for the worst at any moment.

Paul spotted Roxanne with a few of her friends, all wearing T-shirts that read 'Rest In Peace SG Tre, gone but not forgotten.' Paul tapped Ben and said, "See ole girl right there?"

"Which one?" Ben asked as he looked in Roxanne's crew direction.

"The one with the long pony tail," Paul shot back.

"Damn, she nice, what's up with her?" Ben asked.

"That's the bitch I was telling you 'bout off Josephine, remember?"

"Oh that's her huh?"

"Yeah, that's her, let me go see what's up with her," Paul said as he began walking towards Roxanne.

"Long time no see," Paul said to Roxanne as soon as he approached her.

"What's up Joe, how you been?" she said, smiling.

"I been good, just trying to send my homie home in style. We need to get together one day after things get back to normal, and shit settle down if that's cool with you."

"You have my number, just call me whenever you ready. I was telling my friends about you. They all said they didn't know you, or even heard of a Joe from the Melph. My friend Ebony know everybody, or she think she do."

"Well that sounds like a good thing. But, if yo friends ain't never heard of me, then they ain't from uptown," Paul said in an arrogant tone.

The entire time Paul was kicking it with Roxanne, China watched from a distance as her emotions grew. She couldn't allow herself to step to him though. Paul noticed China watching him but he ignored her and didn't pay her any attention. He just continued to entertain Roxanne.

Not only were there hoes from all over, the niggas were there too. Mainly because they knew the hoes would be there. But the more niggas that showed up, the more the tension grew because not only were the niggas out the Melph on point, every group there were on point and that awareness automatically increased the tension level.

When Rell, Creature, and J-Rock pulled up in a black Expedition, niggas immediately zoned in on the SUV. It appeared that whomever was in the truck was creeping because it was moving real slow. But the real reason it was moving slow was because it was so packed at the DJ, making it hard to find a parking spot. So Rell turned into the driveway where he really didn't want to park, simply because if anything went down, he didn't want to be trapped in the driveway.

No matter how many people weren't focused on the truck, Tiger was, and he noticed the truck turning in the driveway, so him and Poppa ran to the cut to see what the play was. When Rell and his crew exited the truck, and headed for the courtyard, Poppa noticed them first and stated, "Ain't that them niggas out the Calliope?"

"Yeah, that's them niggas," Tiger said as he pulled his gun and placed it close to his leg as he and Poppa moved through the crowd to cut them off before they could make a move.

When niggas noticed the play, guns were drawn from several other niggas at the DJ, which got Paul and Ben's attention.

"Get from back here," Paul told Roxanne as him and Ben ran quickly behind Tiger and Poppa.

Little did Rell and his crew know that they were headed into a death trap. Once they appeared from behind the building to enter the courtyard, Ben noticed them and yelled out, "That's my people!" To Tiger and Poppa.

The crowd noticed all the movement and began to scatter. By the time Rell was aware of what was happening it was too late. Guns were already pointed in their direction when he observed Ben running up on him waving one hand as he was shouting, "Don't shoot, don't shoot!" That was the only thing that saved their lives.

The false alarm was so intense, the DJ packed up his equipment and left.

"Say Rell let me holla at cha," Ben said as they moved to the side.

"What's up homie?" Rell said nervously, still fucked up from what had just taken place.

"I apologize for what just happened my nigga, next time call and let me know when you 'bout to swing through. You know how real shit is right now."

"I feel that homie, cause that shit could've got ugly just now." Rell replied.

"But check this out, I need you to tell that nigga Curtis Mitchell that we need to talk."

"I don't think that's a good idea my nigga," Rell said.

"It depends on what we need to talk about that determines if it's a good idea or not."

"Dawg you really think them niggas want to talk?"

"Just relay my message, and if he accepts to have a sit down, give him my number."

"A'ight my nigga, I'll see what its hitting for," Rell said.

The whole time they were talking, Creature and J-Rock were mean mugging because they were in their feelings about the fact that niggas had their guns drawn on them.

When Rell and his crew left from out the Melph, Creature looked at Rell and stated, "That wasn't cool how them niggas did that shit homie."

"What you expect when niggas out the hood killed one of their potners and we show up like ain't nothing going on," Rell said.

"But we don't run with no fucking Cheddar Boys," J-Rock stated. "And with Ben knowing that, that's the only reason why we ain't dead. Homie save our lives, literally. If he was just going on some revenge shit, it wouldn't matter if we ran with the Cheddar Boys or not. They would have killed us simply because we out the Calliope," Rell said trying to get his niggas to look at the bigger picture.

"What the fuck that nigga told you anyway?" Creature asked.

"He wanted me to give his number to Curtis."

"Dawg don't get in that shit, that's them niggas business," Creature said.

"Don't trip son, I got this shit," Rell said putting an end to the conversation.

CHAPTER 17

As soon as Rell, Creature, and J-Rock made it to the Calliope after the incident in the Melph they noticed that the police were raiding one of Je'sus' trap houses, and it wasn't Safe Home, it was ATF and Task Force. That was out the ordinary, because no matter how much the police harassed the projects, ATF hardly ever raided an apartment with or without a warrant.

"I know them niggas head smoking," Rell said when he seen Donte and Black Larry come out the apartment handcuffed.

They were followed by two officers, one holding a Ziploc bag that could have had two thousand bags of heroin in it, maybe more. It was hard to tell with the sun reflecting off the aluminum foil that the dope was packaged in. The second officer wearing latex gloves was holding an AK-47 in one hand, and a clear plastic bag that read evidence in bold black letters, which had two handguns in it in the other.

Curtis Mitchell watched from a distance as they placed Donte' and Larry in the back of a police unit, while he tried to make sense out the whole thing. He couldn't understand what led the people to rush their spot, especially, in a community that's infested with drugs and violence. The thought crossed his mind that maybe they were getting sloppy with their transactions. He didn't rule out the possibility that someone could have given the cops some type of information on them. Why would someone do that after all the months they ran shop with no interference of the law? Throughout the project, they had over ten different sets that traffic drugs, not to mention the murders and other crimes, so why would they spot be targeted? He thought to himself.

Curtis called Je'sus to inform him that one of the spots had been hit, and that Donte' and Larry were in there when the law enforcement rushed the spot.

"Fuck!" Je'sus replied after hearing that half of the package was hit. "That was sixty thousand dollars' worth of dope. I can't afford to be taking losses like that, especially with me owing Giovanni forty thousand. Dawg them niggas stupid," Je'sus continued to complain. "Then on top of that, I got to go bond they dumb asses out."

"Don't trip 'bout the bond money, I'ma give you half of whatever the cost is," Curtis said.

"I know one fucking thing, I want my money back from them niggas," Je'sus said angrily.

Curtis couldn't believe the reaction he got from Je'sus, it was more 'bout the product and money, than the niggas that would lay down their life for him.

"You on some sucker shit right na' homie," Curtis told him with a lil' attitude. "Taking losses come with this game, besides the situation was out their control. Do you really think they were trying to go to jail, FUCK NO, but shit happens? All we got to do is grind a lil' harder, that's all, we gon get that back," Curtis continued.

"I just hope them niggas play it how it go and keep their mouth's closed," Je'sus said.

"Keep they mouth's closed, that's how you feel about the homies, I thought we were family," Curtis questioned him.

"We are family, but you know niggas' crack under pressure."

"Dawg those niggas is solid, and why be involved with a nigga at this level that you have doubts about keeping their mouth's closed?" Curtis asked not understanding Je'sus.

"I may be speaking without thinking," Je'sus said accepting the truth from Curtis. "Let me get in touch with Andrew Dyson and let him know that I need him for a bond hearing Monday, I'ma hit you back."

"Nah, Homie holla at Derek Scott he's the best lawyer for these type of situations," Curtis suggested.

"A'ight, I'm 'bout to see what's up. One."

After the police left, which felt like forever, Rell told Creature and J-Rock that he had to go holla at Curtis who was across the courtyard from where they were standing.

"What's popping?" Rell said as he approached Curtis.

"What's up my nigga?"

"Man, them people been smoking lately. Them motherfuckers at 6th district look like they on a mission, bitches been riding all day. All them shootings and killings ain't making shit no easier for a nigga to make money out chere," Rell said.

"Murder gon' always draw unwanted attention from the law," Curtis said, agreeing that the cops been riding heavy.

Lately, Curtis had been thinking of ways to end the beef between them and the SGs since Tre got killed. He understood that if things continued to go the way they'd been going, everybody was gon' lose, either by dying or going to prison for life.

"How Lou been holding up? I haven't seen that nigga around in a few weeks," Rell asked.

"He just taking it slow, but he good though. He doing better than we expected him to be, but I'ma tell him you asked about him."

"Oh, yeah, before I forget, it's something I need to tell you," Rell said with a mischievous look on his face.

"What's up my nigga?" Curtis asked.

But before Rell could say what he was about to say, his attention focused in on a nigga that was coming towards them wearing a black hoodie. "Dawg who the fuck that is with a hood on hot as it is" Rell asked.

"I don't know who the fuck that is, you strapped?" Curtis asked.

Rell didn't respond, he just pulled his gun from his waist. Creature and J-Rock were strapped also but they were on the other side of the courtyard.

"What's up Dawg?" Rell asked when the nigga got close enough to hear him. When he didn't make a threatening move, Curtis thought it could be a fiend trying to score.

"Y'all trying to buy a gun?" the guy asked while walking toward them.

Rell immediately reacted when the nigga reached for the gun that was on his waist. Boca... Boca... Boca... Boca… was the sound of his glock .40 cal. followed by a hard thump from the sound of the nigga's body slamming hard against the concrete.

"What the fuck?" Curtis said in awe as he looked at Rell.

"That nigga could have been trying anything, and I wasn't taking no chances on letting him grab that gun." Rell explained, but as he walked off he noticed the guy was still moving. So he walked back over to where he laid, pointed the gun at his head and squeezed the trigger once more. Boca...

Once Creature and J-Rock realized what was going on, Rell was already walking away from the scene. Trying not to draw too much attention to himself. Curtis went and stood on a porch about four hallways down from where the body was laying and watched Rell leave the scene.

The police must have been close by because by the time Rell made it to his apartment, a police car was roaring as it headed for the courtyard like they heard the shots. By the time the cops had arrived on the scene, a large crowd of spectators was gathered around the body. The first officers that arrived called the murder into headquarters as they tried to control the crowd before they possibly tampered with the evidence.

CHAPTER 18

When the DJ was over, Paul decided to call Roxanne. It seemed like as soon as the phone rang she answered.

"Hello!"

"What's up Roc, this Joe."

"I know who this is," Roxanne said while smiling. "I'm good though. What's up with you?"

"What you doing, you hungry, want to go grab something to eat, cause I can use some piece of mind right now," Paul asked.

"We can do that, but what was that about today at the DJ?" Roxanne asked.

"What what's was about?" he asked knowing what she was talking about.

"It looked like y'all seen somebody that y'all was about to kill or something. That's why I don't come in those projects. It's always some shit like that happening, but overall I'm glad to hear that you're okay."

"Of course, I'm okay. So what time you gon come through?"

"Boy, I ain't coming back in the project, but you can pick me up whenever you ready."

"A'ight, I'll call you tonight."

"Okay I'll be waiting. Bye."

"Bye."

"It's a good thing I was out here, cause it would have been a triple murder today," Ben said while shaking his head.

"Ha brah, but did you notice how them niggas that was with Rell was looking?" Paul asked.

"How you expect them to look after looking death in the eyes," Ben said with a giggle in his voice.

"So what you about to get into?" Ben asked.

"I'm just 'bout to chill and get this money. I'm supposed to be hooking up with ole girl later on tonight."

"Who dat?"

"The hoe Roxanne that was back here for the DJ. The one off Josephine," Paul said.

"A'ight then my nigga, I'ma fuck with you in the morning, I'm 'bout to go in. Joy been blowing my phone up ever since she left the funeral."

***

After the scene cleared out, Curtis went to holla at Rell before he went in for the night. It was killing him to know what Rell was about to tell him before the murder occurred. Knock…Knock...Knock... was the sound of Curtis knocking on the door. While inside Rell panicked instantly and was about to run out the backdoor thinking it was the police. But Curtis knocked again when he didn't get an answer and this time he yelled, "This Curtis," figuring Rell didn't answer cause he feared it was the law knocking.

"That's Curtis," Rell's older brother Terrance said when he heard the name through the door, but he still looked through the peephole before opening the door.

"What's up?" Curtis said.

"Ain't nothin', what's up with you?" Terrance replied in a defensive tone.

"Let me holla at Rell," Curtis said seconds before he noticed Rell heading to the door.

"What the deal is?" Rell asked.

"Let me holla at you on the porch," Curtis said not wanting to talk in front of his brother.

"What's up?" Rell said the moment he stepped on the porch and closed the door.

"I like how you reacted on that. That was gangsta, ain't no telling what that nigga was up to cause that clown did have a gun on him. What you was about to tell me before that nigga walked up though?" Curtis asked curiously.

"Oh, yeah! Dog me, Rock and Creature went in the Melph to the nigga Tre, DJ and them niggas surrounded us at gunpoint, but the nigga Ben was like they ain't part of the Cheddar Boys, and that's the only reason why they ain't killed us."

"Why would y'all even go back there?" Curtis asked.

"Fuck, we was strapped we wasn't slipping, we just ain't see them niggas coming."

"Then y'all was slipping!" Curtis shot back.

"Well homie, I'm just letting you know, them niggas think or know that y'all killed dude. Either way they held y'all accountable, so keep y'all head up."

"Nice looking out, cause that was definitely some valuable information," Curtis said right before his phone started ringing.

"Hold on," he told Rell as he answered his phone. "What's up, Bae?"

"Nothing. Just wanted to know when you was coming home. De'Ja keep talking 'bout she hungry, and she don't want what I cooked. That's your fault from spoiling her," his girl Kenyatta said.

"Where she at?"

"Here, your daddy wants you," Kenyatta said passing the phone to De'Ja.

"Hello, hey daddy."

"What's up baby girl, what you want to eat?"

"I don't know," De'Ja said in a childish tone.

"What you mean you don't know, why you don't want to eat what momma cooked?"

"Cause I want you to bring me something."

"Okay baby, I'ma bring you something to eat. Tell your Momma to put you on some clothes and we're all gonna go out to eat."

"He said we gon go out to eat, put me on some clothes."

"Girl give me this damn phone," Kenyatta said snatching the phone out her hand. "See, you stupid for her, you do whatever she say. Look at her laughing, that ain't funny."

"You better leave my baby alone, I'll be there in a minute."

"Okay, love you."

"I love you too. Bye."

When Curtis left and Rell went back in the apartment, Terrance was looking at him with a fucked up look on his face.

"Why the fuck you looking like that?" Rell asked with aggression.

"What the fuck that nigga had to say to you, that he couldn't say it in front of me?" Terrance asked.

“Fall back my nigga, let me do me,” Rell said with a sneaky look on his face. Terrance knew Rell like the back of his hand, so he knew that Rell was up to something.

CHAPTER 19

The entire ride home, Ben was thinking about his family, and how he hadn't been spending much time with them lately. He knew that if it weren't for his lifestyle, it would've been difficult for him to live the life he was living. Ben had recently bought a two-story brick house in a gated community that he and Joy lived in. When they purchased the house, they done so with the intention to be secluded from the inner city, and the Stone Bridge subdivision on Manhattan was the perfect location for their desires.

Ben's phone started ringing as he pressed in the code to open the electronic gate that allowed residents to enter the subdivision. As he entered the gate, he looked down at his phone and smiled when he saw it was Joy calling.

"What's up bae?" Ben asked.

"Don't bae me," Joy responded in a bitchy mood.

"What's the attitude about?" Ben asked.

"You saw me calling you, don't play with me Benjamin," Joy shot back.

"Bae stop tripping, it ain't like you didn't know where I was. You chose to leave, when in all reality, you should have been more supportive at a time like this. You of all people should know that Tre was like a brother to me," Ben said hoping she'd understand.

"You right, Bae, but you know I don't like going in the project. When you told me that the repast was in the Melph, I decided to come home after the burial," Joy replied.

Ben pulled up in front of his house, but instead of getting out and going inside, he reclined the driver seat and continued talking.

"Where my son at?" Ben asked.

"He's in his room asleep, that boy been driving me crazy all day," Joy said. "I haven't been feeling good either," she continued.

"What you mean you ain't been feeling good? What's wrong?" Ben asked.

"I been feeling nauseated the last couple of days."

"Joy you trying to tell me something?" Ben asked curiously.

By this time Ben had gotten out of the car, headed to the door and used his key to get in instead of having Joy let him in.

"Bae, it sound like somebody trying to get in the front door," Joy said in a nervous tone. Ben smiled at the fact that she had no idea that it was him, so he played along.

"Listen to me, I'm on my way right now, just relax and go hide in the bedroom closet," Ben said as he held in his laugh.

Once Ben opened the front door he could hear her footsteps as she raced for the room. Moments later he made his way to their bedroom and approached the closet where he found Joy balled up in a fetal position.

"Girl get yo' scary ass up," Ben told her when he noticed how frightened she was, "Then you ain't think about grabbing BJ." he continued.

Joy didn't know if she wanted to be pissed, happy, or maybe both. When she looked up and saw Ben standing there laughing. "You play too much," Joy said as she pushed him out her way because she didn't find what he done funny.

"Come here baby I was just playing," Ben said as he grabbed her around the waist from behind, while trying to kiss her on the neck as she pulled away from him.

"Benjamin, we need to talk" Joy said while taking a seat on the bed.

"Talk about what?" Ben asked not liking the sound of that, knowing it couldn't be nothing good. Joy didn't respond, she simply got up and picked up a condom off the dresser, and held it up for Ben to see it.

"What you doing with that? I know you don't expect for us to start using rubbers," Ben said in more of a statement than a question.

"No motherfucker! What you doing with it?" Joy shot back aggressively.

Ben tried to convince her that he had no idea where the condom came from but it was nothing he could've said to make her feel any other way. The one thing she knew for sure, was that it wasn't hers, so she went on raving about how she's been the perfect woman and that she never considered cheating on him. They argued until the point that he knew he was fighting a losing battle, so he told her that he was going to take a ride to clear his head. Before they both said something that they might regret.

"You think I'm stupid Benjamin, but I'm not. I know what comes with being a hustler's woman, but I don't expect for you to be that careless and bring the evidence home."

"I told you that I didn't have that condom."

"Boy whatever," Joy said as she stormed out the room not wanting to hear anymore.

Ben rolled up a joint then told her that he'd be back in a few hours, and left out the house before she started asking questions. Five minutes after he left, Joy ran to the bathroom to throw up, splashing vomit all over the toilet seat.

***

Paul made a right off S. Liberty onto Josephine, which at that moment he felt very uncomfortable about. Both sides of the street were occupied with niggas who were locked in on his truck with the look of anticipation of some shit popping off.

Paul was well aware of the beef that the Josephine Head Bussers, which is the name of the click that represented Josephine St, was into, so he figured it would be best for him not to stop. So he kept driving as he called Roxanne. Roxanne was looking forward to Paul's call, so she answered on the first ring. "Hello!"

"Yeah, what's up, you ready?" Paul asked ready to get off that hot ass set.

"Yeah, I'm ready, I was waiting on your call," Roxanne answered.

"Which house do you live in?"

"I stay in the third house to the left as soon as you get on Josephine."

"I'm 'bout to pull back on your street right now, so be outside cause they got all them fucking niggas out there looking all in my car and shit," Paul said.

"Boy, they ain't worrying 'bout you," a naive Roxanne said.

"It's clear you don't understand, just be outside."

When Paul turned on Josephine for the second time, the stares were more intense. When he pulled up slow in front of the house that Roxanne described, niggas surrounded his car with their guns pointed. Paul nearly had a panic attack at that point because he found himself in a helpless situation and there was nothing he could do about it. That's when flashes of what Ben had been trying to tell him about fucking with them no good ass hoes came into vision.

He knew it was nobody but God that kept them niggas from executing their ambush. Roxanne ran out the house screaming repeatedly, "That's my friend! That's my friend!" but they never lowered their weapons.

"Don't be bringing them fucking niggas around here," yelled her brother who was one of the gunmen. "Where that nigga from anyway?" he continued.

"Don't worry 'bout where he from, you really think I'ma bring somebody around here that y'all beefing with. Matter of fact, you really think a nigga stupid enough to come around here that ain't supposed to be here. Besides, I can see who I want to see, and y'all don't know that boy anyway," Roxanne said as she was walking toward Paul's truck.

"You lucky we ain't smoke that nigga," her brother said as he was putting his gun on his waist.

When Roxanne opened the car door, the light came on inside the truck and one of the niggas that was out there that was focused on the driver noticed Paul so he walked over to the passenger window to holla at him.

"What's up Paul? Dawg you was 'bout to get it in a major way, we was 'bout to Swiss cheese this bitch," he said pointing to Paul's truck.

"Paul!" Roxanne said confused because he told her his name was Joe.

Paul ignored her outburst and responded to the dude statement. "Dawg if I was on some slick shit, y'all had me like a motherfucker, but I'ma fuck with you though," Paul said anxious to get off that block.

"Stay up nigga, you know it's wicked out chere in these streets," the dude said as they dapped and Paul pulled off.

"You know that nigga?" Roxanne's brother asked the dude.

"Yeah, that's ole boy Paul out the Melph."

"That fool lucky cause I was about to empty the whole clip on his ass," Roxanne's brother said as he was walking off.

It took Paul five minutes into the drive for his nerves to settle down.

"So where you want to eat at?" Paul asked as he lowered down the volume of the music.

"It don't matter, I really want to use this time to get to know you better. I'm attracted to you and want things to go further with us."

'So what do you really want to know?" Paul asked.

"Well, first of all, I want to know your name," Roxanne said looking Paul in the eye.

"I told you my name," Paul said while smiling.

"You did, but Tony called you Paul and you told me your name was Joe."

"Joe is my middle name, and I use that name a lot with strangers, but Paul is my first name."

"A'ight since that's out the way, what's your plans?" Roxanne asked."

"What kind of question is that?"

"I want to know your plans with me?" Roxanne asked again.

"I mean, it depends."

"Depends on what?"

"Depends on your principles and morals, because everybody has a motive that drives them. Trust me if we spend enough time together it will be impossible for me not to peep out your motive."

"Well! It's not hard to find out most niggas motives. Y'all just want to fuck, men are so scared of commitment."

"Speaking for myself, I ain't about to commit to nobody that don't deserve my commitment. But it's far from me being scared, because I'm committed to a lot of things. It's just that I haven't met the women that has the qualities that I look for, that make her worthy of being my ole lady."

"And what exactly do you look for in a woman?" Roxanne asked.

"Now if I tell you, and you live up to those expectations, how would I know if it's genuine?"

"If you tell me and I live up to those expectations, what difference it make if it's genuine or not, as long as those expectations are being met," Roxanne said. "Because sometimes it's important for the other party in a relationship to let their partner know what they expect. What you don't have to tell me is how to be a woman or my do's and don'ts," she continued.

"You have a point, but I would rather things progress naturally, but from the sound of your conversation, it sounds like you have what it takes."

"Maybe, but we'll see how things work out," she said with that same smile on her face that she'd given him the first time they met.

Moments later, they exited on Veteran Blvd, but got held up at the red light.

"Where are we going?" Roxanne asked.

"How 'bout Applebee's?"

"I told you, it's up to you but honestly we can sit and talk because you have an interesting conversation. Something I don't get from the average nigga."

"I ain't average," Paul said with a slight smirk on his face. "And to be honest, you don't appear to be average either, and

I appreciate you uplifting my spirit cause not even twelve hours ago, I watched my close friend get laid to rest. Just in these few minutes we been together you completely took my mind off what I lost and got focused on what I gained."

"And what did you gain?" Roxanne asked anticipating a certain response.

"For right now, let's just say I've gained a friend that I can communicate with, that's on my level."

When they pulled up to Applebee's they found a parking spot in the crowded parking lot and headed for the entrance. Once inside, they were seated and waited for a waiter to take their order. When the waitress arrived, and they ordered Paul whispered to her that it was Roxanne's birthday. So the waitress gathered several other employees and they all approached Paul and Roxanne's table and began singing Happy Birthday. It got the attention of everyone in the restaurant.

"Boy, you play too much," she said as she slapped him on the arm feeling humored and embarrassed at the same time.

Sitting three tables down was Curtis Mitchell and his family, the singing got Curtis' attention. After they finished singing Happy Birthday, the employees went back to their normal work duties.

"Boy, today ain't my birthday, why you told that girl that?"

Roxanne asked while smiling

"You right, it's not your birthday, it's our birthday."

"What you mean, it's our birthday?" she asked confused.

"Because today is the day we gave birth to a new friendship," Paul said.

Roxanne couldn't do nothing except smile at that statement. Curtis' adrenaline was rushing at an all-time high for the simple fact that he had no idea how things would play out if Paul saw him. Him having his family with him made the situation that much more intense.

"What's wrong bae?" Kenyatta asked Curtis because she knew him well enough to know when something was bothering him.

"I'm good bae," but his response wasn't convincing at all.

"Are you sure," Kenyatta asked sincerely.

"Yeah, Bae, but do you have a pen in your purse?"

Kenyatta didn't respond, she simply grabbed her Gucci purse off the floor and dug in it till she came up with an ink pen.

"Here bae," she said as she extended her hand to give him the pen.

"Daddy I want some more soda." De'ja said. "Okay sweetheart I'ma get you some more."

"I got it bae," Kenyatta said as she grabbed De'Ja's hand and headed for the soda fountain.

The moment the waitress brought Paul and Roxanne their food to the table, Curtis' daughter walked over to Paul and handed him a small piece of napkin and said, "My daddy told me to give this to you."

"Who's your daddy beautiful?" Paul asked.

"Him right there," she said as she pointed to Curtis Mitchell.

"Thank you precious," Paul told De'Ja.

Paul opened the napkin which had a number on it, and a note that said: "Give to Ben."

***

After fussing with Joy, Ben decided to go to a strip club to clear his mind, so he drove to Passions with nearly 6 racks in his pocket. If a bitch caught his eye, he was willing to blow a couple dollars on her.

The moment he found a seat and sat down, a dancer who went by the name Cinnamon from Memphis approached him and offered a lap dance for $20. Cinnamon was so beautiful, calling her a dime would have been an understatement.

Ben knew he had to have her for the night so he whispered in her ear and said, "Fuck a lap dance, how much that pussy cost?"

"It cost a hundred dollars for a date," she answered seductively.

As Ben stared at her beautiful body, the blood rushed to his dick which gave him an immediate erection. He looked over at the private booths located on the far side of the club and said, "Get us a booth."

"It cost seventy-five dollars to rent one," she responded as she made her ass shake to the rhythm of the music.

"Do it look like it matter to me? Get us one," Ben said as he was reaching in his pocket.

At that moment, all ten booths were occupied so they waited. Fifteen minutes later still no one had come out. Ben was extra hard as she grinded on him while waiting on a booth. Five more minutes passed and still no booths became available and Cinnamon realized she was losing money by waiting on a booth because she could have made a hundred dollars off of one song. She told Ben she was about to hit the stage, and that she'd try to hook up when him with things slowed down.

"I respect that, go make yo' money," Ben told her while squeezing her ass. Then he went back in his pocket and gave her twenty dollars for her time. When she saw what he was holding, she automatically looked at Ben as a come-up.

"Thank you, daddy," she said softly as she took the 20 dollars.

She immediately went to a dude and pointed him out, who watched Ben closely until he left the club. Maybe 45 minutes passed when Ben decided to call it a night. When the dude saw Ben head for the exit, he got on the phone and gave a description of him.

As soon as Ben hit the unlock button on his key chain, a tall dude came out of nowhere and slapped him across the forehead with a gun. Ben didn't fall, but staggered while panting heavily. He was then hit a second time across the nose, causing him to fall unconscious to the ground. Minutes later Ben found himself looking up at the barrel of a .45 automatic, dazed by the blows he took to the head.

"You know what it is, don't turn this robbery into a murder," the masked gunman said.

"You can have the money, just don't kill me," Ben said pleading for his life. At first Ben thought it was one of those niggas out the Calliope, but his thoughts changed when the gunman demanded money.

"Well up it nigga," the gunman said.

Ben reached in his pocket to give him the money, but before he completely pulled the money out, the nigga cocked the gun. Clock...Clack. At that moment, Ben thought he was going to die. Several flashes appeared in his mind, flashes of Tre, Paul, his girl and son, all kinds of shit ran through his mind until his thoughts were interrupted by the words of the gunman asking, "Is this everything?"

"Yeah, that's everything," Ben answered with fear in his voice.

"Give me your phone and car keys," the gunman demanded.

"Here, take it," Ben complied without resistance.

After getting the phone and car keys, the gunman told Ben to get up. Once Ben got to his feet, he told him to start running. After Ben ran about ten yards, he looked back and noticed that the gunman was running in the opposite direction, so he turned and went back in the club to call Paul to pick him up.

Once he made it inside the club, one of the bouncers recognized Ben from being in there minutes before. Seeing Ben's face was bloody, the bouncer asked was he okay.

"Yeah, I'm straight."

"What happened?" the bouncer asked curious to know what had happened that fast.

"Nothing, I'm good, let me borrow your phone."

"Here, take yo' time," the bouncer said handing Ben his phone. Ben tried to call Paul twice and the phone went straight to voicemail, so he called K-Dog, and after the third ring, K-Dog answered.

"Who this?"

"It's me homie," Ben said happy that K-Dog answered.

'Damn nigga, I didn't know you got a new number," K-Dog said.

"I didn't, a nigga just jacked me."

"Jacked you! Where the fuck you at?'

"I'm at Passions, come scoop me up, the nigga took my phone and keys."

"I'm on my way," K-Dog said.

The nigga that robbed Ben must have thought Ben was gone, so he came back to the strip club and held somebody else at gunpoint. When Ben opened the door to leave out and wait on K-Dog, he saw that same nigga robbing somebody else, so he eased back inside and asked the bouncer to use his phone again. He called K-Dog and asked him how far was he.

"I'm pulling up right now. I'm at the red light on Downman at the bottom of the overpass."

"You strapped?" Ben asked.

"What kind of question is that?"

"Look homie, the same nigga is outside robbing somebody right now," Ben informed.

"Where he at exactly?"

"He in the parking lot on the side of Passions behind the Shell gas station."

K-Dog parked and eased alongside the parked cars where he heard the nigga demanding money. Before he knew it, K-Dog popped up from behind a Charger, gun in hand and yelled, "Police, drop the weapon!"

When the gunman dropped the weapon, K-Dog moved in and told him to put his hands on the wall. He did as he was told, and K-Dog checked his pockets taking all the money off him. He didn't find Ben's phone nor his keys, so he shot him once in the head, blowing his brains all over the wall. K-Dog shot him several more times in the head after his body hit the ground. By then, the nigga that was getting robbed took off running.

Ben heard the shots and came running out the strip club to find K-Dog picking something off the ground. He later found out it was the gun the nigga had, so they jumped in the car and headed to Ben's house.

CHAPTER 20

Early the next morning, Paul was awakened by the sound of his ringtone that was extremely loud in the extremely quiet apartment. He looked at the time on a digital clock that sat on his dresser that read, 6:05 a.m. *Who can this be this early in the morning*, he thought to himself as he rolled over slowly and grabbed his phone off the nightstand. He didn't bother to look at the screen for the caller, he just flipped open his Nextel.

"Hello!" he said as he scooted up against the headboard to sit up.

"Come over to my house," Ben said while trying to use the least amount of facial muscles to minimize the pain that he was suffering from the blows he took to the face during the robbery.

"Nigga you sound like you still sleep too," Paul said informing Ben that he woke him out his sleep.

"I couldn't get no sleep last night, my whole fucking head feels like it's about to bust," Ben said.

"What's up my nigga, you straight?" Paul asked.

"It's too late to be asking me that, if you would have answered your phone last night you would have known I wasn't straight."

That statement woke Paul all the way up. "What happened?"

"Just come over here, we'll talk when you get here."

"A'ight. One." Paul responded jumping out of bed. He got himself together and headed to Ben's house in a rush.

"Baby do you need me to get you anything?" Joy asked Ben with sympathy in her eyes.

"Yeah, bring me a glass of water and two Tylenol."

When Joy came back in the room, she gave him the glass of water and the medicine then sat on the bed next to him.

"Baby, when are you gon get out the game?" Joy asked humbly.

"Not right now Joy, this ain't the time for that, my head hurts like crazy."

"I'm serious Benjamin, when are you gon leave that life alone, because me and the kids need you."

"What you mean the kids?" Ben asked confused.

"I think I'm pregnant," Joy said as she rubbed her stomach. "And I ain't trying to lose you to the streets. Only two things gon come out the streets in the long run, and that's death or jail. I ain't willing to take the chance of losing you for no amount of money. I don't know what I'll do if something happens to you. Look at yourself," she said while pointing to the mirror on the dresser. "You could have easily been killed last night."

"I'll give it some thought bae, but I just want to lay down and relax right now," Ben said not wanting to hear anymore. But deep in his heart, he knew she was right about getting out while he was still ahead, and he felt that he should take what she said into consideration.

"Okay, Bae, get yo' rest, but we'll finish this discussion some other time... Soon," Joy said as she was walking out the room.

Even as a beautiful young lady, Joy was teased a lot by her peers. Mostly for being a nerd because of her devotion to her intellectual pursuits. While her peers were attending school dances and movie nights at the theater, she preferred to stay home and further her education. Some would say she thought she was more than the next person, despite the fact she wore the same clothes, went to the same school, and lived in the same neighborhood as them, but the truth was they envied the morals her parents instilled in her.

With her mother being a high school teacher, and her father being a preacher, Joy's upbringing was totally different from her peers. She was more focused on her studies and more in tune with her spiritual side. For most of her childhood she was never addressed by her name from the other kids, but by The Preacher's Daughter, which she hated dearly. But things changed in the eyes of her parents as well as the neighborhood kids when she established an intimate relationship with Bad News Ben, which is what they called Ben in his precocious years.

Joy's parents were furious at the fact that their innocent little girl gained interest in a hoodlum such as Ben. It was obvious that they were against everything that he stood for. Joy's relationship with her parents started to deteriorate tremendously after they discovered her pregnancy. After they realized that Joy's mind was made up and that Ben was the person she was going to be with, with or without her parent's approval. So eventually, they accepted she and Ben's relationship, and Joy hadn't been with another man since.

Nowadays, her parents refer to Ben as son.

Ben laid back in his bed thinking about all the bullshit that had been happening lately. The back and forth shootings with the Cheddar Boys that resulted in Tre getting killed, Paul getting shot at and him getting robbed and pistol whipped. Maybe it was time to move on to something different like starting some kind of business, and if Tre were alive, Ben knew that he'd agree with Joy one hundred percent.

He thought about his friend Monsta in the process, so he decided to send him a kite letting him know what happened to Tre if he hadn't already heard. By the time he got halfway through the letter, he heard the doorbell ring and he knew that it was Paul. He was the only one in Ben's circle that had the passcode to the front gate besides his mother and Joy's mother.

"How you doing?" Paul asked once Joy opened the door to let him in.

"I'm doing fine. Ben it's Paul," Joy shouted from the living room.

Paul went straight to BJ's room only to find it empty. "Where my lil' man at?" Paul asked Joy who was on her way to the kitchen to fix breakfast.

"Oh, he by my momma for the weekend, he'll be home tonight."

Paul headed to Ben's bedroom, and when he walked in and saw Ben's face covered with multiple contusions his heart fell to the floor.

"What's up, nigga? I was just shooting Monsta a kite," Ben said.

"What the fuck happened last night?" Paul asked not believing how bad Ben was beaten.

Ben told Paul to close the door so Joy couldn't hear what he was about to say. Before he removed his hand from the door-knob, he was asking Ben what had went down.

"I went to Passions, had a few drinks cause me and Joy had a fuss about a fucking condom she found, but anyway, when I left the club I got jacked and pistol whipped. Then the nigga took my car keys, that's why I was calling you."

"Damn homie, I was..."

"Let me finish," Ben interrupted. "It's becoming a pattern that you never there when I need you the most my nigga," Ben said looking Paul directly in the eyes. "It's too much shit going on not to be able to get in touch with you if necessary, and most times it be because a hoe is involved," Ben continued.

"You right dawg, because I did turn my phone off. I didn't want another hoe calling me while I was with that hoe, my bad homie," Paul said sincerely.

"That's why you need to get a line strictly for yo hoes and one for business, because when I call you, I expect for you to answer. You know I ain't gon be calling for no bullshit."

"I'ma take care of that today," Paul said knowing that Ben had made a strong point.

The room got quiet for a few seconds, they both were trapped in their own thoughts. Ben looked Paul in the eyes and asked him, "Can I count on you my nigga?"

"What kind of question is that?"

"The kind I need to know. I don't need to be able to count on you some of the time, I need to know if I can count on you all the time."

"I got cha homie," Paul said while pounding his chest with his right fist. "When me and ole girl was at Applebee's last night, I ran into that nigga Curtis Mitchell and his family, and the nigga sent his lil' girl to our table to give his number to me to give to you."

"What the fuck I'ma do with that nigga number?"

"I don't know the reason why he want you to call him. I didn't say one word to the nigga, but I think it's worth checking out," Paul said as he took the piece of paper out his pocket and handed it to Ben.

"I'ma see what's up, but I'ma be down for a few days so I need you to run things in the project cause I might be M.I.A. for like a week until this swelling go down."

"A week! It look like it gon take a year for that swelling to go down," Paul said playfully as he pointed at Ben's face. "But on some real shit, somehow, some way, we need to find out who the nigga was that pulled this shit off," Paul said changing his mode from playful to serious.

"K-Dog already took care of that when he came to pick me up." Ben responded, just as Joy knocked softly on the bedroom door and asked if he was ready to eat.

"You can come in bae."

When she entered the room, she asked Paul if he wanted to eat, but he declined by saying, "I was just about to leave."
"You sure? We have more than enough," Joy said.

"Yeah, I'm good, maybe next time."

"Okay, you be careful then."

"Careful is my middle name," Paul shot back.

"I'ma holla at you my nigga, get you some rest," Paul told Ben then looked at Joy and said, "Take care of my homie."

"I been taking care of your homie for the last ten years," Joy said with pride.

"I wish I had a woman like you," Paul said before leaving out the room.

"Yo' Paul," Ben shouted before Paul made it to the living room. Paul turned and headed for Ben's bedroom.

"What's up my nigga?" he asked when he peeped his head through the door.

“I need you to do me one more favor homie,” Ben said realizing that his car was still parked in the club parking lot. “I got cha my nigga. Whatever you need done.”

Ben reached in the nightstand and came up with a single key, handed it to Paul and told him to go pick his car up from the club. He wanted him to park it in the project, because he really wasn’t comfortable with anyone else knowing where he lived outside of the few people that already knew. Ben knew if Paul picked up his car, he would have to bring someone with him, so they could drive his truck back.

“I got cha nigga, you just rest up, I’m out,” Paul said, then turned to head for the front door.

CHAPTER 21

After getting things setup in the project, Paul told Ryder to collect the money if he hadn't made it back, because he had to make a run. It would have been much easier for Ben to call a tow truck and have his car dropped off in front of his house, but he decided to let Paul handle it.

Paul really enjoyed the time him and Roxanne spent together at the restaurant, and by him needing someone to drive either his or Ben's car back to the project, he figured he'd utilize this opportunity to spend time with her again by asking her to go with him to get Ben's car. Since that night at Applebee's, Paul had been doing some serious thinking 'bout settling down with Roxanne for the simple fact he felt connected to her. Something he hadn't felt with other girls in the past, and it was weird because he hadn't slept with her yet. They shared similar feelings but neither one was ready to expose those feelings to the other. It was becoming clearer to Roxanne that her feelings were getting involved. It was like they had so much in common, and whenever she was in Paul's company it felt like the right place to be. When she wasn't around him she thought about him constantly. No matter how much she tried to dismiss those thoughts of him, his image would always reappear in her mind. After Roxanne's phone rang four times, Paul came to the conclusion that maybe she was asleep but just as he was about to hang up she answered the phone.

"Hello?" Roxanne said in a tone that led Paul to believe she had been awake for a while.

"What's up wit' cha, I hope I didn't call at a bad time," Paul said as he walked towards his truck.

"When it come to you, it's never a bad time," Roxanne said as she flopped down on her bed.

"I thought you was sleep, as long as it took you to answer yo' phone."

"I was in the bathroom when I heard it ring, so what's up?" she asked as she stretched out to make herself more comfortable.

"What you doing?" Paul asked ready to get to the reason for the early morning call.

"I'm just chilling until it's time for me to go to work."

"Work? You ain't never tell me you work," Paul said as if he was surprised Roxanne had a job.

"I never told you because you never asked, besides how do you think I take care of myself or you ain't gave it no thought at all?" Roxanne said.

"I guess I didn't give it much thought. So where you work at?"

"I work at IHOP in the East."

"What time you have to be to work for?"

"Well today I have to go in at 12:00pm."

"What kind of schedule you got where you have to be to work at 12:00?" Paul asked.

"By me being a manager, my schedule rotates quarterly, but I'm getting tired of it because it's kind of hard for me to make plans. Sometimes they'll call me on my off day if the shift is short and stuff like that."

"Well look here, I need you to ride with me to the East to pick up my homie's car from around Passions."

"Ain't that a strip club?" she asked.

"Yeah, it's a strip club, what difference does it make?"

"Boy it's almost 11:00 a.m., I ain't gon' have time to do all that and make it home to get dressed for work."

"That's why you gon' get dressed right now."

"And how I'm supposed to get my car if I'm going with you to get another car?" Roxanne asked confused.

"Because you not, you gon' take my truck to work and I'ma bring Ben's car back with me."

"Why he can't go get his own car?"

"You gon' fuck with it or not?" Paul asked not wanting to get in to details why Ben's car was left there.

"Yeah, I got you."

"You sho?" Paul asked.

"Yeah, I'm sho, I got you, come pick me up in 20 minutes."

"A'ight, I'll see you then."

CHAPTER 22

Even though they moved their shop to another apartment a half a block away from the one Larry and Donte' got arrested in, Lou was paranoid that they were still being watched. He constantly peeped out the kitchen window, while Je'sus and Curtis sat on the sofa counting money.

"Do you think you can hold down the spot till we get back or do you want to ride with us?" Je'sus asked 9 Finger Lou as him and Curtis prepared to post bail for Donte' and Black Larry.

"Y'all go ahead and bond them niggas out, I'ma stay here and make this money," Lou told them, figuring with Donte' and Larry being in jail he'll stick around to keep the operation running.

"Dawg you know I prefer for more than one person to run shop. Especially, with you not being a hundred percent," Je'sus said.

"I'm a hundred percent as long as I got this," Lou said as he grabbed an AK that was leaning against the love seat.

"Ok hold it down then, we shouldn't be that long, probably 'bout 45 minutes, but my line will be open if you need to call me for anything," Je'sus told Lou who had already began to separate the bundles of dope on the coffee table.

"I'm good homie," Lou said.

"A'ight nigga, we out," Je'sus said as him and Curtis headed for the door.

"So, what bondsman you gon use?" Curtis asked Je'sus as he pulled out the driveway.

"I'ma fuck with William Freeman. Word is he's the most reliable right now and we have to get them niggas out ASAP," Je'sus said. "As a matter of fact, let me try calling him again to let him know we on our way," he continued.

The moment Je'sus flipped open his phone, Curtis Mitchell's phone started ringing.

When Curtis looked at his phone, the number wasn't familiar. "Who the fuck this is?" he said to himself.

After the third ring, he answered the call. "Hello!?"

"I got yo message, what you want to talk about?"

"Who this is?" Curtis asked not recognizing the voice on the other end of the phone.

"This Ben, you wanted me to call, right? So what's up?"

"I'm in the midst of handling some business, I'ma get back with you," Curtis said

"Whatever we need to talk about, we can talk about it right now."

"Like I said, I'ma get back with you, it ain't the time right now," Curtis shot back.

"I see you think shit a game!" Ben said with a lil' aggression in his voice. "Besides I'm out of line even calling you," Ben added.

"I ain't playing no games, I just can't talk right now," Curtis said.

"When you ready to talk, hit me up, you have my number," Ben said and hung up before Curtis could respond.

"Man, them hoes be tripping!" Curtis said out loud to keep Je'sus from asking who that was.

The smell of coffee and cigarette smoke filled the air inside of the small and cluttered office as Je'sus and Curtis approached the desk of the bail bondsman. What they saw was a heavy set bald guy, who looked more like a truck driver than a bail bondsman.

"May I help you," the bail bondsman asked without looking up from the documents he was examining.

"Yeah, I'm here to make bail for two people who was arrested Friday," Je'sus said as he looked around the junky office.

The sound of two got the bondsman's attention immediately. "What are they charged with?" the bail bondsman asked looking back and forth from Je'sus to Curtis not knowing who made the statement about making bail.

"Drug and weapon charges," Je'sus spoke up.

"What are their names?" the bondsman asked as he reached for the phone that was nearly invisible from being surrounded by piles of paperwork.

"Donte' Morgan and Larry Henry."

"Give me a second," the bondsman said as he dialed a number.

As the phone rung he covered the receiver with his hand and said in a whisper, "Let me see if they have a bond yet."

When he hung up the phone, he began telling Je'sus what Donte' and Larry's bond was set at.

"Are you going to pay the bail in full or set up a payment plan?" the bondsman asked.

"I'ma pay it out in cash, all I want to know is how long will it take for them to get out?" Je'sus asked.

"All I need to do is run over to the jail and they will be out by noon."

"That sounds good to me," Je'sus said and began counting out ten thousand in hundred-dollar bills to give to the bondsman.

***

On the receiving tier in the OPP, Donte' and Larry's patience grew thin for the fact that they figured they should have been out on bail already. Not realizing the process takes a little time to be finalized… Sometimes it can take up to 12 hours before a person is released depending on the charge.

Four hours later, Donte' and Larry were called to be released. "Bout fucking time!" Larry said as he began taking off his shoes and undershirt to give to a dude he kicked it with the few days he was on the tier.

While waiting in central lockup to be released, Donte' passed his time flirting with a deputy that work in booking.

"What's up?" Donte asked with a pause before saying, "Ms. Walker," after reading her name tag that sat high upon her full breast.

"You can have a seat and be quiet is what's up," she said with an attitude.

"Damn luv, what the attitude about? Let me guess, you one of those people who allow your job title to define who you are," Donte' said.

"What that supposed to mean?" she asked, a little humbler than with her first response.

"All I did was speak to you and you reacted like I violated you in some way."

"You have no idea what we go through here," she said.

"The only thing I can see y'all go through is hundreds of niggas flirting with y'all daily. When did flirting become a violation, you almost ran me off, that's probably the reason why you ain't married."

"And how you know if I'm married or not?" she asked.

"It's not that complicated to figure out with you not wearing a ring," Donte' said while pointing at her hand that rested on the countertop.

Their conversation was cut short when Donte' and Larry's names were called to a small window to receive their property before being released.

"We need to finish this conversation some other time," Donte' said. "Take my number if you want to finish this," he added.

"What's your number?" she asked picking up an ink pen and a piece of paper.

Donte' gave her his number and asked her what her first name was.

"My name is Stacy."

"A'ight Stacy, I'll be expecting to hear from you."

"We'll see."

CHAPTER 23

Ashley was late for her appointment but came through the door just as Tiffany was about to move on to her next customer.

"Girl I'm sorry I'm late, I had to drop Danny off by his daddy," Ashley said as she removed a bandanna from her head.

"Next time you better call and let me know you gon be running late. I was about to start my next head," Tiffany said pointing at a heavy-set girl who needed her hair done badly. "My time is money, I can't be sitting around waiting on nobody."

"So how you want it done?" Tiffany asked.

"Just wash it and flat iron it," Ashley answered.

The shop kept plenty of traffic, more weed buyers than hair customers. On any given day, you might find a lot of people just hanging out, playing the PlayStation, getting filled in on the latest gossip, or just ducking the summer heat. But parents who were aware of the activities that took place in the shop refused to send their children there to get their hair cut. They feared that at some point the police would raid the shop and didn't want their children to get caught up in a situation like that.

"Girl you heard that the Slum Godds supposed to be beefing with the Cheddar Boys?" Ashley asked Tiffany.

"Bitch you forgot you told me that already," Tiffany said sarcastically.

"I never told you them boys was beefing, because I never knew. I just found out," Ashley said.

"Girl you really need to stop smoking all that damn weed, cause it's messing with your memory. You don't remember telling me that they were shooting at each other on the lakefront."

"Girl you must have took what I said the wrong way. What I told you was, that I was on the lakefront and the Cheddar Boys and the Slum Godds was out there when somebody started shooting. I didn't know who was shooting," Ashley said.

"Girl I misunderstood what you said, I thought you said the Slum Godds and the Cheddar Boys were shooting at each other," Tiffany said realizing that she relayed some incorrect information to Ben and Paul. As they discussed the beef situation, several people overheard how Tiffany had misunderstood Ashley.

"But anyway, they beefing for real, because word on the street is that them boys out the Calliope the ones who killed the boy Tre," Ashley commented, but before another word was spoken, the door burst open with a lot of force and two gunmen with masks on rushed in the barber shop.

***

Je'sus and Curtis Mitchell waited in front of central lockup for Donte' and Black Larry to be released which only took about 20 minutes after they made it to the jail. While Donte' was trying to play Mack Daddy, Larry made the call to Je'sus that they'd be released in no later than an hour.

"There they go right there," Curtis said as he reached for the door handle to get out and greet his niggas who he genuinely had love for, and Je'sus cracked a smile and did the same.

"What's up jail birds?" Curtis said with his arms wide open to hug them both at the same time.

"Nigga you got jokes huh?" Larry said with a big smile on his face.

After they embraced each other, the four got in Je'sus' truck. Before pulling off, Je'sus asked Donte' and Larry where they wanted to go eat. He knew that after spending the weekend in Orleans Parish Prison, nothing would be more satisfying than a decent meal.

"All I want to do is take a shower, I ain't used deodorant all weekend in that bitch," Donte' said while lifting his left arm to smell his armpit.

"That's some real shit," Larry agreed. "But what happened with ole girl? You got that hoe number or you was over there faking with that bitch?"

"Nope that bitch ain't give me her number, but she was feeling me though. I could've got that hoe," Donte' said. "Homie, that bitch wasn't feeling you. If she was feeling you she would have gave you the number," Larry shot back.

"Fuck that shit, now that y'all out that bitch, let's focus on how we gon make up for the loss we took. Man, not only did we lose out on all our profit with the amount of work they took, we have to take into account the money we spent on bail. Not to mention the money we will spend on lawyers to fight the charges because making bail is only the first step to this process," Je'sus said while focusing on his driving.

Donte' wasn't feeling how Je'sus was making an issue on the loss and how much money he had to spend on bailing them out.

"It's like this, that was only half of the package so you don't have to worry about taking a loss. You gon get your money on the back end, so don't trip 'bout that. Me and Larry is the ones who taking the loss, but I appreciate you putting up the money for our bail. Man, you don't have to worry 'bout no lawyers cause now that I'm out, I can take care of that part myself. That's what I hustle for, to make money, and out chere you have to keep a few dollars put away for days like this," Donte' said letting it be known that he can pull his own weight. "But as far as the loss we..."

"Losses come with this game," Curtis said cutting Donte' off in mid-sentence.

"What's up Larry, you good on your lawyer situation?" Curtis asked him. "If you need me in any way, just let me know," he continued while looking at Je'sus as he was talking, and not only did Larry feel the vibe, Je'sus did as well.

"My paper straight homie," Larry acknowledged. But that's some real nigga shit, besides we family, right? That's how it's supposed to be, because if the glove was on the other hand, I'd feel obligated to do the same if it was any one of y'all," Larry stated.

By the time they made it to the project, the vibe was so fucked up that Je'sus didn't bother to hang around. He simply let them out the car and told them that he had some business to take care of, and that he'd be back later.

"What's up with Jay?" Larry asked Curtis, because it was clear that something wasn't right.

"I ain't sho where his head at, but let me look into it," Curtis said knowing in his heart what the problem was.

"Come on dawg, y'all niggas acting like y'all don't see what the problem is, that nigga tripping 'bout that fucking work, like we asked to go to jail. He fail to realize we the ones out chere making all the moves, all he doing is supplying the shit cause he have the plug. For real though, I can score my own shit and do me," Donte' said expressing his feelings about the situation.

"I feel you Dee, I peeped that shit out too. Dawg, I thought I was tripping that's why I didn't say shit ya dig. Now that that shit in the open, I feel like you feel, fuck. We can do us, all we have to do is put our bread together and score something," Larry expressed.

"That's always an option," Donte' said in agreement.

Curtis knew they were speaking the truth about Je'sus because he had the same reaction when he called Je'sus to tell him that the spot had been raided. He also knew without Larry, Donte', and Lou, him and Je'sus wouldn't be in the position they were in. They were the ones that did the ground work from the hustling to the handling the beef shit and without them it ain't no Cheddar Boys. So, he knew it was in his best interest to keep the crew together because him nor Je'sus was cut out for the hand to hand transaction, that wasn't their role. They were meant to be bosses and Curtis knew it was time to start thinking like one, and if Donte' and Larry were seriously considering doing their own thing, that would put an end to that family shit.

***

After fucking around with the homies for a while, Paul decided to head to Roxanne's house figuring he given her enough time to get dressed. When he pulled up in front of her house, she was already standing on her porch in her work uniform looking as good as ever. Roxanne wasn't the prettiest female Paul had dealings with, but never-the-less she was highly attractive to the point where she would catch the attention of any man.

She stood 5'8", weighed 140 pounds with a blemish-free dark brown complexion. She had long black shiny hair that she would normally keep in a ponytail. Most people that knew her would often say that she resembled Kelly Rowland. Those who didn't know her would think she lived in the gym when they saw her, but what stood out the most was the beauty mole on the left side of her upper lip.

A brown and white Pitbull in her yard started barking repeatedly when Roxanne stepped off the porch to get in the truck.

"Shut up, Project," Roxanne said as she paused and looked back at the annoying muscular dog. After she gave her command, Project sat back on his hind legs with his tongue hanging covered with foamy looking saliva.

The moment Roxanne closed the door on the truck, she reached over and gave Paul a kiss on the cheek and started complaining, "I thought I told you I'd be ready in 20 minutes. That was 40 minutes ago," she fussed.

"First of all, don't play me with a kiss on the jaw like I'm a child or something," Paul said as he leaned over the console to give her a more passionate kiss. While holding her firmly under her chin, he kissed her long and aggressively. When he decided to pull away it took her a few seconds before she could utter a single word, because she had to inhale deeply to fill her lungs with air that she desperately needed.

When she did gather herself to speak, all she said was, "Damn."

Paul knew from past experiences the effect his kisses had on women. He already had an idea what Roxanne's reaction would be, so he looked deep into her eyes and asked her did she like it.

"Boy I ain't never been kissed like that before," Roxanne said before she laid her head back on the headrest.

"I told you once before, I ain't the average nigga so get used to it. Once you really get to know me you gon realize that I'm the man of your dreams," Paul said while looking in his rearview mirror before pulling off.

For the first couple of blocks they rode in total silence until Paul grabbed her left hand and asked her why she was so quiet. She hadn't said a single word since they pulled off. Even though he didn't know her all that well, he could tell something was on her mind.

"I'm good, I'm just thinking 'bout my daddy. It's crazy how I can find time to do everything else, but when it's time for me to go see him, I have all kind of excuses."

"Baby don't worry 'bout that, we can fix that. When you get off I'll go with you by his house. It would give me the opportunity to introduce myself to my father-in-law," Paul said with a smile on his face, letting Roxanne know that he's taking their relationship serious.

"That's so sweet of you, but it's only one problem."

"If money can't fix it, then it's a problem," Paul said thinking her father might live out of town or something like that.

"Money can't solve all problems, at least not this one."

"And what's that supposed to mean?"

"My daddy is in prison." Roxanne said.

"When was the last time you seen him?"

"Ever since my mother passed away, we've been kind of distant. I miss the times when my momma would take me and Ronald to see him every month. One time we went to see him about 8 or 9 years ago, and when we got there, he was on visit with another woman. We wasn't allowed to go in until he was finished with that visit so my momma stop bringing us to see him. She ended things all together five years ago, when he finally admitted he had another child on her. She never forgave him for that."

"So, you have a brother or a sister somewhere out chere?" Paul asked.

"I don't know if it's a boy or a girl, cause we never met. I just remember when my mom used to talk about the women my dad got pregnant to her friends."

"I think you need to make plans to go see him. Maybe, you can get the answers to some of your unanswered questions.

"I really can't find the time to go there, my schedule is always full."

"We really have a lot in common," Paul said.

"And what makes you say that?"

"Because my dad is in prison too, the only difference is, me and my momma are still part of his life."

"Can we change the subject?" Roxanne asked because talking about that reminded her how much she missed her mother, and what her mother went through with her own father.

"Yeah, we can change the subject, but always remember, I'm here for whenever you need someone to talk to." Paul said, just as they pulled up in the empty strip club parking lot. Ben's car was nowhere in sight, so Paul called Ben on Joy's phone to inform him that his car was nowhere to be found, and there was a possibility it was towed.

"Uh, look like he gon have to go get his car from the impound," Paul told Roxanne before pulling off. "What time did you say you have to check in for work?" he continued.

"Twelve, why what's up?" Roxanne asked.

"Because I'm hungry, and I could use some pancakes. We can have breakfast together before you check in," Paul suggested.

"Yeah, we can do that," Roxanne answered. They went straight to the *IHOP* location where she worked and had breakfast together. Before he left, he told her to call him when she got off and he'd come pick her up.

***

"I want everybody to get face down on the ground. Don't make me have to kill one of you motherfuckers!" One of the gunmen shouted in an aggressive tone waving around a black semi-automatic pistol that he held in his right hand.

"Bitch hurry up and get on the floor!" The other gunman yelled at Tiffany who was still standing with a look of disbelief on her face.

As he turned back to face the rest of the customers all bunched on the floor on each side of the barber shop, one guy was looking over his shoulder. He was trying to make out who the masked men were but was spotted by the other gunman who quickly approached him.

"Didn't he tell you to lay face down? What you think this shit a game!" he said as he extended his arm to point the gun in the direction of his head, then squeezed the trigger once letting out a deafening sound in the small and confined space.

A kid around the age of 8 was so terrified to where he pissed on himself when the gunshot went off three feet away from his little body.

"Consider that a warning shot, the next one will go in the head of the next motherfucker that take their eyes off the floor," the gunman said.

"Dawg let's get what we came for and get the fuck outta here" the gunman that gave the demands for everybody to lay on the floor said, who clearly seemed to be the one who orchestrated the robbery.

Through the entire robbery, all Duck was thinking was that if he could only make it to his work station to get his hands on his gun that he kept in his drawer, he'd have a chance to defend his shop. But he knew he had no chance of making that happen against two armed thugs that appeared to mean business. So, he done what was in his best interest and remained quiet, hoping that they'd do what they came to do and leave without hurting anyone else.

One of the gunmen moved from person to person, making them place their cellphones in a backpack he held in his left hand. By this time, the other one jumped on the first barber shop chair from the door and moved a square piece of ceiling tile. He reached his left hand in the opening and pulled out three Ziploc bags of exotic weed, one after the other.

"I got it!" He yelled to his partner who was holding everyone at gunpoint.

He then jumped off the chair and placed the weed in a backpack he had on his back and went straight to Duck's work station. When he opened the top drawer, there was a black leather pouch and a custom made .357 revolver with the initials 'D.D' engraved in the wooden handle.

"Look what we have here," he said as he held the nickel-plated gun in the air, before placing it on his waist line. It shined like new money from the reflection of the sunlight that pierced through the window.

When he opened the pouch, he saw a large amount of money and felt like they had everything they came for, so they both fled quickly out the entry door after ordering everybody to remain on the floor. Moments later, everyone in the shop got up from the floor and were shook up at the fact their lives were just in the hands of some dangerous thugs.

What fucked Duck up was how the robbers knew exactly where he kept his stash. Considering how the robbery played out, he knew it was an inside job, for the simple fact that they never approached him in any way. Whoever gave them the inside info on him, only told them where to find the product and the cash. Duck knew he had been betrayed and whoever was behind it was gon get dealt with, because the streets will talk, and eventually it would get back to him.

***

After Paul dropped Roxanne off at work, he went straight to the project to oversee the operation. Not that his presence was necessary for things to run smooth because business was moving like clockwork regardless of who was there.

As soon as he pulled in the driveway, he saw Jack Rabbit and Tiger posted up on their set. His first thought was that maybe, Tiger wanted to score and couldn't understand why he hadn't called like he normally did, but that wasn't the case at all. They were there waiting for Ben to show up, because they needed to speak with the head about the situation that took place in the hallway with K-Dog and Rabbit. With Paul being the next in command Tiger figured that he could resolve the problem instead of waiting on Ben who normally would have been present at that time of day.

Prior to that day, Jack Rabbit explained to Tiger what had really happened when he killed Ken and why. Since all kinds of rumors had spread through the project. He also told Tiger that him and the big black nigga with the dreadlocks, K-Dog, had made strong eye contact that only meant one thing after passing words about hustling in their hallway.

Jack Rabbit played the game by the old rules so he told his nephew that he was gon make a move on K-Dog the first chance he got. Tiger told him to fall back and let him handle it because he knew he could put an end to the beef before it started. The last thing he wanted was to go to war with niggas in his own hood, especially the SG's.

K-Dog didn't think much of the run-in he had with Jack Rabbit, that's why he didn't mention it to the others. He figured Rabbit was one of them old ass niggas that came home from the pen and tried to get in where he fit in. So, when him and Tiger posted up in their courtyard, he kept a close eye on them.

Ryder who was positioned in the same spot when the incident occurred, wasn't suspicious at the fact that Rabbit was hanging out in their courtyard. He watched the whole thing unfold, how Ken stepped to Rabbit, said a few words, then pulled his pistol. In his mind, Ken got killed for trying to rob Rabbit, at least it appeared that way to him, not realizing that it was all behind what took place in the hallway.

By the time Paul got out his truck, Jack Rabbit and Tiger were moving towards him to try and put an end to the tension between his uncle and K-Dog. From where K-Dog was standing, it appeared that they were moving in for the kill, so he pulled his gun and ran down a flight of stairs that led to the courtyard. K-Dog yelled to Ryder to come on as he moved quickly past him in the direction of Rabbit and Tiger, clutching his gun tight in his right hand.

Ryder followed in pursuit as he moved quickly behind K-Dog, causing the people in the courtyard to run for cover. They had seen too many shootouts end with innocent bystanders getting injured by stray bullets. The only thing that stopped them from shooting was that it would've put Paul in the line of fire. So they got as close as they could before letting off any shots, even though Rabbit nor Tiger had a gun in their hand. When Rabbit and Tiger noticed how the crowd scattered, it alerted them both to turn and see what was happening.

"What the fuck?!" Tiger said when he saw Ryder and K-Dog running fast towards them with guns in their hands. At that moment, he thought he was dead because it wasn't much he could have done at that point and he knew that K-Dog and Ryder were real killers.

Paul couldn't understand what was happening so he pulled his gun as well. As soon as K-Dog and Ryder got within 15 feet of Tiger and his uncle, a black Crown Victoria came speeding in their direction. At that same moment, Jack Rabbit was reaching for his gun ready to go out fighting in a gun battle, that's when Lil' Mike's voice came through the walkie-talkie, "Heads up! Five-0!!" he said repeatedly with urgency.

All they heard was the engine roaring as they all took off running in different directions, that way they had to decide on who they would give Paul to. As Paul, Ryder and K-Dog ran full speed heading to Betty's house, the car quickly turned in the driveway in the same direction that Rabbit and Tiger ran. They both threw their guns under a parked car before they ran through a cut.

James, who was standing in a nearby hallway saw where they had thrown their guns and had every intention of getting them. He watched as the police car sped down the driveway heading towards the other end of the projects. He waited a few minutes to make sure they had no other cars in route.

After he figured it was cool for him to make his move he went to retrieve the guns. He knew he could sell them quick, but as soon as he knelt down Tiger came through the cut about 50 feet away. He was wearing a blue and gray RocaWear shirt and some Nike gym shorts after changing his clothes.

"Don't fucking play with me bitch," Tiger said as he stood over James waving him away from the weather-beaten Buick that the guns were under.

"You got 'em nephew?" Rabbit asked as he came through the same cut looking from side to side trying to see if the law was still in the area.

Without looking back Tiger yelled out, "Yeah, I got em unk, just make sure them people don't swing through," as he finally extended his left arm to reach for his .45 cal that slid to the middle of the car.

"I got cha, just hurry up," Jack Rabbit said.

Tiger reached the butt of the gun by a fingertip and slid it towards him making a scratching sound as it slid along the concrete. He jumped up off the oil-stained pavement, dusted himself off and handed Jack Rabbit his .38 special, before placing his own tool on his waist. Moments later, they went in a crackhead's house where they hung out and explained to Poppa and Hood what had taken place moments before Five-0 came speeding through.

"What happened?" Poppa asked angrily when Rabbit mentioned that K-Dog and Ryder ran down on him and Tiger with tools out.

Before Rabbit could respond, Tiger spoke out, "I know shit looked fucked up but…"

"But my ass!" Rabbit said cutting him off. "If the police wouldn't have run them niggas off, they were in the perfect position to off us."

"Dawg I know them niggas don't want to see us," Hood said, then he moved a kitchen table chair so he could look out the window, not looking for anything particular.

"That's why you young niggas now-a-days get killed so fast, because y'all hesitate on making y'all's move. If we ain't talk it out before shit hit the fan, then it ain't nothing to talk about period. How you gon talk a motherfucker out doing what they already set their mind to do, huh?" Rabbit asked not liking the fact that his nephew was trying to down-play this situation.

"If you scared, let me know. If you ain't, let's be the predator and not the prey. Regardless to whether you want to accept it or not, you're just as much a target as I am. I ain't gon sit back and wait till no nigga throw slugs my way, I'm cut from a different cloth than that."

Hood looked at Tiger and said, "That's some real shit OG saying. We really need to see what's up with them niggas.

If it's gon go down, fuck it we built for this shit."

***

"Say brah, what y'all niggas was on?" Paul asked out loud, talking to them both.

"We thought them niggas was about to make a move on you," K-Dog answered.

"Why would y'all think that?" Paul asked.

"Because I been watching them niggas since they came in the court way, and soon as you pulled up them niggas started walking towards you like they was about to kill you," K-Dog said.

"I still don't understand why y'all would think they was about to kill me" Paul asked confused.

"Let me finish," K-Dog stated. "About an hour before that old ass nigga killed Ken, I had to run him off. Cause he was trying to hustle in the hallway."

"What hallway?" Paul asked in disbelief that someone was stupid enough to try to hustle on they set.

"In our hallway, I didn't think much of it. But when I seen the nigga posted up, I just kept my eye on him. I didn't know if Tiger was trying to point one of us to the nigga. So the nigga can make his move on us or what, and my gut told me to react, so I did."

"Let's back up a minute. What exactly happened when you told the nigga not to hustle in the hallway?" Paul asked trying to make sense of the situation.

"Me and Trap was doing what we do when we heard two niggas arguing in the stairway. I went to see who it was, and when I got there they had this old ass nigga trying to serve Ken, but Ken didn't want to score from him. So, he started to walk off until I called him back. I let the nigga know that hustling in our hallway was off limits. I still don't know how he got past you Ryder and you not realzing that he didn't come back out the hallway," K-Dog said.

"Fuck I seen when the nigga went in the hallway but I thought he was going by somebody house or something," Ryder shot back.

"But fuck them niggas, I done that and I'ma stand on that. I'd rather go to war than take the chance of letting them niggas kill you on some fluke shit," K-Dog said nodding his head in Paul's direction. "And we still don't know what those niggas was up to. We know how that bitch Tiger get down," K-Dog continued.

"We don't know what they was up to, but I'm 'bout to find out," Paul said as he flipped open his Nextel.

Before he could actually make the call K-Dog grabbed his wrist and said, "Don't call that nigga, fuck him and his uncle, if it's something to be handled, we gon handle it. Besides, do you really think if they were about to smoke you he gon tell you that, FUCK NO!!"

Three hours later, Paul looked at his watch and realized it was getting close to time for him to pick Roxanne up from work. Before he left he told them to be on point till he got back in about 45 minutes at the most.

In the meantime, they were doing the usual talking shit, smoking weed, and hustling when Hood, Poppa and Tiger came through the cut. Ryder spotted them from the hallway as they moved slowly through the cut. He told Trap to grab two choppers from Betty's house cause if it was about to go down, he wanted some firepower to go to war with.

While waiting on Trap to get back, Ryder and K-Dog pulled the guns from their waists. They walked up to the balcony to make themselves visible, so Tiger and his crew could see them because they weren't ducking nothing.

It only took Trap two minutes before he came running down a flight of stairs carrying two choppers. Inhaling deeply, he handed one each to K-Dog and Ryder. He then took a 40cal with an extended clip off his waist, then they went downstairs to meet Tiger, Hood and Poppa in the courtyard.

When Hood and Poppa saw them come out the hallway toting heat, they pulled their guns but Tiger told them to lower them. He immediately put his hands in the air and said, "This ain't for us homie, I'm just trying to see what's going on. Cause me and my uncle was trying to holla at Paul and y'all ran us down with heaters. What's up with that?"

Parents that seen what was about to take place started screaming for their children to get out of the way. Doors started slamming shut and before you knew it, they were the only people standing in the courtyard, five feet away from each other.

"Dawg a nigga ain't know what y'all was on and you know how we rock homie. Since Tre got killed, we really been on our shit," K-Dog said.

"I told my uncle he was down bad and if he wanted to make some money to sell his shit on our set. But you know them throwback niggas be set in they ways. That's why I was trying to holla at Ben to let him know it won't happen again. When Paul pulled up, I figured I could talk things over with him, cause we ain't never supposed to be on this type of time with each other ya dig?" Tiger said trying to get them to understand where they stood.

"I feel that my nigga, so what's up now?" K-Dog asked never taking his eyes off Poppa and Hood who never put away their guns.

"Whatever the disagreement was, it's over, I'ma keep my people in line," Tiger said while extending his arm to dap K-Dog.

"Dawg that's that same police car," Trap said causing them all to run in a hallway. When the black Crown Victoria stopped, Lil' Dave and Irvin got out of it.

"Where the fuck them little motherfuckers get a police car from?" Ryder asked out loud not talking to anyone in particular.

"Man, you know them lil' niggas always into something," Tiger said.

"Them lil' bitches need to get that car from out the project, all that shit gon do is bring heat on a nigga if them people find that car back here," Ryder said mad at the fact that those lil' niggas moved so recklessly. Not realizing the effect their actions bring on the hood.

"Hold on, you know what? We can use that car to go spin in the Calliope. Them niggas will think we the police and we might get up close on them niggas if they ain't strapped. Ya dig? So, what's up?" K-Dog said.

"What you mean what's up? nigga let's go," Ryder said ready to put in work.

"Say let me holla at cha Lil' Dave," K-Dog said calling the youngster to him.

"What's up?" Dave said defensively knowing K-Dog had something to say about the car. He noticed when they passed through the project that everyone ran thinking they were the law.

"Calm down nigga. Where you get that car from?" K-Dog asked.

"Come on man, you know that's a hotty," Dave replied.

"Let us hold it down for a minute."

"I don't care, y'all can have that bitch, give me 100 dollars," Dave proposed. K-Dog started laughing as he dug in his pocket and gave him ten 10-dollar bills.

Dave and Irvin ran with a lil' crew that called themselves the Hot Riders. They would normally steal luxury cars and sell them to dudes who ran chop shops around the city. That used to be Lil' Mike's crew until Ben took him under his wings. All they did was steal cars and break in houses, but Lil' Mike had more of a drug dealer swag for a youngster. That caused Ben to take a serious interest in him and unlike Lil' Dave and Irvin, Lil' Mike would actually listen.

"We 'bout to go spin in the Calliope, I'ma holla at y'all," K-Dog said to Tiger as he rested the AK on his shoulder.

"Holla at who, nigga we fucking with that," Tiger said as he looked at Hood and Poppa for their approval.

"Let's rock," Hood said.

"Yo, Trap, hold the set down till we get back," Ryder told him. "And make sure your walkie talkie on in case of emergency."

K-Dog got in the driver seat and Hood got in the passenger seat while Poppa, Tiger, and Ryder got in the back seat and headed for the Calliope. After getting in the car they noticed it wasn't a police car. But it most definitely would serve the purpose.

***

Back in the Calliope Donte' was stressing to Larry that he was serious about doing his own thing cause he didn't like how Je'sus handled that situation. He would rather be responsible for his own, than to be putting up with Je'sus bullshit.

"What the fuck going on?" Lou asked being caught off guard with Donte's statement because they swore to be Cheddar Boys for life.

"On the real homie, I don't even want to talk about it, ya dig? Just know Je'sus was on some sucker shit my nigga," Donte' said.

"Y'all niggas tripping, we family dog, we can work out our differences like men." Lou said with a slight grunt from the pain in his stomach.

"If we family, we need to act like one because the shit that nigga was on was like we workers on some shit, and like I said, I don' t need no nigga to do me," Donte' said.

Before anybody could respond, somebody yelled "Five-0!" in the courtyard. When Donte' looked out the hallway, a black Crown Victoria was coming down the courtyard heading straight for their set.

"Give me your gun Lou," Donte' said while extending his arm to get it, knowing Lou could barely move. Once he got it, him and Larry eased inside of the apartment leaving Lou sitting on the Porch, but he was clean, so it didn't matter.

When the doors opened, to Lou's surprise it wasn't the police and by him being sore from his surgery his movement was limited.

Hood was the first one out the car and rushed Lou quickly hitting him with 4 quick shots to the chest, causing Lou to slump back on the porch.

By this time Ryder and Poppa made it over to Lou's body that was stretched out, then Ryder put the chopper to Lou's head and squeezed the trigger 7 quick times knocking out his eyeballs.

K-Dog and Tiger was the last ones to hit him up as they shot at least 35 rounds into Lou's body, ripping his colostomy bag apart.

Donte' heard all the shots and peeped out the window to see K-Dog and his crew shooting inside of the hallway where they left Lou sitting. He opened the window and let off a few shots of his own. Ryder spotted Donte' and aimed the AK at the window that Donte' was shooting from and shot at least 5 shots in that direction causing Donte' to duck for cover.

It seemed like the shooting went on for at least a minute and a half before they all got in the car and pulled off.

Rell stood across the courtyard and witness the whole thing, and soon as the SG's pulled off, he jumped off the porch and started shooting at the car until his Glock 40 cal was empty.

After the shots stopped' Larry ran to the porch to find Lou's body dismantled from multiple bullets ripping his flesh apart.

It was one of the worst murders he'd seen by far.

While still holding his gun in hand, Rell ran across the courtyard where Lou's body was shredded to pieces.

"Dawg, that was them niggas out the Melph!" Rell told Larry. "I seen that nigga K-Dog and Ryder for sure!"

Rell had to snap Larry back as he stood there in disbelief staring at a pile of blood mixed with shit and body organs all over the hallway.

***

The entire day at work, Roxanne thought about Paul and couldn't wait until she got off to spend time with him, even if it was for 20 minutes. She really enjoyed the fact that he dropped her off at work and was going to pick her up.

For years, she witnessed these types of gestures happen for her co-workers and she envied them for that. Not because she wasn't capable of being in that type relationship because she was. She just hadn't found the right guy she was comparable with until she met Paul. Just the thought of him brought joy to her. She hadn't been with many men in her life. If she had to compare Paul to her past relationships, he would have been her best companion hands down.

By his thought process being up to par, she really enjoyed communicating with him. Not to mention he possessed a sense of humor like no other man she had been with. She could only imagine his sexual ability. Feeling positive he would be far from a disappointment, something she was soon to find out.

"Roxanne... Roxanne!" one of her co-workers yelled repeatedly trying to snap Roxanne out of the daydream she was deep into.

"Girl what!" Roxanne answered with the shake of her head, mad at the fact that Kenisha interrupted her thoughts.

"Bitch I don't know what you was thinkin' about but I called your name four times. What's on your mind girl?" Kenisha asked.

"Nothing, I'm just ready to get off." Roxanne said to avoid getting into details of her thoughts.

"Where is your car? I don't see it in your parking spot."

"Oh, I left it at home, my boyfriend coming to pick me up. As a matter of fact, let me call him and let him know to be here at 6:00."

"Before you do that, I wanted to ask if you could you get somebody to cover my shift for me Saturday. I need to take off for Kyra's birthday party," Kenisha asked.

"Let me see what the schedule looks like, I'll let you know by Thursday. How old is she making girl?"

"Girl her womanish ass turning six."

"Don't call her that," Roxanne said giggling knowing that Kenisha daughter is very mature for her age. "I got to get her something for her birthday," she continued, then turned and walked away to place her call.

Paul was on the phone with China when Roxanne called. All his attention shifted to Roxanne when he clicked over, despite the importance of him and China's conversation. Which was based on her period not coming at its usual time and her implying that she was pregnant.

"What's up my baby, you ready?" Paul asked Roxanne immediately after answering his phone.

"Boy I was ready the moment you pulled out the parking lot, but unfortunately I can't leave till 6:00, that's what I was calling to tell you."

"In the meantime, do you need me to stop and get you anything?" Paul asked trying to express how serious he was about their relationship.

"All I need you to do is be here when I get off and not have me waiting."

"I got cha luv," Paul said, then hung up totally forgetting China on the other line.

Paul pulled in the IHOP parking lot 20 minutes before Roxanne got off. He called her to let her know that he was outside and where he was parked at. He figured since he had a few minutes to play with before Roxanne got off, he'd relight a half a blunt of Kush that he was smoking before he got there. He reclined his seat, put a small crack in his window and went in his own zone listening to Soulja Slims, *Years Later* album, waiting on Roxanne to get off.

Paul was locked in on Kenisha as her and Roxanne came out of the restaurant talking. They walked towards the parking lot where Kenisha's black Altima was parked. After talking for a few seconds Kenisha glanced at Paul before her and Roxanne went their separate ways.

Even though Paul put a crack in the window his truck was still filled with weed odor. When Roxanne got in the truck, she was hit in the face with a strong weed smell, and by her not being a person who smoke weed, the smell seemed to be louder than it really was.

"How was work?" Paul asked when she closed the door and placed her Fendi bag on the dashboard.

"It was just work, nothing to brag about," she said then leaned over and gave him a simple kiss on the lips.

China thought that Paul hung up because of what she was telling him about her period not coming down. At first, she was like fuck him, but after thinking about it for a while with tears in her eyes, she wasn't gon let him play her like that, so she called him back.

As Paul waited on the red light on Bullard Ave, before he got on the I-10 bridge, his phone started ringing. When he looked at his phone and saw that it was China he quickly tried to end the call before Roxanne got suspicious. He knew he wasn't going to be able to answer China's call. It was too late because Roxanne noticed how fast he ended the call so she questioned him about it.

Paul tried his best to throw her off by telling her it was a business call and right then wasn't the time to entertain it. It was like Paul had 'liar' written across his forehead because Roxanne wasn't believing him a bit, so she looked him in the eyes and told him, "Paul you ain't a good liar, then again you ain't got to lie to me. I know you probably have girls that you been messing with before we met. It's my job to get all of your attention and eventually they'll get the picture and fade away," but before he could reply, China called again and this time he answered.

"What's up homie?" he said as he tilted his head to the right to make eye contact with Roxanne.

"Don't fucking play with me," China said but before she could finish what she was saying, he told her that he'd hit her back when he made it to the project and for her to give him an hour or so.

Roxanne didn't say a word about the phone call the whole ride home because it was nothing he could say to convince her that that was a business call.

When he dropped her off, he immediately called China, who decided to play a lil' game herself by not answering. For the very first time he found himself calling her back to back because he really wanted to hear what she had to say about this period situation but she refused to answer.

As he pulled off, Tony jumped in the street to flag him down to stop. Paul pulled to the side and rolled down the window to see what Tony wanted.

"What's up my nigga?" Tony said while bumping fist with Paul through the window.

"What it do my nigga?" Paul asked wondering what it was Tony wanted.

"Dawg, it's like this here, we have a steady clientele around here. All we need is a reliable plug to get this bitch jumping for real for real, and that's where you come in at," Tony explained to him.

"Let me get with my people and I'ma get back with you," Paul said before pulling off leaving Tony standing in the middle of the street.

"This clown gonna make me jack his bitch-ass," Tony mumbled to himself while eyeing Paul's truck as it drove down the block.

CHAPTER 24

"Mail call!" the C.O. yelled as he approached the tier with a handful of letters. Once the C.O. entered the tier, he told the inmates to be standing at the bars if he call their name.

"Brian Simmons... Errol Hall... Generio Allen... Rodney Glover... Rondell Martin... James Davis..." When the C.O. got to Monsta's cell he yelled, "Marcus Jackson?"

"Yeah, that's me!" Monsta said.

"What's your number?" the C.O. asked looking at the numbers on the letter.

"336667," Monsta shot back quickly.

The C.O. confirmed that he was Marcus Jackson and handed him the letter. Monsta started smiling as soon as he seen Benjamin Johnson as the sender. *That nigga Ben shot me a kite*, he thought to himself, as he began to open the envelope.

"Sarg? What time you gonna run phone calls?" Monsta asked the C.O. before he left the tier.

"After chow if I have time, if not you have to wait till shift change for the night crew to come on."

"Sarg! You ain't got no mail for Jermaine Williams?" the nigga in cell one asked, as the C.O. was leaving the tier because the C.O. still had several letters in his hand.

"Jermaine Williams!" The C.O. mumbled as he flipped through the mail. "No! I don't have none for you," he said as he placed the letters under his armpit, so he could lock the door.

"A'ight!" Jermaine said in disappointment cause he'd been waiting on a letter from his girl for a week.

When Monsta started to read the letter, his jaw dropped to the floor, and his celly noticed his reaction and asked, "Is everything okay?"

Monsta didn't respond, but the water that build up in his eyes answered for him. The letter read:

> I know you gonna be surprised to get a letter from me, but I couldn't wait until you called to tell you what I had to say. Maybe you heard already but if you didn't hear, Tre got killed my nigga. I know this ain't the type of shit a nigga that's locked up want to hear, but you needed to know. Over the last few months, we been beefing with them niggas out the Calliope, so you know we on it homie. The shit gon get handled for sho, you just focus on finishing that lil' time you have left so you can hit these streets 'cause this is where I need you at. The funeral service was filled with a lot of emotions, Ms. Grace and Ryder took the shit the hardest. Me and Paul covered all the funeral expenses. I can only imagine how you taking this news, because I know how close you and Tre were, but in reality, we all must answer when God's calling. We have no control over our deaths when it's our time to go. We can control our actions though, so it's a

must we ride for Tre. By the time you make it out here next month, we should have closed a couple of those bitch ass niggas eyes. (Dirt nap) Call me when you get this letter. I love you my nigga and stay up.

S.G.

-Ben

Monsta sat on his bunk staring at the letter as if it was a picture. His thoughts were interrupted by the sound of keys rattling as the C.O. opened the door to the tier, followed by the sound of squeaky wheels from the food cart as the cell block orderly rolled the cart on the tier.

"Feed up... feed up!" the orderly yelled as he began to place the food through the tray slots.

Monsta didn't have an appetite after reading his letter so he gave his tray to his celly who tried to convince him to eat. It was the last meal for the day, and being in the hole he would be hungry all night. The only thing Monsta had on his mind was getting to the phone so he could call Ben and find out more about Tre's murder. He couldn't imagine how Tre let them niggas catch him slipping knowing they were at war.

After six o'clock shift change, they began running showers and phone calls. The way they did things in the hole was, each cell had 15 minutes to shower and allowed to use the phone once a week and each inmate could choose any day he wanted. The phones were electronically set up for only one call a week so the C.O.'s didn't have to monitor each inmate that wanted to use the phone. They simply used the phone on their 15-minute shower time. Most people would talk for 10 minutes and use the other 5 minutes to take a quick shower, that was all they needed.

"Shower time!" the C.O. yelled down the tier right before he opened cell 13, which was the last cell on the tier.

Moments later a white boy came out the cell holding a bar of state issued soap, a pack of shampoo that resembled a sample package of some sort, a wash cloth, and a drying towel, as he flip flopped down the tier wearing bright orange shower shoes.

Monsta was impatient and paced back and forth in the cell while his celly tried his best to stay out his way. It was known throughout the prison that Monsta was in the hole for stabbing Thugga 16 times. If it hadn't been for Monsta's homeboy pulling him off Thugga, he probably would have killed him, and his celly didn't want any problems.

An hour later, the C.O. screamed down the tier, "Cell 9 shower!" Once Monsta's cell popped open he headed to the shower and placed his clothes on the shower bars. He then proceeded straight to the phone ignoring a dude that was asking him to grab a magazine from another cell.

"What cell? I got cha my nigga," Monsta's celly asked the dude that was trying to get Monsta to pass the magazine.

"Cell 4, and ask him do he have any more smokes for sell, and if so tell him I want one."

When Monsta's celly walked up to cell 4, a fat dude was already waiting to pass the magazine standing in boxers and shower shoes. While his celly sat on the toilet with his jump suit pulled down to his waist, and tied by the arms to keep it from falling to the ground.

"Ole boy want to know if you have any more smokes for sale."

"Tell him I got a few left so he better get what he gon get while I have them."

"He said he only want one."

"Hold on," the dude said while he dug in his mattress and pulled out a package of loose tobacco.

"Here you go," he said as he wrapped the tobacco in the toilet paper wrapping.

When Monsta's celly handed the dude the smoke, he gave him two stamps for the cigarette and two extra stamps so he could get him one.

"That's what's up," Monsta's celly said as he walked back to cell 4, got a cigarette, then plucked it on his bed before he headed to the shower, because he knew Monsta needed it.

When Ben saw unavailable on the face of his Nextel, he knew it was Monsta, at least he was hoping it was him. Monsta wasn't the only nigga in jail that called him since Charles and Anthony caught an armed robbery case seven months before. They tried to rob a tourist on Bourbon Street during the Essence Festival weekend, who turned out to be an undercover agent.

When Ben accepted the call, he was happy to hear from Monsta.

"What's up my nigga, how you holding shit together out there?" Monsta asked as soon as the operator said thank you and connected the call.

"I'm holding things together like a real nigga supposed to. Did you get my letter?" Ben asked shifting the conversation in a different direction. From judging Monsta's vibe, it didn't seem as if he was aware that Tre had been murdered.

"Yeah, I got it today," Monsta said as you could hear the change in his voice.

"I was wondering why you ain't call in a couple of weeks, cause it ain't like you not blowing the phone up," Ben said trying to lighten the mood up.

"I been in the hole for almost three weeks and you know we only get one call a week, so when I first got put in the hole, I called my moms. Then last week I called my BM, cause I know Jr. be wanting to hear from me. I had to let them know that I only get one phone call a week, so don't be expecting many calls from me until I get out the hole."

"What you in the hole for anyway, especially 3 fucking weeks?" Ben asked.

"I called by the Hot Shop one day and Duck was telling me how them niggas out the Calliope was shooting at Paul. At least Tiffany's good gossiping ass told him that they were supposed to be out the Calliope. You know how I rock, so I ended up stabbing one of them niggas up."

"Dawg you tripping, you trying to catch more time or something?" Ben asked not believing that Monsta was less than a month and a half to coming home and stabbed a nigga up.

"Homie fuck all that, y'all beef is my beef. Nigga you know when it come to the family, I don't give a fuck about no consequences. Have you forgot how I got in here in the first place?"

But before the conversation went any further, the C.O. yelled "Catch your cell, time is up."

"It ain't been no damn 15 minutes," Monsta plead his case.

"You heard what I said, time is up!" The C.O. shot back with a lil' anger in his voice.

"I got to go my nigga, I'ma shoot you a kite, keep your..." Monsta managed to say before the C.O. hit the phone switch.

On his way, back to his cell, Monsta continuously fussed with the C.O. "All you crackers gon do is handcuff a nigga and try to get off. You coward motherfuckers ain't gon approach a nigga without backup."

"Don't trip Monsta, you know how them crackers rocking," someone from the furthest end of the tier said. It was known that if Monsta kept bucking the system the authorities wouldn't have a problem gassing down the entire tier. That would affect everybody on the range.

CHAPTER 25

Two days later, the Cheddar Boys found themselves standing on the blood-stained porch where their friend was brutally murdered at the hands of their enemy. Retaliation was sure to follow, and they knew they had to think outside the box to put themselves in position to make a move. Something that the SG's had done to get up close on them, because they never in a million years thought they'd portray themselves to be the police.

"Dawg I can't get the images of Lou out my head," Black Larry said looking down at the exact spot where Lou's body had laid.

"Me either homie," Donte' said with a shiver of his body. "I had a dream about that shit last night, but see the way them niggas went hard, we just have to go harder. It's mandatory we send a message to all the motherfucker's sitting back watching. We ain't to be fucked with, ya dig?" Donte' continued.

"Yeah, I feel that, but the way them niggas project made it hard to get up close on them. They'll most likely see us coming," Curtis Mitchell said truthfully.

"You talking like those bitch ass niggas is untouchable or something," Larry said with aggression. "Me and Dee already proved that them niggas could get caught slipping like anybody else," Larry continued, referring to the time when they killed Tre and shot Fred.

"So, do you have a plan?" Je'sus spoke for the first time. "Because the way I see it, something has to be done, and soon. It's like Donte' said the streets is watching, so let's give'em something to see,"

"I'ma holla at Rell and see if him and his crew is willing to ride for the cause. I know Rell tried to get at them niggas the other day when Lou got killed." Curtis said.

Standing across the courtyard, Rell and his crew watched the Cheddar Boys holding a discussion. Which they automatically assumed was about retaliating for 9 Finger Lou.

Curtis made his way across the courtyard to holla at Rell. When Rell seen him coming towards him he jumped off the porch and met him in the middle of the courtyard wearing a black pair of Roca wear shorts, a pair of black 95 Air Max and a wife beater which exposed the .45 he packed on his waistline.

"What's up Curt?" Rell said as he greeted Curtis Mitchell with a dap.

"Ain't shit my nigga, we just trying to gather our thoughts on how we gon handle this shit with them niggas out the Melph. By the way, I appreciate how you got down on them niggas the other day."

"Don't sweat it Round, that's what I do, I hold the Calliope down. Besides what the fuck I look like, watching niggas from another hood come in our shit and kill somebody and don't do nothing. Man, cause at the end of the day we all Calliope, feel me?" Rell said.

"That's what I wanted to talk to you about, dawg. We gon need you and your boys to back us up," Curtis said hoping Rell would agree.

"We got cha Round, just let us know when y'all ready to move on them niggas."

"Yeah, I'ma do that," Curtis Mitchell said, then turned and headed back across the courtyard to his set.

"What's up with them niggas?" Creature asked the moment Rell made it back by them.

"They want us to hook up with them against the SGs," Rell answered.

"And you told that nigga we ain't fucking with that right?" Creature asked knowing that Rell didn't allow them niggas to implicate them in to a beef that didn't have shit to do with them.

"I told him that we was gon back them up," Rell shot back.

"Back who up? I ain't fucking with them niggas on that level, they ain't never support us with shit, you trippin' homie," Creature said in disapproval.

"The only way I'll be willing to ride with them niggas is if they make it worth my while," J-Roc said figuring they could use this situation as a come up. Because if it had gotten to the point where they asked for their help, that meant that they needed them.

"Um, you know what? You might be on to something," Rell said as he rubbed his chin using his thumb and index finger.

"Yeah, Dawg you right, let's see what our assistance is worth," Creature said as he looked across the courtyard at the Cheddar Boys. They were being informed by Curtis Mitchell on how he and Rell's conversation went.

"Let me go holla at this nigga and put a proposition on the table to see what we can come up on. Cause if we'll kill a nigga for the simplest shit you know the work we'd put in when dollars are involved," Rell said then headed across the courtyard to where the Cheddar Boys were.

Before he actually made it to the porch where they were, he signaled for Curtis Mitchell to come over. Curtis approached Rell with a look of uncertainty on his face. As if he expected Rell to tell him that they were on they own.

"What the deal is?" Curtis asked hoping that everything was a go.

"I just talked things over with my people and they are willing to back y'all up, but they want to be compensated for their help."

"So, what exactly they interested in and how much?" Curtis asked willing to give them whatever they requested at this point.

"The thing is this, once we get involved and our faces is stamped on this shit, we gon be forced to ride till the end, feel me. For that type of assistance, you tell me how much it's worth?" Rell asked taking full advantage of the opportunity.

"Let me run this by Je'sus and see what he have to say, then I'll get back with you."

"Aight, holla then."

When Rell made it back to J-Roc and Creature, Creature asked him what Curtis was talking about. Rell informed him that Curtis was gon' get back with him on the issue. In the meantime, they just gon' stay on their grind and make that paper, even though business been kind of slow for them lately. Which was strange because they have a decent clientele.

"You should have told that nigga to give us a 9 piece," J-Roc said.

"When you are negotiating, it's best to let the other person make the offer. If it suits us then we accept, if not then we put a number on the table, because if we asked for 9 ounces but they were willing to give more we'd be losing. Feel me? So, let's see what they willing to offer before we make our demands," Rell explained to J-Roc.

"I know one thing, the way them niggas crushed Lou, they better handle they fucking business with or without our help," Creature said.

"Dawg them niggas' punished Lou in a major way," Rell said in a convincing tone. "They shot his eyeballs out his head," he continued giving them a minor detail of what he had witnessed when he looked at Lou's shredded body on the ground.

"What's up y'all?" Brittany said as she stopped by them on her way to the store, wearing a BeBe T-shirt and some blue boy shorts that complimented her ass to the fullest.

"What's up?" they all spoke back. "Where you headed?" Rell asked her.

"I'm on my way to Safe-Way, why? Y'all need something?" Brittany asked.

"Yeah, here, bring me a few cigars and a bag of Skittles," Rell told her as he handed her a five-dollar bill.

"That's it? Y'all sho y'all don't want nothing?" Brittany said looking at J-Roc and Creature.

"Yeah, I want something," Creature said looking her up and down. He'd been trying to fuck her but she never gave him the time of day. It never stopped him from trying though.

"Well you need to make up yo' mind. Come on boy, what you want?" she said in an aggravated tone.

"I want you," Creature said which made Rell and J-Roc laugh. They knew how long Creature had been shooting his stick at her and she always shut him down.

"Yo' ugly ass better stop playing with me," Brittany said as she turned and headed to the store making her loose ass clap in the process.

"I'ma get that hoe one day," Creature said as he looked at the way she was making her ass jiggle in those little ass shorts.

"What's up Ricky?" J-Roc yelled to a dope fiend who passed them on a bicycle headed towards the Cheddar Boys' spot.

Ricky turned around and went to see what J-Roc was talking about, hoping that they had a different package. "What's up nephew?" Ricky said leaning over the handle bars. "You need me to wash yo car or something?"

"No, I'm good on that. I thought you was coming through to score something," J-Roc said.

"I'm is, I'm 'bout to go holla at Donte' though."

"What! You 'bout to go holla at Donte' after all the fucking shorts we take from you?" J-Roc yelled out.

"I'ma be straight up wit' cha, y'all shit been weak lately. A nigga like me need something that can knock the sickness off. The last bag I got from y'all I couldn't even feel the shit. I shoot dope, a nigga need the whole bag to get a buzz with that shit," Ricky told him while wiping sweat off his forehead from the summer heat that was blazing.

"Get the fuck from over here before I jacked yo' ass and you don't get nothing," Creature said while taking a couple steps towards Ricky until Rell put a hand in his chest stopping him from approaching Ricky.

"Just give me a minute, we gon have the best dope back here," Rell yelled, when Ricky rode off. Rell looked at his crew and said, "That's why shit been moving slow, that nigga Rodney served me some weak ass shit."

"I don't know why you be fucking with all them niggas," J-Roc said. "I don't know why you just don't score from Curtis," he continued.

"Because I don't want the same dope them niggas got, that's why I was fucking with Rodney and normally dude have some good shit."

"Well we need to do something, cause we ain't making no money with this shit," J-Roc said while bouncing a bundle of dope in his hand.

"I'ma holla at my people in the Melph, I know he have some good dope," Rell said.

When Brittany made it back from the store, she handed Rell a small brown paper bag that had his cigars and Skittles in it.

"Y'all better watch yourself cause they have a white boy parked on MLK in a gray Expedition," Brittany told them then headed to her apartment.

"Come to think of it, last week I saw a white boy in an Energy Truck parked on Galvez, and it ain't like he was working either. The bitch was just sitting there," J -Roc said.

"Say brah we have to start paying close attention to all details out chere. That will determine how long we gon last out chere ya dig, cause them people been riding heavy over the last couple of months, and I know them bitches ain't riding for nothing." Rell said.

The moment Curtis made it to the porch, Je'sus asked him what Rell had to say. Curtis Mitchell explained to him that Rell wanted to be compensated for getting involved in their beef.

"Compensated! Fuck him and his crew!" Black Larry shouted. "If we gon pay a motherfucker it gon be somebody that will do the job all together. What the fuck we look like paying a nigga to ride with us? You was supposed to check that nigga right there from coming at you with that bitch-ass shit," Larry continued.

"Dawg, I know you ain't agree to some dumb-ass shit like that huh?" Donte' asked, feeling the same way as Larry.

"I told him that I'd talk things over with y'all before I just made a decision on my own that can affect us all, but if y'all is against it, fuck it, we gon do us," Curtis said knowing in his heart that he just wanted this shit to be over without any more bloodshed.

Donte's attention was interrupted by the sound of his phone ringing. Already pissed off about the fact that Curtis Mitchell allowed Rell to come at him with some lame ass bullshit, he answered with an attitude.

"Hello!!" he shouted through the phone with aggression.

"Damn, that's how you answer yo' phone?" Stacy asked in a curious tone.

"Who the fuck is this?" Donte' asked, totally ignoring Stacy's question.

"This Stacy."

"Who?" Donte' asked with aggression.

"Stacy, you forgot my name already?"

"How you get my number?" Donte' asked because the name or voice didn't ring a bell to him.

"You gave it to me, but the next time you decide to flirt with somebody, at least remember her name and where you know her from," Stacy said not believing that Donte' didn't recognize her name. "And I hope the next time I see you it be on the streets and not Central Lockup," she continued.

When she spoke about Central Lockup, that's when the name and face came back to Donte'. "My bad luv, when you called, you caught me at a bad time. I was in the middle of some bull-shit that had me pissed off, but trust me, the attitude wasn't directed to you."

"It wasn't the attitude that offended me, you not remembering my name is what I took personal."

"It's not that I don't remember your name cause I do. It's just that the whole phone call caught me off guard, besides you never told me to be expecting a call from you. I thought you took my number to get me out yo' face. I never thought you would actually use it," Donte' told her.

"One thing you will learn about me, I know how to speak my mind without holding back on my thoughts," Stacy said.

"So, what that's supposed to mean?" Donte' asked.

"If I wanted you out my face I would have told you to get out it, simple as that."

"One thing you will learn about me. When I'm determined to get something or someone in this case, I don't stop until I accomplished my goal," Donte' told her letting it be known that it wouldn't be that easy to get rid of him.

"Is that so?" Stacy asked.

"Most definitely," Donte' told her.

"Now that we have touched basics on the phone, when can you meet face to face?" Stacy asked Donte' who was still trying to stay in tune with the conversation that was taking place prior to her calling him.

"Now that I have your number, I'll call you when I'm finished addressing the situation that I was in before you called."

"Just remember the name of the person whenever you decide to call," Stacy said, playfully.

"If I was to forget your name, do whatever is necessary to make sho I never forget it again in life," Donte' told her before hanging up.

"This is a ride or die situation, we don't need no nigga to ride with us," Je'sus said with authority. "We have to put our trust in each other," he continued to say as he pointed at each one of them. "If we can't rely on each other out chere then we may as well all go our separate ways. We all we got! It's us against everybody. When we make our move, we just have to be aggressive, and the element of surprise is a motherfucker. That's how they managed to kill Lou because we wasn't expecting it, but we don't want to move on emotions, we need to plan our next move and execute it."

CHAPTER 26

Ever since the incident at the strip club, Ben had been spending a lot of time at home, and Joy was loving the quality time that they were spending together.

"Who can this be calling the house phone," Joy mumbled to herself as she was reaching for the phone located on the nightstand. On the 4th ring, she answered.

"Hello?... Hold on…"

"Who that is?" Ben asked.

"I don't know who that is, but you ain't leaving this house," Joy said as she handed Ben the phone with a slight shove.

"Hello?"

"What's up my nigga?" Curtis asked not really knowing how to start the conversation.

"It's obvious that you wanted to talk, so talk. I'm listening," Ben replied.

"I'd rather talk in person, one on one, me and you."

"Pertaining to what?" Ben asked with aggression.

"It's like this, I'm not sho how this beef started, but I'm trying to come up with a solution to put an end to this shit and get back focusing on making this money, because we both know, we can't beef and make money at the same time."

"You know the rules my nigga, once blood been shed, it ain't over til it's over, ain't no squashing it," Ben said wrapping that statement around Tre's murder.

"Don't be so sure about that, we just might be able to work something out." Curtis stated after a moment of silence. The statement caught Ben off guard because he wasn't expecting that response, but it got his full attention.

"So, what you really saying?" Ben asked desperate to see where Curtis was going with this.

"To show you I'm serious 'bout ending this shit at any cost, I'll meet you wherever you feel comfortable meeting at. Anywhere, just name the place."

"I'll tell you what, I just might take you up on that offer, but I'ma get back with you in a few days," Ben said knowing that the situation was going in his favor, especially if Curtis was stupid enough to meet with him alone. Worst case scenario he'd just put a bullet in Curtis' head and be done with it.

"Yeah, Homie you can do that, I'll be waiting on yo' call," Curtis said. "Oh, and Ben, my condolences to Tre's family," Curtis added.

"I am his family," Ben shot back.

"I wish it would have been appropriate for me to show homie the proper respect that he was due," Curtis stated.

"What the fuck you mean by that?" Ben asked with aggression.

"Me and Tre shared a lot of good memories, and I hate that it ended for him like that. That's why it's important for me to make things right despite the fact it won't bring my nigga back," Curtis said trying to keep from choking up.

"Like I said, we'll talk later, so be expecting a call from me soon," Ben said before ending the call.

"What was that about?" Joy asked judging the content of Ben's conversation that it was something serious.

"I'm not sure, but I'll find out soon enough," Ben said honestly.

Ben's initial thought was to call Paul and lace him up on what him and Curtis talked about, but he decided to wait until he was around the whole crew. Even though he was the supplier, everyone's opinion mattered to him, and not just one person making the decision for the entire team. Especially, a decision of that magnitude.

It had been nearly two weeks since Ben last left the house. It was out of the ordinary for him not to be involved in day to day operations. He couldn't wait to let his presence be known so he decided to go out for the day. The first thing he had to do was check on his car. So, him and Joy got dressed and went to the impound to pick it up, but when they got there they were informed that the impound had no records of a silver Monte Carlo that was brought there.

This had been the first-time Ben stepped a foot outside since the robbery and his body accepted the summer heat with pleasure. Even though the cut had closed, leaving behind a minor scab, the scar it left on his forehead stood out like a sore thumb against his red complexion. The last couple of days, he'd been applying a great deal of cocoa butter to the wound 6 to 8 times a day to minimize the scar. That's a technique his grandmother used when he would fall and get a sore, which was often when he was a child. Back in those days, if you were light skin you were considered weak and got picked on a lot, but not Ben. He had a hell of a reputation in his hood despite his light skin, wavy hair, and slender frame.

"Bae, bring me to Enterprise, so I can get a rental until I find out what's going on with my car," Ben said.

He didn't have a particular car in mind, but once they got there a black Dodge Magnum caught his eye, so he rented it for a month.

"Bae, I have something I need to check out. I'll see you when I get home a'ight?" Ben said.

"Okay," Joy responded in a dry tone.

"Come on baby, don't start that. What's wrong?"

"Nothing...," she said but her attitude showed different.

"Listen Joy, I just need to check something out, then I'm coming straight home. A'ight?"

"A'ight, go ahead," she said in a frustrated tone.

"Come here bae," he told her as he walked over to her and gave her a kiss and a tight hug. Before she got in her car, she looked at him for a few seconds before telling him to be careful.

"I'm gon be alright bae. You hear me?"

"I hope so," she sincerely said, as she turned to get in her car.

"I'm 'bout to go get me another phone, I'll call you later"

She didn't respond, she just glanced over her left shoulder and said, "I'm serious Ben, be careful."

Ben headed straight to Nextel to purchased a phone that he so desperately needed. When he got there, he ran into Butch, the person that gave him the game on how to use hoes to get at niggas with money. With Ben having the looks and heart, Butch knew it was gon be easy for Ben to be successful in that part of the game. He'd seen women throw themselves at him.

"Long time no see," Ben said as he approached Butch with his right hand extended to shake his old mentor's hand.

"Badd… Ass… Ben, what's up young buck?" Butch said as he pulled Ben to him with a slight jerk.

He stepped back and looked Ben up and down and said,

"Look like you still doing pretty good for yourself, you still hustling hoes?"

"Naw dawg, I'm fucking with that dope, hitting licks cool, but that ain't shit compared to dope money." "So, what you been off into?" Ben asked.

"You know me, I'm still up to my old tricks, if it ain't broke, it don't need to be fixed, feel me?"

"So, what you 'bout to get off into?" Ben asked.

"Nothing much, I'm just 'bout to get one of my broads a new phone. Some shit went down, and I had to take her phone, so it's best she gets a new phone ya' dig?"

"Nigga you ain't change yet huh?" Ben said with a giggle in his voice.

"You think I'm bullshittin', as long as it's money to be made, change for what, it's better than hustling drugs if you asked me. Why sell drugs when you can let somebody else sell it for you and then use them young bitches to get it from them niggas? Let me holla at you when you finish."

Ben purchased his phone and they walked outside together. "What's up big dawg?" Ben asked.

"I stumbled on a couple of pounds of Kush, you interested in buying them?" Butch asked.

""What you want for them?"

"For you I'll give you a sweetdeal."

"How sweet?" Ben asked.

"Give me four G's for two of them."

"I can fuck with that, you have 'em on you now?" Ben asked.

"No, but I'll swing through the projects and drop them off. Give me your number and I'll call you when I come through." Butch responded as they negotiated a deal and walked toward his car.

"Damn nigga, I see you got tired of driving them old ass cars," Ben said as he checked out the fresh white Monte Carlo that made him think of his shit.

"You know I'm gon always ride old school. I just came up on this shit a couple of weeks ago."

"Where you get it from, the auction?" Ben asked.

"A lil' nigga I had in training jacked some nigga around the strip club. He took the money and gave me the car keys. So, I took it to the chop-shop and changed the VIN number and painted it, but I'ma sell it though," Butch stated. "The shit turned out bad though," he continued.

"How's that?" Ben questioned.

"The lil' nigga got killed 30 minutes after he pulled the jacked off."

Ben couldn't believe what he was hearing. He just found out who was behind him getting jacked and Butch had no idea what position he just put himself in.

"Oh, yeah, I got a tool too if you trying to get a throw-away," Butch said.

"You know I always want to buy tools, I don't care if it's a .25 auto or a rocket launcher," Ben said.

Butch pulled a nickel plated .357 from off his waist and handed it to Ben and said, "I know you like that big motherfucker."

"Yeah, I like it. What you want for it?" Ben asked as he looked at the gun with the initial D. D. engraved in the handle that he knew belonged to Duck.

"I'll take 100 bucks right now for it," Butch proposed.

"Where you get this from?" Ben asked waiting to see if he gon' give details like he did with his car, but he didn't, all he asked was did Ben want to buy it or not.

"You know I can't let you walk away with this big pretty motherfucker," Ben said as he reached in his pocket to give Butch the 100 dollars.

When Butch opened the door to his car, Ben was shocked to see Tiffany sitting in the passenger seat, but neither one said a word to the other. Tiffany didn't have a clue that Butch offered to sell Ben the gun or the weed that was took from Duck's shop, but it won't be long before she did.

***

Tiger and his crew came through the cut that led to Slum' Godds' courtyard where they found themselves hanging more often since they pulled off the act in the Calliope with the SGs. Even though they were allowed to hang out, they would never cross the line and try to make a sell on their set. That wasn't their motive for hanging around. They just liked the setting and the vibe which was totally different from their set even though it was only fifty steps away.

Tiger walked over to Ryder who was sitting on a milk crate by the hallway that they hustle out of. Next to him was a brown and black AK leaning up against the wall.

"What's up my nigga?" Tiger asked Ryder who stood up as Tiger reached out his right hand.

"What it do Soulja?" Ryder said while dapping Tiger.

"I'm just trying to see what the word is cause we know them niggas coming, it's just a matter of when," Tiger said. I can't understand how them bitch ass niggas smoked Tre and made it from back here," he continued.

"When you out chere in these streets, it's fair game. Any nigga can get it, anywhere," Ryder said.

"The same way they killed Tre in his hood, we gave it to Lou in his hood. That's why I'm keeping this half of a man close," Ryder said as he pointed at the AK that was against the wall.

"I can dig that," Tiger said. "That nigga Kev and Snoop heard how shit went down in the Calliope, and was like, the next time shit pop off they want in. They kept stressing how they don't like niggas out the Calliope and shit like that. So, keep in mind if y'all ever need a few good men, those niggas with it," Tiger continued.

***

Paul was the first person Ben called after getting his phone activated. He instructed Paul to get everyone together to meet in Mid-City and also informed him that Fred was already there. After he spoke with Paul, he called Joy like he promised he would once he got his phone turned on. The entire ride, he couldn't get Tiffany's snake ass off his mind. What troubled him most was how he found out that his old friend was behind him getting jacked. He knew Butch had to be dealt with, but how?

Ben couldn't wait to get to Mid-City to be back around his niggas because the lil' time he'd been away felt like a year. Yet more important than anything, he needed to see how the homies felt about him meeting with Curtis Mitchell because their opinion mattered. With 9 Finger Lou getting killed, it could be a setup, but Ben had the advantage being that he was the one picking the meeting location. So, if he decided to go through with the meeting to see exactly what the nigga had to say. He needed to be sure the odds were in his favor.

Ben wasn't concerned with being recognized by his car due to the fact that he was in a rental. Due to him riding with two pistols, he played the rearview mirrors often looking out for the police.

***

Instead of going to everyone individually Paul gave the order over the walkie-talkie for everyone to meet him in the driveway.

"Let me go see what's going on," Ryder told Tiger then grabbed the AK off the wall and held it close to the side of his right leg as he walked across the courtyard to go to the driveway.

It only took seconds for them all to meet up.

"What's up?" K-Dog asked while looking around as if something was about to go down.

"I just talked to Ben, he want us to meet him in Mid-City."

Ryder didn't realize that Tiger followed him and he felt that whatever they were about to discuss was related to drama. A couple of seconds later Tiger approached them and asked was something about to pop off.

"I don't think so because Ben didn't speak with urgency, but if something is about to go down, I'll call you," Paul said.

"A'ight my nigga, I'm here if y'all need me and keep in mind what I told you about Kev and Lil' Snoop," Tiger said looking at Ryder.

Lil' Mike got in the truck with Paul while Trap, Ryder, and K-Dog got in Trap's Gran Prix and headed to Mid-City.

***

By the time Ben made it to the spot in Mid-City, they were already there waiting on him to arrive. After clowning around for a while, Ben got to business.

"The reason why I called this meeting is because I want to hear how y'all feel about me meeting with that nigga Curtis Mitchell."

"What the fuck you have to meet with that nigga 'bout?" K-Dog asked. "If you ain't meeting with that nigga to kill-'em, then explain to me what's the point of meeting him."

"The point is leverage. As long as he willing to talk, we can use that as leverage," Ben said.

"How?" Ryder asked.

"Because as long as I can get that nigga to come to me on my call, we know for sure that we can eliminate another one of them," Ben answered.

"How do you know the nigga willing to talk?" Ryder asked.

Before Ben could answer, Paul explained how the nigga sent his number to him through his baby daughter when him and Roxanne was at Applebee's requesting that he give it to Ben.

"If you were close enough to get his number, you were close enough to kill that nigga. That's all I would have been thinking about if I had run into that nigga," Ryder said.

"It wasn't the time or place for that," Paul told him.

"You should have kidnapped that nigga daughter. Now that would have been some leverage for his ass!" K-Dog shouted out.

"So, do y'all want me to holla at the nigga or not?" Ben asked ready for a decision to be made.

"Fuck talking to that nigga. Tell that nigga to talk to my gun," Fred said. "I ain't sparing none of them niggas," he continued to say.

"Let's get that nigga to meet you somewhere and kill-'em and be done with it, that would be sending our messages loud and clear," Ryder said.

"Can you hear me now?" Trap said which made them burst into laughter. After everyone settled down, Trap continued to say, "On some real shit, see what the nigga talking 'bout cause he sent his number for a reason. What can it hurt?"

"Whoever disagree speak now," Ben said.

"I got one question," Ryder said.

"And what's that," Ben-Dog asked.

"Where the fuck you plan on meeting this nigga at. Matter-of-fact, why the fuck he couldn't say what he had to say on the phone. Don't that make you suspicious?"

"It's some shit you don't talk about over the phone," Ben said. "As far as where, I'm gon tell him to meet me at I really haven't thought that far yet. All it took for y'all to say is that we ain't doing no talking and that would have been that, but since that's out the way I'ma see what's up. Peep this shit out though," Ben continued. "I ran into Butch when I went to get a new phone, and guess who was rolling with him?" Ben asked giving them a moment to think about it before he continued.

"Dawg a nigga don't have time to play no guessing game," Ryder said. "Who it was?" he asked curious because if Ben brought the topic up, then it most likely could affect them knowing what type of time Butch be on.

"That bitch Tiffany!" Ben shouted, but he didn't get a reaction because to them it wasn't a big deal for Tiffany to be with him.

"So, what?" Paul asked while hunching his shoulders.

"This what," Ben said as he removed Duck .357 from his waist and set it on the coffee table before asking Paul if it looked familiar. Paul picked the gun up to examine it, then looked at Ben and asked him how the fuck he got Duck's gun.

"First Butch offered to sell me two pounds of Kush for the low right. After coming to an agreement on that, he offered to sell me a tool and you know I wasn't gon let him walk away with that. After we took care of our business I walked him to his car which was a white MC but I'ma get to that in a minute. Then he opened the driver door and to my surprise, Tiffany was in the passenger seat."

"What you told that hoe?" Paul asked.

"Nothing, we just looked at each other as if we never met before. I knew without giving it much thought that Tiffany was involved in Duck getting jacked. Especially when Butch was trying to sell weed with me knowing he don't hustle drugs.

"You gon tell Duck?" Trap asked Ben.

"What you think? Fucking right I'ma tell that man. I fuck with dude I'd be down bad if I didn't let him know he had a snake right under his nose."

"I feel that," Trap said.

"Now this is the crazy part," Ben said. "When I asked him 'bout the Monte Carlo he was in, the nigga told me in details how he had a nigga in training who robbed a nigga around a strip club for it. But guess who the nigga was?" Ben asked looking around at everyone.

Before Ben said anything else, K-Dog shouted out,

"You!"

"Ain't that some shit, but the nigga supposed to be coming through the project to drop the two pounds of weed off," Ben said with a smirk on his face.

"When he supposed to come through?" K-Dog asked.

"He didn't say, he told me he'd call before he come through and when he do the only way he gon leave is in a bag. I got something for Tiffany snake ass too" Ben said.

"I'd like to get some of that pussy before a nigga off that bitch," Paul said seriously.

"Dawg is pussy the only thing you think about?" Ben asked Paul. "And now that I mentioned it, you was supposed to be with Ryder and K-Dog when they went in the Calliope. Instead you were with a bitch like every time we need you," Ben continued as if he'd been waiting to get that out.

"Dawg check this out. I'm down with the family one hunid, but I can't predict when something gon pop off. Man, if I had that kind of power Tre would still be here ya dig. Fuck, it ain't like I'm ducking shit. I just wasn't round, and don't think for one second that I don't wish I was there. Fuck, the only way I can get some type of closure out this shit is if I punish one of them niggas. I'm still mad I missed my fucking ride the other day when y'all punished dude," Paul said releasing all the tension he'd had built up inside of him since Tre got killed.

Everybody in the room got quiet after Paul spoke out as if they were meditating on what he said until Ben broke the silence.

"Don't get it twisted homie, we know you'll squeeze, and we also know that you are true to the family. It's just that you get side tracked easily when it comes to them hoes, and we done had this talk before."

"If you gon put it like that, something could pop off when you at home, would you say you were side tracked?" Paul asked. "Or would it be that something happened that you had no control over?"

"Man, fuck going back and forth bout who there and who ain't," Ryder said trying to put an end to the back and forth bickering. "Let's be thankful that we are all here today, cause tomorrow ain't promised," Ryder continued as he stood and opened his arms wide for a group hug. After they all embraced, everybody sat back down.

"Man, roll something up," Fred said ready to get his smoke on.

"Now that y'all been updated with the latest info, is it anything that need to be discussed?" Ben asked while looking around the living room at everyone.

"The only thing that I can say is that we need some more work because all we have is this. Which is a little over three ounces, and the way things been moving, these few ounces won't last past today," Paul said then sat a Nike shoe box on the coffee table that was filled with cash. "That's 90 racks right there and that's after everybody got their cut," he continued to say while removing the shoe box top exposing the neatly stacked bills that were inside of it.

Ben was pleased with how Paul held down the operation while he was away, so he got up off the sofa and walked over to Paul and stated, "I knew I could count on you my nigga," he said as he hugged Paul tight, then he looked around the room and said, "I knew I could have counted on all of you, and to show my appreciation I got a surprise for y'all. But first thing's first, let me holla at the plug and put an order in," Ben said as he dug in his pocket to retrieve his phone.

He flipped open his phone and called Ernest but he didn't get an answer. So he tried again and this time Ernest answered on the second ring.

"Hello?" Ernest said in his husky voice.

"What's up Unk? How have you been? I need to speak with Paw-Paw," Ben asked speaking in codes that he was ready to re-up.

"I been doing fine nephew, everything been good. I forgot to tell you, you might need to come out here on the first train smoking."

"Why what's up?" Ben asked because Ernest never told him to come to him. He'd just send it by one of many mules.

"Paw-Paw been sick and he want to see you. I'm tired of hearing him ask for you, it might be better if he come live with you for awhile, to give me a break you know?"

"Okay, let him know that I'll be there tomorrow."

"Alright, I'll let him know, and while you're here, I guess we can go swimming at the house with some bad-ass bitches that I'ma have over. So bring you some swimming trunks."

"A'ight, I'll see you then," Ben said before he hung up.

"We good?" Trap asked hoping that they'd get the package some time the next day. The last thing he wanted was to run out of work. Knowing that if that happened, the dope fiends would take their business to the next available spot.

"I don't know what's up but he want me to come out there," Ben said.

"What the fuck he want you to come all the way to H-Town for? Why he can't send the shit like he been sending it?" Paul asked.

"Dawg you want me to ride with you out there just in case he on some bull-shit?" K-Dog asked seriously.

"Naw dawg, I don't think it's on no shit like that. Maybe it's something he need to tell me that can't be said over the phone."

"You sure my nigga?" K-Dog asked not liking the fact that he wanted Ben to come out there. *Why change what been working all this time?* K-Dog thought to himself.

"Yeah, I'm sure, but that's why I love you niggas," Ben stated as his phone started to ring.

"This might be him calling back to tell me that we gon stick with the usual plan," Ben said. But when he looked at the phone to see who the caller was it was Rell so Ben stated, "This ain't him, this Rell. What's good homie?" Ben said as soon as he answered the phone.

"Ain't much, I'm trying to get something."

"I ain't in the project right now, them people riding like a motherfucker. But if you want to meet me by my spot in Mid-City it's all good."

"Yeah, I can do that. Give me like 30 minutes."

Ben gave him the directions and told him he'd see him when he gets there.

Rell didn't like riding hot, but he saw Brittany sitting on the porch and offered her a few dollars to ride with him to Mid-City. If the price is right she would do almost anything.

He asked her if she had a problem driving cause women are more likely to get overlooked when driving.

"Why would I have a problem driving?" she asked in a sassy but playful tone, as she extended her hand reaching for the keys.

As they headed for Rell's Maxima Brittany told him she needed to stop at a store to grab a few cigars. When she started the engine, she said, "Boy that's a damn shame," when she seen the gas gauge on E. "It look like we need to stop at a gas station before we head to Mid-City, that's if we make it out the driveway," she said giggling.

"I see you got jokes," Rell replied. "Just stop at the gas station on Tulane Ave."

When they made it to the gas station, he gave her forty dollars to put in the tank while he waited to pump the gas. He called Ben and told him he'd be there in five minutes then hung up. When he got to the house, Fred opened the door to let him in. "What's up my nigga?" Fred said.

"What's good young gunner? What y'all niggas up to?" Rell asked curious to know why they were all gathered together in one house.

"We just trying to stay out the way," Ben stated from across the room where he sat on a love seat.

"What you trying to get?" Ben asked.

"I'm trying to get a zone," Rell said as he sat down on the sofa.

"This is what I'ma do for you since you went out the way to come fuck with yo boy. I'ma front you an ounce," Ben said as he tossed him 56 grams of boy.

"That's what's up," Rell said as he was going in his pocket to give him the 2500 dollars for the ounce he initially came to buy.

"How many times I can step on this shit?" Rell asked.

"If you want to get the most for your money you can put a 3 on that shit."

"Real talk," was his response in disbelief that he can make 8 ounces out that shit for 5000 dollars.

K-Dog had just rolled a blunt and asked Rell did he want to smoke.

"No homie I got Brittany waiting in the car."

"What Brittany? Brittany out the project?" Fred asked.

"Yeah, her," Rell answered.

"Why would you bring that hoe to this house?"

"I needed a bitch to drive and she was there, so I asked her to drive. I'm trying to duck them people as much as possible," Rell explained.

The moment Rell left the house, Ryder turned, and asked Paul was that the same bitch he was fucking with.

"Yeah, that's that bitch," Paul said thinking how he 'bout to use the hoe to his advantage.

***

It was a humid night and the fog started to roll in as Ronald and Tony sat on the porch of an abandoned house that was next to Ronald's house.

"Dawg we need to find somebody else to score from cause that nigga Big V be on some other shit. One day he got something, then the next day he don't," Ronald was telling Tony, who was sitting there removing and inserting the clip on his Glock 10mm.

"I hollered at ya boy Paul out the Melph the other night when he dropped Roc off," Tony said.

"And what the nigga said?" Ronald asked hoping that Paul was gon put them on, on the strength of his sister.

"He told me he was gon get back with me, but the way he said it, it was like he was spinning me. But we'll see what the nigga do."

"How did he say it?" Ronald asked out of curiosity because he know how easy Tony get in his feeling. He was the reason why they stayed in so much beef.

"He said it in a dry ass tone as if he was trying to get me out his face. Like I'm a bitch-ass nigga or something," Tony said with aggression as he replayed the scene in his head. "I can tell that he really don't want to fuck with us on that level. He been fucking with Roc lately so maybe he'll fuck with you to get in good with her," Tony continued to say because it wasn't no secret that they needed a reliable plug to score from and being connected with the SGs would be perfect. They both knew that they keep work and they could provide them with whatever they needed.

A white Tahoe with tinted windows horn blew as it passed them going about 12 miles per hour.

"Who that was son?" Ronald asked Tony.

"Dawg I don't know who the fuck that was," Tony answered as he stood up to get a better look at the SUV. "I thought they were blowing at you," he continued.

"Shut up Project," Ronald hollered trying to stop his dog from barking.

"He might want to get out that fucking yard," Tony said as he looked over his shoulder at the dog, that was jumping on the yard gate barking like he seen something.

"He straight, I took him for a walk earlier," Ronald stated.

He stood up and removed his gun from his waist and handed it to Tony. Then he told him that he was about to go take a shit, and went into his house.

The fog started to get thicker by the minute, and normally they wouldn't be outside hustling cause the fog made it hard to see who was coming and going.

Tony got tired of hearing Project bark so he walked over to the yard and grabbed the leash they kept on the gate. He put it on Project and started to walk him up and down the block. Project was a powerful dog, and if you didn't get a grip on the leash, he'd jerk you like crazy.

As Tony walked him, a neighborhood kid was coming towards them dribbling a basketball. To his surprise, he was within ten feet away from the aggressive Pit Bull who was in attack mode as he barked excessively.

"Man, you better get that dog," The nervous youngster said as he ran in the middle of the street leaving his basketball behind.

"You a'ight lil' brother, I got'em," Tony said as it took all his strength to hold the dog back.

The youngster moved slowly towards his basketball that rolled up against the curve. Never taking his eyes off the dog, that was barking more aggressively the closer he got to his basketball. Once he grabbed his basketball, he moved quickly down the street never looking back as he turned the corner.

Tony continued to walk back and forth with the dog until out of thin air a gunman approached the corner on the other side of the street carrying a AK. Fortunately, he couldn't take aim on Tony because when Tony saw the gunman he immediately released the leash which allowed Project to charge him. Before the dog could get close enough to make an impact he was struck with three bullets. One hit him in the face and two hit him in the body. The gunman was distracted long enough for Tony to pull his gun and release several bullets in the gunman's direction. Tony didn't hit him but he did enough to back the gunman up.

Ronald was on his way out the house when the first shot went off, but by him giving Tony his gun, he had to get to the AK that was underneath the abandoned house. But by the time he got it, the shootout was over.

Ronald ran towards the direction the shots came from, that's when he saw Tony running down the sidewalk. By the time Tony made it to Ronald he was breathing heavy and carrying both guns in his hand. He tried to explain to Ronald what happened but Ronald didn't hear a word he was saying when he saw Project lying motionless on the ground. Before they approached the dog, they put their guns up because they knew the police would be there any minute.

As they moved quickly towards Project, Tony yelled out in frustration, "Dawg that was that bitch ass nigga Baby D. out the Magnolia. I saw him when he came around the corner with the K in his hand," he continued to say while he pointed in the direction the Shooter came from.

The Magnolia is one of the most dangerous projects in New Orleans. It's so bad in that project, the police are terrified to go in it. Some rival crews that beef with them refuse to attempt a move on them inside of their project because that would be like committing suicide if they didn't come correct.

For the past year, it's been an ongoing beef between Josephine and the Magnolia, which is also known as the Nolia. The beef started one summer night when Juvenile gave a concert at the House of Blues, and when he came on stage, the first set of words that came out his mouth was, "Where that Nolia at?" and the niggas off Josephine started yelling, "Fuck that Nolia, Josephine rule!" and from there tension flared.

They began to push and shove each other, but security acted on the situation immediately before things got out of control. But Josephine Chris felt violated, so he shouted out at the Magnolia, "Y'all niggas know what's up with Josephine, we don't bar none."

Chris was loyal to his hood, so he was head first behind his niggas. The one who would ride for any cause, but he got gunned down two days later. To this day his murder is a mystery, but Tony and Ronald felt like it came from them niggas out the Magnolia, so they quickly retaliated refusing to let his death be in vain.

"Dawg we about to go in them niggas hood fuck that," Tony said then turned away and headed to get his gun.

"First, we got to get Project to a hospital, we can't just let him die out chere!" Ronald yelled out to Tony after he noticed Project was still breathing.

They quickly picked Project up and placed him in the backseat of Roxanne's car and rushed him to the emergency animal care clinic.

CHAPTER 27

Joy and B.J. stood in the doorway waving as Ben pulled away from the house to meet up with Ernest. But before he left New Orleans, he stopped in the Melph to holla at Paul.

To this day, he still can't understand why Paul is still laying his head in the project, because money wasn't the problem. He had more than enough money to live in any gated community in the metro area of the city.

It's something about the ghetto that had a hold on Paul. Something that refused to allow him to move into a better living environment. His older sister Krystal, who left him the project apartment once she found her a Section 8 house in the East always told him that he needed to move. Because nothing good would ever come out of being in a community that's more of a warzone than a neighborhood.

Most mornings, the traffic on the GNO bridge would be bumper to bumper with working people. They had to cross the bridge to get to work from the West bank to the East bank. And this particular morning wasn't any different.

It took Ben thirty-five minutes to make it from his house to the project. Which realistically should have only taken about fifteen minutes minus the traffic.

James and a few other fiends were the first people Ben saw when he pulled up in the project. To keep from getting out the car he called Paul to tell him to come outside, but he didn't answer his phone.

All the fiends that were out started walking off when Ben parked. Putting as much distance as possible between them and the car Ben was in just in case he was the police.

He knew Paul was home because he saw his truck parked in the driveway. So after he didn't get an answer, he got out and walked over to Paul's front porch and rapidly knocked on the door until Paul answered.

He looked through the peep hole and saw it was Ben, so he opened the door to let him in.

"What's going on nigga?" Paul asked in a half-asleep tone.

"Ain't shit, I'm 'bout to head to H-town to meet with Ernest. "I'll be back later tonight," Ben told Paul who was standing there rubbing his eyes with the palm of his hand.

"So what you need me to do?" Paul asked figuring there was a reason Ben stopped by.

"I don't need you to do nothing. I just wanted to holla at you before I left."

Paul gave him a strange look and then asked, "What's up homie you straight? Cause if you not, I'll ride out there with cha," but Ben declined his offer and assured him that he was good.

"How much dope you got left?" Ben asked.

"Shit I don't know, maybe a bundle or two I'm not sure. Why what's up?" Paul asked.

"Give a bag to every customer that come through till you

run out," Ben replied. "You know, show a lil' customer appreciation, ya dig?"

"That's all good, but I ain't giving them shit till I wake up cause I'm 'bout to go my ass back to sleep."

"A'ight my nigga, I'm out," Ben said as he dapped Paul, then turned to head for the door.

When he got in his car, he went straight to the gas station to get some gas and a few other things for the ride.

***

It was a beautiful summer morning; the sun was shining bright with temperatures in the high 60's. The Cheddar Boys were hanging on their set until Safe Home rushed the courtyard on foot harassing everyone in the area which made them all run inside.

"I can't stand them white motherfuckers," Donte' shouted out in frustration once they all were secured behind closed doors. "We need to start killing them bitches," he continued to say as he peeped out the living room window.

Donte' was a notorious killer, He was well known for pulling off vicious acts throughout the city. His life fell completely apart after the shooting death of his twin brother Vonte' seven years ago. He held the police responsible for his brother's death, not because they killed him, but because they took too long to call the ambulance to the scene. They were more focused on asking him did he know who shot him so they could build a case instead of trying to get him to a hospital. To this day, he hated the police with a passion.
Besides his hate for the police, his brother death brought the worst out of him. Even as a youth, Donte' had an obsession for guns and violence. It became clear when he shot and

killed a childhood friend with a .25 cal handgun. They'd stolen it from an older hustler after they watched him stash the gun in a potato chip bag and placed it under a piece of plywood. Him and his friend Dooney got into an argument about who was gon keep the gun first. They couldn't come to an agreement, so they ended up wrestling for the gun until Donte' pushed him to the floor. Once Dooney got up off the ground, he swung and hit Donte' in his face with a closed fist and with no conscious Donte' aim the gun at him and before Dooney could apologize, "POP" was the sound of the small caliber discharging striking him in the chest, killing him on impact.

A nervous Donte' rushed out of the hallway to tell his brother what had just happened because they were very close and he knew he could have told him anything. Donte' wanted to tell Dooney's mother, but Vonte' told him not to do. He also told him that he didn't know what happened, that he was inside if anybody asked. One hour later Dooney's body was found by someone that came out of their apartment, who called the police.

That was the beginning of the many murders Donte committed, contributing to why killing was so easy for him.

Curtis Mitchell looked around the room at Donte', Black Larry and Je'sus and then said, "Since we all here, it's something that I want to say," as he focused his attention on Je'sus who was sitting slouched back on the love seat.

"What it's about?" Je'sus asked figuring he was gon be the topic of conversation the way Curtis looked at him from his seat.

"It's about how you reacted to the situation when Donte' and Larry went to jail. They feel like you could have..."

But before he finished his statement Donte' cut him off. "We supposed to be family, but the way you acted when that shit happened. You handled a nigga like a worker instead of a partner and when that shit went down like that, I was ready to make the decision to do my own thing. To be real with you, I'm still in my feelings 'bout that shit," Donte' vented being a very outspoken person. He had always been the one in the crew to speak his mind no matter who he was talking to.

"I know I kind of came off the wrong way, but don't get it twisted. I love you niggas and it ain't nothing I won't do for any one of y'all," Je'sus said honestly. "Right now, ain't the time we need to be speaking on separating. The way shit is right now we need one another more now than ever," he continued. "We have to deal with this beef shit, plus try to make this money. And on top of that we got to duck the police."

The 6th District police station continued their investigation on the Cheddar Boys. All they needed was some concrete evidence to support Wanda's allegation.

Lt. Moore knew that he would have to dig deep to come up with something that would stick in order to put the Cheddar Boys away.

Too many times arrests were made and the cases thrown out because of the lack of concrete evidence. So Lt. Moore was trying to do everything by the book to make sure that when they got them they would't be released on a technicality. He wanted to make sure that they all were prosecuted to the fullest extent of the law.

After settling their differences, they reminisced about Vonte' and Lou on all the good times they shared together. It was like Lou couldn't get a break, he was shot in three different occasions.

One of the times was when he got his index finger shot off. He was on his way home one winter night when the brother of a dude he'd killed days earlier jumped out of a hallway as he passed by and pointed a Tec 9mm at him. By the time Lou realized what was happening all he could have done was put his hands in front of his face and attempt to block the bullets. The gun went off once striking Lou in the left hand taking his finger off. Luckily the gun jammed because it was a strong possibility that he would have died that night, and that's how he got the name 9 Finger Lou.

Donte' walked on the porch, by this time the courtyard had been cleared of police. He was told by a dude that was passing by that Ren and Crack Head Joe went to jail. Ren supposedly got caught with a bundle of crack and Joe went for drug paraphernalia, he had a crack pipe in his pocket.

Donte' decided to give Stacy a call to see if she wanted to meet up once she got off because he been thinking about her since she called him. After hearing her phone ring, Stacy ran from the kitchen to her room where she'd left her phone to answer it bumping her shin on the table on her way out.

"Hello?" she said answering her phone as she sat on her bed to rub her leg.

"What's up, how's things going at work so far?" he asked her.

"I'm not at work, I'm off today, but thanks for asking," she said with a smile on her face, really surprised that he'd actually called her back than anything.

"So how you plan on enjoying your off day?" Donte' asked her in a seductive tone.

"Have you eaten breakfast yet? If not I was just about to head to McDonald's if you wanted anything." Donte said.

"I appreciate the offer, but I was already preparing breakfast when you called, and I hurt my leg running to this damn phone, but you don't have to go to McDonald's. When was the last time you had a home-cooked breakfast?" she asked him.

"It sound like you inviting me to your home," Donte' told her not believing that she would let someone that's practically a stranger come to her house.

"Maybe I am," she responded.

"That's cool, I would love to have breakfast with you, but you don't know if I'm a serial killer or not, or do you just invite niggas to your house often?"

"To answer your question, No I don't invite niggas to my house. I haven't been intimate in nearly 6 months since me and my boyfriend broke up and I have a good judge of character about that serial killer statement you made. Besides how do you know I'm not a serial killer, that can go both ways. Especially, since you allowing me to prepare your food without you being in my presence while I'm doing it."

"You have a point. So where do you live?" he asked her.

"I live in Algiers on Tullis St. Are you familiar with that area?"

"Yeah, I know exactly where that's at, I'ma call you when I get on Tullis."

"The address is 2310, the door will be open so let yourself in."

Donte' went back inside and told the fellas exactly where he was going and gave them her address just in case. Twenty-five minutes later he arrived at her townhouse and let himself in like she insisted. When he entered the living room, he did a quick observation and was impressed that the house was up to par.

"I'm in the kitchen," she yelled when she heard the door close.

When he walked in the kitchen, he approached her and gave her a kiss on the jaw. She hadn't been active with a man in so long, that the slightest touch sent chills through her body. Her nipples got hard instantly as they were visible through the sport bra she was wearing.

Donte' took a seat at the table as she placed grits, eggs, ham and toast on the table in front of him.

"Damn this shit look good," Donte' said as his eyes scanned the well-prepared meal.

"I hope you like it," she said as she joined him at the table and began to eat.

"I'm sure I will," he said while digging into the scrambled eggs, never taking his eyes off the plate.

After they finished eating, Stacy cleared the table and walked off. Donte' couldn't help but stare at her ass as she walked over to the sink to place the dishes in it.

"That wasn't bad," Donte' said in approval of the breakfast, as he wiped his hands and mouth with a napkin. "The next meal is on me, just let me know when you up for it, but I can't promise you that it will be a home cooked meal. I'll be the first to tell you that's not my strength," he continued to say as he pushed the chair away from the table and stood up.

"I didn't take you for to be much of a cook, but I'ma hold you to that," she said while fighting the urge to push him on the table and fuck him right there.

"WHENEVER you ready to go out, give me a call," he told her putting emphasis on 'whenever'.

"How about if I call you tonight?" she asked hoping that he would read between the lines and have sex with her before he left.

"Didn't I tell you WHENEVER, if you want to go out tonight, then that what it is," he said then asked her where is her bathroom.

"It's the first door to the right," she told him as she pointed at the hallway.

Donte' knew she was trying to throw herself at him but he was gon continue to give her the impression that having sex with her was unimportant.

When he left out of the bathroom, he could hear her talking to someone so he pulled his gun and eased towards the kitchen where she was talking and peeped around the wall to find her talking on the phone.

All he managed to hear her say was "I'll meet y'all outside, just blow your horn," then she hung up.

The moment she placed the phone on the table he put his gun away then entered the kitchen and asked if she was about to have company. She explained to him that her daughter's father was about to drop their child off. She assured him that she had no type of dealings with him, that they only shared a child together.

"Is that the boyfriend you told me about that you broke up with six months ago?"

"Yeah, that's him, but trust me there is nothing going on with us," she said trying to convince him that it was over between the two of them.

"Out of respect, I'ma push out. Just call me when you ready," Donte' said then he gave her a kiss on her jaw before heading for the door. Before he made it out the kitchen she told him that he didn't have to leave, but he insisted. He told her he had to make a run then got in his car and headed back uptown.

***

The moment Ben walked in the gas station, he noticed the most beautiful girl he ever laid his eyes on. Ben watched her every move as she moved around the store searching for the things she wanted to buy. He couldn't stop looking at her, it's like he actually fell in love at first sight. After she gathered up the things she wanted, she made her way to the counter. That's when she noticed Ben who was making strong eye contact with her. When she approached the counter, Ben eased up behind her totally forgetting to pick up the items he went there to get.

"Can I get 50 dollars on pump eight and a pack of winter fresh?" she requested.

"Would that be all?" the cashier asked as he tapped on the cash register keys.

"Oh, and do y'all have any Golden Nuggets scratch-off lottery tickets," the beautiful female asked.

"I'm sorry we're out of Golden Nuggets," the cashier answered. "Those are the only ones we have at the moment," the cashier continued as he pointed at a plastic case that contained several lottery tickets.

"Give me just a minute sir. I need to call my father and see if he wants any of those," she said while pulling her Nextel out of her Coach purse.

On the second ring, her father answered, "?Hola?"

"Hola Papi, no tiene loteria pepitas."

"D'oro."

"?Queres de los Que hay aqui?"

"Si Amor, dame Que las Que hay."

"Bueno A dios Papi."

Ben, found it astounding to hear her speak in Spanish because she didn't possess any Spanish features, he thought she was the average black female, but when he heard her speak in her native accent, he had to approach her.

"Excuse me beautiful, can I speak to you for a second?" Ben asked as he walked out of the gas station after paying for his gas.

"Sure, but it look like your second is up already," she responded with a smile on her chocolate face.

"Damn luv, you don't have to be so technical," Ben shot back. "But since you put it that way, can I speak to you for a year?" he continued matching her sarcasm which made her smile, exposing her perfect set of teeth.

"Naw I'm just joking, what's up?" she asked while reaching for the gas pump handle.

"Normally women as beautiful as you are don't have a sense of humor," Ben said as he leaned on her CLK Benz. "I been living in this city my whole life and I never ran into a black Mexican."

"I'm not Mexican, Spanish maybe, but I'm no Mexican," the beautiful female said then burst into laughter.

"Heard you speaking Spanish in the store, maybe you can give me Spanish lessons," Ben said seriously. "By the way I'm Ben. And your name?" he asked her.

"My name is Sandra, and the reason why you heard me speak in Spanish is because I'm from Honduras and that's the language we speak. When I speak with my parents they prefer for me to speak in our native language."

"For some reason, I find you to be a very interesting person," Ben told her.

"And why is that?" she asked.

"I'm not sure, but given the opportunity I'll be more than happy to find out," Ben said while looking deep into her eyes. "So how long have you been living in the U.S., because you speak English just as fluently as you do Spanish." Ben asked curiously.

"I've been here since I was 10 years old," she responded.

"I know it's not appropriate to ask a woman her age, but..."

"I'm 20 years old," she said interrupting his statement.

"I don't understand what's the big deal with women not wanting to be asked their age," she continued to say.

"I would love to get to know you better. Not that I know you at all cause I don't, but I most definitely would love to."

"You seem like a nice guy, but my father would kill me if he even knew I was standing here talking to you," she said honestly.

"I wouldn't allow that. I'll take your bullet because without question, you seem like the type to die for."

"I'm serious, my father is, let's just say you don't want to have a run-in with him."

"Ohh, I'm scared," Ben said in a joking tone. "But for real, I'm willing to take that chance," he added.

After exchanging numbers, she got in her car and slowly pulled away, waving as she entered traffic. Ben went back inside the gas station to get the things he originally went there to get. He purchased a pack of Zig-Zag rolling papers, a bottled water and a couple of bags of BBQ corn chips. After filling his tank, he got in his car and headed to Houston.

***

After driving for four hours, as Ben reached the city of Orange, Texas he exited the interstate for a gas and restroom stop. *I thought it was hot in Louisiana, we don't have shit on Texas heat*, he thought to himself when he got out his car to head for the door of the gas station.

Once inside, Ben asked the cashier if there was a restroom available for customers. He was pointed in the direction of a portable toilet on the side of the gas station. To his surprise, it was clean but it wasn't important because all he had to do was urinate. When he finished, he went back inside to pay for his gas, a Red Bull and a bag of peanuts.

Ben called Ernest to let him know that he was in the State of Texas, and that he'd be there in an hour or so. He informed him that he needed his address so he could enter it in his GPS system.

While at the pump he mumbled to himself, "Got damn it's hot out chere."

He couldn't wait to get back in the car to get under the AC. After he activated his GPS system, he got back on the interstate headed non-stop to Houston. The moment he arrived at Ernest's mansion he was seen by the surveillance cameras. The electronic gate opened slowly before he even had the chance to call and tell Ernest he'd made it to his residence.

As he drove down the block long driveway that led to the huge three story brick home, he admired the immaculate landscape that consisted of palm trees, custom designed flower beds and a perfectly cut lawn that resembled a golf course, and he thought to himself that it had to be nice to be able to live like that.

When he made it to the end of the driveway, he was greeted by an armed bodyguard and was ordered to stop the car. He followed the instructions as the bodyguard approached the car and told Ben to get out. Once he stepped out of the car, the bodyguard, who appeared to be black, but his accent said otherwise began to search him for a weapon. He removed Ben's 9mm from his waist and placed it on his waist. "Dis way," he said in a foreign accent.

When they entered the house, there were two more armed guards that stood at the bottom of a spiral staircase. Instead of using the stairs, they used the elevator. Once inside the elevator, the bodyguard pressed the number three button, which took them to the third floor. When the elevator stopped, Ben was ordered to get out.

Ben couldn't believe that Ernest had a home of this magnitude. To the right of the room there's a 15-foot-long bar that contained all the liquor one could want. On the back wall was the largest T.V. screen he had ever seen besides in a theater. On the opposite side of the room there was a snow-white sectional sofa that sat on top of a snow-white carpet. To the back of the room was a black leather recliner which was where Ernest sat.

"Thank you, that would be all Flaco," Ernest said to the bodyguard that escorted Ben through the house. Without saying a word, Flaco nodded his head, turned, and left the two of them alone.

Ernest made his way to the bar and asked Ben what was his choice of drink, and Ben told him Hennessy. He scanned the shelf until he found the Hennessy and poured Ben a shot, then poured himself a shot of Scotch.

Before Ernest got into the details of why he wanted Ben to meet him in person, he asked him did he bring the swimming shorts he told him to bring.

"Damn, I forgot all about that, but I ain't really up for swimming no way," Ben said, just wanting to take care of business so he could get back to New Orleans.

Ernest didn't say another word, he hit a buzzer that was attached to the bar and moments later a beautiful female knocked on the door, and was ordered by Ernest to come in.

When the double doors opened a gorgeous female entered the room and said, "Yes Mr. Mullens, what can I help you with?"

"Can you bring me a pair of shorts for Mr. Ben please? Thank you."

"No problem sir," she said in a Spanish accent but it was fluent enough to understand.

Ernest noticed how Ben's eyes stretched when he saw his servant and asked Ben did he like what he'd seen.

"What you think?" Ben responded with a smile on his face.

"If you think she's attractive, wait till you see what I have by the pool, she's nothing."

A couple of minutes later she brought back a pair of perfectly folded shorts and sat them on a chair near the door then she left without saying a word.

After they finished their drinks, Ernest told Ben to go in the bathroom and change into the swimming trunks. When Ben came out of the bathroom, the same beautiful woman that brought him the shorts was discussing something with Ernest so he cleared his throat to get their attention to let them know that he was in the room.

Ernest turned around to face him and said "Shall we?" as he pointed at the elevator using an open hand.

As Ben approached the elevator, Ernest told him that his maid would put away his belongings. So Ben handed her his clothes, cell phone and watch. The moment the elevator doors closed, the maid searched every thread looking for any type of device. Not because Ernest didn't trust Ben because if that were the case Ben would not have been welcomed into his home. But in this game, you can never get too relaxed or stop paying close attention to details. Because when a person allows that to happen, that's when mistakes and misjudgments occur.

When they made it to the first floor, there was an older heavy set lady standing in the foyer holding two large beach towels. She handed them both to Ernest then asked him did he want her to bring them a beverage or anything. He declined, then headed to the back patio where was a large 3 to 12-foot swimming pool.

"Hey man this has to be the life to have maids who jump at your call," Ben said admiring Ernest's lifestyle. "I have a hard time just getting my woman to run bath water," he continued speaking metaphorically.

"I'm grateful to be in the position I'm in but my life was much simpler before the wealth, the maids and the fancy cars. Things might look glamorous to those who are less fortunate, but when people depend on you to support their families, that comes with a lot of stress. Not to mention you have to put your trust in the people you surround yourself with. Even that can be risky because everybody ain't loyal."

Ben paid close attention when Ernest spoke because the knowledge that Ernest obtained over the years that led to his success was worth listening to.

Ben eyes lit up like Christmas lights when they made it to the pool deck and he saw several beautiful women lounging around in bikinis. Some were floating in the water on inner tubes, and others were laying back on lounge chairs drinking margaritas. They all focused on Ben as him and Ernest came through the side door that led to the pool area.

"This is a good friend of mine, and I want y'all to make him feel welcomed," Ernest told the women just before he pushed Ben in the pool.

By the time Ben came from under the water, he was surrounded by three of the women. Upon contact, one of the women went under the water and grabbed Ben genitals while the other two performed foreplay by kissing on his neck and ears. Ben was there strictly on business but didn't complain about the treatment he was getting from the beautiful females. Ernest entered the pool minutes later and was greeted by the other three women with strong affection.

Forty-five minutes later, they were both dressed and sitting at the table in the massive kitchen for lunch as they ate a crab pasta that was prepared by Ernest's personal chef. As they talked Ernest began to explain that he was about to get out of the game. The sound of that was like a punch to Ben's gut.

"I spoke with my supplier about you and he wants to meet you."

"So when we supposed to meet?" Ben asked.

"As soon as we finish lunch," Ernest responded. "We will meet him at a nearby park at 3:00 p.m. If you want to be successful in this business honor your word, do what you say and say what you mean. This is another thing I want you to keep in mind, when you speak to him, maintain eye contact, cause if he thinks for one second that you weak or can't be trusted the deal will be off. Remember that I'm putting my reputation on the line so don't let me down," he advised. Once they finished their lunch they left the house to meet with Ernest connect.

When they pulled up at the park, there was a soccer game in progress. There were hundreds of soccer fans in attendance cheering for the team they wanted to win.

"Damn, it look like soccer is a big thing out here," Ben said as he observed the large crowd of fans that filled the bleachers.

"It depends on the person and if they like soccer," Ernest responded.

"I never seen a soccer game in New Orleans. That's part of the reason why I don't know shit about it."

When they got out of the car, a real dark skinned African dude that stood 6'2" weighing 235lbs followed by two other men approached Ernest. The African kept his eyes focused on Ben, then looked at Ernest and said, "I see you kind of early," as he shook his hand.

"You know what they say, if you early then you on time, and if you on time then you late," Ernest responded with a smile on his face as he exchanged handshakes.

The African turned to Ben and stared into his eyes for what seemed like an hour, but in reality, it was only a couple of seconds before he extended his hand to greet Ben with a hand shake. "Give me and him a minute alone," the African requested and Ernest and the other two guys walked off giving them their space.

Once they were alone, the African told him that he didn't have all day, that he wanted to get back to the soccer game so he got straight to the point.

"Ernest told me a lot of good things about you. But I need to hear it from you on why I should do business with you."

Ben looked him directly in his eyes and stated, "The product that you provide is Grade A, and the market for your product in my city is unbelievable."

"I'm aware of the market in New Orleans for heroine, I've been doing business in New Orleans for over 10 years. But that don't answer my question on why I should do business with you."

"I can't put it no simpler than this, together we can make a lot of money, and to be honest with you, I ain't here to sell myself. No matter what I say you gon still have your questions even your doubts, but I can assure you that in doing business with me, you won't regret it," Ben said never losing eye contact. "I've been doing business with Ernest for 8 months. I have never been one cent short on his money, and most importantly I kept our relationship confidential. Even my right-hand man don't know who my supplier is, so if you gon do business with me let's do it. If not you can walk away and finish enjoying your soccer game."

"It seems like you speak from the heart, and I like that," the African said. "So, I tell you what, I'ma give you a chance to prove yourself. If you are loyal to me and my organization, I can promise you that you'll be a very rich man in no time."

"I like the sound of that," Ben stated and they shook hands to finalize their agreement.

Before they ended their talk, the African asked Ben how long it will take for him to move five kilos. Ben explained to him that he was not accustomed to moving that kind of weight, that he had a kilo a week clientele but he'd give him a definite answer in a week.

The African went in his left front pocket, then handed Ben a cell phone and told him that he was to use it for no one but him. He made it clear that the phone was to be used for their business purposes only. He also told him that his number is already programmed in the phone.

After they finished discussing business, Ben walked over to Ernest and asked him was he ready to go. When they got in the car, Ernest asked him how things went and Ben told him GREAT with a big smile on his face.

"All you have to focus on is doing straight business with him and he'll give you all the work you can handle," Ernest said. "Remember that older lady who gave us those towels?" Ernest asked.

"Yeah, what about her?" Ben asked

"That's who gon meet you at the airport in New Orleans with your package."

"Man, you serious, you gon use that old lady?" Ben asked.

"That old lady is my most reliable mule, don't worry she good," Ernest assured him. "All I need to do is make reservations for her to fly out tomorrow, then you'll deal with Bambi from that point on. Oh, yeah, this time it will be a kilo so good luck I'm out, the other half a kilo is my appreciation for doing good business with me."

"I appreciate that," Ben said honestly.

"I guess we can go out to a club later tonight and celebrate."

"That sounds like a good idea, but I need to head back to New Orleans and straighten some things out. Maybe in the near future."

"Shoot yourself, you haven't seen a party till you seen one of my parties," Ernest said.

"I imagine you're right, but it's not the right time. I need to head back home," Ben said as they headed back to Ernest's mansion.

When they arrived at the mansion, Ben grabbed a bag out of his console that had $35,000 in it and handed it to Ernest. He told him that he'd notify him when the package was in his hand.

Ben couldn't believe that Ernest was actually about to retire from the drug business. It seemed like it was just yesterday when he met Ernest during a basketball game. The Houston Rockets played the New Orleans Hornets in the New Orleans arena. The more he thought about Ernest giving the game up, the more Joy's voice echoed in his head about him leaving the streets alone. That's something that he'd discuss with her when he got home. He figured that him, Joy and B.J. could live comfortably with a million dollars, so once he reached that he was going to get out. If the SGs wanted to continue to hustle, he'd turn over the connect to whomever wanted it.

Ben thought about all of this as he headed back to New Orleans. He was so trapped in his thoughts that he veered off the road momentarily, but he quickly refocused on the road ahead of him.

Paul called him to see how things was going so Ben explained to him that the trip was a success and that he was headed home at the very moment.

***

Stacy fought the urge long enough so she decided to call Donte' over. When he made it to her house, it was obvious that she wanted the night to end with love making. The lights were dim so they relied on candlelight to focus on each other as they talked over food, drinks and slow music. *Say Yes* by Floetry played low and sweet through the surround sound speakers. When their eyes met, the mood was created by the music, and their unspoken desires for each other was obvious.

"I want you," he simply said as he stood and approached her pulling her towards him, drawing her face to his as he kissed her deeply and tenderly.

He stepped back and pulled his shirt over his head revealing his chest which was covered with a 'Rest in Peace' tattoo in memory of his brother. Her eyes traveled down to the waist of his pants as she took a deep breath at the sight of his naval and the thick patch of hair just below. Following the deep and passionate kiss, he began to take his tongue and lick down the side of her neck back up to her ear.

Remembering how long it been since she'd last been satisfied sexually, he knew that every touch needed to be very sensitive. He removed her shirt and bra dropping them to the floor, exposing her swollen nipples. He then licked circles around them and stroked each one with the tip of his thumb.

"OH... My God...!" she gasped, each word punctuated with pleasure. Reaching between her legs, he searched for her clitoris. Encircling it with his middle finger, he began to slide it back and forth sending pleasures through her body. She worked her hips in rhythm with his touch, and with her eyes closed, she whispered softly in his ear, "Let's go to my bedroom."

Once they made it to the room, she laid across the bed and motioned him to her with an index finger. He continued to give her foreplay as he kissed her body softly until he found his way to her well-groomed pussy, where he moved his tongue in a circular motion to give her the most pleasure.

Gently trembling at first, she began to shudder and cry out softly "OH, OH Donte', that feel good," as she raised herself to a half-seated position, her hands gripped his head to ensure that his tongue stayed on target. She worked her hips in rhythm with him until an erotic sensation took her over the edge and she fell into an erupting, explosive climax. "OOOOH Donte' I'm cumming!!!" Weak from pleasures but aroused again by Donte's masculine scent, she rested her cheek against the thick, soft hair at the base of his dick and ran her fingers through his pubic hairs, up to caressing his stomach and down to his waiting erection.

He guided his dick to her mouth and she took him in small swallows until he completely filled her warm, wet mouth. As she slowly released him, Donte's breathing increased and his hands drew her mouth back for more. Holding his dick in one hand, she slowly licked the length of him, lifting his dick and then sliding her tongue down to his balls. One by one, she sucked them into her mouth, massaging them with her tongue.

He then climbed on top of her, slipping between her parted thighs, and started rubbing his dick against her pussy and clit. Finally, he slowly pushed his large head into her throbbing, hungry pussy. It had been so long and she was so horny that she moaned out in pleasure as he penetrated her tight pussy.

"OH... OH, God, Donte'! Donte' please! OH more! More!" she begged wanting him to go deeper inside of her.

The feel of his penis moving inside of her in slow measured strokes was mind numbing. As she laid on her back, she lifted her head and looked down at their bodies. The sight of his black, thick dick sinking balls deep into her pussy was enough to send her into another orgasm. She fell back against the bed, pushing her hips up to meet Donte' downward thrust, loving the feel of his hot dick as it penetrated through her tight wet pussy.

"Please Donte'! Please give it to me, I'm almost there again please! Don't stop! Give it to me!"

He suddenly cupped her ass in his hands and lifted her hips, pushing his hard dick inside her. At the same time his hot mouth found that sensitive spot below her left ear. She moaned and shuddered, then sobbed with delight and shattered into a million pieces as her body was flooded with pleasures. Donte' looked into her eyes as he pumped her unprotected pussy full of cum. Afterwards, he held her in his arms, kissing her gently as he rubbed his hands across her nipples.

The mood was interrupted by the ringing of her phone. She grabbed her phone off the nightstand and saw it was her baby daddy. Trying to salvage the moment, she ignored his call but he kept calling until Donte' questioned her about who kept calling her. She admitted that it was her baby daddy so he insisted that she answer it. The moment she said hello an argument took place.

It was clear to what he was saying on the other end of the phone because she stated, "Don't worry about if I have company, I'm free to see whoever I choose to, you need to be worrying about your ole lady." She remained quiet for a few seconds, before blurting out "Boy bye!" As the call ended.

"Let me find out you have a stalker on your line," Donte' said playfully.

"He is the last person on my mind, but let's not ruin our night talking about him. I let it be known in front of you that it's over between me and him.

"To be real with you, I ain't concerned with your past relationships, but just out of curiosity who is your baby daddy?" Donte' asked.

"His name is Devin, he from out the Melph so you might know him."

"I'm familiar with most of the people from out the Melph, but I don't know nobody by that name, he must be a lame."

"You might know him by Tiger."

When she mentioned Tigers name, that got his full attention, because he knew that Tiger would lay niggas down in the streets.

"Why you looking like that?" she asked. "What you know him or something?"

"I know of him, but I don't know him like that," Donte' said lying. He knew Tiger well and if Tiger found out that he was dealing with his baby mother, he felt like Tiger would inform the SGs of his whereabouts.

After cuddling together for about 30 minutes, Donte' went to the bathroom and washed off with a warm towel, then got dressed. He told her that he was about to leave and that he'd be in touch with her.

It was raining even harder than it was when he arrived at her house three hours before. So he moved quickly to his car, avoiding the large water puddles in the process. When he got in his car, he looked at the time on his Nextel. It was 9:18 so he tried to call Je'sus, but Je'sus was in the middle of a meeting with Giovanni so he didn't answer his phone.

Donte' went straight inside when he made it to the project. He couldn't wait to tell the homies that he was fucking one of them niggas baby mommas out the Melph.

***

B.J. searched all over his bedroom for a condom he had lost that he received from his sex education teacher. The condom was issued to all boys as a part of the STD prevention assignment they had to complete by demonstrating on a penis like object how to properly use a condom. He went to his mother's room and found the door closed so he knocked on it instead of barging in.

"Come in baby," Joy said to her son. "What do you need?" she asked him when he walked in the room.

"Nothing! I can't find my condom I had for my class assignment tomorrow."

"A condom! What kind of assignment do you have to do that requires a damn condom!?" Joy asked thinking that B.J. was lying about the reason he had a condom.

"In our sex education class, we had to practice on something like a boy thing to show us how to use a condom right."

"Boy I found that damn thing in the hallway by the bathroom. I thought your daddy had that thing."

Joy knew now that she had to apologize to Ben for falsely accusing him of something he had no knowledge of and as a result of her insecurity nearly got him killed.

"No Momma, Daddy didn't have it, it's for me. Where is it?" B.J. asked hoping that she gave it back to him.

"Boy I threw it away. I'll have to get you another one."

"Okay Momma," B.J. said, then went back to his room.

Thirty Minutes later Ben walked through the door. Fatigued from driving he went straight to his bedroom and jumped in the bed fully dressed.

"How did things go?" Joy asked him while taking off his shoes.

Before he could answer B.J. came through the door and jumped on top of him while he laid in the bed.

"What's up Dad?" B.J. asked.

"What's up JR?" Ben said while rubbing him on the head. "You been taking care of your Momma while I was gone?"

"Yeah B.J. said while giggling cause he liked the fact that Ben always told him that he's the man of the house when he wasn't home.

"Baby we need to talk," Joy told him in a humble tone.

"Can it wait till later?" Ben asked her as he nodded his head in the direction of B.J. "Or is it a must that we talk about it right now?"

"No, it can wait, but I want you to know that I love you with all my heart," Joy stated as she looked into his eyes.

"I love you too baby," he responded with a look of concern on his face, and out the corner of his eye he noticed B.J. looking at him. So he looked at him and said, "I love you too JR."

Joy told B.J. to go get ready for his bath so he could eat dinner and get ready for bed. B.J. gave her a kiss, then left out the room obeying his mother's order.

"So, what is it you want to talk about?" Ben asked her as he sat up against the headboard.

"You never gave me a reason not to trust you. I just want to apologize for how I reacted when I found that condom on the floor. B.J. told me that it was his, it was for a class assignment. How would you expect for me to react finding a condom in our house? Especially, knowing damn well we don't use them when we have sex"

"I'd expect you to react just the way you did. If I would have found it, you'd be living back by your momma," Ben stated.

"Boy don't play with me," she said which made Ben laugh and pull her on top of him and gave her a deep and passionate kiss.

"Now I have something I want to say," Ben told her as his attitude went from playful to serious.

"What's up?"

"When I got out there in Houston, my connect told me that he was about to retire from the drug business. When he told me that, I thought about you and how you been telling me that I need to get out the game. So, I figured once I reach a million dollars I'm out bae for real."

"We don't need a million dollars to live comfortable," Joy told him.

"My thing is this, when I do get out I want to find some type of business to invest in. You know when you invest in a business, things don't always go as planned and most times losses come into play. And just in case that happened I don't want it to affect our lifestyle."

Joy is glad that Ben is even considering getting out of the game she'll be so happy when that day come because Ben always had the attitude like he was gonna hustle forever.

"It's one more thing I want to discuss with you," after pausing for a few seconds he asked her was she ready to hear what he was about to tell her.

"Boy what?"

"I'm so lucky to have you as my woman. When niggas talk about they want a good woman in their corner I just laugh because they want what I already have, and I wouldn't trade you for any other woman and I been thinking 'bout making you my wife."

Joy grabbed her chest as if she was catching a heart attack then started jumping up and down as she released tears of happiness.

"Calm down Missy, I said I been thinking about it. I might change my mind," Ben said playfully then stood up and held his woman tight in his arms.

"I love you baby," he whispered in her ear.

"I love you more and today you made me the happiest woman in the world," Joy said. "Oh, yeah, I almost forgot," she continued as she walked over to her drawer, removed a home pregnancy test and handed it to him.

When Ben looked down at the results all he could say was, "You pregnant?"

"You don't sound like you happy," Joy said in a disappointed tone.

"Of course, I'm happy, it's just that I already knew you was pregnant."

"How you knew and I just found out?" Joy asked confused.

"You mentioned that you were pregnant two weeks ago."

"What I said was I THINK I'm pregnant," she said stressing the word think.

"I already knew though, because I know my woman and what made it obvious was your sudden mood swings. And that weird craving you been having. That's what really helped me decide to get out the streets, because you, B.J. and our unborn child is gon need me around. I can't keep risking my freedom or life fucking around in the street forever."

"I'm so happy to hear you talk like you have some sense," Joy told him. "I cooked you some food, you hungry?"

"No, I'm good, I'm just tired. I been driving all day. I need to get some sleep. I have some more runs to make tomorrow.

"Well I'm 'bout to go fix B.J. a plate," Joy said then she left the room.

When Joy exited the room, Ben decided to call Curtis Mitchell to tell him that they were gon meet tomorrow around 3:00 p.m. After the phone call Ben pulled the sheet up to his chin and fell to sleep.

CHAPTER 28

The Cheddar Boys met up at 6:00 a.m. to bag up the new package that Je'sus scored the night before. Je'sus brought them up to speed on the changes of the operation. He explained to them that they were about to expand their clientele and shut down the bag shop because it was beginning to bring too much heat.

Sitting around the table wearing dust masks and rubber gloves, they began packaging up the large pile of heroin into ounces. While doing so, Je'sus made the statement that they would be straight, but it might take a little time to get established because they were transitioning from selling bags to pushing weight.

Curtis Mitchell assured him that he'd handle that part of the operation because he fucked with niggas all over the city. It would be nothing for him to put work in at least four different hoods that had a steady flow of clientele. Donte' asked Curtis what hoods he had in mind because location was important, so Curtis gave him a brief run down.

"I'ma go in the 15th Ward and holla at John Boy in Christopher Homes cause I know them niggas getting money. Then I'm gon swing through the Laffite Project and holla at Chuck cause they have a nice spot down there in the 6th Ward. After that, I'm going in the 9th Ward and see what's up with this lil' Dike bitch that hustle in Press Park. Then y'all already know Pee-Wee and Dre doing their thing in Holly Grove."

"A'ight, that's a start, see what you can do," Je'sus said. He looked at Donte' and Larry and told them to deal with the niggas in the Calliope. He explained that since they were closing the bag shop, somebody would inherit their clientele, and if that was the case, they would need work.

"You know what? We can put Rell and his crew on," Donte' told Larry while shaking his head yes.

"That's a good idea," Je'sus stated. "All y'all have to do is front them niggas until they save up enough to score on their own. That way if they eat, we'll get full," Je'sus continued.

Je'sus had always been a good hustler, even as a youngster. He was the type of hustler that the average nigga wanted to be. By his sophomore year in high school he purchased a Mercedes Benz when most students were catching the city bus or walking to school. He would buy 10 to 15 pizzas from a pizza truck that made rounds around the school and gave them to all the bad bitches that ate during the same lunch period.

He attracted a lot of attention not only from students, but by school staff as well. Away from school, he demanded a lot of attention in the hood. Je'sus and Vonte' would gather up a lot of neighborhood kids and throw hundreds of dollars in the air causing an uproar.

Je'sus was every child in the ghettos dream and every female in his area wanted him to be hers.

Je'sus would get plenty of coke from his cousin Milton until Milton got hit by the Feds for conspiracy. But from prison Milton linked Je'sus up with Giovanni and that's when he formed the Cheddar Boys.

While bagging up the dope, Donte' boasted about how he put it down last night on Stacy. "Dawg that hoe pussy is tight as a motherfucker, you wouldn't even think the bitch have a kid," Donte' explained. "And guess who her baby daddy is?" "Who?" They all asked with anticipation.

"The nigga Tiger out the Melph."

"Even though he don't run with the SGs, that's too close for comfort," Je'sus said. "I think you should back up from that bitch. All it takes is for you to be at that hoe house and dude come over, and y'all crash. You know how niggas be in they feelings 'bout they bitch."

"I wish that nigga would trip 'bout that hoe. We know where his daughter lay her head at now, so we can always use her for leverage," Black Larry said. "It would have been better if it was that bitch ass 'nigga Ben. We could have put an end to this shit today, that would have showed how much fuck-boy love his child."

"Fuck all that, right now we need to be discussing how we gon get this money," Je'sus said as he observed the work on the table.

"After we finish baggin' this shit up, it will be a total of 108 ounces. So, we gon do it like this, we gon sell them three racks apiece and that should bring in 324,000. At the end of the package I need 200,000, that will cover the score money plus my profit and y'all gon split the remaining 124,000." While Je'sus spoke, nobody mumbled a word cause when he started to speak about dollars he captured their undivided attention.

"Curtis, you take two bricks because you gon be dealing with multiple hoods. Off that you gon give me 142,000 so that would leave 74,000 in profit for you," Je'sus explained the numbers to Curtis.

Then Je'sus focused on Larry and Donte' and began to explain how their numbers would break down. "I'ma give y'all a brick, that should be enough to hold the project down with. And off that, y'all gon bring me 58,000 and that would leave y'all with 50,000 to split."

Donte' quickly did the calculation in his head and protested, "So at the end of the day you gon get 100,000, and for what? From having the plug, cause you ain't selling a gram," he directed his comment to Je'sus.

"Then Curtis gon get 74,000 and we supposed to be satisfied with 25,000, it's like we getting played," Donte' continued as he spoke what he felt.

"How you figured that y'all getting played when y'all gon make 25,000 off a half a brick apiece?" Je'sus shot back.

"Why can't we all move the shit together and split the profit evenly. After all we splitting the risk so why not the profit?" Donte' asked.

"Listen homie, I'm just trying to move this shit quick as possible so we can score our own shit. Then we can adjust how the profit get split. Don't get me wrong, I know we can move all the work in our hood. It will take us a little longer to get off it if we only relying on the project. The way I see it, we can get off this shit twice as fast if we spread the shit throughout the city. The quicker we sell this shit, the quicker we stack our fucking money. Feel me homie?" Je'sus said. "I want you to keep in mind that we putting the shit on the street taking a 3 so the shit gon move like clockwork. Cause ain't nobody gon be able to match our prices or potency. So let's get this moving and stop tripping," Je'sus continued.

"A'ight dawg, let's do it," Donte' said as he continued baggin up the dope.

Curtis just sat there in deep thought as Donte' and Je'sus were exchanging words on how they think the money should be divided within the crew. At that moment he came to the conclusion that he would start doing his own thing, cause just like Donte' and Larry, he too felt that Je'sus was playing them all for fools. He also disliked the fact that Je'sus lied and told him that they were equal partners. Curtis knew that if he was in Je'sus position, he would've done things allot better for the sake of the crew.

***

Ben was on his way to the project when he called K-Dog and told him to meet him in the courtyard. When he made it back there, he saw Trap sitting on the project bench eating a hot sausage Po-Boy Sandwich.

When Ben approached him, Trap, with a mouth full of food muffled the words, "What's up nigga?"

To Ben's surprise the courtyard was almost empty so he asked Trap had the police been riding. Trap told him that he hadn't seen them since he'd been out there. K-Dog came out of Betty's house and met Ben in the courtyard carrying a AK. When Ben called telling him to meet him, he thought something was about to pop off.

Ben started laughing because when he saw K-Dog he knew exactly what he was thinking. He told him that the AK wasn't necessary so K-Dog took it back to Betty's house.

While Ben was waiting on K-Dog to come back he went to holla at Paul, who was inside with Roxanne.

"So you the one that have my nigga nose wide open huh? He can't stop talking about you. You Roxanne right?" Ben asked her.

"Yeah, I'm Roxanne, and I better be the only one he talk about," she said seriously but not aggressively.

"So you gon' stay in all day?" Ben asked Paul.

"Fuck, what else you want me to do? We ain't got no work."

"That's what I want to talk about," Ben said.

"Baby I'll meet you in the room," Paul told Roxanne who turned and walked off.

"Dawg we need to get something soon cause everybody going in the middle court to score from Tiger and his uncle."

"Don't trip, let them make those crumbs, we'll be back in power today. Right now, me and K-Dog about to go see what this bitch ass nigga Curtis Mitchell talking about."

"Man, fuck that, I'm coming too," Paul quickly stated.

"Naw chill with ole girl homie, we got this. I don't want to spook this nigga out. Just keep your phone line open just in case," Ben continued.

When Ben walked out the apartment, K-Dog was there talking with Trap. When he looked up and saw Ben, he walked up to him and asked him what was going on.

"I need you to come with me to holla at the nigga Curtis."

"You ready?" K-Dog asked as his adrenaline rushed through his body.

"Hold on let me call this nigga," Ben said as he removed his phone from its clip.

Curtis Mitchell was expecting the phone call so he answered his phone on the first ring and said, "What up Ben?"

Getting straight to the point, Ben told him to meet him at the park by the project.

"Damn dawg, we can't meet nowhere else?" a nervous Curtis asked.

"You the one said you willing to meet me anywhere. Now it's a problem?"

"No dawg it's not a problem. I just wasn't thinking 'bout meeting up in the Melph. I was thinking more of a restaurant or something like that."

"I tell you what, how do you feel about Arnold's on Bienville and Bourbon?"

"That's cool. So when do you want to meet?" Curtis asked.

"I'm about to head that way in a minute," Ben said giving K-Dog a look like it's on.

"Okay, I'm on my way," Curtis said before ending the call.

Ben and K-Dog got in separate cars and headed to the restaurant. It took them 10 minutes to make it to the French Quarters and another 5 minutes to walk from a parking garage to the restaurant. Once they made it, K-Dog stood across the street from the restaurant in front of a bar and blended in with the crowd.

It took another 10 minutes before Curtis Mitchell made it. From where Ben was sitting, he noticed when Curtis went in his pocket and came up with his phone. But before Curtis made the call Ben called his name getting his attention. Ben waved him over to his table and told him to have a seat.

A waitress approached their table and asked if they were ready to order or wanted a menu.

"I'll have a medium bowl of seafood gumbo and a large lemonade," Ben said then looked at Curtis who said that he would have the same but make his beverage an iced tea.

Standing across the street, K-Dog did his best with watching for anything out the ordinary. He was sure that Curtis hadn't come alone just as Ben didn't come alone.

As K-Dog surveyed the busy crowd, he spotted Butch talking to a white girl in front of a strip club. His first instinct told him to rush Butch and leave him there. But he quickly came to his senses because he knew that it was a 1% chance for him to fire a weapon in the French Quarter and get away.

In a matter of minutes, their food was served as they began to talk.

"To end this senseless ass beef, I was thinkin' 'bout giving y'all Donte' and Black Larry for twenty-five-thousand a piece," Curtis said making an offer he knew Ben wouldn't refuse because those two are the S.G.'s biggest threats.

"Nigga you got me fucked up. I aint paying that much to kill no fuckin' beef," Ben spat back with aggression.

"If that's how you feel, then it is what it is, bruh," Curtis replied nonchalantly. "But you know it's gon' be hard for y'all to make money and live comfortably as long as they alive. Besides that's who y'all want, right?"

That statement caused Ben to go into deep thoughts. After a couple of seconds of collecting his thoughts he humbly replied.

"On some real shit my nigga, if I'ma' pay that kind of money, I want the head of the organization," he said, referring to Je'sus because he felt with Je'sus being out the picture, they had a good chance of making more money.

"Fuck no! I can't do that, play boy. Je'sus is like my brother, but if you willing to spend that bread I can for sho' give you a call on the other two."

"Aight my nigga,' but don't take too long to get back with me, because my nigga's is already to the point where they running out of patience. Remember its on you how this shit end.

"Like I said, I can't give you my main man, but I'll be giving you a call on them other two," Curtis said.

"Make it soon," Ben responded.

Ben finished his gumbo, but Curtis had barely touched his food before they both stood to leave. After leaving their tab on the table plus a tip they exited the restaurant and went their separate ways.

Once Ben made it outside the restaurant, K-Dog started walking towards him.

"What the fuck that hoe ass nigga was talking 'bout?" K-Dog asked Ben as they began walking towards the garage.

"I told the nigga that if he wanted to squash the beef, set Je'sus up for us. But he was on some shit like he'd give us Donte' and Larry."

"That's cool with me," K-Dog said. "I would love to punish both them niggas."

"I would too, but if he gon snake his niggas, it's best to go for the head. And if he stupid enough to believe that the beef gon be over once we kill them that's on him. Cause you know we ain't gon stop until all them niggas dead."

"What if he tell Je'sus what y'all discussed?"

"Do it look like I give a fuck? What he gon kill me?" Ben responded sarcastically.

"You think the nigga really gon set his niggas up on some snake shit, or he trying to under mind us. Maybe he was trying to see how close you would allow him to get to you," K-Dog stated trying to keep an open mind about the situation. He felt like no one would get their homies killed, especially for the enemy.

"I don't know if he gon do it or not, but if I don't hear what I want to hear soon. It wouldn't be nothing to call that nigga and set up another meeting, then knock his fucking brains out."

"That's what the fuck I'm talking about," K-Dog said with a mug on his face as they approached their cars that was on the second floor of the parking garage.

"Well look, I'ma meet up with y'all in the project in a hour or so. I'm 'bout to go to the airport and pick up the package," Ben said before they dapped and got in their cars headed in separate ways.

***

When K-Dog made it to the intersection of Martin Luther King and Simon Boulevard, he noticed a parked squad car in the area. So he made a proper right turn by using his blinker. By the time his car straightened up, the police car pulled off and pulled in behind him. Nervously, K-Dog fumbled around with the gun he had which made the car drift into the other lane. With a slight jerk of the steering wheel he was back in his original lane.

Trained for situations like this, the cop believed the driver of the car was in possession of something illegal. He immediately flashed his lights for the driver to pull over. The moment the lights came on, K-Dog pulled over knowing his movements weren't visible due to the tinted windows on his car. So he hurried to pulled up the floor mat under the gas pedal and placed the .40 cal under it, and quickly buckled his seat belt.

The officer approached the car cautiously, with his hand on his weapon because he knew he was in a high crime area. When he made it to the driver's window, K-Dog asked him what the problem was. The officer explained that his windows were too dark and once he pulled behind him he appeared to be nervous because he drifted in the other lane.

"May I see your license and registration?" the officer asked, never removing his hand off his weapon that remained holstered.

K-Dog leaned over to remove the requested documents from his glove compartment. He removed his driver license from the console and handed them to the officer.

"Would you step out of the car sir?" the officer asked as he took a few steps back to put a little distance between him and K-Dog.

Once K-Dog was out of the car, the officer cuffed and searched him before searching his car. Luckily for K-Dog, he didn't find the gun. So, to the best of his knowledge, K-Dog was clean.

"Let me run your name and make sure you don't have any warrants. If not, you are free to go."

When his name was called in, the police captain heard it over the scanner and requested that the officer retain K-Dog until he got there and to contact the K-9 Unit immediately. The captain made it to the scene in a matter of minutes, because the 6th District police station was only three blocks away from the Melph which was where the traffic stop took place.

While waiting on the K-9 Unit to arrive, Rell happened to ride pass the scene on his dirt bike. When he saw that it was K-Dog, he rushed back to the Calliope. He told Black Larry and Donte' that the police had K-Dog on the car and if they didn't arrest him, it meant he didn't have a gun on him. Meaning they'd still have a chance to kill him. Donte' and Larry rushed to their car and headed to the scene. When they got there, K-Dog was cuffed and leaning against the police car, just like Rell had told them.

"Dawg if they let that nigga go, I'ma punish his ass," Larry said as they sat in the car and watched from across the street.

"I'm 'bout to put all 32 shots in that clown," Donte' said while looking at the Glock 40 with the extended clip he held in his hand.

Five minutes later, the K-9 unit arrived and searched the car thoroughly for drugs but came up empty. Although they did manage to find the gun that was hidden under the floor mat. Following the search, K-Dog was arrested, and advised of his constitutional rights via Miranda, and taken to central lockup.

***

Ernest is officially out of the drug business now that his mule is headed to the airport in a cab with a kilo to bring to Ben in New Orleans. She's wearing a full-length dress and a pair of flat slip-on shoes. Taped to each of her thighs were 18 ounces a piece compressed to one inch in thickness and eight inches long.

The mule had made plenty of trips to various states in the past without any interference with the law. She was more than comfortable with transporting large quantities of drugs. When she made it back from this trip, she was sure to talk to Ernest about the sharp pains she'd been experiencing in her chest but had overlooked them for the past few months.

Once she boarded the plane with no problems, a sense of relief ran through her as she moved slowly to her seat. After everyone was seated, the stewardess instructed all passengers to power off their cell phones and to fasten their seat belts.

The mule, whose name is Jackie sat next to a black teenage girl that was 16-years-old who sat next to the window. Ms. Jackie introduced herself to the girl.

"Hi, I'm Ms. Jackie," she said with a smile to make the teenager feel comfortable with talking to her.

"Hi I'm Cyntrell."

Jackie asked Cyntrell was this her first time flying and she politely responded, "No ma'am."

"Do you live in New Orleans?" Jackie asked her.

No ma'am, I'm from Conroe but my father live there and I visit with him at least six times a year and you, do you live in New Orleans?"

"Oh, no sweetheart, don't get me wrong New Orleans is one of the most interesting cities I have ever been to, but the crime is too bad there for my liking."

While they small talked about nothing in particular. The plane departed from the landing strip and they both tensed up for the take-off. The moment the plane leveled off, Ms. Jackie grabbed her chest in mid-sentence as she talked to Cyntrell.

"Are you alright ma'am?" Cyntrell asked repeatedly but she never got a response so she yelled for a stewardess to assist the old lady who appeared to be having a heart attack.

By the time the stewardess made it to Ms. Jackie she was unresponsive. Following protocol the stewardess dispatched required information to the cockpit.

***

Ben arrived at the Louis Armstrong International Airport just as the flight boarded. Upon his arrival, he noticed the paramedics rushing through the terminal with a stretcher as if an emergency had occurred. He didn't give it much thought since it wasn't the police rushing the plane.

All the passengers were quickly ordered from the plane as the paramedics tried to revive Ms. Jackie but they were unable to do so. As the passengers exited the plane, Ben scanned the crowd of people trying to locate the heavy-set, older woman who was delivering his package, but he didn't see her get off the plane. The last person to exit the plane was covered up with a white sheet and being rolled out on a stretcher.

Ben called Ernest to make sure that the mule was on this flight and Ernest assured him that she was. Suddenly he heard voices yelling for everyone to get back, he turned around and saw several police officers running towards the ambulance. He informed Ernest that he would call him back then hung up as his heart fell to the floor.

Ben watched closely as they approached the stretcher and removed two white packages from between Ms. Jackie's thighs. He immediately left the airport in a rush.

***

"Fuck man, I wish they would have let that nigga go," Black Larry said as Donte' drove away from the scene where K-Dog was arrested at.

"Dawg I was gon punish that bitch-ass nigga," Donte' said as he made a U-turn to head back to the Calliope.

"Dawg we have to respect how Rell put us on game even though he didn't want to get involved in our beef," Black Larry stated.

"I mean fuck, I respect that, but if you a real nigga, you supposed to do real shit," Donte' replied while looking through his rearview mirror as he approached the red light at the intersection of MLK and S. Claiborne.

"Oh shit! I just thought of something!" Donte' stated with excitement in his voice.

"What?" Larry asked curiously.

'I'm 'bout to call that hoe Stacy and make a power move," Donte' said while grabbing his phone.

"A power move! How?" Larry asked.

"Just peep game," Donte' said as he dialed her number.

"Hello?" Stacy said when she answered her phone.

"What's up luv? You at work?" Donte asked her.

"Yeah, I'm at work, why what's up?"

"I need you to do me a favor."

"What kind of favor?"

"Hold on," Donte' said then turned to Black Larry and asked, "What that nigga name son?"

"Damn, what that nigga name?" Larry mumbled to himself, then stated, "Kyron Youngblood," he remembered K-Dog name from school when they were in the same math class. Donte' told her K-Dog name. He then asked her to call him when he got released, which she agreed to do for him.

When they made it to the Calliope they pulled in the driveway, parked, and got out the car. As Rell quickly passed by riding his dirt bike on its rear tire, Donte' tried to flag him down, but Rell didn't see them.

"Damn I wanted to tell that nigga that we gon put them on," Donte' said.

"It ain't no big deal, we'll see him sooner or later," Larry said, then headed to their stash house.

***

Roxanne and Paul had just finished having sex for the first time when he heard knocking at his door. Still naked, Paul jumped out of the bed and slipped into his boxers and went to answer the door, "Who is it?" he yelled as he approached the door!

"Open the fucking door," Ryder yelled through the door in a pissed-off tone. Paul opened the door to find Lil' Mike, Ryder and Trap standing there. Once the door was open Paul stepped to the side to let them in. Before Paul could ask what was up, Trap told him that K-Dog had just gone to jail for a gun.

It took Ben 20 minutes to make it from the airport to the project. He went straight to Paul's apartment and to his surprise, Lil' Mike, Ryder, and Trap were there. From reading their facial expressions, he knew that something happened. So, he asked what was going on? Just as Paul said, "K-Dog went to jail for a banger."

Even though K-Dog had several arrests for multiple felonies, and one capital offense, he had never been convicted. The weapon charge was only a state misdemeanor, and even if convicted for the gun he would only face six months, either in prison or on probation.

"He gon be straight, we'll go get that nigga out tomorrow after he go to magistrate court for his bond hearing. Right now, we have a bigger problem," Ben stated.

"What problem is that?" Ryder asked out of curiosity.

"The fucking mule got hit with the package."

"Got hit?" Paul stated in disbelief.

"Yea, Dawg, something happened on her flight. They took her off the plane on a stretcher. I saw the police running towards her and when they got to her, they removed the work from the foot of the stretcher and placed it in a clear plastic bag."

"What else happened?" Paul asked.

"What you think happened? I got the fuck outta there"

"So, what we gon do now big homie?" Lil' Mike asked.

"I'ma holla at Ernest and let him know the mule got hit. That way he can send another package, but it might take a few days to put it in motion."

"Well homie, I think it would be best if you call him right now. To let him know that the package ain't make it," Paul suggested.

Ben took Paul's suggestion, and once he got Ernest on the phone, he explained to him what he witnessed at the airport. Ernest couldn't believe what he was hearing, but his bigger fear was the cops tracing the work back to him. He ordered the plane ticket off his credit card, and he knew that couldn't be a good thing.

While they were discussing the situation at hand, Roxanne stormed in the living room with an attitude. She started yelling and cursing at Paul, "Who the fuck is China, Garineka... Ciera..." she asked as she paused momentarily between punctuation.

"Slow the fuck down, don't you see me in the middle of something?" Paul stated with aggression.

"Do it look like I give a fuck if you in the middle of something? I want to know who these bitches is in your phone," she demanded.

"You ain't have no business going through my phone any fucking way."

"Boy, fuck you and your phone," she said as she shoved the phone in his face. By Paul being forced to protect his manhood, he slapped her in the face with minimum force, but hard enough to let her know that he won't tolerate being disrespected, especially in front his homie.

The impact of the slap was hard enough to burst her lower lip, and with a mouth full of blood she spit in his face, and yelled, "Don't put your fucking hand on..." but before she could finish her statement, she was struck in her eye with a closed fist causing her to stumble backwards. That's when Ben stepped in between them to prevent things from going any further because Roxanne quickly gathered herself and started going after Paul.

"What the fuck wrong with you dawg? You wrong for hitting that girl like that," Ben said.

"Man, you seen that bitch spit in my face."

"Bitch, I got yo' bitch," Roxanne said as she ran to the room to get her things.

"Dawg watch out," Paul told Ben as he shoved him to the side then followed her to the bedroom.

When he got to the room he grabbed her by both arms and stated, "What the fuck you tripping for? Let me see," looking at her left eye. "Look what you made me do," he said.

She didn't want to talk about it, all she said was, "Get your fucking hands off me. I'm 'bout to go home, MOVE!"

Paul released her arms, and she left out the room then heading for the door, passing Trap, Mike and Ben up as she left the apartment. When the door closed, Lil' Mike stated, "If that was me I would have knocked that bitch out."

When Paul came back in the living room, Ben had told them that he was about to head home that he'll see them tomorrow, and explained to Paul that he need to call Roxanne and apologize to her.

***

At the airport, it took a matter of minutes for investigators to trace the plane ticket back to a Ernest Mullen's. Through further investigation they obtained information from a reliable confidential informant who had been assisting the FBI for many years in the North Side area of Houston.

The head investigator in New Orleans contacted the FBI in Houston and explained that an elderly woman, who went into cardiac arrest and died during her flight to New Orleans was strapped with a kilogram, which tested positive for heroin. He included that a Ernest Mullen's purchased the ticket off a credit card and they need to speak with him concerning the situation. The Houston FBI immediately put a warrant out to bring Ernest in for questioning.

CHAPTER 29

9:49AM

Ben and BJ were on their way to the barber shop when they stopped to get a home cooked breakfast from a soul food mom & pop establishment named the Trolley Stop that was located on St. Charles Ave.

Once they arrived Ben placed an order for two plates of fish and grits, which were BJ's favorite and two medium orange juices to go.

After the food was purchased, Ben and his son headed to the *Hot Spot* Barber Shop.

Once they made it there, BJ was nearly finished with his breakfast so he stayed in the car and ate the last few remaining bites, while Ben took his plate into the shop.

"What's up y'all?" Ben said speaking to everyone in one greeting.

"What's up Ben?" some of them spoke back in the midst of distant chatter that took place in the confined space.

He replied, and then he focused his attention on Tiffany and said, "What's up Tiff?"

"What's up Ben?' she responded, unsure as to how much

he knew about the robbery situation.

"Ain't nothing, I'm chilling, just trying to stay out the way."

"That's the best thing to do out here," she stated.

"I didn't know you fuck with Butch," Ben said trying to get a reaction out of her, but she played it cool and casually and responded to Ben's statement.

"Yeah, I been dealing with him on and off for like six months, but it ain't nothing serious between us."

"He good people though, and that nigga will take care of you."

"He cool, but he ain't nobody I can get serious with for several reasons."

"So what's up Duck? You ever get straight on the Purp?" Ben asked.

Never taking his eyes off the person's head he was cutting Duck responded, "Naw brah, I ain't get nothing yet, I need to find out who the snake's that put those niggas on me."

"It was probably Stank and Buck, cause somebody told me that they had some Purp on Forth and Danelle. You know they don't sell nothing but Reggie around there. And after I thought about it, I remembered that they did come in here right before those niggas ran in on us," Tiffany said, trying to put the heat on Stank and Buck. They were two dudes who had been moving weed since they jumped off the porch.

Duck paused for a second and said, "Why you ain't been told me that you heard something like that?"

"I was gon tell you but it slipped my mind," Tiffany said trying to explain herself.

"I don't think they did it anyway. Cause one of the niggas that came in here was kind of tall. I know Stank and Buck voice and none of those niggas sounded like them."

"Ben, give me a second, you're next," Duck said, once he finished cutting the head he was on when Ben first came in.

Ben nodded and went out to the car to give BJ an update. BJ paused his GameBoy, then got out the car and went in the barber shop.

"There go my boyfriend," Tiffany said, smiling as BJ walked in. He was blushing really hard from ear-to-ear.

"Hi Tiffany," BJ greeted.

"Give him the usual," Ben told Duck as BJ got in the barber chair.

Ben started to speak about K-Dog arrest and how he was waiting for him to have his bond hearing, so he could go pay it for him.

"I didn't know K-Dog got hit," Duck said then looked at Tiff, "You mean to tell me that your nosey ass ain't hear that K-Dog went to jail? Well, bout time you missed something," he continued.

"No, I ain't hear that he went to jail," Tiffany said, wondering why she didn't get that information.

"When we finish getting our hair cut, I'ma go pass by the courthouse to see how much his bond will be, but no matter what it cost, he'll be out today," Ben stated.

An hour later Ben was pulling up in the parking lot across from the courthouse. After paying for his parking spot, he made it in the courthouse just as K-Dog name was being called to stand before the judge.

The courtroom clerk stated, "The first matter on the docket is Criminal Number 03-182, Magistrate Section, the State of Louisiana vs. Kyron Youngblood," the court clerk stated.

"On July 29, 2005 Mr. Youngblood was arrested by Officer Stevenson for illegal carrying of a firearm. In the State of Louisiana, anyone carrying an unregistered weapon is in violation for illegally carrying a firearm. I've carefully and thoroughly reviewed your case, and I'm aware that you do not have a criminal record. With that being said, I set your bond at $8,000," the judge said, slamming his gavel before requesting that the clerk call for his next case.

Ben gave K-Dog a look like you'll be out soon, and with a mutual understanding, K-Dog, simply gave Ben a head nod as they took him out of the courtroom. Ben went straight to William Freeman, which was the same bondsman that got Donte' and Larry out. He paid the $800 dollars necessary to attain the bond before he and BJ headed back home.

***

Ronald went to Roxanne's room to wake her up for work. Ordinarilly, she would have been up at this hour, but when he made it to her room, the door was closed. He gently knocked on it, and Roxanne yelled "Come in," through the door,

"You better get up before you be late for work," he stated, once he entered the room.

"I'm taking today off," she replied, still underneath her covers.

Ronald refused to leave it at that, so he pulled her covers off of her and demanded that she get up. When she lifted her head, he noticed the bruise around her eye and immediately went into a rage

"What the fuck happened to your face?" he asked in a hostile tone.

"Nothing, now get out," she told him not wanting him to know that she was abused by Paul. She knew once he found out, he would react in an aggressive manner.

"What you mean nothing, your eye didn't get bruised on its own. Now tell me what the fuck happened," he said insisting on finding out what really happened to his sister's eye.

Even though Ronald is her baby brother, he played the role as if he were the big brother and she knew when he meant business so she gave in to his demands.

"Before you get upset, I want you to know that it was my fault."

"What was your fault, Roc?"

"Let me explain."

"I'm listening."

"Out of curiosity, I checked Paul's phone and when I did, I saw a bunch of female names in it. I was pissed, so I asked him who they were."

"Then what happened?" Ronald asked, forcing her to pause for a couple of seconds.

"Then he snapped about me checking his phone, so I reacted out of anger and shoved the phone in his face, and he slapped me. He busted my lip, so I spit in his face, and that's when he punched me. I know you're mad about him hitting me, but I had no business spitting in his face."

"That nigga ain't have no business putting his fucking hands on you from the beginning. I got something for that bitch-ass nigga," Ronald said, in a revengeful tone.

"I know what you thinking but don't even try it. I'm serious," Roxanne said on Paul's behalf.

"Where your phone at?" he asked, looking around the room.

Before she could answer his question, he grabbed her purse off the door knob and got her phone. He scrolled through it until he found Paul's number then pressed send.

Paul wasn't expecting a call from Roxanne after the way things turned out the previous night, but he was glad that she decided to call him. He felt bad about the way things had gone despite what she had done to provoke him.

"Before you say anything, I want to apologize for..." Paul said as soon as he answered the phone, but he was cut off by Ronald.

"Dawg you have to be out of your fucking mind putting your hands on my sister. You ole bitch-ass nigga."

Roxanne immediately jumped out of her bed while screaming, "Give me my phone Ronald!" she screamed, but before she could grab the phone, he extended his left arm to hold her back by extending and told Paul in a threatening tone.

"I'ma holla at cha though," He said in a threatening tone, and then he ended the call. He threw her phone on the bed and walked out her room. Still angry Ronald headed to the porch where Tony was at rolling a blunt.

The way Ronald slammed the screen door made Tony look up and ask, "What's wrong with you?"

"That bitch-ass nigga Paul beat Roc up last night," Ronald explained to Tony.

"That nigga did what?" Tony asked in disbelief.

"Yeah, Homie, then she trying to put the blame on herself like it was her fault."

"That nigga must be ready to die huh?" Tony stated.

"He must be," Ronald explained.

"Don't trip dawg, you already know what it is," Tony said, "Plus I'm still in my feelings about how he brushed me off when I asked him to start serving us work."

Hoping that Roxanne would answer her own phone, Paul called her back moments after Ronald ended the call with his empty threats. Paul knew if it came down to it, he would have to kill Ronald without thinking twice about it.

"Hello?" Roxanne said when she answered her phone.

"Why would you create a problem you ain't ready for?" Paul asked her in a serious tone.

"Don't worry about him," Roxanne replied.

"I'm not worried, but I don't appreciate how you got your brother calling my phone threatening me and shit."

"I didn't tell him to call you. When he saw the bruise on my eye, he tripped out and demanded that I tell him what happened, so I did; but I' never told him to get involved."

"Well, you need to talk to him before shit end up bad. because I don't take threats lightly. Don't get me wrong, I understand his position as a brother, I respect him for wanting to protect you, because I'm the same way about my sister."

"That's how he is, that's why I tried not to let him see my eye even though it's not that bad."

"Baby my whole night was fucked up after you left. I hate niggas that put their hands on a woman, and I turn around and do the same thing. Roc I promise you that it won't ever happen again."

"I hope not, but it wasn't all your fault, I have to take some of the blame as well."

"Roc, I'm really feeling you. I don't want to bring situations like this into our relationship."

"Let's just leave it alone, I forgive you and I hope you forgive me," Roxanne said.

"You know I'm really glad to hear you say that. Because the way you left last night, I thought it was over between us."

"I would never give up on us that easy. I was just embarrassed with the way you hit me in front of your friends. That's why I left the way I did. If we would have been alone, I assure you that the night would have ended differently."

"I want to make it up to you by taking you out to eat, or whatever you want to do. Maybe we can end the night with some make-up sex."

"A restaurant would be nice, but it will be a long time before we have sex again," Roxanne said.

"You got to be kidding, right?" Paul asked in a desperate tone.

"Yeah, I'm just playing, I think I'd like that," she said with a giggle in her voice.

"Well, you can meet me in the project at 5:00."

"Okay 5:00 it is," she said.

"Well I'll see you then."

"I guess you will," she paused. "Paul, I love you," Roxanne said, totally catching him off guard.

"I don't know if it's safe to say it, but I love you too," he said. "I'll call you later."

* * *

Rell or his crew didn't have a clue that the opportunity they'd been waiting for was about to fall in their lap. They were nearly out of the work Rell scored from Ben, and they needed to score again before they sold out completely. Sitting on the porch was Rell, Creature, J-Roc, and a childhood friend named Pookey who had recently come home two days before from a 30-month bid for a probation violation.

Pookey had been Rell's right-hand man before he went to prison, so Rell wanted to put him in a position to make his own money. But they were barely getting by themselves, so it was going to be difficult for him to put Pookey on his feet.

Pookey was one of those kids that practically raised himself, and for him to defeat poverty at its worst, he learned to survive in the streets at a very young age, by any means necessary.

If he had to rob, steal, lie or cheat to put a meal in his stomach and clothes on his back, he did it. He hadn't been home a week, when he was already making statements about robbing someone to get himself started.

"Pookey, be patient things gon get better, just give it a little time," Rell said.

Rell, Creature, and J-Roc managed to put together $1,000 to put in his pocket, a couple of Dickies outfits, and a pair of wheat colored Timberland boots.

Pookey didn't want to be sitting around waiting on something to happen. He was accustomed to going out and making things happen for himself, so watching niggas get their shine on in his hood only made him more impatient.

"I heard how the Cheddar Boys been making moves out chere, why them niggas ain't put y'all on?" Pookey asked out loud for anyone to respond.

"Them niggas doing them, we don't fuck with them niggas on that level," Rell said.

"Man, y'all been supposed to jack them niggas. Especially, that bitch-ass nigga Curtis. I better not catch that clown slipping, I'ma get that nigga," Pookey stated truthfully.

"I told you homie, just be patient, we gon be good," Rell told him. "We don't need them niggas," he continued to say.

"Whatever you have planned, I hope it happens soon. If not, I'ma do what I have to do to get mine"

Moments later Donte' came through the cut that was located across the courtyard. He walked over to the porch where Rell, Creature, Pookey, and J-Roc sat and asked Rell could he speak with him.

"What's up?" Rell said as he stepped off the porch.

"I got a reliable plug that keeps some good boy, and I want to fuck with y'all because we about to close down our bag shop. That way y'all can pick up where we leave off at and supply all of our clients. I mean, that's only if y'all want to fuck with it ya dig. It's something to think about. I'ma give it to y'all 3 racks, an ounce and the shit is taking a 3, so it's no way y'all can lose. Plus, I'm willing to serve y'all any amount that you think y'all can handle. So what's up, y'all 'bout that?" Donte' asked.

"I mean it sound good but we ain't really got no money like that, we kind of fucked up on the cool," Rell replied.

"Don't trip about that, I'ma front it to y'all. Just make sure y'all save y'all money. And when it's time, y'all can score y'all own shit. Cause whatever y'all spend, I'ma match it on the front tip."

Donte' then pulled a gram out of his watch pocket and tossed it to Rell.

"Make you some sample bags. If it's to your liking get at me and we can start doing business."

"That's what's up," Rell said as he dapped Donte' then turned to his niggas and said, "Man, it's on."

"What's on?" J-Roc asked him.

Rell then explained to his crew what they discussed, which brought a smile to all of their faces. Afterwards, they went in Rell's apartment and started making the sample bags. It was only a gram that they put a 2 on which made it 3 grams, so it took them 15 minutes to bag it up.

Once they finished, Ricky was the first person they gave a sample bag to. The quality of the product spoke for itself as to how good it was. Being that Ricky was found overdosed in a nearby hallway with a syringe still stuck in his arm, but due to the immediate assistance he pulled through.

When the word spread that Rell had some shit that they could overdose on, customers came to score from them in packs, so Rell got back with Donte' that same day and got two more ounces from him on a front.

After they bagged the two ounces up in all 25 dollar bags, they were officially open for business. Between the quality and quantity, of the product, it brought customers from all over the city to the Calliope to score.

Not only did they have all the Cheddar Boys clientele, they also started getting a lot of customers that usually scored in the Melph because for the past day or two the Slum Godds had been out of work. Causing their customers to go in the Calliope to score.

Creature went in a hallway to stash four bundles of dope, which was a hundred bags, in one of his old stash spots. Which was a mailbox to an abandoned apartment. When he opened the mailbox, he saw a key magnet box that he would use to stash his product.

"I been looking for this," he mumbled to himself as he slid the top part of the key magnet to see several small pieces of aluminum foil inside of it. It was the same dope that he accused Cadillac of stealing, he realized that he killed Cadillac for nothing.

Creature had a pain pill addiction. On a normal day, he would take at least 3 Xanax, and one of the side effects was memory loss, which happened often with Creature. At some point he would remember what it was he was looking for, or what he said in a particular conversation. He dumped the dope in his hand and counted 27 ten dollar bags. Instead of disposing of the old dope, he decided to keep it to sell without ever checking to see if it was still worth selling.

Exiting the hallway, Ricky rode up on his bike to ask Creature if he had more of the dope that he got from Rell that made him O.D.

Still holding the old dope in his left hand, he said, "Yeah, I got more. What's up?"

"Let me get seven bags for $150," Ricky stated, then went in his pocket and pulled out a handful of crumpled up bills and began to count out the $150 he was gon spend with Creature.

Once he separated the bills and handed them to Creature, Creature noticed that he still had a nice bit of money in his hand, so he made him a deal.

"For another 50 dollars, I'll give you these 27 bags."

"27 bags for 200 dollars, that can't be the same shit I got from Rell, because that's almost 700 dollars' worth of dope. Why would you sell it to me for only two hundred?" Ricky asked.

"Because these 10-dollar bags, that's why, and Rell gave you a sample of our 25-dollar bags."

"A'ight give'em here," Ricky said accepting the deal. "But don't try to play me cause you know I bring good business to y'all."

"Come on man, when you know of us playing games?" Creature asked him.

"You right, I'ma get back with y'all, just be out chere, cause the money rolling today. When Rell come back outside, tell him to stay posted up," Ricky said then rode off on his bike.

Ricky had been an addict most of his life, but on several occasions, he'd been used as a hitman because he never had a problem with killing, especially if the price was right. When he got to the Shooting Gallery, an apartment where all the users went to do their drugs regardless of what kind it was, coke, rock, heroin, it didn't matter, and the person who had the apartment sold everything from crack pipes to syringes.

When Ricky got there, he got ready to make a fix when he discovered that the dope was sticking to the foil, but he insisted on using it. When he finally scraped the dope off the foil and placed it on a spoon he started to melt it down, so he could draw it in his syringe.

Once he did that, he wrapped his belt around his upper left arm and held it tight by using his mouth. When he shot it, he didn't get the rush he was expecting plus the dope clogged his syringe up, so he immediately got pissed off because he'd specifically asked Creature was that the same dope that he got from Rell. He started replaying the event in his head when Creature threatened to rob him, so he grabbed a butcher knife from the kitchen on his way out the apartment.

Creature was sitting on the porch alone when Ricky approached him. The only other person around from their crew was Pookey, and he was busy trying to fuck a bitch from out the hood.

"Let me holla at you," Ricky told Creature.

The moment Creature stepped off the porch Ricky charged him with the knife stabbing him once in the forearm, and once in his left side.

As Creature began to tussle for the knife, Rell came out of the apartment. At first, he thought that they were fighting until he saw the blood on Creature's side, so he ran over to where the struggle was taking place and pushed Ricky back. That's when he noticed the large knife in his hand, and without giving it much thought, he pulled his .45 cal from his waist and shot Ricky three times in the chest killing him on the spot.

Rell turned to, Creature who was now laying on the ground clutching his side and helped him to his feet. The blood was draining from his wound like a running faucet when someone who ran to the scene yelled, "Don't move him, don't move him. That will cause him to bleed out more, wait until the ambulance gets here!"

"Damn" Rell said, as he laid Creature back on the ground before running inside to put his gun up.

By the time Rell made it back outside, Creature was lying in a pool of his own blood and he was unresponsive, but he still had a pulse. Fifteen minutes later the ambulance arrived and placed Creature on a stretcher, attended to him as he was rushed to the hospital. The paramedics declared Ricky D.O.A.

Rell and the crew went to the hospital to support Creature, but when they got there they were informed that he didn't make it. He had lost too much blood.

***

Strapped with a Glock 9 and four grams of heroin, Curtis Mitchell drove within the speed limit as he crossed the GNO Bridge to go to Christopher Holmes in the 15th Ward. He was trying to track down John Boy because he didn't have a number on him. He exited the bridge on General Degaulle Dr. and in five minutes he was riding through Christopher Holmes. He noticed a large group of niggas, plenty of women and several children as he scanned the crowd hoping to see John Boy.

It was his lucky day because he spotted John Boy leaning in the driver window of a car talking to a female. If he would have driven further into the neighborhood he would probably have gotten ambushed because the car he was driving was almost identical to the one a rival crew member named Doe drove.

He eased alongside of John Boy and tapped his horn twice causing him to turn around. When he looked back to see who it was, he saw it was Curtis Mitchell. So he told the female that he was talking to, to give him a minute, then he turned back to Curtis and said, "What's up nigga, what you doing on this side of the river?" as he leaned in the window of Curtis' Mercedes Benz.

"I came through to holla at you, and I knew I was gon see you out chere."

"I can't make no money sitting on my ass inside. I got to be out chere errday, but pull over though," John Boy told Curtis who then pulled to the side to allow the oncoming traffic to pass by. When Curtis pulled to the side and parked, John Boy approached the car and asked, "What up homie? I ain't seen you since Mardi Gras."

"I'm just chilling, trying to survive out chere in these wicked streets."

"So what you need to holla at me about?" John Boy asked him.

Curtis Mitchell handed him a gram of dope and told him to pass out some samples, and if he wanted to do business after he got some feedback from the junkies, he had ounces for 3 racks that's taking a three.

"I'ma see what it's like, and if it's legit, I'ma most definitely holla back at cha. The shit I'm getting right now, going for twenty-five hundred and it's only taking a one.

"Well look, here's my number, fuck with a nigga."

"Like I said, if the shit one hunid you will hear from me."

"A'ight then, I'm out," Curtis said, as he pulled off and headed to the 9th Ward to holla at a dyke bitch named Goldy who made moves in Press Park.

It took him twenty minutes to make it from the West bank to the 9th Ward. When he made it to Press Park, he saw Goldy sitting on a Milk Crate with a bad bitch sitting between her legs.

He got out the car and walked up to her.

"Look at my fucking nigga," Goldy said as Curtis walked up, "What it do Soulja?" she asked with a smile revealing all the gold teeth in her mouth.

Curtis gave her the same pep talk that he'd given John Boy and handed her a gram. As he got back in his car he headed to the 6th Ward to holla at Chuck in the Laffite Project since he was already downtown. Unfortunately, when he got there, he was told by Yodi, another dude that he knew that Chuck had been locked up for two months, for distribution of heroin and a gun. So instead Curtis arranged for them to start doing business.

His last stop was back uptown as he headed to the 17th Ward to holla at Pee-Wee and Dre in Hollygrove. Curtis had no idea that the niggas in Hollygrove had just had a shootout with another set in the 17th Ward named Pigeon Town an hour before. So, when he drove down Pee-Wee and Dre's street where they hung out, he immediately felt the tension.

He had a number on Dre so he called him. When Dre answered, he informed Curtis he was in the alley and would see him when he passed through.

Curtis wondered what the fuck was going on when he noticed how empty the street was and all the niggas were posted in different alleys. When he pulled up in front of the alley where Dre was, Dre told him to come in the alley because it was hot right now. The police had been riding like a motherfucker since the shootout, even though no one was injured.

Curtis made his point as quick as possible and left from around them niggas even quicker. When he made it back to the Calliope he rushed inside to take a shit and waited on a call from Goldy, Dre, Yodi, and John Boy. He knew that he had given them the best deal they would get, and the dope was good.

***

After leaving the bail bondsman, Ben dropped BJ off at home and went to the project. When he got there, him and Paul discussed K-Dog situation. Ben told him that the bond had been paid and that he'd be released sometime that day. In the meantime, they needed to figure out how they were going to get some work ASAP. They were losing out on money, and if they waited too long, they'd end up losing their customers.

"Did you holla at Ernest to see when he's sending another package?" Paul asked.

"You know what? I can do that right now Ben said as he pulled his phone out his pocket.

Ben made several attempts to call Ernest but kept going straight to voicemail. It was out of the ordinary for Ernest to have his phone powered off, so Ben assumed that maybe he was paranoid because of the Jackie situation. He tried calling

Ernest once more but got the same results. So he went to his car and got the phone that Bambi gave him out of the glove compartment and called Bambi.

When Bambi answered the phone, he didn't give Ben a chance to say anything. He immediately went into details about how the Feds went to Ernest's mansion and took him in for questioning. Bambi said that during questioning Ernest confessed to using Jackie to transport the kilo from Houston to New Orleans and he was being charged for the kilo of heroin. Bambi said he was going to lay low for a while and see how things play out with Ernest.

"Why in the fuck would he confess to that shit?" Ben asked.

"I don't have all the details about what happened yet. That's why I'm not moving nothing until I find out more. If he confessed during questioning I don't know how much he really said. So to be on the safe side I'm shuttin' everything down for right now, but when things get back to normal, you will be the first person I call," Bambi said and hung up the phone before Ben could reply.

Paul noticed the look on Ben's face when he hung up the phone, so he asked him was everything alright. Ben explained to him how Ernest confessed to sending the kilo with the mule, and it had Bambi shook up, so he wasn't moving anything for the time being.

"Damn, we fucked now," Paul said after hearing that the plug wasn't moving nothing right now.

"I got an idea, so don't panic homie," Ben said while staring at the ground.

"What you have in mind?" Paul asked him.

"To see if I can press that bitch-ass nigga Curtis Mitchell for some work. I just need to think how I'ma go at the nigga."

"Dawg, that nigga ain't gon fuck with you like that."

"If I can apply enough pressure on him he will, man, you know pressure bust a pipe. So you know what it will do to a weak ass motherfucker like him."

"That's some real shit," Paul said with a giggle in his voice. "Oh, yeah, you know Monsta come home Thursday, so we need to get him some clothes and shit to have him straight," Paul said.

"Dawg we don't need to worry about that, we can take him shopping once he touch down," Ben stated.

"I hope that nigga don't come home with all that black man this and black man that shit cause you know how those jail house Muslims is" Paul said.

"I'm glad to see that nigga trying to change his life. Cause the way we living, we can't do this shit forever," Ben said trying to open Paul's mind up for ideas.

"So what you trying to say?" Paul asked.

"What I'm saying is we need to start thinking how we can invest our money in some kind of business."

"I mean, I never thought about no shit like that, but what you had in mind a club or something?" Paul asked.

"Right now, homie, I really don't know. I just know we need to do something cause we can't do this shit forever and expect to last, feel me?"

Paul got the sense that Ben was serious about exploring his options to become legit, so he told Ben that he was down with whatever he wanted to do.

"You can believe that I'ma come up with something that gon benefit us as well as our families," Ben stated.

"That's what's up nigga, I see you on your grown man shit," Paul said while dapping him.

"Did you ever call Roxanne and apologize to her?" Ben asked him.

"Yeah, we straightened that shit out. Matter of fact, she gon come through at 5:00, so we can go out eat and talk about the whole situation."

"Five o'clock! Nigga it's ten after four and you need to go take a shower, cause I know your fucking nuts is sweaty as a motherfucker, you been out here in this heat all day.

"For real huh Dawg?" he said as he looked down at his watch, then told Ben that he was about to go shower and get dressed before Roxanne made it there.

"A'ight homie, I'ma fuck with you later. I see Roxanne got your ass right where she wants you," Ben said playfully.

"It's really the other way around," Paul shot back as he walked off.

When Paul went inside, Ben decided to call Curtis Mitchell 'bout the work, but as he scrolled through his call log, he ran across Sandra's number and he decided to call her first.

"Hello, what up beautiful?" Ben said soon as she answered the phone.

"I was just sitting here thinking about you," Sandra said in a truthful tone.

"You couldn't have been thinking about me that much, you ain't pick up the phone and call me. That was my purpose for giving you my number. For you to call me when I cross your mind."

"I was gon call you, I just needed to get my thoughts together before I did. I really don't have much experience when it comes to men."

"Let's get something understood, if we are going to communicate, I need for you to feel comfortable with talking to me, without holding back on your thoughts."

"Who said I was holding back on my thoughts?"

"You did, indirectly."

"And how did you come to that conclusion that I said something indirectly?"

Ben could hear the shyness in her voice when she spoke a little louder than a whisper.

"Because the first thing that came out of your mouth when you answered the phone was that you were just thinking about me. But you didn't call me to share those thoughts. So, what exactly was you thinking about before I interrupted those thoughts?"

"I was thinking about spending my birthday with you, and we could use that time to get to know each other a little better because I am attracted to you. But the only way that can happen is if I get my father's approval, and I really don't know what to expect from him. Being that I have never considered asking him to spend time alone with a man."

"Well if he approves, I will be more than happy to celebrate your birthday with you because I'm so attracted to you also. It would be my pleasure to get to know as much about you as you are willing to let me know."

"Well let me speak with my father and I will get in contact with you no matter what his decision may be."

"You never told me when your birthday is, not that it matters, because if I have something planned for that day, I would cancel it to spend some quality time with you."

"I wouldn't suggest that you cancel your plans, if you had any, but it's August 2nd," she said politely.

"Well, I'll be waiting on your call," Ben said.

"You won't be waiting for too long."

"Okay I'll talk to you then," Ben said before hanging up.

After hanging up with Sandra, Ben immediately called Curtis Mitchell.

"What up brah?" Curtis said as if Ben caught him at a bad time.

"I'm trying to score something. What y'all ounces going for?"

"I can give them to you for three racks a piece," Curtis said in an uncomfortable tone, because he knew that something wasn't right for Ben to call him to score.

"Dawg I got 18 racks. Let me get 9 ounces?" he said in more of a demanding tone than a negotiating one.

"If I do that, then I'm cutting my profit."

"Man, fuck all that, come through for a nigga," Ben said with aggression.

"Nigga, I'm already coming through for you, I'm just waiting on you to come through with that 50 grand," Curtis replied referring to the money for Donte' and Black Larry's demise.

"Speaking of that, what's up with that?"

"Check this out: this what I'ma' do for you: send me seventy-thousand and I'ma make sure you straight on both situations."

"Alright, that's what's up. But dog, don't play no fucking games with me."

"Nigga' I don 't play no fucking games you send that money and I got you, bruh."

***

When Roxanne turned into the Melphomene Project she called Paul and told him that she was outside waiting on him, but he wasn't completely dressed so he told her to come inside. She stepped out her car wearing a pair of blue Apple Bottom jeans that complemented her frame, a white buttonup blouse and a pair of white 6" heels.

When she entered the apartment, she called his name and from the bathroom he answered, "I'm right here baby."

She went to the bathroom to find him drying his dreadlocks with a big towel. She grabbed him around his waist then turned him to face her and gave him a deep, passionate kiss. When they came up for air, he told her that he'd be ready in a minute.

Ten minutes later, they were in his truck heading to Houston's Restaurant on St. Charles Ave. As they drove, Paul told her to remove the sunglasses that she was wearing to hide the bruise on her eye. When she did, he immediately felt guilty when he saw the damage he'd done to her face.

"Baby I'm so sorry, and I promise you that it won't ever happen again. I always remember what my daddy told me about hitting women."

"And what was that?" Roxanne asked.

"That if I have to put my hands on a woman, I don't need her."

"My daddy told me the same thing but from the woman's point of view."

"He told you right, because you don't need to settle for no man that abuses women and that go for me too. That's why I feel so bad because that's not my thing at all."

When they pulled up at the restaurant, Paul parked then turned to her and grabbed her by the chin and guided her face to his and kissed her softly on the lips. Then they got out the truck and entered the restaurant.

When they were seated, Paul ordered two shots of Hennessey while they waited on their ribs and fries to arrive. They talked about their expectations of each other and their do's and don'ts until the food came. When it did, Paul ordered two more shots even though the first two shots had started to kick in as he started to eat the ribs like he hadn't eaten in months.

Roxanne looked up from her plate when she saw how Paul was stuffing his mouth with food and said, "Boy slow down."

"You can sit there and try to eat all pretty and shit, that's on you."

***

Donte' walked across the courtyard to holla at Rell who was chilling on his porch pushing his product. When he reached the porch, he asked, "So how things working out for yall Rell'?"

"It's all gravy on this end, they loving this shit, it's moving faster than I expected."

"Dawg what happened with that shit with Creature?" Donte' asked.

"Dawg I don't know, all I seen when I came outside was them two fighting. So I ran off the porch to break them up because I saw blood on Creature's shirt and when I separated them, that bitch Ricky had a big ass butcher knife in his hand so I hit his fucking ass up. But knowing Ricky he probably was trying to rob Creature or something like that, cause you know them niggas ain't really like each other. That's cold the way Creature went out, man he let a fucking dope vick take him out on some fluke shit."

"Hold on homie," Donte' said when his phone started ringing. When he answered, all he said was, "Thanks luv, I appreciate that," then hung up the phone.

"Say brah I'ma holla at you. I just got a call saying that they just released that nigga K-Dog, I know I got his ass slipping now."

"We can hop on the dirt bike and go catch his ass right now," Rell told Donte'.

"A'ight let me go get my tool," Donte' said.

"Don't trip about that, you can use one of mine."

"Shit let's go then," Donte' said.

Rell went inside and got a 357 magnum out his brother's room and gave it to Donte'. They left and headed around to the Parish Jail to kill K-Dog.

***

K-Dog had just enough charge left on his battery to make a call, so he called Ben to come pick him up. When Ben saw it was K-Dog calling, he cracked a smile then answered his phone.

"I'm headed towards Tulane and Broad, and bitch hurry up. I feel naked without my tool on me, K-Dog said.

"I'm on my way, be by the courthouse, I'll be there in ten minutes."

It only took Donte' and Rell three or four minutes to make it around to the jail from the Calliope. They spotted K-Dog walking down Gravier St., so Rell pulled up next to him giving Donte' an easy target. Donte' shot twice striking K-Dog in his chest causing him to fall to his knees before he could react.

Rell stopped the bike and they both stood over K-Dog and fired several more shots into his body and head area. They quickly got back on the dirt bike and fled the scene leaving behind several shell casings from Rell's .40 cal.

When Ben and Trap made it to the Broad St. overpass, Ben called K-Dog's phone and got no answer.

"Man, where the fuck this stupid ass nigga at?" Ben said when he didn't see K-Dog and he didn't answer his phone.

"Try and call that nigga again," Trap told Ben.

This time when he called, a police officer answered the phone and asked, "Who is this calling?"

"Who the fuck this is?" Ben asked with an attitude.

"This is Officer Wright. Who am I speaking with?"

Ben's first thought was to hang up, but he decided to answer the officer's question.

"I'm a friend of Kyrons. Why?"

"It's no easy way to say this, so I'ma just say it. Kyron has been murdered, can you notify a family member so that they can identify his body? He's in the 3000 block of Gravier."

"I'll be there in a minute;" Ben said before hanging up.

"Who was that?" Trap asked because judging from the conversation, he knew it wasn't K-Dog.

"K-Dog just got killed," Ben said in a depressed tone.

"Ain't no fucking way, we just talked to that nigga," Trap said.

"That was the police who answered his phone."

"Where he at?" Trap asked.

"He said he on Gravier."

"Let's go around there and see what's up."

When they made it to the scene, they saw a witness talking to the police. The only information she had was she saw two men flee the scene on a motorcycle, and they had on helmets, so she couldn't get a good look at their faces.

Ben and Trap walked up to the caution tape and saw K-Dog body laid out on the pavement, they turned and left the scene. When they got back in the car, Ben called Paul and told him what happened.

***

After getting the call from Ben that K-Dog had just got killed, Paul immediately told Roxanne that they had to go. By Paul being slightly drunk, Roxanne told him that she would drive. As she drove, they both were very quiet, trapped in their own thoughts. As she approached the red light at Baronne and Martin Luther King, they were spotted by Tony and Ronald who were in route to the Magnolia after leaving out of the 10th Ward. They'd been trying to creep down on some niggas that they were beefing with, out the St. Thomas Project. "Ain't that that nigga Paul right there?" Tony said while pointing at Paul's truck as it sat at the red light.

"Yeah, that's him," Ronald said when he saw the SG sticker Paul had on the back of his window, as he lifted the SKS from between his legs.

Sitting two cars behind Paul at the red light, Ronald told Tony to pull on the side of him as he climbed in the back seat of the stolen Yukon.

Clutching his .45 cal, Tony swerved around Paul's Avalanche and pulled right up next to it and rolled down the windows and from the backseat Ronald opened fire, Boom…

Boom... Boom followed by shot coming from Tony's gun, Boca... Boca... Boca… as they let off over 20 shots into the driver's window and door.

Roxanne was struck from her left side, taking multiple of bullets in her side causing her to lose control of the vehicle and crash into a telephone pole. Paul was hit once in the upper leg, but Roxanne was dead with her head resting on the steering wheel.

The impact of the crash didn't bother Paul because the truck came to a complete stop and it never picked up speed. Paul held Roxanne in his arms as he sobbed.

"Wake up baby, please wake up baby!" he cried, knowing in his heart she was dead.

Ronald and Tony sped away leaving behind a clean murder scene because all the shells fell inside of the SUV they were driving.

***

Ben and Trap seen the flashing lights from a distance but thought nothing of it until Ben's phone started ringing.

"This Paul right chere, he might be looking for us around K-Dog murder scene."

"What's up homie, where you at?" Ben asked when he answered his phone.

"I just got shot, I'm on Martin Luther King, Roxanne dead," Paul said quickly through the phone.

"You got to be fucking kidding," Ben said then hung up.

"What now?" Trap asked.

"The lights we seen when we hit Martin Luther King, that was Roxanne and Paul, he said Roxanne is dead."

Before they had a chance to park in the project, they turned around and rode to the scene. When they got there they saw Paul being attended to by the paramedics, so they knew he was gon be alright. It was confirmed that Roxanne didn't make it when they saw the coroner pull up and remove the body bag from his van.

Wanting to see their work, Tony and Ronald rode back on the scene only to find out that the person they had just killed was in fact Roxanne. They made it back just as they were removing her body from the bullet riddled truck.

CHAPTER 30

Sitting on the porch in the project, Donte' gave details on how him and Rell killed K-Dog. He looked at Black Larry and said, "Remember I hollered at that bitch that work in Central Lockup."

"Yeah, what happened?" Larry stated.

"What you mean what happened? That hoe come through for a nigga, she told me when the nigga rolled out."

"You down bad dawg. You know you was supposed to come let me know it was going down," Larry said while shaking his head.

"But listen nigga, I was talking with Rell when she called. So me and him went and took care of it, I even had to use one of his guns."

"So how it went down?" Curtis Mitchell asked.

"I was on the back of Rell dirt bike, and Rell pulled up next to K-Dog. I hit that nigga with two quick shots, causing him to fall to his knees. That's when we got off the bike, stood over him and punished that bitch."

As Donte' gave details it made Curtis Mitchell uncomfortable because he knew that Ben was about to come down even harder and wouldn't stop until a lot of people were dead. Especially, if he found out it was the Cheddar Boys who killed K-Dog.

Knowing how Ben would think, Curtis Mitchell tried not to show any guilt. He decided he was gon call Ben about the nine ounces he had asked for the day before. But in reality, he didn't feel comfortable with going through with the call because of what went down with K-Dog. Curtis was hoping that Ben didn't know who killed K-Dog.

He left the porch and went inside, he decided to call Ben anyway.

"What's up? You gon serve a nigga or what?" Ben asked with aggression when he answered the phone.

"Yeah, I gotcha dawg, but I'ma send it by the lil' hoe Brittany. Just let me know when you want me to send her through."

"You can send her right now, fuck."

"Let me go holla at her, she'll be there in twenty minutes."

"That's what's up. Now since that's out the way, what's up with that issue we talked about?"

"Dawg I told you I can't get my main man killed. It won't be nothing to make it happen with Donte' and Larry."

Ben thought about it as he looked around the room at his niggas who were in a depressed mood because of the tragedy with K-Dog. Plus, the attempt on Paul's life that ended Roxanne's life and said, "I'll accept that."

"Then this shit is over right?" Curtis asked.

"Yeah, it would be over, but I want it to happen today."

"No problem but let me go holla at Brittany and send the work. By the time, she drops it off, you should be hearing from me."

"A'ight," Ben said before he hung up. He then went in the room and counted out 70 racks. When he came back, he looked at Lil' Mike and said, "You ready?"

"Ready for what?" Lil' Mike asked confused.

"Ready to put in some work. You always said that they don't know you, so here's your opportunity to put it down for the team, for Tre and K-Dog."

"Dawg you gon send him out there by himself? I think it would be safer if I went with him," Ryder stated.

"It's gon be hard for you to get up on them. They'll never see it coming from Mike, dawg trust me, and with the help of Curtis, he should be in and out like a bank robbery," Ben said.

Ryder gave him a look of uncertainty, so Ben stated, "Trust me homie."

"What's up with the work?" Paul asked as he reached for the bottle of Vicodin for the pain in his leg from the gunshot wound.

"That bitch Brittany gon bring the work in a few minutes, and when she do, Lil' Mike gon ride back to the Calliope with her. I'ma call you when it's time to make your move," Ben told Lil' Mike.

Twenty-five minutes later Brittany made it in the Melph with the nine ounces and gave them to Ben like she was told to. Before Ben gave her the money, he called Curtis to find out how and when the hit was gon go down. Curtis playing in the hands of the enemy told him to wait by the swimming pool for his call, thinking that Ben was gon put the work in himself.

When they hung up, Ben handed her the money and told her that he would give her an extra $1000 to let Lil' Mike hang out in her apartment for a little while. If money was involved, Brittany was down with whatever.

Moments after Curtis Mitchell hung up with Ben, Je'sus called "What's going on in the project?" Je'sus asked.

"Me, Donte' and Larry just chilling."

"Y'all better make sure that those niggas don't catch y'all slipping."

"We good homie."

"I'm on my way in the project right now, and when I get there we gon go in the Melph cause I know them niggas won't be expecting for us to make a move so tell Dee and Larry to be ready," Je'sus said.

"You sure you want to go in the Melph right now?" Curtis asked nervously.

"You acting like you ain't 'bout it."

"Come on dawg, don't start that bullshit."

"Well if you 'bout it, act like it. We can't stop laying them niggas down until we kill all them niggas. Especially, the way they did Lou."

"A'ight homie, I'll see you when you make it in the project."

***

Brittany gave Lil' Mike the key to her apartment when they made it in the Calliope, while she went to give Curtis Mitchell his money. Donte' and Larry were sitting on the porch when Brittany walked up and asked them where Curtis Mitchell was.

"He inside," Donte' told her, then moved to the side to allow her to pass. As she approached the door, but before she knocked, Curtis opened the door.

"Here you go," Brittany said as she handed him the money that was in a big brown paper bag.

"I appreciate that," he said and told her to come inside the apartment so he could pay her for her service. Once she got paid she left and went to her apartment.

Curtis was overwhelmed with guilt at the fact that he was about to get his homies killed. Although the more he thought about it, the more he realized that Donte' nor Larry were the problem. As long as Je'sus was alive, the war would never end. Je'sus had the mindset that he wouldn't stop till they were all dead. So, Curtis made the most difficult decision he had ever made, and that was to give the Slum Godds who they wanted.

From Brittany's hallway, Lil' Mike could see Donte' and Larry sitting on the porch. He wanted to put his identity to the test and if the opportunity presented itself he was gon make his move.

While heading towards Donte' and Larry, they never once paid Lil' Mike any attention. When he noticed that, he reached for his gun, but before he could actually get it out, his phone rung, so he stopped to answer it.

"What up?" he asked Ben.

"A white Range Rover is about to come through, punish that nigga."

"A white Range Rover, gotcha," Lil' Mike said then hung up. He turned and headed back towards Brittany's porch.

The moment he approached the stairs, he saw the white Rover pulling up and started walking towards it. By the time he got to it Je'sus was closing the driver's door and when he looked up, Lil' Mike had the gun pointed at him. Lil' Mike started shooting rapidly hitting Je'sus twice in the head killing him instantly. As he turned towards Brittany's apartment, a undercover police officer jumped out of a Durango and yelled, "Drop the weapon!" but Lil' Mike turned around and opened fire, striking the police in the vest.

When Donte' and Larry heard the shots, they pulled their guns and started shooting in the direction of the undercover police officer in plain clothes. After exchanging over 25 rounds, Lil' Mike ended up getting hit in the neck which killed him immediately. By the time, Donte' and Larry realized it was the police, several police rushed the project. They were focused on Je'sus and Lil' Mike, allowing Donte' and Larry to get away unrecognized.

Twenty minutes later, Rell showed up on the scene. He pulled the Cheddar Boys away from the crowd and told them that Lil' Mike was indeed one of the Slum Godds.

"I seen Lil' One walking towards us. Then he got a call and tuned around, but I didn't pay the lil' dude no mind," Black Larry said.

"We was probably the target if you seen what you seen before the call," Donte' said. "Then Je'sus pulled up and that changed their plans, but how the fuck they knew Je'sus was about to show up?" Donte' continued. "But most importantly, why would they spare us when we the real threat?"

"I don't know, but them niggas must have been watching us the whole fucking time. But from where?" Curtis Mitchell questioned as he looked around the courtyard.

Rell stepped to the side and called Ben to tell him that Lil' Mike had just gotten killed. In five minutes the Slum Godds along with Tiger and his crew stormed the scene. They got the attention of everyone as they made their way through the crowd passing up the Cheddar Boys in the process. Uncomfortable stares were exchanged between the two crews, but neither side said a word, but if looks could kill, everybody the SGs laid their eyes on would have been dead.

The undercover officer that did the initial shooting explained to his captain from the 6th District police station that he was conducting a surveillance on a group of young males that went by the name *The Cheddar Boys*. They were believed to be responsible for at least one murder, attempted murder, drug trafficking, and weapon charges. He explained that Victim #1 was the head of the group, and that Victim #2 approached him and murdered him. He continued by saying that once he identified himself as an officer Victim #2 turned and opened fire striking him in the vest. Which forced him to put the perp down.

The Slum Godds had seen enough so they left. That's when Rell walked over to Donte' and told him he knew a spot in Mid-City where they hung out at, then gave him a description of the house.

***

China called Diamond because she hadn't heard from her in a week or so and she was used to hearing from her every day.

"Hey girl," Diamond said when she answered the phone.

"Bitch what's up with you, you acting funny huh?"

"No girl, my momma been sick so I been bringing her back and forth to the hospital. So, any lil' spare time I manage to get all I can do is go to sleep," Diamond responded.

"Girl tell Ms. Sylvia I said I wish her the best and I hope that she gets well soon."

"Alright. So, what's been going on?" Diamond asked.

"Nothing, I was worried cause I ain't hear from you in a while. Oh, yeah, bitch you missed it. Gabriel and Ozoneisha tore it down behind that boy."

"Bitch what boy?" Diamond asked confused.

Girl the boy Bul, it was a big thing and he just stood there and watched."

"So what happened?" Diamond asked loving the gossip.

"Something about Bul was messing around with Ozoneisha, and Gabriel approached that girl instead of checking him. You know how Ozoneisha is. It went down, bitch you should have seen it, them hoes really tore it down, I ain't gon lie, both them hoes know how to fight."

"I bet your ass was all in," Diamond said while laughing.

"Bitch you know I was," China replied.

"So what you doing tonight?" China asked.

"It depends. But if I'm able to get away, what's up?"

"It's supposed to go down in Sam's tonight. It's an allblack party so let me know what you gon do."

"Alright, bye girl," Diamond said.

"Bye bitch," China said as she ended the call.

CHAPTER 31

"Even the air smells different," Monsta said to himself as he stepped off the Greyhound bus and inhaled deeply once he made it to New Orleans.

Wearing prison blues and carrying a bag that contained his most valuable possessions. His family pictures, law work and letters mainly from his girl Miecy who held him down the whole five years. He walked in the bus station and went straight to the pay phone to call Ben to come pick him up.

By the time Ben made it to the bus station it was 3:15 pm. When he looked around Monsta was nowhere to be found. Until he looked towards a far corner, that's when he saw him on his knees praying the Asr Salat. His new religion required he pray five times a day which he did. So Ben waited patiently until Monsta was finished before welcoming him home.

When Monsta rose to his feet, Ben greeted him with a long hug. "Welcome home baby," Ben whispered in Monsta's ear.

"It feels good to be home," Monsta said with a smile on his face.

"Well let's get out of here, the homies can't wait to see you," Ben said as he led the way to the car.

When they pulled out the parking lot and headed down Earhart. Monsta was looking out the window as if he were a tourist in his own city.

"Where we going?" Monsta asked when they passed the project.

"We have a spot in Mid-City where we get together and hang out when we need to get out the project."

When they made it to the house, the first thing Monsta noticed was all kinds of drug paraphernalia. There were plastic bags, small digital scales, and heroin residue that had been left on a plate from filling small bags that sold for twenty-five dollars.

"I haven't been out a day yet. I don't need to be around this. I'll end up violating my parole before I even visit with my P.O. for the first time," Monsta said, but his voice was drained out by multiple voices that was screaming at the same time.

"My fucking nigga is home! What's up, Homie? That's one of the Original Slum Godds," Ryder said.

Fred waited until everyone greeted Monsta. He then walked over with a slight limp and introduced himself by extending his right hand to dap Monsta.

"What it do, Homie?" Fred said.

Even though Monsta spoke back, his facial expression motivated Fred reply, "I know you don't know me, but I'm Fred. I been rocking with the team for a minute now."

Monsta looked at Ben, then back to Fred and said, "I'm Mon...", but before he could finish giving him his name, Fred cut him off.

"I know who you are, I was just waiting for the day to meet you."

"I don't know what you heard about me, some of it might be true, and then some of it might be exaggerated. But, I live a different life now."

"Come on dawg, don't come home with that jail house ass shit," Trap said from across the room.

"I'm serious, I don't desire anything the streets has to offer. From the looks of things, it don't seem like the streets have much to offer. Looks to me y'all is in the same position y'all was in when I left 5-years ago."

"That's where you're wrong at," Ben stated. "We're on another level for real homie."

"Y'all might have a little more money, if that what you was insinuating, but trust me, y'all on the same level. If them crackers lock y'all up today or tomorrow, how long would y'all family be able to support the house after the money ran out. Because one thing about drug money is this, if it ain't coming in on a consistent basis, it will get away from you. If y'all got it like you say y'all got it, y'all would start thinking like the white man. Investing into a business instead of blowing your money on high priced clothes and cars. At least a business could possibly be around for generations." As Monsta spoke, he had everyone's attention.

For a person like him to be speaking on that level, they had to take what he was saying into consideration.

"While I was locked up I took a real estate class and y'all would be surprised how easy it is to buy some of this property right here in this city."

"It ain't nothing like dope money," Fred stated.

"That's exactly how the white man want you to think Lil' Brother. That's why they pump hundreds of kilos a month into the black community, so we can think just like you."

"I like the idea," Ben said. "But I don't know the business, the streets is all I know, and that's what I'm good at."

"The only way you gon learn anything, is you have to apply yourself. Like I said I've learned the business, so if you want to get involved, I'll teach you everything I know about real estate."

"We gon talk later, but right now we need to get you out those clothes. So let's go to the mall," Ben said.

"I really wanted to go see Miecy first. But, I guess I can go after we come home from the mall," Monsta said while looking down at the clothes he had on.

Trap was the first one to the door. When he opened it, Donte' and Larry had just turned on their street and spotted Trap the moment his feet touched the second step. So Black Larry took aim through the window and opened fire. But, with his quick reaction Trap was able to rush back in the house pushing Ben and Monsta on the way.

"How the fuck did them niggas know where this house is?" Trap said after he slammed the door shut and pushed himself up from the floor.

"It had to be that nigga Rell," Paul said. "He the only person besides us know about this house. Ben, I been told you not to trust that nigga."

"Naw homie, he ain't do no shit like that because he know the finger would point back to him," Ben said.

"But if the plan was to get us killed, then what difference would it make?"

"It probably was that bitch Brittany," Fred said. "That's why I said he shouldn't have brought that bitch over here."

"I forgot he had that hoe with him. It's known that she be fucking with them niggas because she dropped that package off for Curtis. She probably did tell them niggas 'bout the house." Ben said.

"That hoe got to get it," Ryder said with an evil look on his face.

"I need to get the fuck out of here before the police come. Right now, just thank Allah that no one was injured." Monsta said.

"Well let's go to the project," Ben insisted as he handed Paul his crutches.

***

"Where you going nephew?" Jack Rabbit asked Tiger when he came out of his apartment and headed towards a cut that led to the Slum Godd's set.

"I'm about to go holla at these niggas and see what really happened with K-Dog. I didn't see them niggas none yesterday," Tiger said.

"Listen brah, that's they problem, let them deal with it, we need to focus on what we got going on. What you need to be doing is trying to score something."

"I'ma holla at Paul about that too. But, at the same time I fuck with them niggas and I ain't about to stop now just because they beefin'. Say brah I do what the fuck I want to do anyway, ya heard me?"

"Yeah, I heard you, but when I was young, doing what you wanted was reserved for grown folks. You talkin' like you obligated to fuck with them niggas, but I don't see them niggas fucking with you like that. The most I see is y'all doin' business, and that's it. The niggas I see you fuck with on a daily basis is Hood and Poppa, but do you nephew?"

Without responding, Tiger went through the cut and when he entered the courtyard he seen all the SGs walking towards Paul's apartment. He yelled for Paul to stop because he was the last one out the crew to make it to the porch because he was on crutches.

"What's up playboy?" Tiger asked when he made it to him.

"These fucking crutches killing me," Paul replied as he struggled to walk with the crutches.

"I'm sorry to hear what happened to your girl," Tiger said with sympathy in his voice.

"I appreciate that homie, but she was dealt a fucked-up hand, she ain't deserve that."

"I feel that, but you know what they say, the good die young, and the bad die even younger," Tiger said.

"It would mean a lot to me if you, Poppa, and Hood come to her funeral at New Hope church Monday."

"What you asking is nothing, we'll be there. But what I want to know is who that was that done the shooting."

"Like I told Ben, all I seen was a black SUV pull up then the shots went off," Paul said.

"What's popping Tiger?" Trap asked as he waited on the porch to help Paul up the stairs.

"I'm trying to find out what's popping."

Ben came back to the porch to see what was taking Paul so long only to find him and Trap talking to Tiger.

"What's up Soulja?" Ben asked.

"Shit, you tell me, you already know I'm with it."

"Come in," Ben told him.

"We got to make it quick cause I'm already running late to go see my little girl. So how this shit going down?" Tiger asked the moment he walked in the living room where everyone was.

Ben didn't want to mention anything about the shooting in Mid-City because nobody really knew about the spot and he wanted to keep it that way.

"We need to catch all them niggas at one fucking time. Cause I'm getting tired of this back and forth shit," Ben said.

"On the real, cause we've lost three niggas already," Ryder said.

Monsta sat quietly as they discussed what they thought needed to be done. He knew that if they didn't leave the game alone, eventually they would all end up dead or in prison.

What we gon do with Rell?" Paul asked.

"Look homie, I'ma be in the Middle Court, holla if you need me. Oh, yeah, I'm trying to get a two and a quarter if you straight," Tiger told Ben.

"I got it," Trap told Ben then went in the kitchen and removed a plastic bag out of a cookie jar. He weighed out 63 grams and served Tiger.

When Tiger got the work, he left out the kitchen door which led to the driveway.

Ben then called Rell and told him to meet him in the project. However, Rell told him he was already in route and he'd be there any minute.

"Let me go wait on the porch, dude said he'll be pulling up any minute," Ben said then walked outside.

Just as he spoke, Rell pulled up in the Melph a couple of minutes later. Ben went to meet him as he got out of his car.

"Say brah, I ain't accusing you of no shady shit, but my spot in Mid-City got shot up today. You the only person that knew about the house besides my niggas."

"You said you ain't accusing me, then you turn around and accuse me of some bullshit like that. I thought you was calling 'bout that money I owe you but you on some other shit. Nigga I been 100 with you since day one, so I don't know why you'd think I'd do some shit like that. Nigga if I wanted you dead I would've been killed you. You tripping homie, but you know what, that bitch Brittany's most likely the one who told them niggas bout the house. I saw her go by their trap house yesterday, that dirty bitch," Rell said as he dug in his pocket and gave Ben the money he owed him. "But my fault for bringing that bitch to your shit, but I'ma clean up the mess I made."

"So what you have in mind?" Ben asked.

"It ain't but one solution to this problem homie," Rell responded.

"We'll handle it then," Ben said.

"Don't even worry about that, it will get handled SOON!" Rell said stressing the word soon.

***

As Donte' was expressing his frustration for missing the SGs when they were in Mid-City, his phone rang. He didn't bother to look to see who the caller was, he just removed his phone from its clip and flipped it open.

"Hello."

"Are you busy?" Stacy asked him.

"Not really... Why… what's up?"

"I need to talk to you," she said in a demanding tone.

"A'ight, go ahead I'm listening."

"I'd rather talk in person, can you come to my house now?"

"Yeah, I can do that, I'm on my way, but what's it about?"

"We'll talk when you get here."

"A'ight," Donte' replied then hung up.

"That was Stacy, she told me she need to talk to me. From the vibe she had it might be something serious."

"You want me to ride with you?" Larry asked.

I don't think it's nothing like that, it might be something concerning that nigga K-Dog."

He grabbed his gun off the coffee table then left the apartment and got in his car to head to Stacy's house. It only took 15 minutes to make it there because the traffic was light.

***

"We can't bag the shit up right now. We ain't got no cut, we used the last bit we had on that last package," Poppa said.

"Well look, I'm about to go see my lil' girl. I'll stop and get some cut on my way back," Tiger said.

"Ain't shit going on right now. I'ma take that ride with you," Hood said.

"Well fuck it, I'ma take that ride too," Poppa said.

Before hitting the interstate to go to the West Bank, they stopped at a corner store and bought a cigar, rolled up a gram of purp and got back on the road.

When they tuned on Tullis Dr., the street Stacy lived on, a police car was riding slowly on the opposite side of the street as the officer looked at Tiger's car. Tiger almost panicked knowing they were all carrying weapons but luckily the police moved on and didn't conduct a traffic stop.

When Tiger pulled up in front of Stacy's house he saw another car parked in her driveway.

"That look like that nigga Donte' car," Hood said from the backseat, when he noticed Donte blue BMW.

"I know that nigga ain't fucking with my bitch," Tiger said.

"I'm glad I still have a key," he continued to say as the three of them got out the car.

***

"I thought you told me that that boy was your friend," Stacy said looking Donte' in the eyes.

"Who the fuck you talking about?" Donte' asked.

"That boy who got killed by the jail, please tell me you ain't have nothing to do with that."

"What kind of question is that? That's the reason why I ask you to tell me when he was about to get out. So I could have been there when he stepped out of Central Lockup. By the time you called me, he had already left the jail. I'm thinking you was gon call me when he first started getting processed for release. If you had, my fucking homie would probably still be alive."

"I'm sorry," she said as she scooted closer to him and tried to give him a hug but he pushed her away and said, "Sorry ain't gon bring my nigga back."

"You trying to make it seem like what happened to him is my fault."

"Momma, can I have a freeze pop?" Devine asked when she walked into the living room. As she noticed Donte' she said, "Hello Mr. Donte'."

"I can't get a hug?" Donte' said.

Devine smiled, revealing the four silver caps on her front teeth, walked over and gave him a hug. Just as Devine and Donte' embraced. Tiger entered the house using his key.

Bitch you playing with me, you got this nigga around my lil' girl," Tiger said with the sound of death in his voice.

"Give me my key Devin, you lied and told me you lost it. You ain't got no business being in here."

Tiger pulled his gun and told his daughter to move away from Donte'. When he did that Hood and Poppa pulled their guns as well. With no way out of the situation, Donte' grabbed Devine and put his gun to her head.

"Donte'! What you doing?! That's my baby! Please Donte' let her go!" Stacy said pleading.

"It's two ways this can go down, y'all can back away and leave. Or the murder rate can rise starting with her," Donte' said while holding the gun to the little girl's head.

"Please just leave Devin!" Stacy cried out between sobs as she ran and grabbed her phone.

"I'm about to call the police!"

"Come on dawg, let's get the fuck outta here," Poppa said. "Daddy I'm scared," Devine said with a face full of tears.

"Dawg it ain't the time right now," Hood said. "But we gon most definitely get that nigga."

Looking at his daughter, and the position she was in Tiger lowered his gun and started to back out the house. Before he made it completely out the house he told Donte' that he was gon see him again. Donte' responded by telling him, when he sees him again, it won't be in the same situation.

When they got in the car and pulled off, Donte' looked out the window to make sure they all got in the car. At that point he ran quickly to his car and left Stacy's house.

***

While counting money in the kitchen, Black Larry and Curtis Mitchell discussed their next move on getting more work once they ran out of what they had.

"We should be 200 plus strong when we finish with this package. All we need to do is find a reliable plug," Curtis Mitchell said.

"What we gon do with Je'sus' share of the money?" Larry asked.

"We gon cover whatever expenses it cost to bury him and we'll split the rest between us."

"You don't want to give his momma the rest?" Larry asked.

"We can but she'll be able to keep the insurance policy if we cover all the funeral expenses." Curtis answered.

"Yeah, you right."

"But this is what I was thinking, Je'sus owe Giovanni a hundred racks right?"

"Yep."

"So if I can find a way to pay him what Je'sus owe him. Plus spend a hundred racks with him, we might end up with the plug."

"That would be Sweet, but how you gon get in touch with him?"

"That's the only problem but we'll think of something cause the money can't stop coming." Curtis said.

While they were discussing business, Donte' stormed in the apartment and slammed the door.

"That's you Dee?" Larry yelled from the kitchen.

"Yeah, this me," Donte' replied. "Je'sus told me not to fuck with that stupid ass hoe."

"What hoe?" Larry asked.

"That hoe Stacy."

"What happened?" Curtis asked.

"Man, I wasn't by that bitch 20 minutes when that nigga Tiger and two of his homies come in that motherfucker. When that nigga seen his little girl hugging me that fool tripped out and upped his tool. When he did that the two niggas that was with him upped something with extensions in them."

"So, what happened?" Larry asked with an attitude.

"It wasn't nothing for me to do but grab his daughter. When I did, I put my gun to her head and told them niggas we can go out blasting or back the fuck up. With his lil' girl's life on the line he backed down and left allowing me to get the fuck on. But if his daughter wasn't there I'd be dead like a motherfucker homie."

"That's why we need to lay low. The way shit going, the Feds gon fuck around and get involved. We most definitely don't need them bitches on our line," Curtis said hoping he could get Larry and Donte' to fall back with the beef shit. He told them to just focus on getting money but as usual, Donte' was rebellious.

"Nigga lay low?! Fuck that! We in too deep to even consider laying low. Those niggas most definitely ain't talking about laying low, and now, Tiger and his crew is involved we already know those niggas is more reckless than the SGs. when it come to this type of shit. So right now it's all or nothing ya dig. I ain't 'bout to back down from no nigga out chere, I'd rather die first."

Before Curtis Mitchell could comment, his phone rang.

"This is what it's all about right chere," he said when he saw it was John Boy calling.

"What up homie?" he asked when he answered the phone.

"Dawg, they loving that shit, we need to meet ASAP," John Boy said.

"We can arrange that; can you meet me uptown?"

"Yeah, where uptown?"

"Meet me on Earhart and Galves.

"I'm on my way right now, it's the same shit, right?"

"Yeah, nigga, hit me up when you make it around here."

"A'ight. One," John Boy said then he hung up.

"Listen my nigga," Curtis Mitchell said once he hung up his phone, "I agree that we in too deep, but we can't get caught up in the beef shit and or allow it to blind us on the things happening around us. The war ain't just with the SGs, it's against everything and everybody that's not with us. Think about it, didn't you say the police that y'all was shooting at had on plain clothes?" he asked Donte'

"Yeah but…"

"Hold on listen to me. What do you get out of that?"

"Out of what?"

"See what I'm saying? You so caught up with the beef you losing focus. Because the way I see it, if an undercover was right on the scene when Je'sus got killed, then most likely he was already there watching us. It was plain luck that they didn't notice y'all shooting or we wouldn't even be having this conversation. How many signs you have to get to realize them people on us. As long as we on this shoot 'em up bangbang shit, it's gon increase our chance of getting hit. For right now we have the luxury of being away from the block and still make our money."

Twenty-five minutes later John Boy called Curtis back. He told him he was approaching the red light at Claiborne and Earhart, so Curtis gave him the directions to his location. Shortly after John Boy pulled up in a Grand Prix. When Curtis spotted him, he walked up to his car and asked him how much he was trying to get. John Boy told him he wanted 4 ounces. Curtis only had one ounce on him so he gave it to him then ran in the apartment and got the other 3 and gave them to John Boy as well. John Boy then handed Curtis a fist full of cash.

"Do I need to count this right now?" Curtis asked as he looked at the large knot of cash.

"If it was me I would count it, but it's all there," John Boy said.

A'ight nigga. Watch them people, they be hot up here homie."

"That's why I'm 'bout to get the fuck from up here."

"A'ight baby holla."

When Curtis got inside, he threw the money on the table, "It took five minutes for us to make 12 racks, that's gotta be better than beef."

Curtis phone started ringing again, this time it was Goldy calling.

"What's up Red?"

"You. What's up, come fuck with me," Goldy told him.

"I'm tied up right now, you can't come up here?" Curtis asked.

"Yeah, I can do that. Have me a two and a baby ready when I get there."

"How long you gon be?"

"Give me about 30 minutes."

"A'ight Red, I'll be waiting on you."

CHAPTER 32

Saturday 10:30 A.M.

Flashes of the incident that claimed Roxanne's life had filled Paul's head ever since it happened. The closer it got to the funeral the more he couldn't block out the images of Roxanne's bloody body as it rested motionless on the steering wheel.

Sticking to the plan, Paul went to the barber shop to try and steer Tiffany away from it, but he decided to get an edge up while he was there. That way he would have minimized his suspicion. When Paul walked through the door on his crutches he noticed that the shop was filled with the normal Saturday crowd.

Several people expressed their sorrow for his loss. Some of them genuine, and others just felt like it was the right thing to do in this situation. Many of them told him that they were there for him if he needed them to help out in any way.

"The only way y'all can help at this point is by keeping your ears open and let me know who the shooter was," Paul said as he made his way to a seat.

"That's a shame how that girl got killed," one female said while shaking her head under a hair dryer.

"You really don't know who it was?" Tiffany asked Paul while she ran a comb through the hair of a client.

"Not really. Who was it?" Paul asked as his body tensed up.

"I heard that it was her brother, they say he tried to kill you but made a mistake and killed her."

"Girl you lying," a customer stated in a surprised tone.

"I'm just saying what I heard," Tiffany said.

Then she asked him when did they start beefing because that's the first time she heard some shit like that. Paul's mind went blank after hearing Tiffany mention that Ronald was the reason why Roxanne was dead, but, in all reality he knew he was the reason. It would have never come to that if he would not have hit her.

"You alright Paul?" Tiffany asked him when she noticed the distant look on his face and he didn't respond to her question.

"Yeah I'm good," he said when he snapped out of his thoughts.

"Where did you hear some shit like that at?" Duck asked Tiffany.

"You know I got my sources, but like I said that's what I heard."

"I think you got the wrong information this time," Paul said hoping that wasn't true.

"One thing about it, Ms. Tiff don't get the wrong information, I get the 411 straight off the press," Tiffany said which made some of the people burst into laughter.

"Come on Paul, you know she Channel 4, 6, and 8 News, that bitch in everything but a casket," one girl said while laughing.

It won't be long before she be in one, Paul thought to himself. Paul rose to his feet and told Tiffany to let him speak with her outside for a minute. When they got outside, Paul told her that he gon need her to help him get some things in order for Roxanne's funeral. She told him that she'd help out in any way she could. She figured it would be easier to find out everything that was going on if she was personally dealing with the situation at hand.

"What time you gon get off?"

"I have one more head to do after the one I'm doing. Let's say I'll be finished in about 3 hours."

"That's perfect timing just call me off the shop phone when you ready."

"Why I got to call off the shop phone?" she asked curious, because something didn't seem right about that. But her love for gossip clouded her better judgment.

"It's a long story, just call from the shop phone."

"Okay, I gotcha'," Tiffany said before going back into the shop.

Paul didn't go back in, he just peeped in the door and told Duck that he would holla at him later. Then he left and headed to the house in Mid-City where Ryder, Trap, Ben and Fred were waiting on him.

***

"Babe, what time do you have to see your parole officer?" Miecy asked Monsta from the bedroom.

"Any time before 4 P.M.," he yelled from the bathroom as he brushed his teeth.

Even though Miecy stood by Monsta's side throughout his bid, she had become involved in a relationship with a dude by the name of Macho. Though she never allowed him to come in between what she and Monsta had.

When Monsta finished in the bathroom, he entered the bedroom where Miecy was changing out of her night gown and in to a pair of Capri jean shorts.

"So what's your plans now that you're out," she asked as she put on her clothes.

"I took a real estate class, so I'm leaning towards getting involved with that."

"Boy it gon take money to get involved in a business like that."

"I already know. I talked to Ben about that though."

"Please don't tell me you plan on getting back in the streets already," Miecy said cutting him off.

"Come on babe, give me some credit, I gave you my word that I'm done with the streets. It may take a little money to get started but not much. I want to target duplex housing that's up for foreclosure."

"So how you gon come up with the LITTLE MONEY that you gon need to get started?"

"Like I was saying before you jumped into conclusions, I talked to Ben and he wants to invest in my plan."

"I haven't saw that boy in a long time, what is he into?"

"Let's just say ain't nothing changed with him."

"You ready?" Miecy said as she grabbed her clutch purse off the bed.

"I guess I'ma go to the P.O.'s office on Franklin Ave., cause I know I don't have to go to the one on St. Charles Ave."

"They ain't tell you which one you have to go to?"

"My release address is a downtown address so most likely I have to go on Franklin."

"Okay let's go see," Miecy said as they left the house.

When they got in the car, Miecy told him that she wanted him to have a phone when he came home but it slipped her mind. So she told him once they finished at the parole office, they'd go get him one.

***

When Paul made it to Mid-City he told the crew that everything was set up for Tiffany to contact him. Four hours later, once the shop cleared out Tiffany called. She asked him did he want her to meet him somewhere or was he going to pick her up.

"I'll come pick you up but be outside so I don't have to worry about getting out the car."

When Paul picked Tiffany up the first thing she asked was whose car he was driving. Next she asked him what they were about to do, so he told her that he wanted her to help him pick out some flowers. As they rode around, Paul was real quiet. However, he noticed that Tiffany kept looking at him, so he asked her why.

"Normally you would be flirting with me. With you being so quiet it lets me know you really liked that girl."

"Yeah, I did."

"I know this ain't the time for this, but if you want to get together and hang out when we finish, I'm cool with that." Tiffany said, after being quiet for a few minutes.

"Naw I'm good, maybe some other time."

When they made it to the Mid-City area, he told her that he needed to stop by his cousins to pick something up. The minute they made it to the house, he asked if she would hand him his crutches. She got out and grabbed his crutches off the backseat and handed them to him. Once he got out he leaned up against the front fender before heading to the door.

When he opened the door, he glanced over his shoulder and asked her in. When she entered the house, something just didn't feel right. Especially, when she saw duct tape and a rope on the coffee table plus all the SGs in the living room.

"What's up Tiff?" Ben said once the door closed, but the way he said it was real creepy.

Before she could have possibly answered, Ryder grabbed her around her neck and slammed her really hard on the floor. She was so scared she urinated on herself while she was crying and screaming.

"What's he doing Ben? Please stop him!" She cried.

"Tie that bitch up!" Ben told Ryder who picked her up off the floor like a bag of feathers and slammed her in a wooden chair using all his strength.

Fred picked the rope up off the coffee table and started tying her hands and feet to the chair. Once she was secured to the chair, Ben called Duck and told him to come to the address he gave him ASAP. He also asked if he would stop to get some firecrackers.

When he hung up the phone he slapped Tiffany hard across the face. Demanding that she tell him where Butch was.

"I don't know where he at. I swear Ben, please let me go!" she cried out.

"Man let's just kill that bitch and be done with it," Fred said while holding a gun in his hand.

"Naw brah, we ain't gon kill her. We just need to know where that nigga at," Ben said convincingly.

"I don't know where he at Ben! I swear!" she continued to cry out.

"Bitch you knew how to get in touch with him when you set Duck up," Ben snapped.

When he said that, her eyes stretched as wide as saucers as she cried out, "Ben! That wasn't me! I ain't have nothing to do with that!"

Ben slapped her again and shouted, "You lying bitch, remember when I saw you with that nigga. That's when he told me you set Duck up to get jacked, you snake bitch."

"That wasn't me Ben I swear," she said with a tremble in her voice.

Ben's phone started ringing and when he answered, it was Duck asking the address again so he gave it to him.

"Hold on, tape that bitch's mouth up, I'm sick of hearing her."

"What's going on over there?" Duck asked.

"You'll see when you get here."

***

When Monsta and Miecy left the parole office they went straight to get him a phone. Once he got it, Ben was the first person he called.

Ben thought it was Duck calling, so when he answered, he said, "You still can't find the house?"

"Who you think you talking to?" Monsta asked him.

"Oh my bad, I thought you was somebody else. So what's up homie?"

"Just trying to see what y'all off into before I come around, cause I ain't trying to get caught up."

"Right now ain't a good time, is this your number?"

"Yeah, the babe just got it for me."

"Where she at?"

"She right here."

"Tell her I said hello."

"Babe, Ben said hello."

"Tell him I said hi."

"Well look I'ma go holla at Moms. Get at me when you finish taking care of your business."

"A'ight my nigga, one"

"One," Monsta said then hung up.

***

When Duck arrived at the house in Mid-City, he had no idea what was waiting for him on the other side of the door. He grabbed the bag of fireworks off the passenger seat before he got out of the car.

Tap, Tap, Tap, Tap, Tap, was the sound of the knocks that echoed off the wooden door when Duck rapidly tapped on it. When Ben opened the door, Duck couldn't believe it when he saw Tiffany tied up to a chair with tape over her mouth.

It was obvious that she had been beaten. Her face had multiple contusions, her eyes were swollen to the point where they were nearly closed, and her nose was twice the normal size and leaked a mixture of blood and mucus.

"What the fuck going on?" Duck asked trying to make sense out of what he was seeing.

"Close the door," Ben demanded.

When Duck closed the door he asked Ben once more, what was going on. Without responding, Ben pulled Duck's .357 magnum.

Duck quickly put his hands in the air and asked, "What you doing homie?" in a nervous tone. At that moment, he noticed his gun and immediately assumed that the SGs were the ones who robbed him, so he asked Ben where he got it from.

At that point Ben removed the tape from Tiffany's mouth and she instantly started pleading.

"I'm sorry Duck! I'm sorry!" but he had no idea what she was sorry for.

"That's the bitch that set you up to get robbed and the nigga that robbed you is the same motherfucker that's responsible for me getting robbed. I'ma deal with him, with her help," Ben said as he slapped her in the back of the head.

Duck was too shocked to say anything, he just looked at Tiffany with pity in his eyes because he knew she wasn't leaving the house alive. Ben handed him his gun and told him he'd better deal with her or he would.

When Duck did speak, all he could ask her was, "Why! Why did you do it Tiff?!"

"I'm sorry Duck, he made me do it!"

"Fuck all that bullshit, where can we find this nigga?" Ben aggressively asked.

"I don't know where he at!"

"If she ain't gon tell us where he at, then we don't have no use for her," Fred said when he put his gun to her head.

"Hold on," Paul said as he hopped over to her with one crutch. When he got to her he started pulling her pants down and stated, "I told you I was gon get some of this pussy one day."

"What you doing?" Duck asked when Paul pulled down her pants and underwear exposing her pussy.

"Damn her pussy fat," Fred said as he looked between her legs.

"It's gon be even fatter when I finish with her," Paul said as he dug in the bag of fireworks and pulled out a M-80 firecracker.

"Please don't hurt me, Paul," she begged with trembling lips.

Paul lit a firecracker to give her an example of what she'd be facing if she didn't give them Butch's location. The sound of the firecracker was as loud as a 9mm pistol. He then reached in the bag and grabbed another firecracker and told her that the next one will go inside of her pretty little pussy if she didn't tell them what they wanted to know.

"Okay, Okay," she cried. "All I know is where his momma live, she lives on the Louisiana Parkway in a brick house with yellow trimming."

"Don't let me find out you lying, but just to show you I ain't bullshitting..." Paul said before he stuck the firecracker in her pussy and lit it. The pain was so excruciating that Tiffany passed out.

"Oh shit!" Fred shouted when the firecracker popped and ripped her pussy apart causing blood to ooze out.

Ben looked at Duck who was just standing there holding his gun with a disgusted look on his face, and said, "What you waiting on?"

Duck stuck the .357 between her legs and shot her once in her pussy, then he placed the gun to her head and shot her five more times. The force of the large weapon knocked her and the chair to the floor.

"That's what I'm talking about," Ryder said as he looked over at her body.

"Man, let's throw that bitch's body in the backyard or something," Fred said.

"Fuck no, we ain't gon put that hoe in the yard. We'd be asking for an investigation," Trap said.

"Throw that hoe on the streets, put her under the house, I don't care, we just need to get her outta here," Paul replied.

"I know a spot where they would never find her body," Ryder said.

"And where is that?" Ben asked curiously.

"They have a spot in between Slidell and the East, ain't nothing out there but swamp, I promise no one will ever find her."

"How you know about a spot like that?" Paul asked.

"How you think?" Ryder said with a chuckle.

"Well that's settled then, you and Trap go get rid of her body, and me and Fred gon check out the house she said dude momma live in," Ben said as he gave Fred a head nod towards the door.

"I guess I'm supposed to sit back and chill huh?" Paul asked.

"What you can do is go to the project and get Betty to clean this mess up," Ben told him looking at all the blood that splattered over the living room.

"That's a good idea," Paul said.

They left the house and went their separate ways, while Ryder and Trap stayed behind and wrapped Tiffany's body in a blanket before moving it.

When Ben and Fred made it on the Louisiana Parkway they spotted a house that matched the description that Tiffany gave them. Ben noticed his Monte Carlo so he parked in front of the house. Ben sent Fred to knock on the door because of his non-threatening appearance.

Fred knocked on the door and Butch's mother looked through her peephole to see a young kid and decided to open the door.

"Are you all right sweetie?" she asked when she opened the door, that's when Ben rushed in from the side of the door and held the gun to her.

"Where the fuck is your son?" Ben demanded to know as he pushed her further into the living room.

To his right was the kitchen, that's where Fred saw Butch counting money at the table. Butch looked up but it was too late to make a move. Fred was on him in a flash pointing his gun before saying, "Don't move pussy, get over here," signaling him to the living room where Ben had his mother at gunpoint.

"What you doing Ben?" Butch asked when he saw Ben holding his mother at gunpoint.

"Karma is a motherfucker."

"What the hell you talking about?" Butch yelled at the top of his lungs.

"You know what the fuck I'm talking 'bout. You fucked me, you got me jacked, pistol whipped, and almost killed me. So since you fucked me, I want you to fuck her," Ben barked pointing to Butch's mother.

"Leave my mother out of this, she has nothing to do with it. What the fuck you talking 'bout, nigga, I ain't got you jacked, I would never do that. And how do you expect me to fuck my mother? You got me fucked up."

"You heard what I said, and from the looks of it, you ain't in no position to play tough," Ben said.

"Dawg you might as well kill me cause I ain't doing no shit like that," Butch growled.

"If you don't do it, I'ma kill her first and make you watch, then I'ma kill you."

"Just do it Jerome, it ain't worth us both dying," his mother insisted.

"NO momma! I can't do it!" he declined.

"DO IT!" his mother said as she started to take off her dress.

"What you gon do? You gon listen to your mother? Or are you gon go out like a Soulja?" Ben asked.

Tears started to roll down his face as he unbuckled his belt and the moment his pants dropped to his ankles Fred shot him three times in the head.

Butch's mother started screaming hysterically, "OH MY GOD Jerome!" until Fred shot her twice in the head.

"Grab that money," Fred told Ben who moved quickly to the kitchen and stuffed his pockets with the money.

"I got it, let's get the fuck," Ben said then they left the house in a hurry leaving Butch and his mother dead in the living room.

CHAPTER 33

Strapped with more guns than a shooting range the Slum Godds and the Thalia Court Boys entered the funeral. It was obvious that the streets were aware of the rumor that Ronald mistakenly killed his sister in his attempt to kill Paul because once they entered the church, they instantly became the center of attention.

Paul noticed people whispering and pointing in his direction. The thought crossed his mind that maybe he shouldn't have shown up, but the love he had for Roxanne overpowered any discomfort he was feeling at that moment.

When Ronald realized that Paul had shown up the tension in the air became thick as mud and it felt like at any second, bullets were about to fly. The hate they developed for each other since Roxanne's death was mutual because they held each other responsible.

Paul's crew took a seat on the back row. As soon as they sat down Fred asked a group of girls sitting in the row in front of them, why they were looking in his face. But they didn't respond they just whispered among themselves.

Paul moved slowly towards the casket to see his love for the last time. As he got close he noticed someone viewing the casket that was dressed in an orange prison jumpsuit with D.O.C on the back of it. When he made it to the casket to his surprise it was his father standing there with tears in his eyes.

"Pop, what you doing here?" Paul asked his father with a confused look on his face.

"Why you think I'm here? I'm happy to see you show up to your sister's funeral because for so long your mother kept you away from her and your brother."

Paul was under the impression that he was there for his girlfriend, but in reality, he was actually at his sister's funeral. Paul became sick to his stomach to find out that the woman that stole his heart was, in fact, his sister.

Ronald noticed his father and Paul holding a discussion, so he walked up to ask his father what was up, while looking Paul directly in the eyes.

"I want you to look out for your little brother," he told Paul when Ronald walked up.

"My brother?" Ronald said out loud.

"Yeah, brah, your brother. Why am I getting the feeling that y'all had no idea that you are brothers?"

"Because we didn't know," Ronald stated.

"So why are you here if you didn't know that Roxanne was your sister?"

Paul didn't respond, he just looked at his father with pity in his eyes.

"It's a long story dad," Ronald told him but by that time his father had figured out that Paul was dating his sister.

"I just want to know one thing…"

But before his father asked his question, Paul said, "Yes," figuring that he was about to ask if he'd had sex with her.

"It's my fault because I didn't do enough to make sure that all my children knew each other," his father said while dropping his head.

"What happened to your leg?" he asked Paul.

"We were together when she got killed."

He looked at Ronald and Paul and told them that it's a must that they get whoever was responsible. Without revealing that Ronald was the killer they both agreed that they'd work together to find out who did it.

The pastor stepped to the podium to begin the service. But before Paul went to his seat, he kissed Roxanne on the forehead. The service was beautiful, hundreds of people were there to pay their final respect to Roxanne, even the mayor was in attendance.

After the funeral, Ronald and Paul talked and as a result, they agreed to amend their differences. While they talked, the SGs and the TCBs stood close by because the Josephine head busser stood behind Ronald like secret service does for the president. Despite the fact that several officers were present, Ryder and Fred never removed their hands from their weapons.

Once they finished talking, both crews relaxed as they headed for their cars before heading to the cemetery for the burial ceremony. Fred never took one step though, he just stood there watching them hard as they walked away until

Tony looked back and saw him. Which made him stop and face off with Fred until he heard Ronald speaking to him, "Come on Tee let's go."

On their way from the cemetery, Sandra called Ben to remind him that it was her birthday and that her father was looking forward to meeting him. He explained that he had to make one stop to drop off a friend and he'd be on his way.

When Sandra hung up her phone her father looked at his watch then he approached her.

"Ese tipo que te interesa, a que hora va a llegar?" her father asked.

"El llegara pronto, cabo de hablar con el." she replied.

"Que no se atreva dejar mi muneca esperando." he stated before walking off.

Sandra was receiving the most expensive gifts one could ask for from her relatives. She really didn't have many friends, so she celebrated her birthdays and holidays with her family. She was hoping that Ben showed up because she really liked him and it was important that he didn't give her father a negative outlook of him by not showing up.

***

After dropping Paul off in the project, Ben rushed to Sandra's house. Fifteen minutes later he arrived at the entrance gate of EASTOVER, a gated community for the rich.

"Who are you here to visit?" the security guard asked Ben when he pulled up to the security booth.

"Sandra Martinez," Ben responded.

"Hold on one second," the guard said before calling to get Ben's visit verified. When he hung up the phone, he allowed Ben to enter and told him to have a nice day.

This is the first time Ben had ever been inside of EASTOVER subdivision. He was in awe, at the sight of the huge mansions that he observed in every direction he turned. He was even more impressed when he pulled up to Sandra's house which was directly across the street from Cash Money Records CEO Brian "Baby" Williams. Parked in front of Sandra's house were Lamborghinis, Ferraris, Corvettes, Range Rovers, and a white Porsche Cayenne with a big red bow on it. The least expensive car parked at her house was her CLK Benz.

"God damn, her people got to have that cake!" Ben said to himself as he exited his car carrying a large teddy bear and a small gift wrapped box.

Ben was relieved when Sandra was the one to answer the door.

"Happy Birthday beautiful!" Ben said as he handed her the presents.

"Thank you," she said politely as she accepted them with gratitude.

"Judging what I've seen in your driveway it's gon be impossible for me to compete with the presents you've probably already received."

"You don't have to compete, believe it or not I'm not impressed with all those fancy things. I'm more of a simple girl," she said bashfully.

"I wouldn't be either if I had been showered with the best things all my life."

"Boy shut up and let me introduce you to my parents."

"All these people are your relatives?"

"Yes, they are cousins, aunts, uncles, etc."

"From the sound of it, none of them speak English," he said because it sounded as if he was inside a Mexican bar.

"They all speak English, they just prefer to speak Spanish when they are around each other."

"Mother, Father, this is Ben, they guy I was telling you about."

"What kind of name is Ben," her father asked but before Ben could respond her mother told her father not to be rude, then she greeted him with respect.

"Hi, I'm Sandra's mother."

"And as you were told, I'm Ben, the guy with the odd name."

"Sweetheart, don't mind my husband. He'll loosen up in time, until then feel free to mingle," she said and walked out of the kitchen taking Sandra by the hand as she did. Which allowed Ben and her husband time alone to get to know each other.

"Come," her father said as he led Ben to a room that was set up more like an office.

Her father offered him a seat as he sat behind an office desk. When he sat down he removed a .357 from one of the drawers and sat it on top of the desk, which Ben found funny and smirked at the action.

"Do you find something funny?" her father asked.

"Your scare tactics ain't as intimidating as you would like, but that is a nice piece," Ben said.

"If I wanted to intimidate you, trust me you would be."

"Fair enough. So what's the purpose for this one on one?" Ben asked.

"I wanted to see what type of person you are because my daughter really likes you. But if you hurt her in any way, you won't have a chance to be intimidated."

"Your threats don't move me, but it's not my intention to hurt her. But what happens if she hurts me?" Ben asked looking him directly in his eyes.

"Let's just say things get serious between you and my daughter, how would you provide for her. As you can see her standards of living aren't average. So what do you do for a living?"

"I run a pharmacy," Ben stated.

"Bullshit," her father aggressively said as he slammed his fist down on his desk. "I know your kind, and if you can't be honest with me you can get up and get the hell out of my house. So I'm going to ask you again, what is it you do for a living?"

"I'm a Street Pharmaceutical Rep.," Ben replied as he stood to walk out of the room.

"Sit down!" her father demanded.

"You wanted the truth, so there it is. I'm a drug dealer," Ben said expecting him to be against a drug dealer. Especially, one that's trying to date his daughter, but to his surprise her father continued asking questions.

"What and where?"

"What you mean what and where?

"What do you sell and where do you sell it at?"

Ben remained silent for a few seconds before he answered. "Heroin and uptown in the Melphomene Project."

"Do you move alone or with a crew, and if you move with a crew, what's your position in the crew?"

"Daddy, what are you doing in there?" Sandra asked through the door.

"We'll be out in a minute sweetheart. Now, where were we?"

"You asked do I move with a crew or alone," Ben replied.

"Do you move alone?"

The whole-time Ben was being questioned the thought of her father being a plug never crossed his mind. He just assumed that after that day, he wouldn't be allowed to see her again.

"I move with a loyal crew, and my position is, how y'all say it, I'm the Jefe."

"I can sense that you have leadership skills."

"You can huh?"

"Yeah, I can. And if you want to make some real money, I can provide you with an unlimited supply of Grade A heroin."

"You can do what!" Ben asked with excitement in his voice.

"You heard me correctly."

"So that explains all those foreign cars out there in the driveway."

"That's nothing," her father said boastfully. "But I don't just sell drugs, I'm very successful in the real estate business, I own multiple car lots, a few clubs, and I have clothing stores as well."

"Make me understand this, you don't know me from a can of paint. I could be a snitch, the Feds, DEA but you openly exposed your hands to me. Why?" Ben asked out of curiosity.

"I have resources that can tell me when you took your last shit, so trust me I'd know if you were Fed or even a snitch. I already knew who you were, and what you did for a living. I'm also aware of the war between your crew and Je'sus' crew, and if he hadn't wanted to handle the situation himself, you and your crew would have been dead. When the war started, I knew that eventually the situation would interfere with my money. But now since Je'sus is dead, I need somebody like you to fill his shoes. Do you think you can handle it?"

"To be honest with you, Je'sus' shoes is too small for me. If you did your homework like you said you did, you would already know that."

"Let's go celebrate with my daughter. We'll continue our talk later, and by the way, my name is, Giovanni," he said as he extended his hand and dapped Ben.

When they joined the party, Sandra's mother announced that it was time for Sandra to open her presents. She received everything from jewelry to clothes. Although the present she adored more than anything was the big white teddy bear Ben brought. After she opened her last present, everyone sang happy birthday. Before the evening ended she took several pictures with her father and Ben before he left. He said his goodbyes to her family and left the party thinking about the conversation between her father and him.

CHAPTER 34

"Dog where the fuck Pookey at?" Rell asked J-Roc.

"I haven't seen that nigga none this morning and I been out chere since 6:00am catching this early morning rush," JRoc stated.

"Try to call that nigga and see what he gon do," J-Roc told Rell.

Rell removed his phone from its clip and called Pookey.

"Hello," Pookey said half asleep.

"What's up bruh, you going to the funeral or what?"

"Yeah, I'ma fuck with it," he said as he sit up in the bed.

"Where you at? You shoulda been up and ready by now."

"I'm by Brittany's house, dog I fuck that bitch all night."

"Where she at right now?"

"If she was able to get up this morning that would mean I didn't put it down right."

"So you saying she still asleep?"

"The way I punished her, she might not get up til 3:00pm."

"Say bruh open the back door, and be ready to leave when I get there."

"What you ..." but Rell hung up before he could finish.

Rell entered her apartment through the back door because he wanted to minimize his chances of being seen entering or exiting her apartment.

When he got to her room, Pookey was putting on his shoes, when he looked up he seen the .40cal in Rell hand, but before he spoke a word Rell put his hand over his mouth implying that he wanted him to remain quiet, then signaled for him to leave.

Once Pookey left the room, Rell took one of her pillows to muffle the sound of the blast as he put the gun to her head and releasd two quick shots, then fled the apartment.

Waiting in the car was J-Roc as Rell and Pookey fled the scene.

"Dog you need to get rid of that gun, you got like 4 bodies on it," J-Roc told Rell.

"Since when a nigga started getting rid of their guns because it has a body on it if that was the case, nobody would have a gun."

"I'm telling you homie, you need to get rid of that bitch," J-Roc said trying to convince Rell to throw the gun away or trade it with somebody.

"Man fuck all that, let's go," Rell told J Roc who was driving.

Rhodes Funeral Home is only a few blocks away from the Calliope so they got there in no time. Before the service started Curtis Mitchell, Kenyatta, and Deja walked up to Je'sus mother and hugged her real tight all at once.

"Baby I just hope you change your life because it is not worth dying for," she told Curtis Mitchell who couldn't believe how strong she was because the average mother who lose a child be emotionally weak, but it was different with her, it's like she had expected for him to get killed.

"My life changed the moment Je'sus died, Ms. Edna. You know better than anybody that Je'sus and me was like brothers, and without him around, my life would never be the same."

Donte' and Larry also attended the funeral with their family.

Many people came to pay their respect as the funeral home quickly filled up, mainly with people out of the Calliope Project.

Je'sus funeral was everything people thought it would have been. He was laid to rest in a gold-plated casket and had more than a hundred flowers alongside it.

Waiting outside was a horse and carriage, accompanied by the Hot 8 Brass Band to send him home in a traditional New Orleans style second-line.

After the funeral majority of the people went to the Rest Haven cemetery for the burial ceremony.

While everyone was gathered around Je'sus plot, a black Cadillac with limo tint pulled up slowly. Some people assumed it was the Feds, others thought that it was members from a rival gang until Giovanni stepped out of the SUV, dressed in a black tailor-made suit.

Many questioned who he was, but the moment Curtis Mitchell seen him, he started walking towards him.

"I'm sorry to hear what happened to Je'sus," Giovanni said when they met up with each other.

"I appreciate you coming," Curtis replied while extending his right hand to shake his.

"It's only right that I show my respect, after all we were successful business partners."

"I was hoping that you show up, because I know that Je'sus was in debt with you for a hundred thousand and I have it for you, so let me run and get it."

When Curtis Mitchell made it back from his car with the bag of money, Giovanni asked him why didn't he keep the money because he would have never known that he had it, and Curtis told him that he was trying to establish trust hoping that it would lead to them doing business.

"I tell you what, here's my number, I want you to call me Wednesday at 4:00 sharp, not a minute before or a minute after," Giovanni told him as he handed him his number on a piece of paper that he took out of his wallet, and before he turned and walked away he said, "Don't make me regret it."

"You won't," Curtis assured him then they shook hands in agreement.

After they left the cemetery, Curtis met up with Rell in the project, that's when Curtis found out that Brittany had been Murdered.

"I wonder who the fuck killed her," Curtis Mitchell asked Rell.

"I don't have a clue, it's not like she had enemies," Rell responded.

Britany crime scene was cleared out, the only thing that was left behind was the caution tape that littered her hallway.

"That's some fucked up shit," Curtis stated.

"Heads up!" someone yelled as Safe Home rushed into the courtyard.

Rell threw his gun and ran through a cut and by Curtis Mitchell being clean he decided not to run.

"Put your fucking hands up motherfucker!" a police officer yelled as he moved close to Curtis Mitchell with both hands on his weapon as he pointed it at him.

While Curtis was being searched, another officer searched the area and found the gun that Rell threw.

"I got something," the officer said as he kneeled down and picked up the .40cal by the back of the barrel using his index finger and thumb.

"That ain't my gun," Curtis protested.

"Tell it to the judge," the police told him then cuffed him to place him under arrest.

Curtis was placed in the back of a police car while they finished searching the area and when' they were done, he was taken to central Lockup to be booked. with possession of a firearm.

Curtis didn't really trip because he knew that he would make bond the moment he get one, but things would soon make a turn for the worst.

CHAPTER 35

After getting Ben's number from Sandra, Giovanni' called him. He told him to go to his clothing store on Manhattan and tell whoever was at the counter that he was sent by him to pick up a pair of Air Force Ones.

When he entered the store, he did what he was told. He talked to a female in her mid-thirties who went to the back of the store. When she came back she had two kilos in a NIKE shoe box and placed them in a bag before handing them to Ben.

When he got in his car, he called and told Giovanni that the shoes fit then hung up. When he made it back to the project, he went straight to Paul's apartment and put the work up. He called everyone in the crew and told them to meet him by Paul's house. Once all the SGs made it, Ben sent Trap to go get Tiger and his crew.

"While we waiting for Trap to come back somebody help me roll up a few blunts," Ben said as he pulled out 14 grams of orange Kush.

"That's what I'm talking about," Fred said as he grabbed a Keep Moving cigar off the coffee table and cut it open using a key.

Just as they rolled up three blunts, Trap came through the door with Tiger, Poppa, Hood and Jack Rabbit. Ben tossed Tiger the bag of weed and told him to roll them something to smoke. After catching the bag, Tiger, put it to his nose, inhaled deep, and said, "This smell like some gas,"

"If it ain't gas we don't want it," Ben replied.

"I'ma roll it. You be rolling the shit too tight," Poppa said. "So what's all this about?" Tiger asked.

"It's like this, I got a crucial plug. It's gon be more than enough for all of us to eat, so if y'all want to make some real money let's do it, if not that's cool but I'm telling y'all it's going to be love because we bout to lock the whole fucking city down."

"So what you need us for?" Jack Rabbit asked.

"I don't, but on the strength of the relationship I have with your nephew, I'll like to see him and his crew eat, and like I said the plate will be big enough for all of us to eat from, but don't get it twisted, I don't need y'all."

"Give me a minute," Ben said when his phone started ringing. "What's up Soulja?" Ben said when he answered it.

"Where y'all at in Mid-City cause I don't see none of y'all outside." Rell asked"

"Who you with?" Ben asked him.

"I'm by myself. Why what's up?"

"Go ahead and park, I'ma meet you on the porch."

When Rell got out the car, he looked up at the 4th floor where Betty lived, but Ben called him from Paul's porch.

"What's popping homie?" Rell asked when he made it to the porch.

"Let's go inside," Ben said as he headed for the door.

When Rell walked in the house and seen Tiger and his crew alone with the SGs he asked Ben what was going on.

"Ain't nothing going on, we were just discussing how we gon take over this city. So what's up with you?"

"I was just passing through to let you know that the issue with ole girl is handled."

"Yeah, I heard about that."

"You know my word is law if I say I'ma do something it's considered done."

"I feel that homie. But what's going on with them niggas?"

"Right now, that nigga Curtis Mitchell is in jail so it ain't nothing but Donte' and Larry left out chere. When I think, those niggas slipping I'ma call you and let you know when to come through. If I can get away unnoticed I'll handle it myself."

While they talked, Jack Rabbit saw through the facade that Rell displayed and immediately developed a dislike for him. But he remained quiet, because the rules that he went by told you not to tip your hand under any circumstances.

"Yeah, you do that homie cause it's a must that we get them niggas."

"I got cha my nigga, I'ma holla at cha though," Rell said, then he left the apartment.

"That's y'all's problem right there," Jack Rabbit said when Rell left.

"What's our problem?" Ben asked.

"I know it ain't my place to be telling y'all shit, but that nigga that just left is y'all's problem. Y'all niggas act like y'all can't see through that weak ass game that nigga running on y'all."

"I don't know what you think you see, but that nigga is a hunid," Ben replied defensively.

"I don't know that nigga, but I know his kind. That nigga is a snake. The crazy part about it is, he got y'all niggas fooled, but I know better."

"Man look, we here to talk about making money," Ben said trying to avoid sticking to the Rell topic.

"Yeah, what up with that?" Tiger asked impatiently.

"What I'ma do is, I'ma give y'all two bricks for 50 thousand a piece. Do y'all think y'all can handle that?" Ben asked Tiger.

"Fucking right we can handle that!" Hood shouted out before Tiger could respond.

"What's the catch?" Jack Rabbit asked.

"The catch is, I'm trying to put y'all in the position to eat instead of petty hustling ya dig? Like I said, it's enough money out chere for us all to be straight, but I ain't twisting your arm my nigga, it's only a proposition. You can fuck with it or not, it really don't matter to me. At the end of the day, me and my boys gon eat regardless. So, what it gon be?" Ben asked.

"We fucking with that," Tiger said eagerly feeling like it was an opportunity of a lifetime to touch two bricks.

"How many times can we step on them?" Poppa asked.

"That's the thing, when I give it to y'all its gon be ready to hit the streets like it is," Ben stated.

"So that's the catch," Jack Rabbit mumbled to himself.

"So, we can't put NOTHING on it?!" Tiger asked.

"That's why I'm charging y'all 50 apiece, that way all y'all can make a profit, and the shit gon be the same shit we puttin' on the streets. I tell you what, you can make a sample package straight off the brick and if you get a complaint I'll give you a 9 for free."

"Naw homie you don't have to do all that, but it's gon be the same shit y'all put on the streets, right?" Tiger asked.

"The exact same shit, so you know the shit gon be A1"

"A'ight! Let's do it!" Tiger said.

"Let me go get the shit ready, and I'ma get with you in a few hours," Ben said.

Before Tiger and his crew left, Tiger told Trap to let him hit the weed. But instead, Trap gave him the piece of blunt then told him he could roll with it. When they left, the SGs started cutting the dope. They stepped on each kilo three times turning two kilos into eight kilos. Ben put two on the side for Tiger and his crew.

"Dawg that nigga Jack Rabbit was getting on my fucking nerves, I don't even know why you putting them niggas on," Ryder said through the dust mask that he wore.

"You know how them old niggas is, they over analyze every fucking thing," Ben replied.

"I don't like that nigga," Fred said.

They bagged up one kilo in one gram packages and planned to sell them for 50 dollars apiece, that way they'll make 50,000 off each brick so by the time they sold out they would have taken in 400,000 off the two kilos Giovanni gave them, so they would profit 200,000.

It took them nearly seven hours to cut and bag up the dope. Ben delivered the work to Tiger personally. Once he got it, him and Hood went inside and started bagging it up for distribution.

CHAPTER 36

Ben and Carl went to the local jeweler to get six customized chains made. They requested for the SG emblems to be crusted in white diamonds. Since they were purchasing six chains at once, they were given a discount at 5,000 apiece.

They were told that they would be ready by Friday afternoon.

"It don't make no sense to get the chain and not the watch," Paul said as he looked at a blue face Rolex that was in a glass case.

"That is a nice watch, but I ain't trying to get off that kind of money right now. The chains will have to do for now."

"They making money, they just gon have to get their own watch if they want to come correct," Paul said as he made up his mind to buy the watch.

He then turned to the jeweler and asked how much was the watch. "It's priced at 8,500, but it depends on how many y'all buy, the price would drop," the jeweler said.

"What you want to do homie?" Paul said as he looked back and forth from the watch to Ben.

Ben looked at the jeweler and asked him what he will sell him them two for.

"Um' I'll knock off 500 for each one."

Ben thought about it for a few seconds and then said, "Have them ready when I come to pick up the chains."

"Will do," the jeweler said with a smile on his face.

"Them niggas gon like the chains," Paul said as they walked out the store.

"We gon throw Monsta a surprise party at the Venue Saturday, that's when we gon come out with the SG chains," Ben said.

"After all the shit we been through in the last month, we really can use that time to kick back and enjoy ourselves," Paul said speaking about the party.

"I wish Tre, K-Dog, and Lil' Mike could have been with us," Ben said in a humble tone.

"What you mean you wish? As long as we breathing them niggas gon live through us," Paul said. "Matter of fact, we should get some T-shirts made with all their pictures on it and wear them to the party," Paul continued.

"Fucking right, that's what we gon do. We can go get them made later," Ben said with excitement in his voice as they got in the car.

It looked like Mardi Gras when Ben and Paul pulled up in the project and seen the massive crowd of dope fiends that flooded the courtyard to score.

Today is the first-time Monsta actually hung on the set since he been released from prison and he can't believe the type of clientele his homies had accumulated.

The way Trap was selling the product Monsta knew he

would be where he wanted to be if he made one run.

Once Ben got out the car, he immediately chirped Trap off his Nextel.

"Yo Trap, what's up?"

"Man, where the fuck y'all at, I need some more work, this shit moving fast as a motherfucker."

"How much you have left?" Ben asked.

"Dawg, I'm almost finished."

"What you mean you almost finished? That was a whole thang and it ain't even 6:00 yet."

"Man, half of that shit was gone in the first four hours, they loving this shit."

Tiger must have been waiting for Ben to come in the project because as soon as he seen Ben he approached him.

"Let me holla at you round," Tiger said when he made it to them.

"What's popping Soulja?" Ben asked as he walked up to him.

"It look like this shit is only designed for y'all to eat."

"I don't know what you talking about homie. Where you getting at with this?" Ben asked as his body tensed up.

"I'm saying, you put a nigga on, but we can't sell our 25-dollar bags as long as y'all serving grams for 50."

"Check this out my nigga, I gave y'all two bricks, y'all free to sell them however y'all want to, but I do understand what you saying, so this is how it can work. Monday through Friday we gon run shop from 6 to 6, after that every dollar that come through is strictly for y'all, and y'all can have the weekends to sell y'all selves, we won't sell shit on Saturdays or Sundays."

"So what you telling me is that we can't sell shit until 6 o'clock and the weekends?" Tiger asked with a funny look on his face.

"Naw homie, you got it confused. Y'all can sell whenever y'all get ready, I'll never try and dictate how and when y'all make y'all money. What I'm saying is y'all don't have to worry about competing with us after 6 o' clock and weekends."

Tiger thought about what Ben said for a few seconds, then he shook hands with Ben in agreement.

Monsta waited until they finished talking before he approached Ben.

"So this is what you meant when you said y'all on another level huh?" Monsta said as he observed the huge crowd.

"I tried to tell you, now you see for yourself, shit real," Ben said in a boastful way.

"As much as I hate to say it, it look like I might have to get down until I touch a few chips to get myself started with the business plans I put together."

"Naw homie, you don't have to get your hands dirty, I'll give you the start-up money you need, don't trip on that."

"I respect that, but you know how I get down, a real man get off his ass and make something happen for himself. I can't sit around and wait on handouts."

"Is this what you really want?"

"What it sound like, let's put him on," Paul said.

"This ain't what I want, this is what I need, but what I want is some more fucking clothes. I only got two new out fits left."

"A'ight, let me go holla at Trap first, then we gon go to the mall after that," Ben told Monsta as him and Paul started to head to the hallway where Trap was.

Trap was surrounded by several fiends that was trying to get a fix as Ben and Paul was heading to the second floor.

"Back up, back up," Ben yelled as he made his way through the crowd. When he made it to Trap, he got all the money that he had on him then he told him to finish off what he had left and close for the rest of the day, then he looked at Paul and told him to get Fred and start baggin' up another kilo until him and Monsta make it back from the mall.

Before they went to the mall, Ben went to Paul apartment to look through some pictures Paul had in a shoebox and found pictures of Tre, K-Dog, and Lil' Mike, then he went on Canal St. to a T-shirt shop to get the R.I.P. T-shirts made with the pictures on them.

Paul started covering the table with newspaper before dumping the kilo on it. Staring at the mountain of dope, Fred's curiosity started to get the best of him.

While they were baggin' up the dope, Fred eased a gram in his pocket, then removed the dust mask from his face and told Paul that he needed to take a shit.

He went into the bathroom and locked the door. Nervous at first, Fred just held the dope in his hand because this is the first time he ever considered trying dope, giving that he watched this type of addiction ruin many people lives. Not knowing how much to use he opened the bag and dug in it with his pinky finger and scooped up a very small amount of dope and sniffed it up his nose.

He closed the bag up then flushed the toilet to make it seem like he actually used the bathroom.

"This shit ain't nothing," he said to himself before leaving out the bathroom.

By the time he made it back to the living room, he started to drain and right before he made it to the table where the dope was, he vomited all over the floor.

"What the fuck?!" Paul shouted as he jumped up from the table to see Fred throwing up all over the floor. "You got to keep your mask on when you fucking with this shit, the fumes alone are strong enough to get you high," he continued thinking that Fred just inhaled too many fumes.

"Dawg I need to lay down for a little while," Fred said as he headed for the living room to lay on the sofa.

"So I guess I have to clean this shit up huh?" Paul stated as he looked at the vomit covered floor while shaking his head. "I guess so," he said when he didn't get a response.

***

When Tiger made it back to the Thalia Court after talking to Ben, he gathered up his crew and explained to them what Ben said in reference to them selling the work.

"Say brah, y'all letting them niggas handle y'all any kind of way," Jack Rabbit told Tiger after he finished explaining.

"What you mean by that?" Tiger asked.

"I'm saying this nigga's gonna try and put a timeline on when we can hustle."

"If you think about it, it can really work in our favor," Tiger stated. "Cause if we only focus on hustling after 6 and the weekends and still make 50,000 a week, plus we using their work to do it with, it's a win-win situation because we never have to invest our money to score, we could just sit back and let them bring it to us for FREE."

"All that shit sound good, and it would be a nice bit of money to make over the week, but if we making that, imagine what they making."

"Man, fuck what they making, as long as we good, that's the only thing that matter," Hood stated in Tiger defense.

"Dawg, we'll make more money in 4 days than we make in 3 weeks and if they could afford to take the risk and front us two fucking bricks, you know they gon make more money than us, so fuck what they making," Tiger stated.

"Everybody ain't cut out to be bosses. Some niggas is put here to be workers," Jack Rabbit said as he pulled a lighter out his pocket to light his cigarette.

"I don't give a fuck bout working for a nigga as long as I'm eating," Tiger said with strong body motions.

Jack Rabbit looked at him for a couple of seconds then shook his head and said, "You ain't nothing like your daddy, he would have took all them niggas shit."

"When you a dope fiend, you'll do just about anything to get that monkey off your back. So I believe he would have tried to rob them too, but when you a hustler, the most important thing you want is a plug, and that's what I got when fucking with them."

"You looking at them like a plug, but in reality, you ain't shit but competition to them."

"Say brah, you don't have to fuck it if it's a problem, but we selling two bricks in 25 dollar bags and if things continue to move at this pace we can sell them in 3 to 4 weeks." "That's a whole month," Jack Rabbit said.

"Yeah, it's a whole month, but we wasn't selling nothing but a half a brick in a month. This love, you trippin', Unk!"

While engaged in their disagreeable conversation a dope fiend approached them to score.

"Let me get a gram," the addict said in a slur.

"We only sell 25-dollar bags right chere," Tiger said.

"Damn man, I drove all the way from Hammond to get that shit," the addict said angrily.

"You have to go through that cut if you trying to score a gram," Tiger said as he pointed in the direction of the SGs set.

"That's what I'm talking about right there," Jack Rabbit said not liking the fact that they were letting money pass them by to go straight inside the SGs pocket.

"You think the only reason why they selling grams is to stop us from eating? FUCK NO, cause if that was the case, they'll run they shop 24/7," Hood said. "And on some real shit we have two options: One we can go to war with them and nobody get paid, OR we can take advantage of this opportunity and get this money while we have this plug."

'I don't know about y'all but I rather kill the chicken and eat before I wait on an egg to get laid," Jack rabbit said then walked off.

***

Ben and Monsta headed back to the project after spending two hours in the mall.

"Ain't no way they bagged up a whole brick," Ben said when he made it to the project and seen Paul outside talking to China and Diamond.

Carrying several shopping bags, Ben and Monsta walked over to Paul.

"What's up homie? Y'all finish already?" Ben asked Paul as he sat the bags he was carrying on the ground.

"Dawg Fred can't handle the fumes, he almost fucked the shit up when he throwed up everywhere."

"He throwed up? Why didn't he have his mask on?" Ben asked.

"What's up Ben, you acting funny," China asked because Ben acted as if he didn't acknowledge her presence.

Before Ben replied, Monsta looked into Diamond face and said "You look familiar. What's your name?"

"My name is Diamond," she said in a flirty tone.

"You Cash's old lady, right?" Monsta asked her casually.

"Where you know Cash from?" she asked in a more serious tone.

"That was my celly, he used to show me every picture you sent him," Monsta said in a tone that played with her conscience.

"He showed you what?" she asked quickly.

"Yeah, he showed me all of them. That is the ones that was appropriate for me to see," Monsta said because whenever Diamond sent her exclusive shots Cash wouldn't let him see them. Monsta respected that because he knew that she was his girl.

"I'ma tell him that I ran into you," Diamond told him in a relaxed tone.

Monsta pulled out a fist full of cash and peeled off 150 then handed it to her.

"Put that on his books, and tell him to let me know when he need something. Here take my number so you can give it to him."

"I'll give it to him when he calls and thanks for the money."

"You can thank me by showing up at this lil' thang my homies put together for me at the Venue Saturday.

"Bitch why you ain't tell me about this lil' thang he talking about at the Venue?" Diamond asked China.

"Girl this is my first time hearing about it," she stated in a sassy tone as she rolled her eyes at Paul.

"Well actually don't nobody know but y'all, because they just came up with the idea. But since y'all know make sure y'all invite all y'all friends and tell them to bring a friend." Monsta said.

"Alright, we most definitely gon be there," Diamond said.

As they were talking, Miecy pulled up in her Nissan Altima. It was obvious what she thought she saw. Because when she parked, she quickly got out of her car and rushed over to Monsta who was still engaged in the conversation with Diamond. Miecy let it be known that Monsta was hers. She walked up to him and gave him a long, deep kiss, then asked to be introduced.

"I'm not interested in knowing who you are," Diamond said.

"Bitch, was I talking to you?" Miecy replied.

"It's seems like you was talking to me when you asked to be introduced."

"What you tripping on?" Monsta asked Miecy.

"All I asked was for you to introduce me and this hoe gon start running her fucking mouth. You gon take her side and say I'm tripping like you trying to impress her or something. What you fucking her?"

"Come on bae, if it was like that, do you think I would have told you to come pick me up?"

"I don't know what to think right now. This bitch running her mouth," Miecy said pointing aggressively.

"Make that your last bitch," Diamond said in a threatening tone.

"BITCH!!" Miecy said with aggression as Diamond charged at her. But Monsta and Ben got in between them to prevent them from fighting.

"Get her from back here," Paul told China who was trying to calm Diamond down.

"Come on girl, let's go," China said as she pulled Diamond by her arm.

As they walked away, Diamond continued to make threats towards Miecy who wasn't affected by them at all. By the time, Diamond and China made it to their car, Ben started picking the bags up off the ground to help Monsta put them in Miecy car. Once all the bags were in the car, Monsta and Miecy left. You could tell they were fussing as they pulled away.

CHAPTER 37

Lt. Moore is the lead investigator for the 6th District precinct. The moment he was notified a weapon was recovered during the raid, he instantly ordered that a thorough ballistics be done immediately.

It was confirmed that the .40 cal. Curtis was arrested for was involved in several shootings including three recent murders.

The head District Attorney was notified about unsolved cases the gun was related to, so the D.A. recommended that Curtis Mitchell be denied a bond until a further investigation could be done.

When Curtis Mitchell was informed by his lawyer that the weapon he was charged with was linked to several violent shootings and murders he went in to a rage.

"How many times do I have to tell you, that's not my gun!" Curtis Mitchell yelled through the phone during an attorney visit.

"Right now, it's your word against theirs," his lawyer told him. "We need something concrete if you want to get exonerated from this charge."

"All you have to do is tell them to check the gun for fingerprints and I promise mine won't be on it."

"Do you have any idea whose gun it is?"

"Yeah, I know who it for but if I wanted to snitch, I wouldn't need you!" Curtis said angrily.

"I'm not asking you to snitch, what I'm insisting is that if you know whose gun it is, you can get that person to sign an affidavit stating that it's their gun."

"What type of motherfucker gon do some shit like that?" Curtis asked.

"You'll be surprised how many people sign affidavits, it's worth the shot," his lawyer stated honestly.

"Let me make a few phone calls to see what I come up with," Curtis stated.

"Remember, your freedom is riding on this," his lawyer told him before he left out of the visiting room.

Minutes after he returned to the tier from his attorney visit he was brought back to Central Lockup to get rebooked with attempted murder for Louis '9 Finger Lou' Reed and Robert White who accidently got shot around the Hotspot. As well as the murders of Brittany Green, Jimmie Adams and Kyron 'K-Dog' Youngblood.

While in inmate booking, Curtis Mitchell had to get his armband changed from orange to red. Orange bands were placed on inmates that had been arrested for felonies and red bands were for capital offenses such as murder of any kind, rape, robbery, etc.

Throughout the entire booking process, the only thing that was going through Curtis' mind was Rell, and how they allowed him to undermine them.

He was transferred from the HOD which was short for House of Detention, a ten-story jail that housed felony offenders to OPP which was short for Orleans Parish Prison.

When he walked on the tier carrying his mattress and bed roll he scanned the tier quickly. Trying to see if he recognized anybody he knew. But didn't so he found his bunk, made it up and laid down.

As he laid down Curtis Mitchell started to think back to when the beef first started and how he always knew that the whole situation didn't add up. But now that the truth had come to light that Rell's gun matched the bullets that were removed from K-Dog, Brittany and Lou's bodies it all started to make sense.

He started to think about the F-150 that was parked on Erato with bullet holes in it, also about the time Rell told him that the SGs surrounded him and his crew in the Melph. The thing that stood out most was when Rell told them that he knew a spot in Mid-City where the SGs hung out. For him to know that, he had to be dealing with them.

"The whole time Rell's snake-ass was playing both sides, he the one behind this whole fucking beef," Curtis mumbled to himself.

Curtis laid in his bunk looking at the ceiling with both hands under his head. He began thinking 'bout how his life made a turn for the worst, after he thought about his promising future as a basketball player before he got involved in the drug business.

Curtis was an elite basketball player in high school. He was

a record setting player at Booker T. Washington. Curtis and All State point guard Trevon 'Tre' Miller led the school to two state championships. He also set the Louisiana State record for the most career points with 6,457 total points. Every college in the nation wanted to recruit him especially, his home state LSU Tigers. But he let the street life get the best of him.

As a youth, he fantasized about playing in the NBA. However, those dreams were shattered by the lust of the lifestyle he was exposed to by his long-term friend Je'sus. Curtis knew that the streets gave him something he couldn't get in the NBA and that was street credit.

Growing up young in the Calliope projects gave Curtis a different outlook on life. He was surrounded by peer pressure so that made him want to be a part of what he saw going on in the hood. He was the perfect example of a good kid that became a product of his environment. By the time, he made it to high school he was known to have the best weed amongst his peers. He got arrested once for selling weed on the school campus, but due to his basketball talent, the principal pulled some strings to get the charges dropped.

Curtis Mitchell's mind was racing as he got out of his bunk. He went straight to the phone to call Donte' and let him know that if Rell wasn't going to own up to the weapon, it would be in their best interest to kill him the first chance they got.

***

Donte' told Larry what Curtis Mitchell told him about getting Rell to sign an affidavit. Larry knew it would be a waste of time trying to get Rell to admit that the gun was his. But, Donte' insisted on confronting Rell about it, he figured it couldn't make things any worse.

Donte' looked across the courtyard and saw Rell sitting on the porch with Pookey. He tapped Larry on the shoulder and signaled for him to follow. Heading across the courtyard to holla at Rell, Larry asked him was he really going to ask

Rell to own up to the gun. But it was obvious because Donte' moved towards Rell in a rapid pace as his black Air Force Ones scraped the ground with every step.

"I'ma just throw it at the nigga and see how he responds to it. You never know," Donte' replied.

As they approached the porch, Rell stepped off to meet them before they actually made it to the porch.

"What's up homie?" Rell asked sizing up their demeanor.

"What up my nigga?" Donte' said while extending his right fist to dap Rell then Larry did the same.

"Say brah, I just talked to Curtis Mitchell and he asked me to holla at you about getting with his lawyer and signing an affidavit 'bout that tool," Donte' said.

"What tool?" Rell replied as if he had no idea what Donte' was talking about.

"That's the kind of games you gon play with a nigga?" Donte' asked.

"Fuck no, I ain't signing no affidavit," Rell retorted with aggression.

He automatically expected them to make some type of demand or threat. But to his surprise Donte' said, "I told him the same thing. That ain't no nigga 'bout to come and admit to some shit like that, because I wouldn't do it for the simple fact that a nigga know how that shit go."

"On the real, then it ain't nothing but a gun charge," Rell said in a less aggressive tone.

"So how business?" Donte' asked.

"For the last two days' shit been moving slow as a motherfucker somebody must got some tarcher, that's the only way shit slow up like this," Rell responded.

“Well look, when y’all sell out, come fuck with a nigga,” Donte’ said then him and Larry headed back across the courtyard.

“We got to kill that nigga,” Donte’ told Larry as they walked.

“I don’t like the way that nigga was talking when you mentioned the affidavit,” Larry said.

“I didn’t like that either, that’s why I had to dumb it down, because I didn’t want to alert him.”

“You know that nigga ain’t stupid, that bitch be on game,” Larry stated.

“Let me see if he peeps game when we take his ass somewhere and knock his fucking brains out.”

“Nothing beat the cross but the double-cross,” Larry stated in agreement with Donte’s statement as they approached the stairwell that led to their apartment.

Rell had been out hustling all day and only made a thousand dollars. Since business was slow, Rell decided to go in the Melph to kick it with the SGs for a while. When he made it to the Melph, he thought he had ran into a murder scene because people were everywhere.

As he parked and got out of his car, he realized why business was slow in the Calliope. It appeared as if every heroin addict in the city was there to score.

“I wonder what the fuck these niggas selling back here to get this type of traffic,” Rell mumbled to himself as he walked through the courtyard looking for Ben.

Fred spotted Rell coming in his direction, so he called Rell name and waved him over.

"What's up my nigga?" Rell said when he walked up to Fred.

"Ain't shit popping, what's up with you?" Fred asked.

"I'm just passing through to holla at Ben, where that nigga at?" Rell asked.

"Them niggas in the hallway shooting dice," Fred told him as he pointed in their direction.

"I got 100 more he hit it," Ryder was saying when Rell walked into the hallway.

"I bet that 100 he don't," Tiger responded.

"What's the point?" Rell asked as he pulled out his money to get into the game.

"The point is 10," Ben said as he shook the dice rapidly in his right hand. "You better ride with me!" "I got 50 he hit it," Rell said.

"I bet he don't," Tiger said then threw 50 dollars on the ground.

When Ben shot the dice, they landed on six, four, on the first roll. "Big Ben Backdoor!" Ben yelled, while picking his money up off the pavement.

"Dawg you have to roll the dice," Tiger said while he watched Ben pick up his money.

"I can shoot how I want to, if you don't like the way I shoot, don't fade me," Ben said as he got ready to shoot for another point.

***

"Say brah, you know them niggas supposed to have that party for Monsta today at the venue," Black Larry said.

"You want to go pass in the Melph and see if we can catch them niggas slipping?" Donte' asked.

"You ain't saying nothing, let's go," Black Larry said as he stood up and placed his gun on his waist "I can't wait to lay one of them niggas down," he continued as they left the apartment.

"Hurry up and put the AC on, it's hot as a motherfucker in here," Donte' said, when they got in the car.

"You ain't lying," Larry said as he rushed to place the key in the ignition so he could turn on the AC.

When they made it to the Melph, their adrenaline began to pump at an all-time high. They both knew it was like entering a death trap. When they turned onto S. Robertson the outside courtyard was packed with people. It was too congested for them to lay eyes on the SGs. But, what they did notice was Rell's Maxima parked in the Melph.

"Ain't that Rell's Maxima right there?" Larry asked Donte', even though he knew the answer.

"Yeah, that's that nigga's shit. I thought Curtis was just saying that shit since he was in his feelings cause he went to jail for dude's gun."

"Ain't no telling how long he been fucking with them niggas," Larry replied.

"Dawg we got to punish that nigga for real homie," Donte' said while looking at the crowd in the courtyard.

"We can always get at Rell. We need to focus on how we gon catch all these niggas slipping. You must remember that it's only us two. We ain't in no position to go to war so when we strike on them, we have to kill them."

"I feel that Round, but if he fucking with them niggas, he's a bigger threat to us than them. So we have to kill him ASAP," Donte' said.

"Let's just focus on catching them niggas after the party tonight, then we'll deal with Rell," Larry said, pulling off and heading back to the Calliope.

***

Ben hadn't seen Sandra since her birthday so after he finished shooting craps, he called her and told her to meet him in the project. While waiting for her to show up, Ben explained to his crew that they would park their cars in the club parking lot ahead of time. That way they would have immediate access to their cars by being in front of the building.

When Sandra pulled up in her new Porsche, it got the attention of everyone there. Ben walked to the driver's side of the truck to open her door, but she refused to get out as she stared the ghetto in the face.

"I'd rather stay in the truck. But, what's up?" Sandra commented as she continued to observe her surroundings.

"Tonight, my homeboy is having a welcome home party and we want to park our cars in front of the club. So our cars will be right there when we come out."

"Why would that interest me?" Sandra asked.

"I need you to drive to the club with us so we'll have a ride back. Afterwards me and you can spend some time together if that's cool with you."

"I don't see why that would be a problem."

A'ight, let me go get that nigga," Ben said, taking a few steps away from her truck to signal Ryder.

Ben and Ryder got in their cars and pulled away slowly and she followed. The further she rode uptown, the more she understood what poverty was really like. But, what she found really amazing was the number of luxury cars she saw parked in front of houses that were barely standing.

When they made it to the club, Ben and Ryder parked their cars close to the entrance and got into Sandra's truck. On their way back to the projects to drop Ryder off, Sandra's father called.

He asked her where she was, and Sandra told him that she and Ben were together. Giovanni asked to speak with Ben, so she handed him her phone.

"Who is it?" Ben asked as he raised the phone to his ear.

"It's my father."

"What's up G," Ben asked when he got on the phone.

"How's everything going?"

"I done ran a hole in those shoes already," Ben said.

"Well come over to the house so we can talk about getting you another pair."

"Alright, we'll stop by," Ben said then passed the phone back to Sandra.

When they made it to the projects Ryder got out of the backseat and walked over to Fred and Paul and said, "Dawg that motherfucker ride nice."

"I can see me in one of them," Paul said. "I might look into getting one," he continued to say as he watched the truck pull away.

"What them people gon do about your truck," Ryder asked.

"By it being involved in a murder, they gon keep it till they finish investigating, but I'ma see if I can claim it as totaled and let the insurance pay me for it. If they do I'm most definitely gon cop something nice."

"I heard Chill was trying to sell his Grand Prix for 8 racks, when I get my money straight, I'ma buy it from him if he still got it," Fred said.

"Nigga you should have 8 racks to spend. What the fuck you doing with your money?" Paul said.

"Yeah, I got it, but I ain't trying to be broke rushing to buy a car."

"That's all you got?" Ryder asked in disbelief.

"You crazy as a motherfucker for wanting to buy a car from Chill. A'in't no telling how many niggas waiting to see that car to shoot that bitch up, he's in all kinds of beefs," Paul stated.

"I ain't tripping, I can get it painted another color," Fred replied.

"You really must want a Prix huh?" Ryder asked.

"Dawg I been liking those cars for a long time, and now that I'm making money, I'ma get one."

When Sandra pulled up in front of her house, her father was already waiting outside for them.

When she parked, her father was there to open her door. "Thank you, father."

"You're welcome precious," Giovanni said as he moved aside to allow Sandra to exit her SUV. By the time, Giovanni had shut her door Ben had gotten out and gone around front to greet him.

When they made it inside, they went to a conference room similar to where they'd gone the night of Sandra's party and started discussing business.

"So you finish with the two keys already?" Giovanni asked.

"You mean eight keys, but yeah, I'm done with everything but maybe one."

"You must be whole selling them," Giovanni asked.

"Fuck no! I'm breaking everything down into grams."

"And you sold nearly eight kilos all in grams?" Giovanni questioned.

"My business is moving a kilo a day, and that's only because I close down at 6:00 p.m."

"Well if that's the case, it looks like I'll be seeing you more often than I expected. Nevertheless, if you want to limit the number of trips you take, tell me how much you need to last you a month."

"I really can't say what will last a month or not, but whatever you give me, I'ma try to pay you off as soon as possible. So what you have in mind?" Ben asked.

"How does 5 kilos a month sound?" Giovanni asked.

"It sounds like we have a deal," Ben said as he reached over the desk to shake hands.

"Well let me get things together for you, and I'll call you with the date and place to pick it up."

"I'll be waiting," Ben said then he left the room.

As Ben walked down the long hallway that led to the living room, he was met by Sandra and she asked if he was ready to go.

"Yeah, I'm good. We can go," he replied.

When they got in her truck, Sandra placed her purse on top of the console. To Ben's surprise, he saw the handle of a firearm, so he pulled it out still inside the holster and held it in the air.

"So, you're into guns huh? I would have never guessed you were into guns."

"My daddy bought it for me. Guns aren't my thing. I just keep it in my purse to satisfy him. What! Why are you looking at me like that?" Sandra asked curiously.

"I was just wondering if you know that me and your daddy are doing business?"

"What kind of business? He's never spoken to me about doing business with you."

"Well if he didn't tell you, he must think it's in your best interest not to know."

"Maybe you're right," Sandra said with a slight attitude.

"Oh daddy little girl mad!" Ben said teasing her.

"I'm not mad, but if this business you talking 'bout involves drugs, I'll be disappointed. I'll be so happy when he stops dealing with that stuff. I just want to start living a normal life."

"Your life is normal. You live in a house with both parents, you're financially secure, you don't have to worry about how you gon pay your bills, or where your next meal will come from. You are riding around in a brand-new Porsche. What's not a normal life is when you see your mother sell her body for drugs. Or your father abuses you sexually, or you're living in a house with no lights, that shit ain't a normal life. What you living is the American Dream. So explain to me what is your idea of a normal life?"

"I understand exactly what you're saying but all those people you're talking about are free to move like they choose to. Even with all the money and cars, I still feel like I'm trapped in an overprotective world and at times it can be stressful."

"That's why I am here to relieve you from all that stress," Ben said seductively.

"Don't even think about it," Sandra said smiling.

Thirty minutes later they arrived at the River Walk. This was Sandra's first time actually being on the River Walk, so Ben walked her around to sight-see as if she were a tourist.

They ended their evening looking over the river as they watched the currents slamming into the wall.

"Do you ever ask yourself is it worth it?" Sandra asked over her shoulder as Ben stood behind her with his arms around her waist.

"If you talking 'bout my lifestyle, yeah, it's worth it. When you came up like I did, survival comes at any cost. But, at the same time I want to leave it all behind someday and start my own business."

"If you thinking about starting a business, what you need to be doing right now is learning the ins and outs of whatever you're thinking about getting involved with."

"Lately I been thinking about getting into the real estate business."

"How much do you know about real estate?" she asked as she turned to face him.

"Not much, but my homeboy took some classes and he gon give me a few pointers."

"If you are serious about what you're saying, I can point you in the right direction."

"I just might need your help," Ben said as he looked at his watch. Reading his facial expression, Sandra asked him was he ready to head home. She knew he might need to take care of some loose ends for Monsta's party.

"Yeah, we can go, but I want you to know that I really enjoy hanging out with you."

"I like hanging out with you also, and I really enjoyed myself. This is one of the few times I really felt free."

When she finished talking, Ben looked into her eyes for a few seconds. At that point he leaned over and kissed her gently on her full lips before they took off for her car.

After dropping Ben off at the project, she went to Barnes and Noble to purchased a book before going home.

CHAPTER 38

Club Venue was packed wall to wall and they still had at least 100 people waiting in line to get in the club. When the SGs entered the club, all eyes were focused on them. As they moved towards their section it appeared as if they were acting out a movie script in a mafia movie. Especially, the way Ben clutched a small leather bag in his hand.

Everyone was there except Lil' Fred, because he was too young to get in the club, so he stayed at the project. The whole crew sat in the VIP section of the club, where they were accommodated with bottles of Crystal. The dance floor was jam-packed, and everyone was facing the stage waiting on Magnolia Shorty and Big Freddia to perform.

Hanging over the stage was a large Welcome Home Monsta banner. Monsta didn't know if the club was packed with people that were there to support him. Or if it was just a regular crowd, but no matter what the reason for it being packed, he was pleased with the way his homies put it together for him.

While sitting at the table, Ben grabbed the leather bag from the sofa and placed it on the table. Before unzipping the bag, he looked at his crew and said, "First of all, I love you, niggas."

"Come on dawg, don't get all sensitive on a nigga," Paul said in a joking tone.

"Never that, but on some real shit, I know its been a crazy summer. But, through it all, you niggas was there, so to show my appreciation, I got these for y'all," Ben said as he pulled one of the SG chains from the bag and placed it on his neck.

They were waiting on him to pass them out, but instead he asked what they were all waiting on with a sly smile. At that point he then reached in the bag and began handing out the chains.

Ben extended a fist towards the middle of the table and said, "Slum Godds for life."

"Slum Godds for life," they all repeated.

"Now that that's out the way, let's see what's up with these hoes," Paul said as he bobbed his head to the music.

DJ Pee Wee announced from the DJ booth that the show would begin in 15 minutes. Everyone rushed to the bars to get their drinks before they took the stage.

"You can let 'em in? They with me," Ben told security working the VIP section when Tiger, Poppa and Hood approached the velvet rope of the VIP section. They all greeted each other once they were allowed in.

"Y'all niggas representing, I like that," Ben said speaking about the black T-shirts they wore with TCB in big bold white letters going across the chest.

"If y'all would have told us that y'all was gon wear R.I.P. T-shirts, we would have got 'em on the strength," Tiger said.

"I see y'all shining too," he continued to say as he reached for Paul's chain.

Monsta spotted a dude name Tron who he did time with, so he eased from their section and began making his way through the crowd to holla at him. But, before he could make it to him someone reached out and grabbed his hand. When he turned to see who it was, it was Diamond, looking good as ever.

"After what happened in the project, I'm surprised to see you show up, but thanks for coming."

"I wouldn't have missed it for the world."

"A'ight, I'll see you around, let me holla at my potner right fast."

Before Monsta walked off, Diamond told him that she wanted to holla at him before he left the club.

Tron had made it to one of the bars and was flirting with a bitch that had the total package of a stripper. Small waist, big ass, a perfect size chest, and some light brown eyes that could have been contacts.

As he was talking, Tron noticed Monsta coming his way.

"I can't really make out what you saying over this music and shit. Give me your number and we can talk later," Tron told the female just as Monsta approached him.

"What's up homie?" Tron said after he got her number.

"I'm good, my nigga," Monsta said as he greeted him with a hug.

"I heard you was home. So whatcha in to?"

"Right now, I'm just weighing my options, feel me?"

"It look like you doing something, you rocking ice and shit."

"Naw this shit ain't nothing. You gon know when I'm doing something."

Moments later, Rell and his crew made their appearance dressed like they were attending a funeral. They were dressed in all black with custom made fitty caps that read CP3 on the front of them.

Even though the music was playing, the moment they were noticed, it seemed as if everything got quiet. The crowd was filled with anticipation that Rell and his crew were about to get stumped out. Because they were letting it be known that they were from the Calliope because the CP3 stood for Calliope Project 3rd Ward.

From the VIP section, Trap noticed how all the attention was focused on the entrance. That's when he saw what had everyone's attention.

"Yo Ben, ya boy Rell and his crew just came through," Trap yelled over the music.

When Trap said that, they all looked. Ryder didn't like the fact that they showed up at a Melph party wearing shit with the Calliope on it, so he spoke out about it.

"I know them niggas don't mean no disrespect. But, they out of line wearing that shit in here with the whole city knowing we at war with they hood."

Monsta had made it back to their section. When he did, he asked what was up with those niggas at the bar with that CP3 shit on their hats. So Ben explained to him that they were cool. Ben noticed how the other crews from the Melph started to move towards them. So he moved as quickly as he could through the crowd to stop whatever they were planning to do to Rell and his crew.

"What up with y'all?" Ben said when he made it to them.

"Ain't shit popping, just 'bout to get us a drink," Rell said.

"Y'all don't have to wait in this long line for drinks. We got a section and more than enough bottles of Chris, and we got that loud so let's roll."

As they were headed to the VIP section, everyone got on their feet when Magnolia Shorty took the stage and got the club jumping. When they walked in VIP, everyone spoke except Ryder who was sitting back sipping on his drink.

"Come on babe, let's go take some pictures," Miecy told Monsta the moment Rell and his crew sat down.

While they were waiting to take pictures, Diamond watched from a distance. The more she watched, the more she realized she was highly attracted to him.

Out of the hundreds of people that were in the club, Monsta and Diamond caught eyes. But, he didn't think anything of it.

The night was winding down and Miecy was ready to go home. The truth of the matter is, she wasn't the club going type of chic, she was only there to support her man.

While Miecy went back to the VIP section to get her purse, Monsta went to see what Diamond wanted. China tapped Diamond on the shoulder and told her that Monsta was coming their way. When she turned around, she was face to face with him.

"So what's up? Cash straight huh?" Monsta asked.

"Yeah, he good."

"Well, what you want to talk to me about?" Monsta asked curiously.

"I wanted to ask how you felt about taking a picture to send to Cash."

"I would love to do it, but you know how my girl be tripping."

"It sounds like she got you wrapped around her finger."

"It ain't that. It's just that she so jealous and I ain't for the bullshit tonight."

"I hate an insecure bitch. She the type that make a bitch want to fuck her man just to show her that..."

Before she finished her comment, Miecy walked up and aggressively shoved Diamond in her chest. Telling her to stay the fuck from being around her man.

Diamond shoved her back causing a big commotion. For the onlookers who didn't actually see what was going on it was somewhat confusing. Many thought that two rival crews had gotten into an altercation. By the time everyone realized that was not the case security had defused the situation and ordered everyone to leave the premises.

Donte' and Larry noticed that everyone was leaving the club so they knew that the SGs had to come to the parking lot to get their cars. But they didn't know they'd be waiting in vain because the SGs had their cars parked directly in front of the club. So there was no need for them to go to the parking lot.

The moment Tiger and his crews turned the corner to get their cars, they were recognized by the TCB t-shirts they had on.

"I got that bitch ass nigga now," Donte' said as he got out of his car and kneeled down beside it and Black Larry did the same.

While Tiger and his crew were walking heading for their car, they spotted a group of females then stopped and started flirting.

"Let's go," Donte' said as he raised up with his gun in his hand.

They got within 30 feet of them when one of the young women started running and screaming, "Watch out girl, they got guns!"

If Tiger and his crew have had their guns, things might have turned out different by them being alerted. But, since they didn't, things went exactly the way Donte' and Larry had predicted.

Hood and Poppa managed to get away unharmed simply because they weren't the target and all focus was on Tiger.

They rushed Tiger and shot him 9 times as he tried to run from the gunfire and ended up collapsing a half block away. The only reason they didn't stand over him and continue shooting was because there were entirely too many potential witnesses. So they tucked away their guns and fled the scene.

When the SGs left the club, they all went straight to Paul's apartment. As soon as they entered, they noticed the kitchen floor was littered with broken glass from the window. After further observation, they also noticed the kitchen door was ajar as well. That's when it became clear that someone broken in.

Paul moved as quick as possible on his injured leg to see if the money and product were still in its place.

"Fuck!" Paul yelled when he saw that they were both gone. "Where the fuck Fred at!?" Paul asked out loud.

Without saying anything, Ben called Fred's phone but got no answer. "He ain't answer his phone," Ben said in a confused tone, and just as he said that, his phone started to ring.

"Here he go right chere," Ben said flipping his phone open without looking and asked, "Where you at?"

"We at the hospital."

"Who this is?" Ben asked in an aggravated tone.

"This Hood, say brah them niggas from the Calliope just hit Tiger up and I don't know if he gon make it."

"A'ight homie, we on our way, we'll see y'all there," Ben told him and then hung up.

"Where that nigga at?" Paul asked curious to know where Fred was so he could get some answers because that's a kilo of heroin and 175 racks missing.

"That was Hood. He said something about some niggas out the Calliope hit Tiger up."

"It probably was that nigga Rell and his crew," Ryder said with confidence.

By the time, they made it to Charity Hospital, Tiger had been taken into surgery. That was a good thing because that meant he was still alive.

As they were all gathered in the emergency room, Monsta stepped out to answer his phone. By him not logging Diamond's number in his phone, he didn't know who was calling because the number was unfamiliar.

"Hello?" he said when he answered the phone.

"Are you okay, because somebody got shot around by the club," Diamond asked.

"Yeah, I'm good, but did you hear anything about who did the shooting?"

"I don't really know them people uptown like that. So where are you?"

"I'm at the hospital."

"Is Paul with you?"

"Yeah, why what's up?"

"If he ain't too busy, tell him China said to come by my house and you can come with him."

"Why would I want to come with' him," Monsta said.

"That would spoil the surprise if I tell you."

After everything was under control, Paul and Monsta went to the St. Bernard Project to kick it with Diamond and China. Thirty minutes later they arrived at Diamond's house. China opened the door with a big smile on her face because she was happy to spend some time with Paul.

"I miss you so much," China told Paul then started kissing on his neck.

Paul walked her backwards until he ended up on top of her stretched out on the sofa.

"Diamond is in her bedroom," China told Monsta between kisses.

Monsta knocked on her bedroom door and she told him to come in. When Monsta entered, he found her laying across her bed in her lingerie, listening to Usher's *You Make Me Wanna.*

"Why you looking like you never seen a bitch in her lingerie?"

"Because I wasn't expecting this."

Diamond got out of her bed exposing her flawless body, then walked up to Monsta and pulled him down on the bed. At first Monsta felt bad for allowing his homie girl to approach him the way Diamond did. But, once he felt her small warm hands grab his manhood, his hormones took over. They ended up indulging in sexual intercourse for over two hours. Monsta fucked her in every position his mind could think of.

Other than Miecy, Diamond was the only female Monsta had indulged in sex with since he'd been released from prison. If he had to describe her sex skills, let's just say Diamond fuck like an experienced porn star.

As they were laying down Monsta glanced at the dresser and noticed a prison picture of Cash and thought to himself that bitches ain't shit.

"

CHAPTER 39

The next day, Donte' and Larry walked to Safeway grocery store to purchase a newspaper to see if it had an article in it about Tiger, but there was none. They expected for Tiger's homies to retaliate. So to avoid a shootout right then, they stayed in their apartment until they were ready to lure Rell away from the project and kill him.

***

The SGs had never been faced with a situation such as the one they were facing at that point, because in the project, home invasions were non-existent.

Ben made several attempts to call Fred, but he hadn't gotten an answer up to that point. In the midst of trying to track Fred down, Ben contacted Giovanni about purchasing another package.

Giovanni instructed Ben to go to his car lot on the I-10 service road and ask for Myron. He explained to Ben that by the time he made it there, Myron would be filled in with the details of his visit.

While heading to the car lot, Ben tried once more to get in contact with Fred, and just like the other times, he didn't get an answer. From a logical standpoint, Fred was expressing his guilt, but Ben's better judgment kept telling him that Fred wouldn't have crossed those lines. He was already in the position to accumulate money just as the others.

Then his train of thought changed, maybe he was dead somewhere or went to jail. So Ben came up with the conclusion that he would find a way to check with Fred's mother and ask if she'd seen him lately.

Once he snapped out of those thoughts, he told himself that he'll get Rell to go over to Fred's mother's house and ask her if she had seen him.

When he pulled into the car lot, he was greeted by a car salesman.

"May I assist you with anything, or do you want to look around first?" the salesman asked.

"I'm here to see Myron. Would you mind pointing me in his direction?" Ben asked as he looked around the car lot.

He was told that Myron's workstation was the first cubicle to the right once he walked inside of the dealership.

Carrying a briefcase Ben approached Myron, who was sitting behind a messy desk and introduced himself as Giovanni's friend.

Once he did that, Myron left his station for a couple of minutes, then came back carrying a medium size duffel bag and placed it on the side of the chair that Ben was sitting in, and then took the briefcase and placed it under his desk.

Myron called Giovanni from the company phone and told him that the parts arrived, and while still holding the receiver to his ear, he told Ben that their business was done, so Ben left the dealership and headed back to the project.

***

Rell went to Wanda's apartment to check on Lil' Fred. He knocked on the door with great force because no one answered, until finally Fred opened the door without asking who it was.

When he saw it was Rell, he asked what he wanted in a slur. "Ben asked me to come and check on you. He hasn't seen you, and you ain't answering your phone, you might want to give him a call," Rell told him while looking at several pieces of foil on the coffee table.

"A'ight, I'ma holla at him," Fred said then closed his door.

On his way back from Wanda's house, Rell decided to stop by Donte's spot and see if they were still in business since Curtis Mitchell was in jail.

Donte' and Larry were standing in the hallway when Rell approached the stairwell that led to their apartment.

"What's up homie? You still straight cause I'm trying to score something," Rell asked Donte'.

"We ain't got shit right now. But, we was just about to go holla at our potner in East Shore and get somethin'. You can ride with us out there if you want to," Donte' told him.

"A'ight, let me go get my money," Rell said then took off across the courtyard...

We got that bitch ass nigga now," Black Larry told Donte'.

"Look, soon as we turn off Haynes Blvd. by Compact Food Store I'ma tell you to pull over so I can take a piss. That's when I'ma smoke that bitch," Donte' said.

Ten minutes later, Rell made it back to Donte' and Larry's spot. "What's up y'all ready?" Rell asked them.

"Yeah, let's go handle this right fast," Larry said.

As they were riding, Rell noticed that Donte' kept watching him through the rearview.

"How's things going with Curtis?" Rell asked trying to strike a conversation. Something about the quietness made him feel very uncomfortable.

"His lawyer said that he'll be out soon because Curtis' fingerprints wasn't on the gun," Donte' responded. "But like I said homie, I wouldn't have took that charge either," Donte' continued.

"You know how the game go," Rell stated.

When they exited the interstate on Downman, Rell really felt that something wasn't right. It seemed as though their moods began to change, along with the fact that Donte' kept watching him through the rearview.

They rode down Haynes Blvd, because it was somewhat secluded. The further they rode, the faster Rell's heartrate increased. Donte' made a mental note on how he was gon execute the murder. As soon as the car stopped he was gon turn around in his seat and kill Rell before he knew what hit him. They were a block away from the Compact Food Store and the closer they got to turning off on the side street, the more Donte's adrenaline rushed.

"Pull over and let me take a piss," Donte' told Black Larry as planned. But, the very instant the car stopped, Rell shot Donte' in the back of his head once. He immediately turned the weapon and shot Black Larry twice in his head before he could react to the situation.

Nervously, Rell pulled them both out of the car. Using his shirt, he wiped the little blood spatters from the windshield before pulling off in Larry's car. When he felt, he was close enough to the project, he wiped his prints off the steering wheel and walked quickly toward the project.

Once he made it home, he took a quick shower then went in the Melph for two reasons. First, to tell Ben that he stopped by Fred's mother's house and he was there. Secondly, to explain to him that it appeared that Fred was getting high. Based on the slur he spoke with, and the empty foil packages that he saw on the coffee table.

When he made it to the Melph, he saw Ben and Ryder sitting on the project bench. Rell enjoyed the fact that his plan was coming together, and that he only had a few more people to eliminate. He figured that it would do him more harm than good to kill Ben. So Ben would be one of the few people that he would keep around. Simply because Ben was the way to the plug, and without a plug, everything that he accomplished would be in vain.

"I got some good news for you," Rell told Ben when he approached him and Ryder.

"Spit it out then nigga," Ben replied.

I don't know how long it's gon take before they find their bodies, but I handled that issue with Black Larry and Donte'."

"That's what's up. Where did you end up putting their bodies?" Ben asked.

"I dumped them niggas bodies in East Shore on Vincent St. You know it ain't too much traffic right there. But, by tomorrow morning they should be found."

"So what I owe you for your services?" Ben asked, because he was more than willing to pay a fee for the job, cause that's two less niggas he'd have to worry about.

As they were talking, Ronald and Tony pulled up in Roxanne's car. Ryder knew that the car looked familiar but, he couldn't put a finger on it until he saw Ronald step out.

"I wonder what them niggas want?" Ryder stated as he watched them come closer.

"I guess they looking for Paul," Ben stated.

"What's up with y'all?" Ronald said as he was walking up to them.

"What's popping Soulja?" Ben said.

"I need to holla at Paul, he around?" Ronald asked.

"Yeah, that nigga inside," Ben said as he pointed them in the direction of Paul's apartment.

"A'ight my nigga, y'all be cool out chere," Ronald said as him and Tony headed for Paul's apartment.

"Now back to you, what I owe you?" Ben asked.

"I ain't gon charge you for no shit like that because I fuck with you. What you can do for me is front me some work for a good price though," Rell said.

"Are you sure homie?" Ben said with a little concern in his voice.

"Real niggas do real shit, ALL THE TIME," Rell replied.

"A'ight homie, I'ma give you a call tomorrow," Ben replied.

"Oh, yeah, I went by Fred's mother's house and that's where he was."

"I wonder why that nigga ain't answering his phone," Ben responded in a confused tone.

"If I had to say so, dude getting loaded."

"Why would you say some shit like that?" Ben asked with a little hostility in his voice.

"Because he was ducking when he answered the door. Plus, I seen boo-coo pieces of foil on the coffee table."

"I appreciate that my nigga," Ben said as Rell was about to leave.

"Give me Rell's number," Ryder told Ben.

"Why, what's up?"

"Nothing just let me get his number."

Without further questions, Ben gave him the number. Five minutes later, Ronald and Tony came out of the apartment followed by Paul. When Ronald and Tony left, Ben asked Paul what it was that they wanted.

"Ronald want me to put him on his feet."

"So what you tell'em?"

"I told him that I'll start him off with two and a quarter and we'll go from there. You know, show a lil' brotherly love."

"That's cool with me. But, that's your people so you deal with him."

I got this homie."

Well we good then, but I'm 'bout to shoot home and spend a lil' time with the wifey and B.J."

Before he left Ben told Paul that he'd be back to the project early so they could start baggin' up the dope.

When Ben left, Ryder went to holla at Paul about Fred.

"Say brah, who you feel is responsible for stealing our shit?" Ryder asked Paul.

"On the real, I can't put that shit together to save my life. Who'd you had in mind?" Paul asked.

"Think about it dawg. We never had no fucking problem like this until we brought a new nigga in."

"Who you talking about, Rell or Tiger?" Paul asked.

"I'm talking about Fred. A nigga break in and steals the work and money then all of a sudden, he come up M.I.A. Plus he was the only one in the project."

"You know what? I never thought about that," Paul said. "Rell said he went by the mommas and he was over there loaded as a motherfucker."

"Off what? Weed." Paul asked.

"Fuck no! Dope!"

"Get the fuck outta here with that bullshit."

"For real homie."

"I know that nigga ain't rocking like that," Paul remarked.

"Man, fuck all that, what you want to do about it?" Ryder asked.

"You really think the lil' homie would do some shit like that?" Paul replied.

"THINK! Man, I know that nigga done that shit!"

"You already know what time it is then. We got to rock him," Paul said.

"But how we gon find out where his momma stay?"

"Don't worry about that, I'ma handle it."

In the process of them talking, Monsta pulled up in Miecy's car.

"I didn't tell you that nigga Monsta fucked that hoe Diamond last night?"

"He did? How he ended up pulling that one off?" "Them hoes called us when we was at the hospital."

"What's up my nigga?" Paul said with a smile on his face.

"Ain't nothing, just talked my way back on Miecy's good side."

"What's up with that hoe Diamond?" Ryder asked.

"Dawg that hoe fuck like a nympho, prostitute, and porn star all wrapped in one."

As Monsta gave details about him and Diamond sexual encounter, Paul fantasized about sexing her.

"But fuck all that. Where is everybody and why is all the customers going to the Middle Court to score?"

"The way we doing it, since they got our work we just let them have the weekends, cause when our shop is open they don't be able to sell shit."

"I see y'all got this shit organized."

"When doing business, structure is very important. But, fuck all that let's go ride on the lake front and check out all the bitches."

"Man, I ain't been on the lake front since 99, it still be going down out there?" Monsta asked.

Like 4 flat tires." Paul responded

Let's dip then," Monsta said as they headed for the car.

Later that night, Ryder called Rell to find out exactly where Fred's mother lived because he wanted to go check on him.

When you a snake, you think like a snake. So Rell gave him the address over the phone to keep him from having to meet Ryder in person.

Ryder went to the address that he was given by Rell and watched the apartment closely as he sat in his car. It was a quiet night, there was little to no movement at all. Tired of waiting Ryder decided to get out and walk up to the porch. He was about to knock on the door, but had a premonition to check the door to see if it was unlocked and to his surprise it was.

He didn't want to just barge into the apartment, because he wasn't sure of what was waiting on the other side of the door. Standing there Ryder thought about his next move. He placed his ear to the door to see if he heard any voices or movement. But, all he heard was absolute quietness, so he turned the knob and slowly opened the door.

When he entered the apartment, he saw Fred nodding at the kitchen table, which was filled with a large amount of cash. Ryder watched him nod for a couple of minutes before deciding to put an end to Fred's life by firing two quick shots to the back of his skull. Before Fred's body hit the floor, Ryder was gathering up the money and placing it in a paper bag that was on the kitchen counter.

"Where the work? Where the work?" he kept mumbling to himself as he looked around the roach-infested apartment.

Starting with the kitchen, Ryder searched the apartment for the kilo that was stolen. However, he didn't find anything but crack and heroin paraphernalia.

"FUCK!" he yelled when he didn't find the kilo. Ryder knew that it had to be somewhere. It wouldn't have been possible for Fred to have gotten rid of it that fast, unless he sold it wholesale.

Ryder walked out of the apartment as calm as he could as he headed for his car. When he made it back in the Melph, he went by Betty's and counted the money.

"Eleven racks. Where the fuck is the rest of the money?" Ryder said as he slammed the money on the table. "Whatever he did with it, he paid for it with his life, so fuck it," he continued.

He tried to call Ben and let him know how things turned out, but Ben had his phone turned off. *Well I'll see him in the morning,* Ryder thought to himself before he went in for the night.

CHAPTER 40

The next morning, all the SGs met up at Paul's apartment to cut and package the product, that's when Ben asked did anyone see or hear from Fred.

Ryder started to explain to Ben about the event that transpired the night before. He tried to get Ben to understand that it was best to get rid of Fred, because the last thing they needed was to have someone around that they had to second guess.

Ben was emotionally distraught, because he looked at Fred as a son. Deep down inside, he didn't think Fred was responsible for the break-in. Even if he was, killing him in cold blood without any proof was below the belt.

Even though he felt like Ryder was wrong, he never spoke out against him. He knew that Ryder had been loyal since day one, and if he made a move such as the one he made, he'd done it with good intentions to protect the crew. That's exactly the type of people he wanted to surround himself with. The kind that's willing to do what it takes for the good of the entire crew.

Without saying one single word, Ben walked out of the apartment to get a breath of fresh air. Ryder removed his dust mask and followed Ben to the porch. It was obvious that Ben didn't condone the murder of Fred.

"What's good homie? You straight?" Ryder asked Ben once he made it to the porch.

"To be honest with you my nigga, I ain't straight," Ben said as his eyes filled with water. "I truly don't think he deserved that."

"After what Rell told us, and what I saw for myself when I got to his mother's apartment. It was only a matter of time before our lives were put at risk by the hands of our own," Ryder said. "Remember back in the day when I was using that shit?" he asked.

"Yeah, I remember, how could I forget, but we pulled you away from that shit now look at you. You all about the paper instead of the high."

"Between you and Tre', y'all helped me to get clean. But come on man, Fred didn't have the history we had with each other. All I know is that dope will bring the worst out of anybody and Fred was dangerous enough without the influence of dope. You'd never understand unless you've walked in those shoes. A heroin addiction will run you out of your conscious, I'm speaking from experience. When you have that monkey on your back, and your body is yearning for a fix, you'll rob anyone that can provide you with the money to get that fix. Even if that person knows the consequence is death. Before I pulled the trigger, I watched Fred duck for a couple of minutes. What I saw was the image of myself sitting at that table."

Ben tried his best to hold back his tears. But, as Ryder gave further details of how he killed Fred, tears rolled down Ben's face like an avalanche. Before they went back into the apartment, Ryder asked Ben what they should do with Fred's SG chain.

"If I didn't think his crackhead ass momma would try and take it, I would like to bury him with it on. We'll figure it out, right now let's go help these niggas bag that shit up," Ben said as he reached for the doorknob.

When they entered the apartment, Monsta asked was everything straight.

"Yeah, everything good," Ben said.

"Well put y'all dust mask on and help us finish this shit," Monsta said in a muffled tone as he spoke through his mask.

Between food and smoke breaks, it took them a little over 5 hours to bag up two kilos into one gram packages. Fatigued from the constant work, everyone decided they would call it a night and start fresh in the morning. Before Ben left the apartment, he called Rell and told him to come through any time the next day between the hours of 6 and 6, then he headed home.

Trap went by a females by the name of Pinkey that lived in the project who he dealt with from time to time. Monsta was about to call Diamond to see if she wanted to get together. But just as he grabbed his phone from his pocket, Miecy called to ask when he'd be home which changed his plans all together.

Ryder didn't have anything planned for the night so Paul asked him to take him to the hospital to visit Tiger after he showered. An hour later they arrived at the hospital smelling like a pound of marijuana.

When they walked through the lobby, to their surprise, they saw Diamond sitting in the waiting room in distress. She was leaning down crying while holding her face in both hands.

Since Paul was more acquainted with Diamond, he approached her and questioned her about why she was crying.

She looked up at him with pity in her eyes. Through her sobs she told him that her mother was very sick and that she was just told by the doctor that it wouldn't be long before her mother passed way.

That was part of the truth, but the main reason was because she was told that her mother couldn't use her blood to have a blood transfusion because she tested positive for H.I.V.

Diamond didn't have to give much thought to how she contracted the virus. Monsta was the only guy she'd had sexual intercourse with since Cash went to prison.

Paul displayed his condolence, by taking her hands and raising her to her feet. He gave her a tight hug, and then whispered how sorry he was to hear the discouraging news.

"If there's anything I can help you with, let me know a'ight," Paul said as he looked into her puffy eyes.

"Paul I don't know what I'ma do," she said in a low pitch as she dropped her head.

"If you want to go have a drink or something to clear your head, we can do that," Paul told her trying to take advantage of her vulnerability.

"I might take you up on the offer," Diamond responded.

***

While connected to a heart monitor, and with an IV running in his arm, Tiger laid in his hospital bed while Jack Rabbit sat and observed him.

"Don't try to speak, all I need you to do is listen to me," Jack Rabbit said as he looked down at his nephew.

"I know how it is when you fuck with niggas and they beefing, you feel the need to ride with them. But I tried my best to keep you from getting involved in them niggas beef. I've seen too many times in the past, when two sets start beefing, either they all end up dead or go to jail for a long time. Leaving the streets busted wide open for the next crew to step in. We're supposed to be that next crew, and you damn near got your ass killed. But it's gon be all good when you get out of here, cause while y'all was at ole boy's coming home party, I broke in them niggas shit. And guess what? They had a brick and 175 cash in that motherfucker"

"You did what!" Tiger asked in a whisper.

"If you in this shit to win, you have to take advantage of every opportunity, especially when hundreds of thousands of dollars are involved."

"This shit gon end up bad," Tiger struggled to say.

"Trust me nephew, we will be the last ones they suspect, due to the fact they fronting us two fucking bricks, but I don't want you to worry about that, all I need you to do is focus on getting well so we can get this money."

Tiger knew that the SGs weren't the niggas to be fucking with especially when it came to their money. Now his uncle was about to create a problem that they weren't equipped to deal with, because the SGs had enough money to send several hit men at once and completely wipe them out.

"What you thinking about?" Jack Rabbit asked him when he looked into Tiger's distant eyes.

"Nothing," Tiger replied.

"Well look brah, I'm 'bout to push out, I'll stop by tomorrow," Jack Rabbit said then leaned over and kissed Tiger on the forehead before leaving.

After talking with Diamond, Paul and Ryder headed for the elevator. Once the elevator stopped and the door opened, Jack Rabbit was getting off.

"What's up young-bloods?" Jack Rabbit said when he seen Paul and Ryder.

How's he doing?" Paul asked sincerely.

"He gon be a'ight," Jack Rabbit replied.

"A'ight School, we gon holla at cha later," Paul said then pushed the #2 button on the elevator.

Paul and Ryder visited Tiger for 30 minutes before leaving the hospital. When they made it back to the project, they seen Jack Rabbit and Poppa standing in the cut. Ryder was about to go hang out with them but he decided to call it a night.

"I'ma see you in the A.M. my nigga, I'm gone," Ryder told Paul as he left.

CHAPTER 41

Curtis Mitchell was told by his girlfriend Kenyatta that Donte' and Black Larry were found dead in New Orleans East. The news was like a punch to the stomach and he hated to hear it, but at that moment he was fighting for his life. The only thing that was on his mind was not getting indicted for the gun or the charges linked to it.

In Orleans Parish, they have a thing called the 60-day rule, and what that means is that the Grand Jury must indict a person within a 60-day time frame, and if not the accused party must automatically be released unless he/she has some type of hold on them that prevents them from being released.

Curtis Mitchell was being represented by one of the best criminal lawyers available. So his chances of being acquitted on the charges are high, and without proof that he was in possession of the firearm Derek Scott would beat the case in his sleep, all Curtis had to do was be patient.

Curtis Mitchell found himself talking with an old convict that was back in the Parish from Angola State Penitentiary on an appeal. He was told that if the police raided a neighborhood, it's impossible to charge one person with the contraband they find especially if it wasn't on that person, and Curtis was ensured that if he obtained Derek Scott to represent him he was sure to walk on the charge.

CHAPTER 42

Ben woke up early in his home on the last Sunday in August, 2005. He had slept only three or four hours, because he couldn't get Lil' Fred out of his mind.

Prior to he and Joy preparing for bed the night before, it was announced on the radio that a powerful storm by the name of Katrina was sure to hit New Orleans.

The National Hurricane Center categorizes every storm based primarily on the strength of its winds, therefore, based on the radio information, Katrina would be a Category 3 storm.

As Ben watched the news early the next morning, it was reported that Katrina had upgraded to a Category 5 and was expected to hit the New Orleans region within the next twelve to twenty-four hours. Ben didn't think much of it, because, there would normally just be a lot of wind and rain damage, but nothing severe.

As Ben was tuning into the news broadcast, Breaking News flashed across the bottom of the television screen. He thought that it was something about the storm. That's when they showed Giovanni, Sandra, and her mother being escorted out of their residence in handcuffs.

"What the fuck!" Ben yelled as he eyed the TV.

"What happened bae?" Joy asked as she came running in the bedroom.

When she looked at the TV and the arrest being made, she asked Ben did he know those people. Ben didn't answer her but his silence screamed yes loud as a bullhorn.

"Who are those people?" Joy asked Ben, because the worried look he displayed on his face while watching the TV was easily recognizable.

"That's someone I was doing business with," Ben replied as he tried to listen to the news spokeswoman.

"After a 5-year investigation for drug trafficking and money laundering, local and federal authorities worked together to bring down Giovanni Martinez, the largest drug distributor in the Southern Region. Authorities confiscated $1.5 million in cash, two firearms, and 10 kilos of heroin out of a wall safe that was hidden behind a bookcase. Giovanni Martinez is facing a life sentence in federal prison if convicted."

Ben's mind was racing at the fact that he didn't know how much information the authorities knew, or if they were onto him at all. He started to explain to Joy that if he were lucky enough to escape prison this time that he was getting out in a week or two.

"I hope so Benjamin, because I don't know how much more of this shit I can take..."

"You have my word bae, when I am done with this package, I'm out, but just in case they come back for me, I want you to get in contact with Raymond Marrero. He's an expensive lawyer but he's worth every penny."

"Why would they come back for you?" Joy asked as her heart rate increased.

"I didn't say they will, but just in case they do, I need you to follow my instructions and hire Raymond Marrero to represent me, but let's hope it don't come down to that," Ben said as he stood up then he told Joy that he was about to go in the project to get some things in order.

The moment Ben pulled out of his driveway, paranoia started to set in. He felt like he was being followed so he made several unnecessary turns while in route to the projects. When he made it to the projects, just as expected, he ran into a massive crowd of heroin users that were there to score.

When he got out the car, he looked around for Paul, but there was no sign of him. He approached Monsta and asked him why he was serving the customers. He was told that Paul wasn't around so instead of waiting for his day tomorrow, he decided to take Paul's day and Paul can have his day tomorrow.

"Did you try calling him?" Ben asked as his mind wandered in the direction of Paul being arrested.

"Yeah I called him but I didn't get an answer, let me try again," Monsta said as he reached into his pocket for his phone.

When he placed the call, Paul picked up on the third ring. "What's up homie?" Paul answered.

"Where you at my nigga?" Monsta asked.

"I'm at the hotel with a friend."

"You trippin', brah, you know today is your day and you laying up with a bitch."

"Oh shit! I'm about to get up now."

"Don't trip, I'ma hold you down for the day."

The entire time Paul was on the phone, Diamond was performing oral sex on him. He and she had sexed each other all night and they both agreed to keep their sexual encounter between the two of them.

When Monsta ended the call, he told Ben about Paul's whereabouts and all Ben did was shake his head and then said, "That nigga would die for some pussy."

Trap and Ryder came out of Betty's apartment and saw that Ben had made it into the project, so they went to ask if he picked up the cut because they needed it to bag up more dope.

"Fuck, I forgot all about that shit, I'ma go get it before they close. But, the reason I came to holla at y'all was to tell y'all the plug been all over the news."

"I thought they picked him up in Houston, why are they showing him on our news?" Trap asked.

"No homie, I'm talking about the new plug," Ben responded.

"What! They got Giovanni!" Trap asked in disbelief because Giovanni was their only heroin supplier since Ernest got arrested.

"Yep, the news says they got him charged with drug trafficking, money laundering, and possession of firearms."

"What did his daughter say about it?" Ryder asked.

"That's the crazy part, they arrested her and her mother too."

"Damn that's fucked up. So what we gon do now," Trap asked.

At that moment, Ben made his final decision that once he sold that package, he was getting out of the drug game while he was ahead. Since lately everyone around him was dying or going to prison.

"After we finish with these bricks, I'm done with this shit."

"Yeah, right," Trap said sarcastically.

"I'm serious my nigga, when we done with this package, I'm done."

"Like I told you before, we can get involved with that real estate shit," Monsta stated.

"Speaking of real estate, y'all know that storm supposed to be hitting. What y'all gon' do?" Ben asked.

"What you gon' do?" Ryder asked him.

"Me, Joy, and, BJ gon' dip to Houston, we gettin' the fuck outta here. There's supposed to be a Category 5 storm coming in."

"Dawg a nigga ain't got time to be leaving and shit, waiting in all that fucking traffic. I haven't seen a storm yet that affected these bricks," Ryder stated.

"Well that's on you, I'm getting the fuck away from here. Besides we can use this time like a vacation," Ben said.

"I'm thinking about leaving too. Miecy wants to go by her family's place in Baton Rouge."

"I'll probably just stay in the project with Ryder," Trap said.

"I'm 'bout to go home and help Joy pack some things for the trip. I'll be back in a few hours with the cut," Ben said before heading to his car.

"Hold on Ben, drop me off at home," Monsta said as he began walking behind Ben.

After dropping Monsta off at home Ben went straight home and began packing.

***

The next morning word spread throughout the Calliope project after the news broadcast that Donte' and Black Larry were found dead. They were found in the East by an elderly man who was taking his dog for a morning walk.

Residents of the Calliope were trying to figure out who they were with at the time of their deaths. The shots to the back of their heads clearly indicated that someone was in the backseat when the murders took place. Larry's car being found a block away from the project also suggested that the killer or killers might be from the surrounding area.

J-Roc and Pookey were sitting on the porch smoking a blunt, wondering what they would do now that the only plug was dead.

"Say brah, if we can't find a plug, we gotta start jacking these niggas. I ain't about to sit around and do bad while these fake ass niggas eat out chere," Pookey said.

"If push comes to shove, that's what we gon' do, but let's use up all our options. Rell might know somebody that got some work, you know he fuck with niggas all over the city."

"Where the fuck he at anyway?" Pookey asked.

"Ain't no telling where that nigga at. But, we wouldn't be in this situation trying to find a plug, if he hadn't thrown that gun by Curtis when Safe Home hit."

"On the real homie, he was down bad for that shit. If it had been the other way around, he would have been in his feelings. Not to mention that fool has like four bodies on that gun," J-Roc continued.

"Speaking of bodies, what went down that made him kill Brittany?" Pookey asked. "I'm laying up with the hoe and he called and told me to get dressed and to be ready to leave when he got there, then he smoked the girl."

"Dawg I didn't even ask him what that shit was about, I just rolled with the punches," J-Roc said. "But lately he's been doing a lot of slick shit without telling us. When we ask him about it, he'll brush a nigga off by saying shit like, 'Fall back I got this.' But, at the end of the day, he always put us in position to eat so a nigga don't push the issue."

As they were talking, Rell came from across the courtyard from a crackhead named Nicole house where he regularly got his dick sucked. The moment he approached the porch where J-Roc and Pookey were, J-Roc started complaining about their need for work. He was concerned they were going to end up losing their customers if they didn't get a package soon. Rell assured them that they would be straight. Since he knew that he was going to get some work from Ben.

"So who you gon' score from, because we need that shit right now," J-Roc said.

"Fall back and let me work my magic. If everything goes as planned, the streets will soon be ours, all we need to do is be patient."

"Patience ain't going to put food on the table, we need to be focused on eating right now," Pookey said.

"Not only would patience put food on the table, it will put enough on it for us to feast year in, and year out," Rell replied.

"How much patience we need, cause right now we ain't eating shit," J-Roc stated.

"By tomorrow, we gon' be where we want to be. Within a week our conversations will be based on where we can hide all the fucking money we 'bout come up on."

"Now that's a problem I wouldn't mind having," Pookey said with a smile on his face.

***

Jack Rabbit and James were standing at the end of the driveway when Rell pulled up in the Melph. Rell noticed that the courtyard was almost empty for that time of day, so he asked James where everybody was. James told him that Ryder and Trap were by Betty. When Rell pulled off, Jack Rabbit told James that he didn't trust Rell at all.

Rell parked and went to Betty's apartment. Inside he found Ryder and Trap counting thousands of dollars on the kitchen table.

"What's up with y'all?" Rell said when he closed the door.
"What's popping homie?" Ryder said as he continued counting the money.

"Ben told me to come through, and that he was gon' serve me. Where that nigga at?"

"That nigga talking, about he gon shoot to Houston for the storm. I told that nigga he was tripping. I ain't going nowhere, you want me to call him for you?" Ryder asked him.

"No, you ain't got to call him, I'll get with him later," Rell responded, looking at all the money on the table. Rell knew that it was at least a hundred thousand easy.

"It looks like the game been treating y'all good," Rell said never taking his eyes off the money.

"We been doing a'ight, but we ain't nowhere close to where we supposed to be," Trap said.

"So what, you was trying to score?" Ryder asked him as he stop counting the money for a second to look up at Rell.

But, when he did he was looking down the barrel of the .45cal, and before he could have gotten another word out of his mouth Rell squeezed the trigger striking Ryder in the face. He quickly pointed the gun at Trap and told him to put the money in a bag.

"You can have the money, just don't shoot!"

"Shut the fuck up and do what the fuck I said!"

"Damn homie! I thought we were on the same team!" Trap said while trying to buy some time.

Trap know they keep a gun stashed in the bottom cabinet under the sink.

"Hurry the fuck up!" Rell said aggressively as he nervously looked back at the door.

Betty came from out of her room fussing, "What I told yall bout playing with them guns in my... OH SHIT!" She said when she seen Ryder dead on the floor and Rell standing there with the gun in his hand.

"Shut the fuck up and get on the ground!" Rell demanded her.

"Just do what he says Betty," Trap told her.

When Trap opened the cabinet to get a bag, he quickly grabbed the 9mm that they kept stashed and managed to fire one round before Rell shot him three times killing him before his body hit the ground. Rell quickly grabbed a bag and placed the money in it then fled the apartment.

Jack Rabbit heard the gunshots, so all his attention was focused in the direction the shots came from, that's when he saw Rell running from the apartment with a bag in his hand. Rell moved quickly and cautiously as he headed for his car.

Once he made it to it, he tossed the bag of money onto the passenger seat through the driver window, then got in the car. The moment he pulled off, Jack Rabbit ran up to the car from the driver side firing a .44 magnum. One of the three bullets struck Rell in his face causing his car to crash into a dumpster. Rell's head slammed into the steering wheel real hard on impact.

Between the bullet injury and the head injury he suffered during the crash, Rell was defenseless. Jack rabbit walked up to Rell, who was out of it at the time, and placed the gun to his head and fired one shot, completely dismantling the left side of Rell head.

Jack Rabbit looked around for a brief second then ran around the car to the passenger side and grabbed the bag of money, which at the time he had no idea what it was, then he ran to the Thalia Court.

When Ben pulled up in the project after leaving the store, anger set in when he noticed Rell Maxima taped off within a crime scene.

"I know them niggas ain't kill that fucking dude," Ben said to himself when he looked through the crowd and didn't Ryder and Trap.

"Up here! Up here!" Betty was screaming from her fourth-floor balcony.

The commotion alert police officers that may be someone else was injured.

"What the fuck happened!?" Ben asked Paul who had walked up to him with a confused look on his face.

"I don't know what happened, I heard a few shots so I came out on the front porch to make sure it wasn't our people, that's when I seen a lot of people running towards the driveway , and when I followed the crowd , I seen Rell car, so when I walked up to it to see if he was aight, I noticed half of his face was gone."

"Where the fuck Ryder and Trap at?" Ben asked. But before Paul could answer, James walked up and told them that Ryder and Trap didn't make it, that they were dead in Betty house.

"They what," Ben said as he dropped to his knees.

"Come on Paul, help me bring him inside," James said.

Just as they made it to Paul's apartment, Paul's phone started ringing. When he looked at the screen and seen that it was China calling, he ignored her call. China called three more times back to back getting Paul very upset, so he decided to just answer.

"Hello!!" He answered aggressively.

"I talked to Diamond a few minutes ago..."

"Look bitch, don't be calling my fucking phone telling me about that hoe, fuck you and that bitch!" Paul said then hung up the phone.

A couple of seconds later she called back and when he seen it was her again he started not to answer it because he thought she found about him fucking Diamond, but he answered anyway.

“What the fuck I told you?”

"Listen Paul, this is important," China said before he could hang the phone up.

"What's important?" He asked curiously.

"You might want to tell your friend Monsta to get himself checked out, because Diamond told me she tested positive for HIV."

“She was tested what?” Paul asked then he got lightheaded.

"That's what shc just told me," China said.

"Aight Ima holla at him," Paul said then hung up in her face.

After hanging up with China, Paul immediately called Monsta to inform him bout the murders of Ryder and Trap, he also told him what China told him about Diamond testing positive for HIV, but Monsta wasn't fazed by the news because he used a codom when he sexed her.

After Ben gathered himself, they returned back to the scene, where they found Ms. Grace taking her son’s murder real hard. By this time, Monsta and Miecy had made it on the scene. Ben walked over to Ms. Grace and held her tight in his arms without saying a word because at the moment it was nothing he could have said to make her feel any better.

When the paramedic removed Ryder and Trap bodies from Betty's apartment, Ms. Grace charged them as they done so while screaming, "Let me see my child!"

"Would somebody please control her!?" One of the paramedics yelled.

Two police officers grabbed her by her arms and escorted her away from the scene. Jack Rabbit watched the scene frcrn a d istance before he decided to step to Ben. When he felt like the timing was right, he done so.

"I tried to tell you about that nigga, but yall thought I was tripping," Jack Rabbit said when he approached Ben. "If yall would have listened to me, none of this shit would have happened, at least not like this. I'm just glad I was there before the lil nigga made it out of the projects," he continued to say.

"I'm glad you were there too, at least we got some type of closure. But on the real old school, you can have the project if you want it, I'm done with this shit."

Their conversation was cut short when Joy called.

"What's up bae?" He asked Joy when he answered.

"The mayor just ordered a mandatory evacuation, so you need to hurry up before the interstate be bumper to bumper."

"Okay bae, I'm on my way," he said in a depressed tone.

"What's wrong, why you soulld like that?" Joy asked, because she knew that something was on his mind.

"I'll talk to you about it when I get home, I'll be there in a minute."

When Ben hung up, he told Monsta and Paul that he was about to head home, because Joy was tripping about the evacuation.

"I love you my nigga!" Monsta said as he hugged him.
"I love you too homie."
"So, you and Miecy leaving right?" Ben asked Monsta.
"Yea man we gon leave."
"What you gon do homie?" Ben asked Paul.
"Ima go by China, and if she didn't decide to leave, Ima ride with her."
"That's what's up, but when we get back we gon get this business shit started," Ben said then he headed for his car.

Monsta and Miecy left moments after Ben pulled off. Paul called China to come pick him up. She arrived thirty minutes later, and they went to her apartment in the St. Bernard project where they plan to stay for the storm.

***

Word got back to Terrance, Pookey and J-Roc that Rell was murdered in the Melph.

They swore to avenge Rell's death even if it cost them their lives. They armed themselves with high power assault rifles and headed towards the Melph.

AUTHOR'S COMMENT

I know you're probably holding this novel in your hands saying to yourself that this was a great read. I truly agree with you one hundred percent. You're also probably saying that it gets wicked in the streets of New Orleans and once again I agree with you one hundred percent. Just to make it clear to the world, we do not snake each other for other hoods in my project. That goes against everything we stand for. So please don't do it in yours. This is only entertainment.

Things that happen in this novel could possibly be the outcome when you have a group of individuals such as hustlers, players, gangsters, snakes, and fakes in the same crew. So always be aware of who you surround yourself with. It's always best to surround yourself with people that have the same qualities as you. That way you'll always know what to expect. Loyalty Is Everything....

Kennaire "CP3 Bul" Mathieu

We didn't only write this novel for ourselves but for our city as well. For so long we have been missing in the Urban novel world. But now that we're here, we aren't going anywhere but to the top of the charts.

Devon "Oreo" Wilson

ABOUT THE AUTHOR'S

Kennaire Mathieu and Devon Wilson both were raised in public housing projects in New Orleans, Louisiana. They discovered their passion for writing in Federal Prison while serving lengthy sentences for drug trafficking and fire arms. Their goals are to become successful and also motivate others to know that anything is possible if you put your mind to it.

Made in the USA
Columbia, SC
07 March 2025